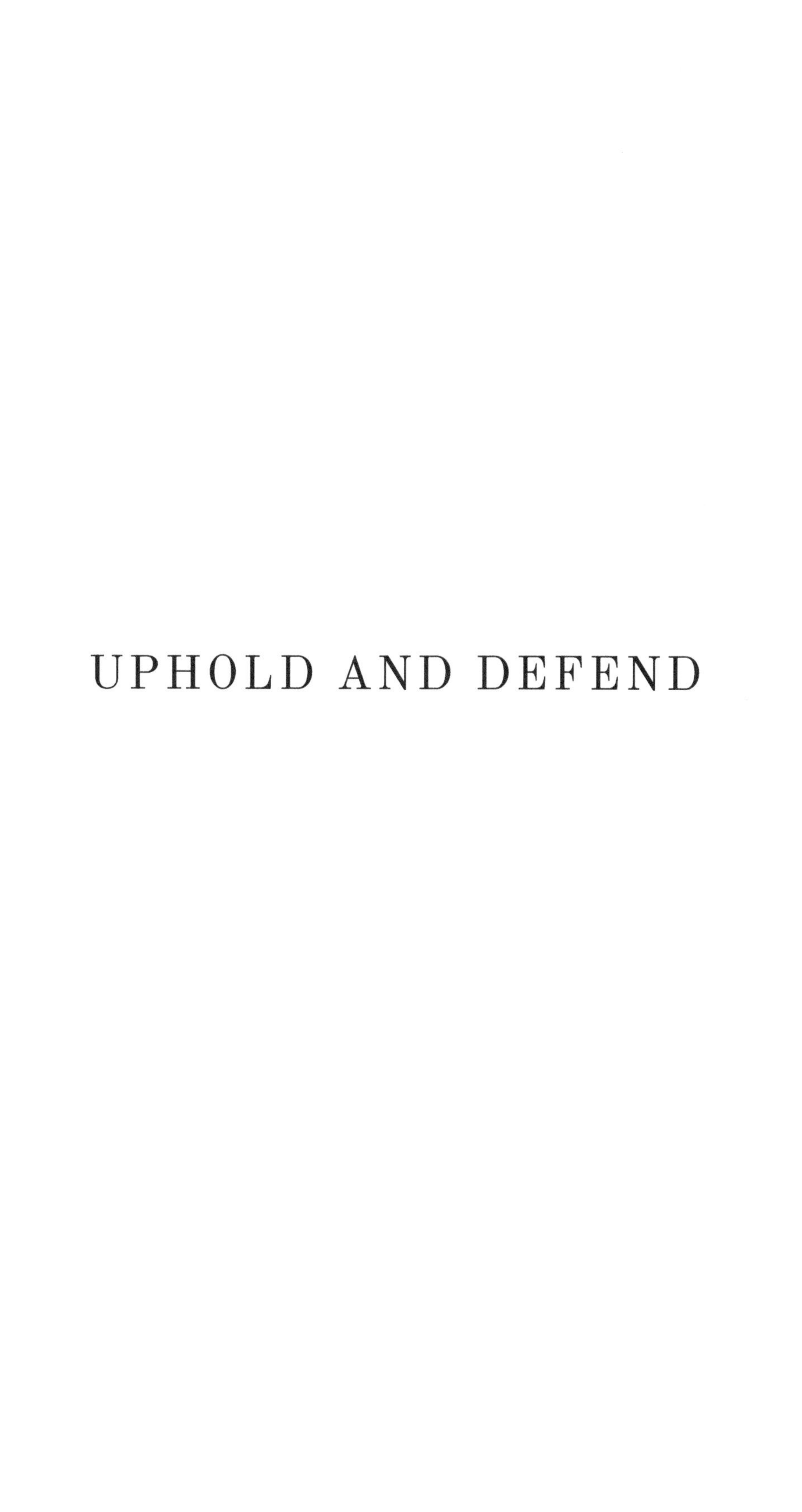

UPHOLD AND DEFEND

UPHOLD AND DEFEND

SUNSET ON THE AMERICAN DREAM

Stephen S. Hoag

IngramSpark

Print ISBN 9798988466314

First Printing, 2023

Illustrator: Linda Hoag
Tenny Hill map by SSH
Cover Design by: SelfPubBookCovers.com/VonaArt
www.upholdanddefend.life

Disclaimer Statement

It is important for the reader to note that this is a work of fiction and that any reference of characters to real people is purely coincidental and unintended. This is pure entertainment, any reference to real agencies, places or businesses are simply for situational orientation only. No affiliation or endorsements exist, and defamation is certainly not the purpose of mention.
The author and the publisher are not responsible or liable for any injury, damage or loss incurred by an individual attempting to misuse any information or act on any fictitious plot depicted in this novel. This novel is not intended to be an instruction manual, and readers are not advised to use it as such.

I dedicate this book with a heartfelt thanks to the men and women of our armed forces, our Police and all the people who work with emergency response. My son is in the Air Force, and my daughter is a Firefighter so a special thanks goes out to them for their service and for their courage to serve their country and their community. Their effort is essential for the protection of American principles and for the survival of our Republic, our constitution, and the Bill of Rights. I would also like to express a sincere 'thank you' to my wife, who deserves my gratitude for putting up with me and supporting me through the many years that it took to finish this project. Without her, I would not exist in the same capacity.

I would also like to express my sincere thanks to 'Dixie' (my daughter's dog) for the times she nudged me while I was typing and looked up at me with those puppy dog eyes. The message was clear "You need to take a break (with me)" she would say. Thanks 'Dixie', those breaks we had together were really special.

Contents

If the American people continue down the path they are on, some aspects of the fictitious scenarios set up in this novel could very well become a reality. It's up to us, "We The People", to change direction and avoid the devastating consequences of a violent reaction to an economic downturn.

Stephen S. Hoag

Do you think the American government should be "progressive" and guide its citizens with a living breathing constitution that is updated and changed to reflect modern times? If you answered yes to that question, it means that you are one among a generation of people who don't know or have forgotten the underlying premise that fueled the birth of this country's political authority. It's not your fault. The brilliance of that document is something that many people working in and outside of our government are doing their best to obscure and make sure that you do not understand. Yes, the constitution can be amended, but the principles that made America great cannot. They are the pillars that stood us up and separated us from other failed nations. The principles set forth in the American constitution should never be compromised or we shall suffer the same fate as with the socialist countries whose leaders disparage them.

In the United States of America, our government isn't supposed to be steering the country in any direction, 'We The People' are responsible for maintaining that course. 'We The People' entrust and bestow the job of running our government upon politicians whose sole responsibility is to study circumstances to a greater degree than we ourselves can do, thus (in theory) enabling our representatives to arrive at decisions that will create a better outcome for the majority of constituents. As it is with financial advisors endowed with fiduciary responsibility, Politicians too are expected to act in a fiduciary manor and govern with the best interest of their constituents in mind. Unfortunately, we have arrived at a point in American history where most of our politicians have relinquished their responsibility to honor the country and are now acting more in their own best interest than in the interest of the people they serve. By their actions it seems they believe the relationship, once defined as "government by the people and for the people", is now "government by the elite and for the elite", for we are truly working our lives away in a not so free "free market system", all in an effort to support and pay an outrageous amount of our income to the government in the form of taxes.

Too many in government have fallen victim to the age-old quandary that has plagued human beings ever since we appeared on earth- Power and the desire to control. In the relatively short span of time that our government has been empowered, the "Great American Experiment" has shifted and is building momentum to swing to the other side of "land of the free, home of the brave". For a long time now, arguably from the day our country was formed, the Progressive agenda has focused on removing the rudder from the hands of "We The People" and has sought to place it in the hands of the deep state elite. Their agenda has successfully shaped our political system and empowered our government with an ever-increasing demand for control, power, and money. Right in front of our eyes our system has transformed into something that would surely dishearten the people who founded the Constitution and the Bill of Rights and designed the negative liberties that define the boundaries our government must adhere to.

It's up to us to understand the limitations that the U.S. Constitution places on our government and the reason why the concept of negative liberties is so vitally important to the wellbeing of 'We The People'. We must recognize that we are poised to lose the power of curtailment, an inherent ability of the people bestowed upon us by our constitution (that is if we haven't lost it already). If we lose it, it will be impossible to get it back, not without a fight and not without a fight that will surely involve violence at an unprecedented level. People entrenched in the profit of corruption won't give it up easily. This is a serious statement considering what we went through during the Civil War. I suggest we avoid it.

"We The People" should demand that our government restrain its action to existing parameters as defined by Constitutional law. We are not demanding it, our politicians are not, our Justices are not, the FBI is not. Why? In my mind I can still hear my grandfather say "Give them an inch and they'll take a mile". How true this is especially as it applies to government. History shows us that it is human nature for a percentage of the population to think that they are smarter than everyone else and they strive to affect control over others and express it through political influence. They place themselves on a pedestal with an "I know what's best for you" mentality; they're supposed to, but they don't, they only know what's best for themselves.

Corruption in the American political system has manifest itself to the point where our law makers are only acting to generate wealth in their own bank accounts. Proven by the fact that the 'Speaker of the House' is now personally worth over three hundred million dollars. How are our politicians' becoming millionaires off a government salary? The fix is in, and it can clearly be seen when just before their seven-week vacation congressmen vote themselves a raise on top of their $175,000 dollar a year salary. In addition to that they have been given expense accounts, government gas cards, security equipment, security guards and compensation that includes a "cover everything" Cadillac health care plan offering benefits that are unavailable to the common citizen. Then on the sly for example, they vote against public opinion and pass Obamacare which forces the population to buy substandard health care plans (at higher ever-increasing cost), and with outrageously high deductibles. Common citizens are forced to give up their family doctor for one supplied (approved) by the government's preferred insurance companies, quite the opposite of their own Cadillac government health care plan which includes prescription drugs and has none of the same limitations.

History has shown repeatedly that politicians gravitate towards a totalitarian form of government with socialism being the first spoonful of "fix" that is fed to the masses. Our government is creating the problem and then offering us a disguised solution which is in fact

Socialism. With its siphoning nature, socialism weaves its way into the fabric of society disguised at first as a promising idea. But with every previous example of its implementation, societies have collapsed and disintegrated into something far less desirable.

> **Socialism runs parallel with failure. Jealousy and resentment guide believers into a downward spiral. Misery ends up as its main byproduct to be experienced by all except those at the very top.**
>
> Stephen S. Hoag

The great American experiment has been the most successful system of government ever created. It has led to individual growth and widespread personal prosperity at a level never achieved before in the history of mankind. The American free market system is now under attack and is being threatened by an aspect of human nature that succumbs to the use of force to take the profit out of success and secure it for themselves under the guise of giving freely to the unproductive (yet able to be productive) in our society. There is a very real problem that creeps in after this concept is applied. Eventually the profit they are tapping into shrinks to insufficient levels. (Note: I said "able unproductive people", for there are always people in need who truly require and deserve our support).

The storyline in Uphold and Defend is weaved with the intention of exposing underlying issues so they can be brought up for debate, not to promote any type of violent reaction. I hope that you the reader, will ponder and consider the underlying topics seriously and debate them fairly on their own merits rather than getting hung up on any idiosyncrasies or errors in my writing. If anything, I am hoping that readers become invigorated and are moved to get up and go vote to stop our country from getting deeply entangled in socialist policies which inevitably will lead to a tyrannical, authoritarian, fascist/communist style of government. No, you say? Ah, it is already happening to people in countries that never thought it could. Venezuela anyone?

CHARACTERS IN ORDER OF APPEARANCE

- Kaiden Alvin Sawyer- Student at Tenny Hill Academy.
- Roman P. Sawyer- Kaiden's dad.
- Mayor Carvey- New York City's newly elected mayor.
- Master Kwong- Teaches Choy Lee Fut Kung Fu.
- Master Chow- Well known Martial Arts Master.
- Master Lee- Well known Martial Arts Master.
- Si Hing Joel Young- Kaiden's Wing Chung teacher.
- Mr. Bentner- Kaiden's High School history teacher.
- Neil- Gang member from the 88's.
- Raymond Carzone - Banshee gang member.
- Aaron Grimes- Student in Kaiden's High School (Mr. B's class).
- Sanchez- Student in Kaiden's High School (Mr. B's class).
- Kip Taylor- West Point cadet.
- Emory Hill- Bus driver working for the Academy.
- Ciera Lowman- Kaiden's true love.
- Nick Oberman- Ciera's boyfriend. Senior Captain of the Cadets.
- Candy- Kenny Carlson's girlfriend.
- Raymond- The RA in Kaiden's dorm.
- Rio Linda- The village where "seekers" live in tents called Hogan's.
- Kenny Jay Carlson- Kaiden's roommate.
- Julianne Ingle- Professor Jim Ingle's wife.
- Jim Ingle- Professor "Jing". Head of the agricultural department.
- Chancellor Roger Gentry- The president of Tenny Hill Academy
- Professor Mike Nailor- Head of the Science department.
- Professor Pellegrin- Head of the mathematics department.
- Professor (Major) Jaz Ray Monett- Head of the Phys Ed department.

- Professor Harry Coin- Jaz Monet's partner in the Phys Ed department.
- Mortimer Latti- Professor teaching Kaiden's American government class.
- Mr. Benelli- Fellow student in Kaiden's American history class.
- Anthony Knowles- Head of the IRS and the ART program.
- President Richfield- Recently elected President of the United States.
- Mr. Jong Tao Wing- Chairman of the Peoples Republic of China.
- Nadd Coulomb- Senator from Illinois.
- Lyle Koneham Mr.- Head of the ATF.
- Gartner, Mr.- President Richfield's public relations manager.
- Daugherty, Mrs.- Last owner of TH property- donated to the founders.
- Darleen Rose, Mrs.- Runs the campus infirmary.
- McKinney, Mrs.- Donated a sum of money to the Academy.
- Clyde Bennett, Mr.- Tenny Hill Academy treasurer.
- Allen McKinney, Mr.- Mrs. McKinney's grandson who graduated three years prior. Now works as a purchasing agent for the outpost program.
- Mount Tenny- The Mountain enclosed in the boundaries of Mt. Tenny Academy's property.
- Bill Sanchez- Head of maintenance, runs Academy ground keeper's department.
- Mars Lacy, Mrs.- Runs the stable at the farm and the corral on campus.
- Dell Arleen and his wife Judy and family- Run Stockman's farm.
- Adrian Joe Phillips- Captain Phillips- Head of campus security.
- Marlene Phillips- Captain Phillips wife.
- Harry Konic, Mr. - Dean of administration.
- Waters, Mr. - School Chaplin, head of the theology dept.
- Jimmy Venudo- Major Monett's #1 the first year he taught at the school.
- Master Bow Nak- Visiting Tai Chi master teaching a seminar.

- Chester Fairmond- Second in command of the Cadets.
- Carl Roughett- Cadet Supply Sergeant.
- Mallory Hicks- Assigned as ATF "TF" Commander.
- Earl McKafree- Platoon "C" First Lieutenant.
- Manny Stern- Cadet Cell Sergeant.
- Seal Hutchison- Cadet 1st squad Sergeant, promoted to Lieutenant.
- Irene Stalouti- Cadet Company Lieutenant.
- Shane- Kenny's friend at the RL party.
- Candy- Kenny's girlfriend.
- Ivan- Kenny's friend at the RL party.
- Pico- Kenny's friend at the RL party.
- Shelly- Kenny's friend at the RL party.
- Ricky- Kenny's friend at the RL party.
- Gore- Kenny's friend. Real name- Erin Mengore.
- Brute Winiker- Kenny's friend and fellow Cadet at the RL party.
- Shiloh Mead- Candy's friend at the RL party.
- Professor Margaret Hayer - Teaches "Water filtration".
- Stanley Rotterman- Professor Teaching "Tactics and strategies".
- Al Slack- Gun store owner.
- Roy Atkinson- In Charge of the IRS ART (Asset Reclamation Team).
- Shenki Kadisu- Roy Atkinson's team leader.
- Dean Minolta- ART leader (IRS Asset Reclamation Team).
- Curtis Mead- Grocery store owner in Delhi New York.
- Sergeant Lee Pointer- Campus security team leader
- Candon and Riley- Cadets who made the first run to Florida for supplies.
- Erin Stots (Shots)- Instructor for the school's hunting class.
- Jones Herring- A student hunter who shot a deer in the meadow.
- Dale Coonrod- Patrol leader, also in Kaiden's Military Tactics class.
- Mary Sterling- Chancellor Gentry's secretary.

- Henry Welch- State trooper assigned to support Fed's raid on campus.
- "Money"- Carleton Forbes. Kaiden's next door neighbor in the dorm.
- "Peck"- Another next-door neighbor. Body builder type.
- Rolf Wiggum- BTAFE agent that confronted Carl in the Armory.
- Bastone, Officer- State trooper supporting the Fed's raid at the Academy.
- Moran, Officer- State trooper supporting the Fed's raid on the Academy.
- Remy Horton- Kaiden's partner on the "Pickup and delivery".
- Romondo Velez- Kaiden's truck driver from the old neighborhood.
- Murray Adel- sent to the school to represent the FDA.
- Mr. Creaton- the FDA's rep at the meeting with Captain Phillips.
- Mr. Alfonso Marr- Head of Homeland Security.
- Avery's farm- The farm is located at the end of Mt. Tenny Road.
- Russell Diggens- Owner of the local Getty Gas Station in Delhi.
- Lenny- A Patriot Pioneer outpost member.
- Dr. Allie Wright- Patriot who works at the Hospital and at the "Ritz".
- Stan, Earnest, Cindy and Galloway- Members of the Patriots Outpost.
- Kathy Benninger- Woman that held Romondo's fancy at the Ritz.
- Nathan Dixon- Romondo's first patrol leader after he joined the Patriots.
- Glen Kingston- Patriots squad leader on the roadblock raid.
- Gil Agreskie- Governor of New York.
- Clark Benson- Student who took charge of the RCO operation.
- Mr. and Mrs. Craig Hommel- Their home was where Ciera and Jing fled after the Woodstock massacre. Sergeant Rutledge- ATF agent.
- Samuel Case- Security clerk on duty the morning of the school's closing.

- Chuck Hempro- Administrator assigned to the security department.
- Kevin Morrow- School office staff member.
- John Listen- Ham operator and teacher of the Ham radio course.
- Clewy Riddell- Remote Controlled Observation course instructor.
- Tray Greenfield- President of the Delta cluster. Outpost #1
- Deston Minor- President of the Zulu cluster. Outpost #2
- Miles Delear- Head honcho of the Beta Cluster. Outpost #3
- Chance Shorebird- Zappa cluster president. Outpost #4
- Neal Lee- Zeta Cluster president. Outpost #5
- Steven Manila- Pi cluster leader. Outpost #6
- Ben Marlin- Cadet sergeant promoted to Lieutenant after the massacre. 1st squad's leader.
- Raul Whitaker- Cadet 3rd squad's Sergeant.
- Spanner- ATF agent in charge of the Roadblock on Route 10.
- Tungston, Al- Technician operating the Wave Tracking System.
- Rickert, Shawn- IRS agent sent in to Tenny Hill Academy (first claimed to be FDA) to monitor the school's activity. Observer/ witness to the First Action Force that closed the school.
- Sistren, Ned- #1 agent sent to Mt. Tenny Academy to help confiscate weapons. Assigned as Captain of task force one.
- Jim Lawrence- BearCat driver.
- Ponce Cowfin- Cadet sniper partner.
- Jeremy Latino- Cadet sniper.
- Stephen Tobin- Commander Shots staff sergeant.
- Hutchison, Seal- Third squad leader. Security building.
- Coonrod, Dale- Fifth squad leader. Bunker security.
- Jamison, Ernie- Second squad leader assigned to the cafeteria.
- Ben Marlin- First squad leader at the roadblock.
- Robert Saga- Six squad leader at the Theater.
- Fred Angstrom- Cadet seventh squad leader at Delta house.
- Perry Klingemann- Cadet 3rd squad leader
- Mark Brown- Lieutenant. Fed TG1 leader assaulting Delta House.

- Reynold Bond- Sergeant. Fed TG1 leader assaulting the security building.
- Trooper Gibbs- New York State Trooper assigned to roadblock detail.
- Marty Slag- Cadet who worked on cutting the OP trail.
- Connors- Federal agent, acting Special team leader.
- Haskell- Federal agent, acting team leader during attack on the school.
- Terry Pride- Outpost team leader on the mission to save the gold.
- Dixon- Lieutenant leader of the Patriot Pioneer team.
- Crenshaw- Sergeant leading Patriot Pioneer team.
- Clance Driscol- Homeowner where Patriots stayed at after the attack.
- Deloris Driscol- Wife.
- Steve West- Cadet they met on the trail after fleeing the Academy.
- Jones- Patriot Pioneer and Crenshaw's go too guy.
- Rene- The daughter enslaved by the roadside bandits.
- Frank- Leader of the bandits.
- Gregory Dean- Local homeowner the troop met on their march.
- Melvin Brooks- Chief security officer at Clear Water Farm.
- John Shay- Head director of Clear Water Farm (Outpost #5)

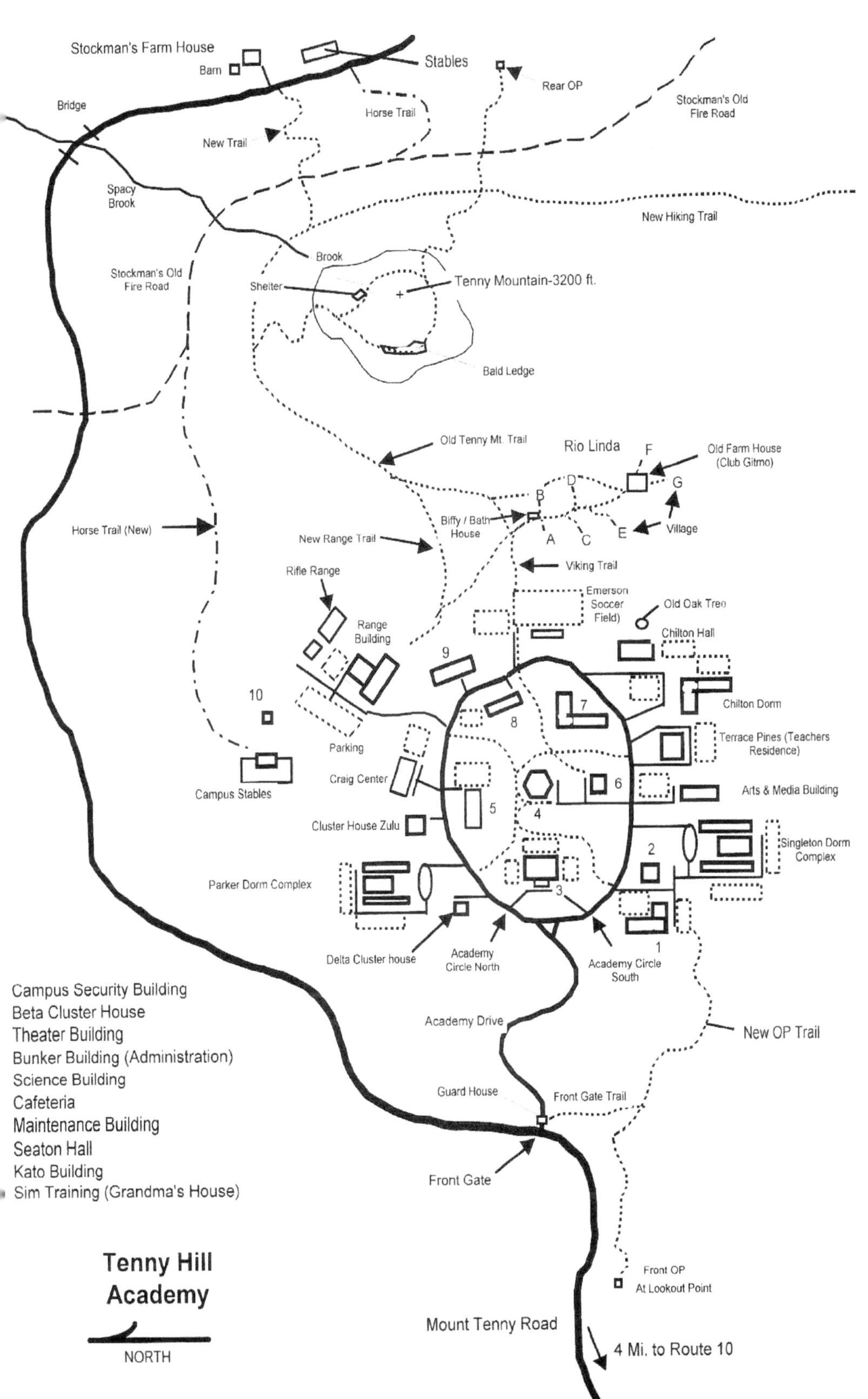
Stockman's Farm House
Barn
Stables
Rear OP
Bridge
Horse Trail
Stockman's Old Fire Road
New Trail
Spacy Brook
New Hiking Trail
Brook
Stockman's Old Fire Road
Shelter
Tenny Mountain-3200 ft.
Bald Ledge
Old Tenny Mt. Trail
Rio Linda
F
Old Farm House (Club Gitmo)
D
G
B
Biffy / Bath House
A
C
E
Village
Horse Trail (New)
New Range Trail
Viking Trail
Rifle Range
Emerson Soccer Field)
Old Oak Tree
Range Building
Chilton Hall
9
10
7
Chilton Dorm
8
Parking
Terrace Pines (Teachers Residence)
Craig Center
6
Campus Stables
Arts & Media Building
5
4
Cluster House Zulu
2
Singleton Dorm Complex
Parker Dorm Complex
3
1
Delta Cluster house
Academy Circle North
Academy Circle South
Campus Security Building
Beta Cluster House
Theater Building
Bunker Building (Administration)
Science Building
Cafeteria
Maintenance Building
Seaton Hall
Kato Building
Sim Training (Grandma's House)
Academy Drive
New OP Trail
Guard House
Front Gate Trail
Front Gate
Tenny Hill Academy
Front OP At Lookout Point
Mount Tenny Road
4 Mi. to Route 10
NORTH

1

Putin' On The Git Go

Kaiden looked up and hoped to God he was seeing Greyhound bus #53 roll around the corner. What a relief, yes, there it was. The young man edged forward from his perch against the concrete column drawn to this moment by hours of anticipation.

"Bout frickin' time" he said out loud while humorously envisioning his words flashing across the electronic billboard above the Greyhound Terminal. The long dog "Greyhound" logo painted on the side of the incoming bus came into view. Kaiden strained to see the number above the front windshield and then confirmed it. "Yup, number 53, that's her".

In his hands, literally, was his ticket out of here. Or as they say in New York "At a heea". The young man with crew cut hair and a crew cut beard looked at his watch and calculated that it took twelve hours to complete the normally three-hour Philadelphia to New York leg of its route.

A top-heavy design made the bus sway dangerously to one side as it made the turn and rounded the corner. Lumbering into the terminal staging area, the "shoebox" parked in slot #8 with the classic hiss, chirp, and squeal of air brakes as it came to a complete stop. No sooner had the doors opened than a steady stream of passengers stepped off and looked around in awe at the buildings that towered above them. There were smiles all around and pats on the back from friends who walked up to meet them. Most of them looked happy that they had finally reached their destination. Some looked disgusted.

"How strange it is that anyone on board could actually be glad to have made it to New York" Kaiden thought as he watched them.

Departing passengers picked their way through a crowd of people standing there next to the bus with a ticket in their hand. All of them looked anxious to secure a seat of their own. Kaiden was one of them. For him and a large portion of the others, any other destination besides N.Y.C. would have been a major improvement.

A buzzing noise from above increased in intensity as a PD-40 drone slid into view and hovered in the air over the crowd on a four-prop turbine engine. The Media called them PPD's (Police Patrol Drones). On the streets they called them a "Snitch" or a "Sniffer" or just "Oh shit, here it comes". These drones are equipped with a rotary camera with camera stabilization technology and took twelve mega pixel stills as well as video in 1080 HD standard. Instantly the images were beamed back to a base computer to be analyzed.

The camera on this drone was active; it scanned the crowd at the station analyzing faces through an updated version of FRT (face recognition technology). Nowadays it was not uncommon to see these drones buzzing around the streets of New York attempting to get a good look at someone or some group of people. This one stood still, hovering above the sidewalk as the camera lens focused on the stream of people walking underneath it.

People looked up and stared at it. Not because they wanted too, they had too. It's the law. In New York City if you saw one you were required to look up at it for a minimum of six seconds to allow it to identify you. If you didn't, it would follow you and maneuver around to get a better view of your face. If it couldn't determine your identity, it would search its data base and determine if your profile was a possible match for someone on the government's list of wanted. If it labeled you in the high percentile, a squad of sniffer police would pop out of cars and out of the shadows to detain you until they could determine why you didn't want to be identified. Of course, this was all in the name of National Security and for maintaining public safety.

Kaiden A. Sawyer stared at the sniffer for the required six seconds and then settled back against one of the six huge thick concrete pillars supporting the front of the Greyhound station terminal. The buzzing noise hung in the air for a few moments before the snitch moved on down the line. He leaned on solid concrete and waited patiently for things to die down a bit so he could board the bus. The pillar behind him was massive, it had to be to support the tall skyscraper that towered above him and the hundreds of people who now lived at its base. "I wonder how much weight this column is supporting" he thought as he felt it with the palm of his hand. Unable to come to any figure at all he resigned to calculate how long he had been standing there. "I've wasted five hours and fifty-nine minutes of my life waiting for this bus". The bus was now six hours and fifty-five minutes late. At that moment, the sniffer must have gotten a hit on somebody because police in black tactical gear showed up in force, popped out of vans and swarmed around a man. They took him away in handcuffs.

If you saw Kaiden standing there, it was instantly apparent that he was a member of a gang. The tattoo "88" was inscribed on his arm in a fancy font with the numbers resting on a bed of thorny vines, of course much to the dismay of his parents. It was deliberately conspicuous under the rolled-up sleeve of the T shirt he wore. Although he looked military with that buzz cut, the baggy black pants and tight shirt pulled him far away from any misconception. Now he was done with the "88's", but parts of that gang life still lingered. The story behind it was the reason he held the ticket in his hand.

In his other hand Kaiden held a black leather jacket. He stood there holding it with both arms folded across his chest exuding an aura that radiated "attitude". It came naturally for him. He shifted position, grabbed the heavy duffel bag at his feet and slung it up over his shoulder with one clean jerk. At a tad over 6' 2" Kaiden carried his strong muscular physique on a large boned frame. It was obvious that he was no stranger to the inside of a gym, but he lacked the bulky swollen muscle look of a body builder. On the contrary, his was a youthful tone with broad shoulders and a thin waistline that created that "Y" shape and six pack abs that women swooned over. Along with the scruffy beginning of a beard, his hard knocks look gave him an instant air of authority. When he glanced at you with those strong blue eyes it grabbed your attention if not just for a moment. His strikingly handsome facial features lent millions to a first impression which in most cases fostered an instant friendship. The same effect allowed him to easily slip inside a women's fantasy.

Most people got a positive impression after meeting Kaiden, it gave him an edge. He exuded a certain charm that was capable of disarming someone's negativity. But of course, it didn't work with all. In this world there are always those indignant few, male, or female, who see strength or a perception of strength as a threat and will instantly reject someone deemed guilty of wielding it. Yet indelible first impressions never fade. For those seeking an advantage in relationships they quickly made the connection and saw Kaiden as someone they wanted on their side. Even now, at the age of twenty-one, Kaiden was completely aware of how to use this to his advantage with friends, foe and even more importantly, with the ladies in his life.

2

The State Of New York

In the entire history of New York there had never been a depression as deep as the one New Yorkers found themselves in now. After fifty years of a continuous pounding by progressive politicians (on both the left and right), New York had slithered into the same deplorable depths achieved by Chicago, Detroit, Los Angeles, and Seattle. A host of others were following suit at this very moment. Soon the list would get longer. Between that and the Middle East war, Kaiden and the people waiting at the bus terminal were reeling from the effects. Thanks to our politicians, nowadays there are a multitude of immigrants and homeless people who tout the Greyhound bus station as their home address. They all transformed the location into what is known as "Greyhound Tent City" or just "GTC". Sure, the immigrants had been given a driver's license but here, in these times, all they could do was walk.

Strewn about the parking lot and alleyway were tents and cardboard box shacks of every color shape and size. Some were more elaborate than others with plastic bags taped to them like shingles for some semblance of an attempt at water proofing. Sleeping bags and bed rolls of all kinds lined the wall of the parking lot and all along the adjacent alleyway there were small areas where each person had staked a claim. About six hundred squatters sporadically settled themselves anywhere they could find without concern for design. Multiple barely discernable pathways led into the mishmash of people and snaked between groups of staked tents and lean-tos. In the last five years there had been an ever-increasing number of jobless people accumulating here and at other sites just like it.

Locations that had access to large public bathrooms were the initial attraction for early settlers. This Greyhound terminal had a large accessible men's and women's public bathroom with multiple stalls. The availability of potable water from the sinks was the essence of sustenance for the multitude of downtrodden. The one stall next to the drain in the floor was turned into a shower but it was such a pain in the ass to use. If you didn't reach out from under the stall with your foot and continuously clear the drain of garbage the entire bathroom floor would fill up with water by the time you were done, and it did that on a regular basis. On any given day you would have to walk through gray dirty water to use the toilet. The bathrooms became so busy that there was a waiting line out front almost twenty-four hours a day.

Many Americans who had just lost their jobs were mixed in with the illegals and the Middle East refugee population, all of them reeling from the latest economic downturn. "Depression number three" they called it or "The Triple Dipper" but this one has lasted for so long now that most didn't know what to call it. They just said "The depression... again".

Depressions came in waves but now the down turns have become the new "norm". Instead of naming the Depressions people were starting to name the upturns. It was becoming increasingly difficult for Americans to dig themselves out and reverse the trend especially when competing against refugees who would work for just about anything. The Progressive party believed it was America's responsibility to take in our share of the refugees pouring out of the Middle East to escape the violence. It was estimated that just last year alone nine hundred thousand came pouring into the waiting arms of the US welfare system. This new influx was in addition to the millions of illegals coming in over the border with Mexico. Politicians kept the country grinding down this path to inject a greater number of people who were comfortable with a "socialist agenda". They achieved their goal by building up a significant voter block of socialists as well as a large Muslim population by accepting unrestricted numbers of immigrants from Mexico and now refugees from the Middle East that were sympathetic to the Democrat agenda. An agenda whose goal was not to generate an increase in prosperity but to simply stake out a larger piece of the American pie by removing it from the hands of the middle class and placing it directly under their control.

Maintaining an edge at the voting booth was paramount and that took precedence over initiating the kind of change that would support the old capitalist marketing system. The younger generation was taught and the people in power believed it to be, outdated and old. Politics as usual continuously inserted resistance into the path of the U.S. free market system.

Americans who lived from paycheck to paycheck were especially vulnerable. Most survived the initial stages but now they found themselves unable to pay their mortgage or rent and suddenly became homeless before they knew what was happening. It was bad; it became exceedingly difficult to live in the city. It got even worse with the onset of war where Russia, China and the US were slugging it out in the Middle East and With Taiwan in the East China Sea. That caused energy prices to skyrocket. The draft had been re-enacted and was responsible for pulling a significant percentage of America's youth into an ever-escalating situation. The number of casualties and "KIA's" were a major concern and was positively the catalyst for Kaiden's father to seek other alternatives for Kayden's future. It was difficult and took all the strings he could pull to keep his son out of the conflict and send him to college. They had been here over the three-year limit, but since Kaiden's family was technically here on a diplomatic visa and not considered a full fledge citizen, Kaiden's father was able to get an exclusion from the selective service for his son.

Equally as difficult to obtain was the bus ticket that Kaiden now held in his hand. The cost of one rose from seventy-nine dollars ten years ago to three hundred eighty-one dollars today. That was the going price for Greyhounds famous "Anywhere Fare" ticket, a ticket that no longer took you everywhere. Plus, the cost of one will change daily depending on the price of oil.

It would have been interesting for anyone watching Kaiden to see him standing there among the derelicts hanging out around the station. Drug addicts hovered around newcomers and bothered them for handouts but avoided the gang member standing there against the concrete column. If a homeless person walked by, Kaiden stared them down with that hardhearted face he wore until the guy turned away and walked on. It was Kaiden's "internal warrior" that came out and surrounded him like a shield. He could turn it on conveniently generating "bad ass" at will, totally designed to make you think twice. He had it turned on now for the benefit of all the misfits that hung out around the terminal. None of the derelicts dared to come up and beg him for money. These times forced a defensive strategy to the forefront and made it prudent and necessary. Danger lurked around every corner.

Most famous were the first and largest TC that took shape and grew on the north side of Central Park. It started 'way back when' as a refuge for the Occupy Wall Street crowd but it turned into a permanent hangout for the homeless and the thousands of illegal immigrants. When the dispossessed were kicked out of everywhere else, they migrated and collected here. Off and on for years' people hung out here. Every so often, they would participate in a protest, a "sit in", a "live in" or a "love in" (whatever) to attract attention to their plight. At first the cops were instructed to kick them out and directed them to local shelters but the shelters near the park on Madison and Fifth eventually capped out and couldn't handle any more. The crowds increased in number and many homeless started tenting and hanging out on various street corners and alleyways within a few blocks of the place. That caused a major complaint from residents and businesses alike. When the Cops came and made them move along, they just ended up back at the park again. There was no place else to go.

To keep the peace, the cops were forced to capitulate and tolerate their presence to keep some semblance of order around the parks. They looked the other way and unofficially allowed the trespassers to take refuge there. At least they wouldn't be bothering the downtown district. Hence the Tent Cities expanded. Mostly it was an expansion of an existing shelter where there happened to be a space, parking lot or alleyway next to it to expand into. There was the one down on Chester and Clancy Street and the one on 172nd and 33rd. But the most famous eye sore of a TC grew rapidly under the Brooklyn Bridge on the east side of Manhattan. It was painfully visible to all those who entered and exited the city from the boroughs and from Long Island. The same thing happened to three other shelters located in Manhattan and there was more whose status was growing from "Town" to "City" at an alarming rate.

For newly elected NYC Mayor Carvey, it became the first major battle of his political career. The problem grew into a political football from the start, handed down to him by the previous administration. Mayor Carvey inherited the full brunt of it and right off the bat he had to deal with the emergency. His administration decided to tackle the problem by launching a major effort to bus the overflow of licensed illegals into upstate NY and to other parts of New England and even across the border into New Jersey and Connecticut. The theory was that these new refugees would filter back into society with minimal consequences mimicking the national plan espoused by the White House as it pertained to immigrants coming across the Mexican border.

Unfortunately, there were not enough jobs in the Northeast to support them. Crime rose dramatically in all the areas where they were deposited. Towns, Cities, and then entire States caught on and refused to accept them. New Jersey's Police now actively sit on the border manning roadblocks set up to monitor all incoming traffic. They stop buses and vehicles to search for illegal personnel and contraband. Any item considered contraband is confiscated and they force all the illegals to turn back. Other States followed suit and are now "monitoring" their borders in the same manor due to this exact problem. To travel anywhere nowadays means going through multiple traffic jams created by police checkpoints designed to weed out the undesirables. Even some interior counties have adopted the practice. That and the excessive cost of gasoline forced people to stop driving.

* * *

Here they were, immigrants, unceremoniously dumped back into the pits of NYC. Due to open boarder policies, the influx of an exorbitant number of immigrants taxed the system to where existing funding is way past insufficient and additional funding is out of the question due to the state of the government's financial predicament. Welfare programs the system set up to support these people proved inadequate and could not absorb all the economic casualties. Tent Cities, all of them looking and smelling just as bad as this one, were here to stay.

Kaiden looked around as he stepped onto the line in front of the bus. "I am so glad I'm getting out of this hell hole" he said to himself. The sad state of the American economy was only one of the reasons recounted as to why he was getting on this bus. Other problems intensified over the last year when he started getting into trouble with the police. On top of his latest run in with the law, violent union riots were on the rise. That's when his father decided to send him to the Academy to remove him from the source of his woes. Kaiden pictured his father with that finger of his pointed at his face saying "A military school is just what you need to turn yourself around young man. You'll learn to direct that energy of yours in a more positive way".

Kaiden didn't say anything or even resist like some adolescents would. He took a long look at his prospects and thought that his father might be right. He sure didn't want to continue down the path he was on. Thinking about it, he pulled out a quote from memory. More precisely from a character "Trinity" in an old movie made in 1999 called The Matrix. She said it best "It's only a dead end down that way, and you know exactly where that one leads Neo". He felt like Neo, he felt like he had let his father down and more importantly, his mom too. At that moment he made up his mind to turn his life around and do something with the second chance he'd been given. He decided to "follow the white rabbit"; only in this case it was a greyhound running out of New York City.

3

The State Of The Union

Last year the value of the US dollar dipped to an all-time low of thirty cents against the Euro. Due to a fully open spigot of out-of-control spending, the Chinese and the five major oil conglomerates held an emergency summit meeting in Copenhagen. All six unanimously agreed to switch the "currency of exchange" (the currency that oil was traded in) from the Dollar to the Chinese Yen. They dropped the Dollar and declared the Chinese Yen as the new exchange currency of the "New World Order". To top that the Chinese themselves were on the verge of switching to their own Chinese bit coin. The whole effort was spearheaded by the International Monetary Fund to link all the economies of the world together. Since 1792 Oil had been traded in transactions that were pegged to the US dollar and now the New World Government turned their backs on the weak US currency.

Switching and pegging trade to another currency was something all the experts said would never happen. "The Oil Conglomerates could never switch currencies, it's impossible to do" critiques said. But they were wrong. The world's oil producing nations bailed out from underneath a sinking ship. It was "phase one" in the global plan to start moving towards a "One World Economy". The US dollar lost. The most profound indicating statement of the year was "any other currency would have been an improvement".

The improvement part wasn't exactly true. Oil traders profited from the weak dollar. They received more dollars for their product with the 3.35 Dollar to Euro exchange rate which increased their purchasing power. What Europeans feared was that someone in Washington might just see the light, reverse direction, and start to shore up and improve the value of the dollar. Then they would lose millions on transactions as the value of the dollar climbed and billions if it ever reached a one-to-one ratio with the Euro. The higher the dollar goes the fewer Euros you get in exchange, effectively lowering the buying power of the person holding Euros. Therefore, millions of dollars poured into the Democrat party election campaign to sustain the status quo and keep America moving in a declining direction.

Progressive liberal politicians during the Obama administration started it off and the Biden presidency put the nail in the coffin by spending and borrowing at an unprecedented level. To an ever-increasing degree they allowed the treasury to continue printing money disregarding all the warnings from economists against doing so. The steam roller grew larger and larger and reared up behind them. If they stopped now, it would roll right over their backs. The liberal mantra to "Spend our way out of recession" continued as the most favored prescription, only it was taking such a long time to cure this disease. They and many external sources blamed the capitalist system for the failure and fueled the fire with sentiment arrayed against the people who profited most from it. It was the poor and the middle class against Wall Street, the rich, and elite politicians.

To those who bothered to look, it was becoming clear that the government's love affair with spending wasn't just to pull America out of a depression; it was to expand the power of the Federal Government and the people who ran it. Then a while back the Chinese Virus hit. It was just the "emergency" needed to pass legislation as fast as possible, so the public didn't have enough time to fully understand the ramifications of the proposals they installed. Economic reform was the excuse used to force socialist policies down the throats of Americans with unprecedented speed- while they had the chance. "Never let an emergency go to waste" was the politicians common "don't quote me" quote. And the gullible portion of the American public bought it.

Back in the day, famous outspoken people like Ross Perot, Glen Beck and Rush Limbaugh sounded the alarm but most people just thought of them as conspiracy theorists. Way too many American citizens never even bother to 'fact check' the propaganda and just dismissed conspiracy theories all together. Our politician's real intent only became evident after it was too late. As time went on people began to see the result of socialist policies that crept in and slowly bled out the country's economic prosperity. Markets went into a downward spiral and never rose back out. Informed people found themselves outnumbered at the polling booth. There were too many people who voted for the politician that told them everything they wanted to hear and who promised them the most benefits in return for their vote. Only, the benefits never seemed to materialize.

It wasn't just one political party; it was all the Democrat progressive politicians along with some Republicans who allowed it to get to this point. Together they consistently guided America ever closer to the European model. President Obama and the progressive agenda had only been slowed by Trumps brief reign. After which the movement got kicked into overdrive by Biden. The progressive movement molded the free market system into a bastardized version of socialism while waving the banner for a New World Order. Progressives argued that a surge in the printing and spending of the US dollar would bolster the GDP (Gross Domestic Product) which is the total market value of all goods and services produced in a year, and the supply of money would counteract the deflationary trend in the real estate market by creating inflation. They are right about the first one. The GDP will level out or rise if the Government spends enough money. They are in effect taking up the slack in the private sector spending slump. You can see the results of a policy like this when the Japanese tried the same thing back in 1992. Their economy tanked due to actions that looked all too familiar to the way the US is trending now. Amidst huge stimulus packages and bailouts Japan still couldn't stem the tide of a steep deflationary collapse of their real estate market. Japan's Commercial properties fell by 60% in just three years and settled at an amazing 87% loss over a fourteen-year period.

Japan was in a much better position to fight off deflation and instigate a recovery than the US is today. Their GDP grew because they still had customers in nations with growing economies who were strong buyers of Japanese exports. Their large export sector benefited from a weak yen and put them in a much better position to fight off deflation. The US export market is not only weak but has been steadily shrinking further and further over the last few decades. It started in earnest when our politicians' sent jobs and industries overseas by passing the trade bill N.A.F.T.A (North American Free Trade Agreement). They told us "Our economy will become an economy based on technology and information instead of one based on production". But what happened was that we became dependent on other countries for our material needs. So much so that our entire supply chain was dumped into the waiting arms of China. Yes China, who's communist government considers us an enemy.

With the benefit of a weak dollar America's exports were declining as imports were rising. And with this recession, the entire world economy was going down the tube. The whole thing compounded and added to the erosion of our export trade due to an ever-increasing lack of buyers. The world's monetary system became so tightly wound together due to the increase in popularity of the "New World Order" that the entire world felt each pang of the depression as intensely as a single country did.

Interest rates on US treasury bonds soared. It was a natural market response to try to make them more attractive to investors. In 2012 America was borrowing over one hundred and fifty billion dollars a week just to pay their obligations and stay afloat. The total (interest) paid out on the debt would have knocked over the uninformed voter if they knew. It was staggering. Today the payout is just over three billion dollars per day. To be forced into paying that high of an interest rate shows the sad state of the underlying investment. America had to bribe them with higher rates to make it more attractive to lend them money. Paying that kind of interest multiplied the "cost of money" by seven-fold. That burden became a noose that hung around the neck of the American People.

Bank bailouts forced the government to print trillions of dollars in multiple stimulus packages to attempt to stem the tide of the Chinese virus and save the economy. Recently, they put out another job creation stimulus package (#2) for three trillion. Once again it was supposed to create jobs that the previous one didn't. Of course, they started calling it something else besides "stimulus". A bail out in various forms was a popular method for politicians to throw money at a problem so they could say that they were doing something about it. The money injection just kicked the can down the road and mostly went to pay back corporations and donors who kicked the money back into re-election campaigns.

Only certain companies that played ball received favored tax status, some also received subsidies. The ones who didn't were overshadowed and either shrunk into insignificancy or went out of business altogether. You can say that the catalyst for the extinction of the middle class was the government shutdown after the virus hit. But the policies continued well after the pandemic subsided. The after effect devastated the small business sector which just couldn't recover after such a slack in revenue. Looking back, it seems like it was all part of the plan to eliminate competition for the government's preferred constituents.

Three out of ten people ended up working for the government due to the constant flow of money that poured out of the National Treasury and into government projects. Naturally, those people became proponents of the government's fountain of monetary flow and voted for maintaining the tax and spend status quo. They argued that the government isn't supposed to "make money" from any venture they might embark upon. Ok, but are they supposed to lose money? The founding fathers gave us the "guiding principles" that the government was supposed to abide by, driven by a philosophy based upon minimal government involvement in the economics of the country. Following these original principles ushered in an age of prosperity that anyone could experience if they sought it out and worked hard to achieve that end. The flower born out of that relationship is more commonly known as "The American dream". The difference between America and other countries was that it was not some unobtainable pie in the sky notion. No, it was something obtainable- until now. Momentum swung all the way to the failure side of that concept.

As evidenced by the soup lines at the Greyhound Tent City, the homeless became dependent on government handouts for their daily existence. One good thing that came out of it was that it solved the obesity problem. The average weight of an American dropped from 235 pounds in 2010 to 175 pounds today. But that was offset by the fact that the life span of an American declined as well.

"We The People" no longer had the same healthcare system that was once so prominent and effective in America. Now Healthcare is controlled by a government who will never have "efficiency" listed as one of its attributes. America is in a serious decline, and many believe that this is exactly what the elite intended. Why else would anyone continue to do the same things that had produced economic ruin for other countries in the past? There was plenty of warning. Many signs, but the politicians continued to do what politicians do... spend money they don't have.

4

On The Other Side Of The River

It was almost twelve o'clock midnight. Not the normal hour for gas delivery at Mr. Bill's Gas & Go convenience store. Bloomfield, New Jersey was normally a bustling city, but not at this time of night. Bloomfield was located just north of Newark and was a convenient stop along the driver's route, convenient because it was located just one exit shy of his drop location and far away from the seeing eyes of his boss at the Bayway Refinery in Linden N.J., it was a perfect spot.

For the driver Jonathan Cook, dropping off a load of gasoline was routine, he had done it every working day of his life for the last fifteen years. His next stop would be the last drop of his working career. With this, he would move south with his wife and retire somewhere in Costa Rica.

Cook jumped down out of the cab with enthusiasm hoping to get this over with quickly. According to the story he was going to have to weave, he was just stopping here for an emergency break to use the bathroom and get something to drink. Only this pit stop would end up being a little different.

Minutes after Cooks arrival a tan Chevy Avalanche drove in and parked in the #1 spot in front of the convenience store. The driver got out and entered the store with just a slight glance in the direction of the tanker. When the passenger emerged from the store five minutes later and climbed back into the Avalanche, once again he gave the tanker a cursory glance. This time he locked eyes with Mr. Cook for just a moment. Then he got back into the SUV and drove off.

Mr. Cook climbed back aboard his cab and drove off in the same direction. He no longer could afford a GPS on his phone, so it was back to reading an old-fashioned map again which was hard to find because they had stopped printing them. Also, since he hadn't used one for years, he found that reading it was a lot harder than he remembered.

Cook drove on for a half hour dividing his attention between the map, road signs and traffic. When he reached the exit for Denville he turned off. Without a wrong turn he crisscrossed various roads where one of them led his tanker over a set of railroad tracks and into an empty lot next to a vacant building. It was an out of the way place but not so out of the way that it would be too long before discovery.

Ten minutes later the same tan Chevy Avalanche that Mr. Cook saw at the last pit stop pulled up and parallel parked next to his tanker. He got out and walked towards the three men that exited that vehicle. They shook hands when they met yet it was serious faces all around. The men talked but got busy when another cab minus its trailer pulled into the parking lot. Cook helped unhitch the tanker from his cab and allowed the new arrival to back his cab up into the hitch. Minutes later his tanker with a full load of gasoline was on its way out of the parking lot to parts unknown.

A short conversation ensued before one of the men produced a bag. That man walked with Cook back to the curb next to his rig. "You're not going to make me wear that thing, are you?" Cook said. "Yep" is all his accomplice said as he tied his hands behind his back and put a gag in his mouth. When he was done tying him up, he placed the black bag over Cooks head and tied it around his neck.

"Hang on dude, we'll call in a sighting to the cops to speed this up, you won't wait here long don't worry. Just keep thinking about the one hundred grand! Well meet you on the other side of this to square up. Keep the story straight, don't get flustered and you'll be alright. Got it?".

All Jonathan Cook could do was mumble and nod his head. "For a hundred grand I can put up with this" he said. Only he hoped he wouldn't have to sit here long before being discovered by the police. His boss would have no choice but to believe his story about his rig being hijacked by thieves. Cook was certain he wouldn't lose his job; he'd be cleared from any responsibility. All he had to do now was to put up with a little fall out and he'd be a hundred grand richer tomorrow morning.

"Ok sit down on the curb and wait for the cops, you'll be alright here" one of the men said while helping Jonathan Cook sit down on the curb. The other two men scanned the immediate area around them looking carefully to make sure there were no witnesses. The man asked Cook "Not too tight?" as he pulled a gun from a holster tucked in his belt behind his back. Without pause he placed the barrel of the gun against the driver's head and pulled the trigger.

5

Last Look Over The Shoulder

The last few passengers on bus #53 disembarked and spilled out onto the ramp. For those, New York City was their last stop. They faced the high rises, the smell of acrid city air and a hell of a lot of foot traffic while bumming out at the sight of New York's Greyhound Tent City with all its misbegotten. The significance of it was clear; if they didn't have something going for them already, it was doubtful that they'd find anything lucrative here in a city where people affectionately called it "The rotten apple" or "New York Shitty". The travelers collected their luggage and then most wandered around aimlessly with a "what am I going to do now" expression on their bobble head faces. There was an air of disparity here that seemed to suck the spirit right out of you even before getting the full gist of the situation dawned on you.

Kaiden pitied them. They were just arriving and he, along with a bus load of people, were getting the hell out of here. The last couple of months flashed before his eyes as he pushed off and stepped onto the bus.

Throughout his high school years Kaiden roamed his neighborhood with a gang called the "88's". They were just one of the many gangs whose membership and power had recently grown in the rapidly deteriorating social conditions of NYC's urban neighborhoods. Every kid had to belong to a gang. It was how you survived in the big city. It was a smart thing to do, to plow through as a "loner" in today's urban environment exposed you to a lot of risk. You would be an easy target and preyed upon by the criminal element that was so prevalent in the streets of New York. The loners were the ones who got picked on, robbed, or beaten up. A kid was always stronger and better protected in numbers. Being a member of a gang was a welcomed alternative.

Kaiden was in trouble with the Police, his girlfriend, parents and probably even God himself. That last one worried him, Kaiden still held a firm belief in God. He was a devoted Christian in a world that seems to have outgrown it. Yet even with the wrath of God Kaiden too found it difficult to keep his feet planted firmly on the golden path. His father Roman P. Sawyer saw to it that Kaiden grew up a Christian. Figuratively speaking Roman had "old style" written in ancient script all over him.

Borne in the hills of Scotland, Roman had the profound roots of Christianity handed down to him from his parents. In turn the man ruled his family by the same virtues that they had handed down to him. Roman instilled the teachings as best he could into his family and son and continued to do so even after moving to the United States. A job transfer to the United Nations as an interpreter promised monetary rewards that Roman was unable to turn down. Yes, his motivation was "for the money" and not for the privilege of living in the U.S. He just wanted to put in his ten years and then get back to the homeland.

Kaiden's father spoke English, Irish and Chinese fluently. Irish was considered a language by itself due to the heavy accent which many could not decipher upon first hearing it. Roman's parents were stationed in Taiwan back in the mid 1900's during World War II where Kaiden's grandfather worked in the Irish Embassy. He ended up staying on for more than twenty years after the war. Roman grew up and went to school in Taiwan and naturally learned both Mandarin and the

Cantonese versions of the Chinese language. He followed in his parent's footsteps and worked as a Chinese/English interpreter for the UN.

If Roman could stand living in New York City for the fifteen-year contract, he would be able to cash out and return to Scotland with the ability to retire very comfortably. So, he up and moved the whole family to NYC when Kaiden was 9 years old. There, he started his pursuit of a piece of the American pie.

The Sawyers were the essence of a typical catholic family, very devoted to family and church and were filled with gratitude for the Lord thy God and yes, he came to admire the United States of America for what it stood for. But his mother, Miriam Sawyer, found living in NYC to be repulsive although she graciously acquiesced and gave up her preference for the promise of someday living their lives in comfort back in Ireland. Roman embraced the teachings of the Bible and made sure that his son Kaiden received a deep understanding of Christianity as seen through the eyes of the Catholic Church. He guided his family abiding by Gods law and adhered to the customs dictated by Catholicism. It was church school every Sunday when Kaiden was young, Mass every Sunday morning and even on Wednesday nights when he was older. He was constantly involved with the Church ever since he can remember. Ironically his father saw the old way as the only way to live in a new world that was moving in the opposite direction.

Kaiden's father was determined but he wasn't blind to the needs of a kid growing up in the city. The same year they moved to New York he used his contacts in the Chinese Embassy to obtain recommendations for a good martial arts school. It was of utmost importance to give his son an education in the art of physical survival. He wanted Kaiden to literally have a fighting chance in future battles that his father knew would be forthcoming. To him, it was imperative that Christians were strong and capable of protecting themselves as well as able to verbally defend their beliefs. It would happen whether Kaiden wanted it or not. Luckily it wasn't necessary to push Kaiden at all. He was excited about the whole idea and looked forward to the excursion into New York's "China Town" with his father.

As Kaiden followed the people in front of him online for bus #53 it reminded him of that first Saturday's trip into China town, his mind floated back to that day. From the bus ride downtown, to the crowded subway train ride back home, he pictured his father sitting there beside him. In between they spent the whole day walking around visiting various martial arts schools. It was so much fun and Kaiden smiled from the fond memory of his dad. It seemed like such a long time ago.

"The first school we visit Kaiden will be one that teaches a martial art called "Choy Lee Fut" his father outlined their schedule while riding the "E" train going into Chinatown. "It's a style of what Americans call Kung Fu which in Chinese means 'a skill learned over a long period of time'. The word can be applied to many things, not just martial arts.

Choy Lee Fut is one of 140 different styles of martial arts that can trace their roots back two thousand years into the depths of ancient Chinese history. Choy Lee Fut kung fu is the combined innovation of its three founding fathers- Mr. Choy, Mr. Lee, and Mr. Fut, all of whom were Masters of their style of Kung fu. They combined the best aspects of their arts into one and it became one of the most popular styles of pugilism on the Chinese mainland. Students honored the founding fathers by naming the art Choy Lee Fut".

It was a day that Kaiden will always remember. Visiting martial arts schools with his father made a major impression on Kaiden. Immediately after seeing students practicing in the studio Kaiden became enamored with the idea of becoming a martial artist. It amazed him that there were people walking around with swords and spears. They did dances with them called "forms" while turning, swinging, and artfully twisting each weapon around their bodies and all without cutting themselves. He was impressed with the energy of the practitioners and kept shouting "awesome" with a "did you see that dad" about a million times. They also did bare hand forms that Kaiden thought were the "razz" as he used to say. It was just like an old Jackie Chan movie playing out right in front of him. Only this was real!

From one strong stance to another a whole class of students stepped in unison with their arms flailing in a whirlwind of circular motion. A block became a strike, and a strike quickly turned into a block all in one swing of the arm. The teacher, Master Kwong, did a special demonstration just for the benefit of Kaiden and his father. He had multiple students attack him at the same time and he successfully defended against them all. His arms turned into fan blades and students bounced off him at every attempt to penetrate his defenses.

"This is just like the movies!" Kaiden excitedly told his father.

Using the unique techniques of Choy Lee Fut, Kung Fu Master Kwong struck simultaneously in two directions striking opponents both in front and behind him at the same time.

"I wanna learn that one Dad!" Kaiden squealed as he marveled at a student performing an energetic routine with a spear. "This must be the place where people in the movies come from". Roman smiled at that.

Next, young Kaiden and his father walked to the famous Preying Mantis Martial Arts School just a block away from the first school just off Church Street. Master Chow greeted them, and his father showed him the letter of introduction he obtained from an emissary at the Embassy. Master Chow was impressed by the fact that Roman spoke fluent Chinese. He was so impressed that he demonstrated the main characteristics of the art himself. They were told later that this was a rare privilege because the Master hardly ever "performed" for anyone.

Then Master Chow directed his top students to demonstrate a few of the other Preying Mantis forms. They performed the first and second form and then did some wild free style sparring. It was a very aggressive style designed to take control and tear an opponent apart with movements that mimicked the Preying Mantis insect. The teacher would stop them and explain an error, then he would show them how to do it right and direct them to try it again. They also practiced with wooden swords with protective gear and fought each other with such ferocity that Kaiden thought they were really fighting. Even at that young age Kaiden took it in and loved every minute of it.

After visiting the Choy Lee Fut School, they had a fantastic lunch at a Chinese restaurant just a few blocks away. The place was highly recommended by someone at the Chinese consulate. The waiter feigned an inability to speak English and was very surprised when Kaiden's father responded in perfect fluent Chinese when he ordered. Right then and there Kaiden swore that he would learn Chinese so he wouldn't starve when he came back to China Town.

It went like that all day long, people at every place they went were pleasantly surprised when Roman conversed with them in fluent Chinese. Kaiden saw students, waiters and strangers pull a comrade to the side and point at the two of them. One of the students they met stated in broken English "I'm sorry I only speak Cantonese". Roman freaked him out by smoothly switching to the "Cantonese" dialect and continued the conversation. It made everyone look at each other with big smiles and a sense of admiration for the man and his son. It was very rare to find an American who appreciated the Chinese culture enough to become fluent in their native tongue. Most people never take the time to learn another language and learn it well. A lot of people they met that day were left wondering "Who is this American?".

After lunch they walked to the next "Kwoon" which is what the Chinese call their martial arts gym or training room. According to directions, they walked the three blocks from the restaurant to an obscure alleyway. At the end of it they found a door without any markings that led down a dark hallway that led to another door. They knocked and someone slid open a movable slot in the door and peered out.

What do ya want? The eyes in the slot said.

His father responded "We're looking for the Wing Chung School of Martial Arts. Are we at the right place?".

The guy answered by slamming the slide back over the slot in the door and after some fumbling with the lock it opened, and the mystery person beckoned them inside. Kaiden thought it was weird, if they didn't have precise directions, they would never have found the place.

Again, introductions along with the letter from the Consulate softened the man's demeanor.

"Come inside" he said. "Master Lee's not here but I'll get Si-hing Young (the senior student) to show you around".

A small waiting room was just off the main training facility and when Kaiden walked through that door he walked into a different world that was as amazing as it was intriguing. After the introduction letter was presented to Si-hing Young, they were accepted with a bow, and they all shook hands. Names were exchanged and Si-hing Young gave them the tour of the facility and showed them the inner training areas. He told them he was a disciple of Master Lee's and described himself as the curator of the Wing Chung School. Young was of American decent, which was great because he communicated easily with Kaiden and Kaiden took to him right off. With Young there wasn't the barrier that other Chinese martial artists seem to have when you first meet them. Most of the instructors they met that day spoke Chinese and varying degrees of English. With some of them it was impossible for Kaiden to understand anything they said.

Si-hing Young told them "No one is accepted into the Kwoon right away for various reasons. Generally new students are not accepted before first proving themselves to be a worthy recipient of the art. If you go to another school in China town an American will not get the same degree of training that someone of Chinese origin would get. Here, everyone is treated equally. There will be many character and physical tests that you will have to pass, then and only then will you be fully accepted as an inner circle student".

The key was the letter of introduction. That broke down barriers that they never could have overcome otherwise if they just found the place and walked in. People who do that are treated with suspicion and are never allowed to see anything except basically the door on their way out. You had to know somebody to be invited to join. This was a secret society that only gave certain people the privilege of even inquiring about the school.

Si-Hing Young gave Roman and Kaiden a full explanation and description of the Art of Wing Chung. Kaiden asked a million questions, and the instructor answered them in a way that got Kaiden really excited about joining this school. Especially when he told Kaiden that Wing Chung was the original style that Bruce Lee studied before he became famous. He learned that it was an art that trained in sensitivity exercises that concentrated on teaching the student real useful fighting skills.

"It's nothing fancy like some of the other styles" Si-Hing Young explained. "We concentrate on learning how to fight. Not just learning forms". Si-Hing Young pulled a few students away from their practice and asked them to demonstrate the main form of the art. They performed the movements together with each mirroring the other's movements to the tee. It was a relatively simple form that was not done with all the wild punching, kicking, twisting, and turning that they had seen at other schools. This was more of a boxing style where low kicks were integrated into it with a lot of fast punching techniques.

First the form was done slow and precise by the two students and then Si-Hing Young got one of the senior students to perform the same movements only faster and with power in the punches and kicks. They also did the same movements on a partner that resembled a sparring exercise where one would punch and the other would block. Then they would switch with the other one doing the punching.

Kaiden was impressed when the two of them started to pick up speed. They quickly traded punches with blinding fast hands that flew all over with short quick kicks in between. Luckily for the recipient, each kick was blocked and a punch or a kick was returned instantly right back at the attacker. Well, almost every kick was blocked. Every so often one would get the better of the other and a body would hit the floor. It was a unique block and counter type of exercise that trained close in fighting techniques with excellent results.

If that wasn't enough, Kaiden saw a student walk up to this thing that Si-Hing Young called a "wooden dummy". The guy started wailing away at it with punches, blocks, and kicks. It looked like a wooden man on a stand with a telephone pole size body. Two thick sticks came out of it at shoulder height which represented arms. One thick wooden tree branch in the shape of a bent leg came off at waist height and pointed down to the floor mimicking the shape of a man's bent leg.

Si-Hing Young knew that Kaiden would be fascinated with this unique training device, most people are, so he led Kaiden and his father over to it for another demonstration. He explained the basics of what they were doing and showed him how one practices punching and kicking on the "wooden dummy". The instructor started off slowly punching the dummy with various techniques. Then he sped up and was moving to each side of the dummy with kicks and punches striking multiple places rapidly. The whole dummy shook on its stand and even the floor seemed to vibrate when he struck it. You could see and feel the power in his strikes. Kaiden couldn't believe that a person could hit a solid piece of wood that hard without getting hurt. He looked at Si-Hing Young in awe and was hooked from that moment on.

Kaiden looked at his father. "Dad, I want to learn this".

That was that. Kaiden was accepted as a student on a temporary basis. They made him aware that as a beginning student you had to work hard to prove yourself before you were fully accepted. From that day on at least twice a week and sometimes three, Kaiden's father either brought him himself or made arrangements for his son to travel down to China town for Wing Chung lessons.

Kaiden moved up online, but he wasn't paying attention. He stood there outside the bus flipping through a few hard-won memories like he was turning the page of a scrap book in his mind. He remembered being there in the City training with all the good friends he had made and yes also the fights he had gotten into with all the assholes he had to deal with on the street. Kaiden smiled as he fondly remembered the Chinese restaurant and the soup he loved to eat after class and all the lessons he learned on that same block in downtown China town. Mostly he remembered "Shou ping" the Chinese girl that he fell in love with. That happened to be the cause of most of the fights he got into. She was so cute, even now he could picture her straight black hair and every detail of her pretty face. Back then Kaiden found out very quickly that Chinese parents (along with their brothers) were so protective of their blood line that they strictly forbade their daughters to date anyone outside of their race. Defiantly Kaiden and a buddy of his pursued a relationship anyway. Each of them had fallen in love with a Chinese girl. Because of it, both the parents came down hard on their daughters. They were beaten and chastised for their transgressions and then forbidden to leave the apartment except to go to school. They too were best friends and together the girls wallowed in their grief. The two of them became so distraught and overcome with sorrow that in protest against their parent's intolerance, hand in hand Shou ping and her girlfriend both jumped off a ten-story building and killed themselves.

To Kaiden all that seemed like a long, long time ago. Yet it had become an intricate part of him and molded his character in a way that most people will never experience at that age.

6

What Is But What Should Never Be

Violence and rioting were on the rise, not only in New York City but everywhere. During the past year. Unions organized strong protests which turned out crowds of unhappy workers and illegal immigrants who took it upon themselves to break things. Large masses of people threw violent temper tantrums because a wage, a benefit or a pension was put on the chopping block. Municipalities, Cities and States were forced to cut back on budgets. Pay raises were out of the realm of possibility. Even promised pension contracts were broken and nullified. The Unions had no leverage; there was no more room for bargaining. Many municipalities including some States were not only broke but owed millions if not billions of dollars in loans. There was simply no more money to hand out to pay for the ever-increasing expenditures.

Except for Fox News, footage the media showed was heavily one sided with an overwhelming number of segments covering police beating people and arresting them than clips of rioters destroying property and setting buildings on fire. When cops were shown manhandling a protester, captions underneath described them as "innocent students". When the video showed bands of union workers throwing flaming Molotov cocktails at police and buildings, captions described them as citizens fighting back. New York, Chicago, and San Francisco were hit hard. The media painted a picture of the participants as "Victims of a failed capitalist system".

Prominent progressive leaders interviewed on TV skewed the point and deflected it by saying protesters "deserve and have the right for a free college education". This even though the majority are not paying anything into the Federal tax system at all (50% of the US population pay no Federal taxes). They went on to demand that the wealthy pay for it because "the wealthy have made their money off the backs of the downtrodden people of the world". The parody of this being that the modern capitalist system can claim sole responsibility for bringing more than a billion people out of the throws of poverty since its conception, something that no other system has been able to do- ever. Still the liberal media wove the story and added jabs of distrust directed toward the wealthy while throwing stabs at Republicans who they said "...were trying to cut spending and take what little we have out of the hands of the poor".

Eventually riots would be contained and restricted to an area by police who protected certain buildings and areas within boundaries. Lines formed by police decked out in riot gear were common. Apparently, there was a policy of "non-interference" with the rioters and generally no orders to move on the crowd were ever given. At least not unless the violence turned deadly. Liberal City mayors allowed their people the freedom to express themselves and the freedom to destroy. Therefore, several union organizers took it upon themselves to take it to the next level. In many cases they pushed back hard against police defenses. On way too many occasions gunshots rang out and bullets flew in both directions. More and more the fight against police turned ugly and included an increasing number of shootings that ended in the death of a cop or a citizen. Of course, the "other side" was always the one who started it first and "guns in the hands of citizens" was the problem with gun control being the solution.

Kaiden wanted no more of it. It was not a total rejection of the way he was brought up. No, it was more like a magnetic repulsion of opposite poles that developed and accumulated over the years. Growing up in the dismal grind of that section of NYC took its toll. The City forced the skills needed to survive to the forefront and imposed a dark spot on the psyche of anyone who had to endure it. It was bad enough during normal times let alone in these times of great turmoil. That was the reason why Kaiden was so ready to put it all behind him and was so thankful for this opportunity to get out and start fresh.

A Greyhound employee wearing an official "Greyhound Bus" uniform stood by the luggage compartment door taking tickets and checking luggage. Kaiden showed him his ticket and gave him his duffel bag. It was accepted and the man motioned him on. Kaiden moved up and stepped onto the bus and then picked his way down the aisle toward the back. Surprisingly the first available was next to a window. The digital display on the front of the bus changed from "New York" to "West Point" designating the next stop on the route. He stuffed his small carry-on knapsack underneath his seat and pressed the button to allow him to push it back into the reclining position. Settling into a soft cushioned chair was refreshing. Automatically he checked the comfortable factor by nestling his head back against the headrest. His head rolled to the side, and he looked out the window while contemplating the course that had been chosen for him. Thoughts continued to pop into his head and flash across his mind like intermittent scenes from a movie. For the umpteenth time he thought about the possibilities that lay before him. In his mind's eye he tried to see the future but that seemed so vague and elusive. The attempt gave way to painful memories of the past. Those were strong and solid.

Kaiden was a member of the 88's. For two years Kaiden had worked his way up through the ranks of the organization until they voted him in as leader just short of eight months ago. All the gang's activities centered around Public School District #88 in Queens NY, NY, they claimed the entire east side of the neighborhood as their turf. Rumor had it that the members had taken their name from the obvious designation of their school "PS 88" but anyone in the know knew that it originated from the movie "Kill Bill" in which the Chinese sword fighting gang was called "The crazy 88's".

The 88's didn't have just one leader. They have what you could call a "board of directors" of which Kaiden was considered the chairman. They were probably the only gang in NYC where decisions were put to a vote. It was unique in that business was conducted democratically rather than revolving around the whims of one impressionable leader as was the case with other gangs. This was undoubtedly an offshoot of the "Bentner effect" which was a nick name given to the phenomena that seemed to transpire when anyone stood in the presence of Mr. Bentner for any length of time. Mr. Bentner was PS 88's history teacher.

Major opposition to the efforts of the 88's came from the "Banshee's". Their identifiable script could be seen written in graffiti all over the west side of PS 88. They were a rival gang who claimed a large section of street that ran from Broadway all the way up to 20th Ave. The 88's claimed to have everything from Steinway east. PS 88 was located in the neutral zone between the two. Boarders and terms of a truce had previously been delicately negotiated with the help of Mr. Bentner. He had become a mentor to many of the students over the years and found himself in the middle of such disputes. Mr. B or "Professor" as he was fondly called was a large man of the past. Meaning quite literally he used to weigh a solid 295 pounds. Mr. B had lost 75 pounds recently and looked quite different than he did in the picture on his driver's license. He was a balding man of 54 years of age, of average height with grey/black wisps of hair on both sides of his head. Most of the time he combed it straight back, but mostly it just kind of stuck out giving him that wise man Einstein look, positively the "whole nine yards" look of a teacher.

Mr. B spent 18 years as a kid growing up in Kansas, then six years at Penn. State University where he finished his master's degree in history. Then it was back to Kansas for four years before finally venturing out and heading back east. One job he landed was in Philadelphia; there was also one he took in Washington DC. Nobody knows why Mr. B turned down these more lucrative positions in lieu of a history teacher's job at PS 88 in the heart of New York City. That was a mystery that manifested itself just nine short years ago.

The "Bentner Effect" was something that captured the hearts and minds of students and influenced quite a number of people with his own style of care and devotion. He showed genuine concern and even a little magic that seemed to happen to everyone he encountered. Mr. Bentner was a once in a lifetime teacher rarely found in the dark dungeons of the New York City Public School system.

Yet even Mr. Bentner's magic couldn't stop the inevitable battle between the Banshees and the 88's. One night the Banshee's initiated an incursion into the 88's territory which everyone knows is against common law. That fateful Friday night was the start of the whole turn of events for Kaiden Sawyer. The excursion took place on the basketball courts in Winchester Park located off 31st street. The 88's considered this their home base of operations and many members hung out there at all times of the day and night. The gang moved into the old home team baseball dugout of the park and used it like an office. "Homie hometown" was written in graffiti on the concrete ledge above the steps.

It didn't make no never mind to any of the locals. No ball games had been played there in that neglected park for quite a few years now. Everyone knew it was home base for the 88's but even the people who lived in the neighborhood tolerated their presence. Rival gangs were supposed to respect their claim to the territory and in turn they would respect the others. All of that had been fought for and settled a long time ago. Intrusions into the hood were rare.

Yes, it's strange to say that residents "respected" the gang. Who really respects a gang? But they did in one way. Gangs in the urban areas of the cities had become so common that most kids of all ages belonged to one. Some parents even encouraged it. Inevitably they'd be better off, which really came down to being better protected in numbers rather than being alone. Or rather than being picked on and robbed of your school lunch money on a daily basis, protection achieved by being a member of a gang was accepted. It literally gave your kid a fighting chance. Many times, that's exactly what it took to survive in the city... a fight and a chance.

Basketball was still the game of choice and was played vigorously on the rusted dilapidated hoop and backboard at Winchester Park. It was a full-sized court that sat adjacent to the baseball field separated by the fenced in batter's cage. At one time the double sectioned fence helped keep foul balls from sailing out onto the court. The home team dugout was almost at the center of the park and made a great protected structure with a strategic commanding view of the area. Over at the courts, for most hours of the day and even into the night you could hear the dribbling of a basketball and the shouts of someone arguing about the last point. It might not have been the best-looking park by far but there was always some form of activity or human presence there in one form or another. There were the kids and parents at the playground during the daylight hours, local drunks and druggies took it over in the evening and the hookers seemed to be there at all times of the day and night. Mixed between all of that were members of the 88's and their girlfriends.

On one significant night, it all started from the back seat of a sedan as it drove slowly down 31st Street at 11:00PM. It was the only drivable street adjacent to the west side of the basketball court. The windows rolled down and immediately loud shouts with an audible array of insults poured out from both the front and back seats, positively with the intention of provoking a response.

"All you fuckin 88's can't shoot for shit you's sons a bitches! I just saw your girlfriend lyin' on her back scorin' better than that... look at you wimpy ass mutha fuckas with your frickin sponge bobbin nickel-odeon game!

The car's front wheels started "bopping" as the passenger switched the hydraulic switch on the handheld control box from "on" to "off".

The air shocks bounced the front end of the car up and down in a blatant attempt to gain attention like a peacock spreading its wings.

"Fuck all you's and yo nasty ho freaking' ma ma's too".

With a little skill in timing and hitting the hydraulics just right, the car's front wheels came up off the ground and the whole front end would then slam back down again jarring and bouncing the inhabitants of the car up and down. It bounced as it drove slowly down the road making quite a racket while displaying the trendy use of modern hydraulic technology. The car shook the occupants silly as they held on for dear life. It succeeded in turning the heads of people loitering nearby and some of the ones hanging out on the sidelines around the basketball court. Some of the 88's immediately got the gist of what was going down and automatically raised middle fingers shouting back with matching nasty euphemisms. Others caught on and joined in by slapping the bicep of one arm into the palm of the other and raising their fist in the air. A few showed no fear and started strutting toward the intruder's car while yelling back with insults of their own.

"Come on mother fucker, come on" you could hear them join in.

More slanderous words about how the other "sucked" flew back and forth between the two entities like a mad ping pong ball. Soon some of the players stopped in the middle of their basketball game to look. They too joined in and shouted in an all-out show of solidarity against the intruders who dared to mock them. A group of guys got serious in their demeanor and their attention soon became focused on the car. If this was allowed to escalate and the poor occupants in that car were caught, a serious fight was inevitable.

Before that could happen, the sedan stopped bouncing and three quick gunshots accompanied by flashes of light erupted from the open window. The unmistakable bang of a .357 magnum halted everyone in their tracks. Everyone ducked as they realized it was gunfire and heard bullets zinging through the air in their direction.

One of the boisterous males in the group of men hanging out at the courts, moved defiantly toward the car in an aggressive manner. He was the first one to get struck by a bullet. The young man clutched his leg and went down fast. Kaiden and three of his 88's were standing near the dugout and pulled guns while running toward the street as the car peeled out and accelerated down the road. Kaiden and his guys made it into the middle of the street only to point their pistols at the taillights of a car speeding away from them. Everyone in pursuit stood there for just a second- thinking, and then a decision was made. One gun went off and others followed shortly thereafter. All four guns fired randomly in a vain attempt to somehow strike back. Other members who followed, stood behind them with arms held straight in the air, middle fingers extended, in a kind of Hitler style "fuck you" salute. It was more like they had to shoot, a response to the anger that welled up inside. Bitter hate came out in the form of bullets that spewed out at the car as it sped off down the block.

No one could tell if they hit the car or not. But the car's occupants knew. They heard the distinct sound of punctured metal as two bullets slammed into the trunk of the car. The driver flinched; all the others ducked in case one came through the rear window. His flinch caused the car to swerve; it banged against a parked car and then skidded sideways across the road as they entered an intersection. The car disappeared as the driver made a sharp left turn. It careened around the corner with a squeal coming from the tires.

The full insidious nature of the cowardly act was instantly apparent when Kaiden walked back and saw his friend Neal withering on the ground in agony. Clutching his leg, he screamed inaudibly through clenched teeth as a pool of blood formed underneath his leg. Kaiden quickly tore off his shirt and wrapped it around the site of the wound, not allowing the victim's painful screams to deter him. The bullet had torn through the guy's calf entering with a small hole and exiting the other side where a big chunk of skin was hanging off. Unknown at the time, the bullet had skimmed off bone and broke the fibula before exiting.

Blood quickly soaked through the shirt. He heard someone say "Put a tourniquet on it man". But Kaiden knew that that should be held as a last resort. Applying a tourniquet dramatically increases the risk of losing the limb. Kaiden opted to wrap another shirt around the first and apply pressure to attempt to stop the bleeding. Only if a main blood vessel was severed would he resort to the tourniquet. He couldn't tell exactly how bad it was, but he had seen quite a few gunshot wounds before and this one didn't seem to be as life threatening as the others. He kept telling Neal "Don't worry, you'll live".

Eventually the cops came but they took their sweet time in getting there. When they finally arrived, they didn't even bother to get out of the patrol car until backup arrived five minutes after that. It was a full 55 minutes before the ambulance showed up. The paramedic said that Kaiden's decision not to use a tourniquet probably saved Neal's leg.

Inevitably tension built up between the 88's and the cops due to being late and their blatant lack of concern for acting on the information they were given. Arguments ensued as the cops went through the motions of an investigation. They wrote down a few names but the 88's knew they weren't going to do anything about it. One of the cops accused the 88's of somehow provoking the attack with some kind of antics of their own. The last straw was when the cop insinuated that the victim got what he deserved, that's when a gang member decided to defend their reputation with his fist and ambushed the cop with a right hook. A brawl ensued and Kaiden jumped in to try to break it up only he got caught up in what turned out to be a rumble. Three of them were hauled off to jail. Unfortunately, Kaiden was one of them.

Heated arguments ensued between Kaiden, the cops, his lawyer, parents and ultimately with his girlfriend as well.

The shooting, Kaiden later found out, was instigated by Jack Albert Kahn. Kahn was the new leader of the Banshee gang. Everyone called him "The Jackal". The Banshee's main line of income was dealing drugs, but they sidelined into robbery and more recently, due to bad economic times, it was anything that paid well. Methamphetamine and heroin were the drugs of choice with ecstasy coming in a close third. Because the Jackal was a user as well as the main supplier for the area, his mind was as warped as the drug can make you.

Information filtered back to the Jackal that one or more of the 88's was selling "product" in their territory (which ended up being true). Protecting their business interests became paramount in the mind of the Banshee's leader. It only took a fleeting thought of revenge that blossomed into reality on that night.

Kaiden never sanctioned the drug dealing side of business, but he couldn't control it either. Some fringe elements of the gang who weren't as loyal as he would have liked had dealings that Kaiden didn't approve of. But he had no power to stop it. Drugs were the mainstay of monetary support for some of the 88's but not for Kaiden. Either way the die was cast.

"Ok, we're goin to have ta respond ta dis, we got no choice" one of the 88's said at a meeting held just after the incident. Another chimed in "Yeah we all agree, cops ain't interested in putting themselves in harm's way just to stop a few drug deals".

Kaiden was all in and offered a plan. "We'll do a sting; it won't be that hard to set up wit dees guys. It'll require some very convincing acting on the part of an outside accomplice. But he's got to be an unknown to anyone in the Banshees gang. I know a guy who'll play the part for a fee...". Kaiden explained the rest of his plan and they all agreed that it was doable. It involved setting up a buy which ended up being the easy part, in the environment that hovered around the city the Banshees were eager to make a buck anyway they could.

Word put out on the street said that a high roller was ready to pay big bucks for a quantity of product that was a little different than what the Banshees normally dealt with, weapons. The Banshee's responded to the 88's bag man and took the bait. A deposit of two thousand was given with a promise of a final payment of 35K upon delivery of the goods. A special list of weapons they wanted was given. The 88's knew the Banshees didn't have a ready supplier that could fill the list of required items. No one on the street did. They had to coax the Banshees out of their neighborhood, and into a trap with an item that was hard to find. Drugs were out. They were readily available, and the Banshees already had plenty of anything you might want. No, the Jackal could get all that crap. It had to be something the Banshees didn't have in stock and couldn't get a hold of very easily; it had to be something they would need to steel.

The list of guns was extensive and precise; "10" Colt AR-15 semi-automatic rifles of various models, preferably .40 caliber. "10" Beretta 9 mil, 40 or 45 caliber 1911 handguns (any model). 10 Kel Tec .223 or .76 mil tactical semi auto rifles, "5" Ruger Mini 30's or 14's. The list was precise.

Kaiden had previously taken inventory of all the pawn shops and gun suppliers in a 50-mile radius, and it just so happen that the closest one who could possibly supply that quantity of arms with those specific manufacturers was a local wholesale gun dealer "Calvary Arms". They were the only dealer authorized to sell to the police and who had the AK's" that were on the list. Conveniently they were located close by just a few blocks down on Grand Ave. If the Banshee's did their homework and if they preferred it to be a one stop shopping spree, they would come to the same conclusion that Kaiden did, that this particular gun dealer was the perfect place where they could hit and steel all those weapons in one shot. The "buyer" played the part well and amazingly even suggested where the order could be filled. He told them that he would never attempt the heist himself and needed a motivated group to do the deed for him. "Oceans 13 style" he threw in as a joke. The only stipulation was that he needed the product delivered within two weeks. The Jackal took the contract.

The rest of the plan was easy although it was a risk. The Banshees just might have been able to steal the guns in multiple robberies at various other shops to fill the order and would not show up at Calvary Arms as predicted. They didn't. Four days later at 3:30am, a stolen pickup truck pulled up in front of the Calvary Arms Gun Shop. The pickup turned away from the entrance of the shop and stopped perpendicular to the front door. The driver looked hilarious with the football helmet he was wearing but its purpose became clear when he slammed the truck into reverse and hit the gas. A high-pitched screeching tire pierced the night as it burned rubber in reverse and peeled with billowing smoke emanating from the rear of the truck. It flew backwards and jumped the curve just missing a parking meter. Then it slammed into the front of the store with a blast of shattering glass and crumbling brick. A loud alarm went off, but a member of the Banshees calmly got out of the van, took off his helmet, threw it to the ground and reached into the truck bed. He quickly came up with a 3-pronged steel hook that was attached to a thick steel cable and hooked it onto the iron bars on the door that were now loose but still covering the ruins of the front entrance. A slap to the side of the pickup sent a signal to the driver.

Instantly the truck's tires spun and propelled the truck forward this time as fast as it had in reverse. Slack in the cable disappeared. With a loud "tong" the cable went taught and the iron bars jolted snapping right off the window casing. The whole grid flew 20 feet before hitting the ground with a loud crash. Sparks flew from the metal grate making quite a show as it tumbled and slid across the pavement. The truck swerved down the street looking almost out of control either from over exuberance by the driver or by simply over correcting on the steering. The truck fishtailed and sped off out of sight.

Seconds after, a van pulled up and backed up to the gaping hole in the entrance of the store. The rear doors flew open, and 3 guys scrambled out. All of them had stockings pulled over their heads and gloves over their hands. Two of them carried baseball bats. They scrambled over debris that littered the ground and disappeared into the dust and smoke-filled store.

After abandoning the damaged pickup its driver suddenly appeared by the van. He took his post and became the lookout.

"You know exactly where to go, now do it as we planned" one of the gang members said to another. They ran quickly over to a rack of assault rifles on the wall. "Cut it! He said in an excited tone. His partner produced a wire cutter and cut the cable that secured the guns to the rack. "Get as many as you can". Both feverishly started grabbing AR15's and sliding them into a duffel bag. Another one of the robbers stood over a display case, swung a bat up and over his head and brought the full force of the mighty slugger down on top of the casing. The glass countertop disintegrated in front of him. He moved to another and struck that one too. Access to the handguns inside was achieved in a matter of seconds. Pillowcases pulled from his belt were used to stow the handguns and as many as could be carried were swept off the shelves and hurriedly thrown into bags. Both teams of robbers ran out with the first load and tossed the bags into the van before running back into what was now an abnormally smoke-filled room.

They were fast. But on the second trip their speed had noticeably decreased. It looked as if they were getting tired. One even paused and looked up at the other giving him a silent question mark with a quizzical look on his face. "What's that smell" one of them said to the other. He glanced around at the guns as if he didn't know which one to take before finally choosing one and dropping it into the duffle bag. His partner pulled two rifles off the gun rack and calmly placed one on each of his shoulders and started marching out of the shop like a soldier. They all slowed down to a fast walk, then to a slow walk while seeming to have trouble maintaining their balance as they stumbled over the glass and concrete chunks that covered the floor. One thief crumpled to his knees and then fell over. His partner marched out of the store and sat down on the rear bumper of the van. With a pillow-case of goodies in his hand he sat there and stared back into the store from where he came without moving. The other accomplices never came out of the building.

Police responded and arrived at the Calvary Arms Gun Shop shortly after the attempted robbery. After clearing the building, they roped off the crime scene and started their investigation. Security video showed exactly what happened but not entirely who did it and why. They suspected the owner of the gun shop rigged an ambush in anticipation of a robbery. The act was positively illegal. The owner had a lot of explaining to do. But the mystery was why one of the thieves was lying on the ground next to the van with a bullet hole in him. Paramedics were busy kneeling beside him tending to a serious wound. After they administered first aid to stop the bleeding, they got him on a stretcher and quickly rushed him into a waiting ambulance. While frantically working to set up a blood transfusion, the doors slammed shut and the vehicle sped off to Belleview Hospital.

Camera recordings didn't show who fired the shot that night, so it was impossible to prove who did it. The cop's investigation went along with the same lack of enthusiasm that was selectively applied to cases such as these where the bad guy got what was coming to him. If it wasn't for an anonymous tip, they never would have suspected Raymond Carzone as the shooter. The caller revealed that he was a member of the 88's and gave revenge as a reason for ratting them out.

Everyone connected with the 88's gang was brought into the police station and interviewed. The suspicion shed a negative light on Mr. B's past involvement with them, which triggered a special meeting of the school board. The next day, school board members held a vote on whether to revoke the group's extracurricular authorization status which would effectively kick them off school grounds. Even Kaiden's parents were interviewed by detectives.

Luckily for Kaiden, he wasn't the lookout that night, he had an airtight alibi confirmed by his girlfriends' parents. Still, the police and Kaiden's parents held the suspicion that he was somehow involved. Certain pieces of the puzzle came to light that implicated him and they threatened to charge him with the crime. They believed Kaiden was either an accomplice or was the actual brains behind the sting/robbery. So, they offered a deal of immunity in exchange for revealing the identity of the attempted murderer which required Kaiden to testify against him. The truth and what it indicated alarmed Kaiden's parents to the degree that it became the catalyst that drove their decision to guide their son in a different direction. If he continued, surely he would have ended up in jail or dead.

What Kaiden wasn't saying was this; The week before the robbery an informant inside the Banshee's gang tipped them off as to which gun shop the Banshee's were going to hit, but (she) couldn't say exactly when they would do the deed. They did know that they wouldn't have to wait long for them to make their move.

Previously Kaiden had reconnoitered the Calvary Arms building and gathered information on the structure and its roof. It was a two-story building, and the roof was flat with a glass dome over the middle of the open two-story showroom floor. The dome allowed natural light in, but it was covered with thick iron bars making it impossible for anyone to break in that way. It was perfect.

On that night, 88 member Raymond Carzone had volunteered for the assignment to stake out the Calvary Arms gun shop. In the cover of darkness Ray, dressed in black with a mask on, found his way unnoticed to the back alley of the gun store where he snuck up on one of the security cameras. He didn't' worry about the camera overlooking his approach. Only if something bad happened would someone go back and look at the video. If they did, he was positive that no one would recognize him. Ray continued and hoisted himself up on top of the dumpster which enabled him to reach an old fire escape ladder. It wasn't a hard climb from there up to the roof. From his perch on the roof, he had a commanding view of the front entrance and due to the flat type of roof, he could easily move to the back and observe both sides undetected. From there he could peek his head up over the parapet wall and get a good view of the storefront and the street, all with one glance. He was keyed up about his part in the sting because it was his best friend Neil who had been shot by these guys.

Raymond was a member of the 88's who, in the early stages of planning, voted to go much farther than the plan they finally approved. Ray was one of those guys on the fringe. If he had gotten his way, it might have involved murder as well. As it worked out, he pulled the shift on the same night the hit went down.

"Neal's my best friend and I can't stand the fact that these assholes put him in the hospital with a zinger man" he argued to the others in his gang. "I'd go to any length for a little Banshee pay back. Let's give 'em the same thing they gave us- a lead splinter".

Luckily the group reined him in, and they all settled on payback that might get rid of the Banshees without the possibly of serving jail time themselves.

The time rolled into 3:30 in the morning, Ray awoke in a sitting position with his eyes bugging out from the realization that something was going down. The sound of screeching tires out in front of the building pierced the calm of night and caught him by surprise; he had been asleep with his chin resting in the palm of his hands.

There was no time to think about the mistake he had made by dosing off. His head popped up over the parapet wall just in time to see a pickup truck burning rubber in reverse and heading backwards straight at him, straight towards the main entrance of the gun shop that is. His eyes popped wide open as he realized that this was it. He turned and ran over to the glass dome in the center of the roof. On the way Ray grabbed a short piece of 2x4 he had placed there earlier for the express purpose of accomplishing his task. His legs were numb from sitting in the same position for a long time, so he hobbled over with a weird looking walk. Then, using the 2x4 as a club, he brought it up over his head and swung it down as hard as he could onto the homemade gadget that was nestled perfectly between the iron bars of the dome window. The gadget sat directly on the glass, and when he hit it, his mighty swing smashed the window which sent a vibration throughout the building. Ray felt the reverberation strongly in his hands going down to his feet. His strike happened to land at the same instant the pickup truck's tires screeched and it peeled off down the road.

From inside you could see glass in the dome window brake and the "gadget" as it dropped down onto the floor of the gun shop. A large sprinkling of shattered glass "tinkled" to the floor all around it. It bounced a few times and rolled up against one of the counters. The "grenade" was hissing, and white smoke began to spew out of it. The security camera caught it all on video and showed smoke steaming up from the floor mixing with the cloud of dust that came from the destroyed front entrance. The gang moved into the cloud of smoke undaunted and quickly went to work robbing the place.

In no time at all it became obvious to police observers watching the video that their bodily functions were affected in an adverse way by the smoke. On the second trip in, they all seemed to lose their initial enthusiasm for speed and started having a little trouble with coordination and picking out guns. Finally, their balance went altogether, and they started to stumble around. The two who were caught inside the store eventually slumped to their knees, unable to move. One of them had fallen face first onto the floor and the other collapsed and crumpled to the ground.

Ray ran back over the roof to the front wall and looked over to survey the scene on the street side, his heart was racing. Outside, and right down below him, the Banshee's look out was pacing nervously back and forth trying to speed up his accomplices. When the lookout turned, Ray recognized the face. "Holy shit, it's the Jackal himself!" Ray almost yelled it.

The image of the Banshee leader's face came back to him, retrieved from memories of the shooting on that hectic night in the park. He saw the Jackal leaning out the car window and then the gun going off-Bang...Bang...Bang. The smile on his face as he fired was imbedded in his mind. It made him furious. The Jackal was now right in front of him nervously pacing back and forth behind the getaway van without a clue about what was happening inside.

Watching from his perch, Ray was ecstatic that he was about to catch the Jackal himself. But the Jackal never went into the building and was never affected by the gas. He stayed outside and managed the operation, helping to place the stolen goods into the van. When one of his goons came out and slowly walked over to the van and unexpectedly sat down on the bumper, the Jackal went nuts. He hit him hard on the shoulder to get him going and started yelling in a thick New York accent "What the fuck's a matta wit chew?" He kept glancing nervously towards the building looking for the others.

Ray could hear him screaming and cursing, it made him smile.

"What in the world are you doing you fucking idiot" the Jackal yelled at the top of his lungs. "Get up and get the hell back in there!".

But to no avail. His partner didn't move he just sat there staring straight ahead. Nobody else came out of the smoke-filled store.

The Jackal stopped and quickly sized up the situation. He realized that something was wrong. The job was now compromised beyond repair. Police sirens sounded in the distance; they were just minutes away. He threw his cigarette down, turned and suddenly sucker punched his partner clean in the face knocking him back into the van. But instead of throwing his feet in and shutting the doors, he grabbed his feet and pulled him out! The guy's head and limp body hit the pavement at the same time with an audible thud. He shut the doors to the van and ran towards the driver's side.

Ray saw this and realized that the one person he wanted to burn, the one person he wanted dead, was about to escape the trap and get away. The leader opened the door of the van and hesitated. Just before he stepped in, he gave a last glance at the store entertaining a fleeting thought that his partners in crime might emerge from the gun shop at the last second. But no one did.

Just before the Jackal jumped into the van, from the edge of his vision he caught movement up on the roof. When he looked up, a shot rang out. The Jackal stared for a few seconds at the person on the roof trying to understand what just happened and why he couldn't move. As he tried to focus, his eyes glazed over, and his body fell to the ground while staring up at his assailant.

Ray stood on the edge of the roof in plain sight. A gun was in his hand with smoke emanating from the barrel. A sick twisted smile formed on his face expressing satisfaction with what he had done. Sirens could be heard in the distance. He turned and ran across the roof to the back of the building implementing the first part of his escape plan.

* * *

"An education will get you out into the world. Open your mind and possibilities will emerge" Mr. Bentner always said.

Hearing consistent statements like that, on a sub conscious level if nothing else, helped Kaiden to consider Mr. Bentner with more respect than some of the other kids did. Bentner was an excellent history teacher of the likes that hadn't graced the halls of PS 88 in many years. When Kaiden turned thirteen he found himself attracted to Mr. Bentner's style of teaching (some said preaching). Suddenly he felt like he was getting something rather than constantly having to give something up. That led him to Bentner's extracurricular class, the class of 88's. The members put Kaiden's application to a vote and they voted to allow him to join. That was how it was done. The group met mostly after school (sometimes on Saturday's) for extracurricular lessons and discussions on how history related to current events. The whole thing was voluntary. The class was sanctioned by Mr. Littner, the High School principal, who let Mr. B conduct the class on school grounds even though he disagreed with Bentner's entrenched conservative viewpoint. That was unbelievable in a school system where the "Liberal" mind-set prevailed. But the principal realized that these students needed help in any form they could get, and he surely wasn't going to stand in the way. Who would deny a teacher who was willing to spend so much extra time on PS 88's students?

The group was formed out of students who displayed a superfluous desire to learn. There weren't many takers in the beginning, but over time, and the more the economy turned south, the larger the group became. It seemed that more and more kids were looking for a better way out of this mess and Mr. Bentner gave them ideas which led to some answers. They were striving to understand the reasons that led them into the predicament they were in and were afraid for what the future had to offer. For the first time in American history the descendants of the previous generation were worse off than their parents. Surprisingly these students wanted to learn more about the past. It was a desperate effort to educate themselves as to the best way to proceed.

Liberals blame capitalism for every evil known to mankind and touted "The Government" as the best way to get the job done. Mr. B. taught the other side of the story, with facts, never attempting to influence by playing the emotion or the race card, but by catering to the student's common sense and intellect.

One of those classes stood out in Kaiden's mind. Mr. B addressed the class and asked them "Name any major program the government has ever created or any business that the government has ever gotten involved in and let's discuss how they've done".

Students raised their hands with various answers and Mr. B wrote them on the blackboard. 1) Welfare. 2) Medicare.

"Cars for clunkers!" someone yelled, and everyone laughed.

"Yes, #3 the cars for clunkers deal. I'll allow that. It's not a business but it is an attempt by the government to steer public buying power. OK, come on, you can think of more than that".

"How about the Post Office?" a student said.

"OK, #4 the Post Office".

"The Military?" another student shouted.

"Well, you can convince me that it is a business, but I would respond by saying that this is really the sole purpose of the government, to protect its people. It is an entity embedded into the system as a cost. I hope and I pray that the Military always succeeds at defending the American people and on the other hand I pray that it will always fail at making a profit. For if it ever turned into a profit-making business- oh my god, watch out! So, I don't include that as something the government has expanded into.

"Social Security" yelled a student in the front row.

"OK good, #5 Social Security" Mr. B said. "The business of securing our financial future". Then he looked at the class. "Anymore?".

A student in the back yelled out "Amtrak!" and Mr. B wrote that down as #6 saying "Good, Good, anymore? How about Finny Maylee and Mac Fruddle mortgage company? Let's write those down as #7.

"How about GM?" a student said.

"Ok, that's #8. Anymore?".

"Solar Energy" someone shouted.

"Ok that's #9".

"SanMonto" another student yelled.

"OK, SanMonto #10. The results are not in on that one yet and that one just might prove me wrong. SanMonto might be the first venture that the government will actually make money from".

Sanmonto wasn't even going bankrupt when the government forced them to take bail out money. They saw the importance of controlling the food industry and set out to do so by capturing the industry leader. Hence, they stepped in as SanMonto's controlling partner.

SanMonto genetically alters seeds. They successfully transformed the industry into one that would now be dependent on the US government for every successive crop. Genetically modified hybrid seeds do not produce viable annual seeds for re-planting; the farmers would have to buy new lots of seeds each year from guess who? The SanMonto Company. It's now illegal to plant non-GMO seeds. They control what farmers grow by restricting the type and quantity of seed they sell and of course to whom they sell it.

"But okay I'll write it down here as #10 although the full extent of the damage done to the food industry and the true "cost" of this acquisition will not be fully understood for many years to come. Let me be clear that with this one the "loss" here is not necessarily due to a lack of profit, at least not now, but more because of the adverse effects of their engineered seeds and genetically modified foods on both the environment and on the population. Increased rates of disease and cancer have been linked to the consumption of food products produced and chemically treated by Sanmonto. And that right there makes me label this as a failure. I'll allow it with prejudice.

OK, that covers most of the government's major attempts at running a business. But not the ones they are attempting to take over at this very moment. Now, how successful have they been at these businesses? How has the government done with the businesses they have run and or subsidized to the point where they are running it?".

Mr. B. pointed to the blackboard and went over each one individually with a generous explanation. "Look at the Post office. They are losing billions, yes billions of dollars a year. At the same time, privately owned UPS is making a profit. Why is this? The 'Cash for clunkers' project produced thousands of used cars that flooded the market. It made new car sales go down! This produced the exact opposite of what was intended. Amtrak rail service is owned by the government and is losing money in the same manner as the post office. The Solar Energy business. They tried forcing people to buy photovoltaic electric generators and no one wanted them, to the point where billions were lost in that endeavor too... In conclusion" he said after discussing the last one "All of these projects that the government has undertaken have failed! They're all losing money and require huge amounts of support in the form of tax credits or subsidies or both for the business to exist except for the SanMonto Company which I have already explained.

Aaron Grimes who was sitting in the front row spoke up "Wait a minute Mr. B, they did a great job with welfare. That can't be run badly. I mean how can they screw up handing out money!" Laughter ran through the class as that answer seemed to throw an undisputable truth into the discussion.

Mr. B responded "Don't be cute Mr. Grimes. If we look at the welfare program closely, it turns portentous really quick. There's a word for you- 'portentous'. Let me ask you a question Aaron. You do have a point that they can't screw up handing out money, but did it fix anything? Isn't the value of a program measured by its positive results? I'm here to tell you that there are still poor people in the US even after handing out over twenty-two trillion, yes trillion with a 't', taxpayer dollars since Lyndon B. Johnson implemented the program. Welfare is a black hole that has sucked up more and more money each year without anything to show for it. There were 14% of Americans on welfare when the program started, today there's a whopping 15% on welfare which is a hell of a lot more people when calculated against the increase in population. Are we any better off?".

"No!" the class registered their vote almost in unison.

"Welfare is another term for redistribution of wealth. It's a concept practiced by socialist governments in which the government is empowered or self-empowered to take from the haves and give to the have-nots. Why doesn't handing out money solve the problem? I mean the concept sounds great right? But is it a good thing for society?".

Some of the class voiced their approval while others moaned with displeasure, but it all melded into a low volume mumble that reflected an ambivalent response.

Mr. B tried to explain... "Mr. Grimes. Do you believe that in order to get an "A" in this class you would have to work really hard?

Aaron sat up and replied with a little sarcasm "Yes Mr. B we all know how hard we have to work to get an 'A' in YOUR class". The class burst out with conciliatory laughter.

"OK" Mr. B. said as he moved in front of the student and placed his hands flat on Mr. Grimes desk. He got serious, lowered his voice, bent down and looked him in the eyes. "Please be truthful and answer this next question honestly. If you did get an "A" in my class Mr. Grimes, by working hard, do you think that 'you' as a person would be better off? In other words..." he looked up and spoke loudly to the whole class "...do you believe that you would be better prepared as a citizen of the United States to help solve the countries problems if you learned these lessons at an "A" level rather than at a "D" level?

The entire class overwhelmingly responded with "Yes of course Mr. B".

"Would you Mr. Grimes?".

"Yeah, I guess I would agree" he confirmed.

"You guess?".

"Ok, Ok, I would be better off".

"Would the world be better off Mr. Grimes?

"I'd like to think that it would" Aaron said with an air of sincerity that Mr. B accepted as authentic.

"Ok. Mr. Grimes says he would be 'better off' and the world would be 'better off' if he and all of you performed at an 'A' level. OK, now think about this. Mr. Grimes happens to be one of the people in this class who is producing at an 'A' level, that's why I picked on him for this. I'm going to take Mr. Grimes here and anyone else in the class who is doing 'A' or 'B' work and I'm going to take some of that 'A-B' work of theirs and give it to the students that are getting D's and F's. That would be you Mr. Sanchez!" Mr. B directed his comment to a student in the back of the room.

Mr. Sanchez smiled and then laughed when his buddies around him patted him on the back and high five'd him. "All right Sanchez!" his buddies taunted.

"That would bring everyone's lower grade up to a C and of course everyone's higher grade would come down to a 'C'. As the head of this class, I now proclaim..." Mr. B said it as he opened his arms wide and gestured towards the ceiling... "I am now omnipotently proclaiming that everyone here is going to get a 'C' from this point on, C's for all of you, regardless of what you do. Let's take 'what you do' out of the equation".

Mr. B. danced around the room waving his arms wildly in the air and doing circles like he was Merlin placing a spell on the class.

The students all looked at each other in disbelief as they pondered what Mr. B was saying.

He explained "In other words I'm going to take from the top performers and give to the bottom performers. What do you think about that?"

Some of the students, especially Mr. Sanchez, cheered with new-found enthusiasm that they would now be passing this class without any extra effort and of course Mr. Grimes was looking shocked with equal disappointment and contempt for the new grading system. Still others just sat there without comment trying to think about how this would affect them.

Mr. B's dance ended with his arms coming down with a BOOM on top of Mr. Grime's desk again. The room fell silent. "What do you think Mr. Grimes? We already know how Mr. Sanchez feels about it".

He took a few seconds to respond and then Grimes stated emphatically "I don't like the idea that I can't get an A in this class".

"Oh, boo hoo Grimes" came from someone in the back of the room.

"Why" Mr. B asked him.

"It won't look good on my record for college" Grimes replied.

"Oh, poor Grimy won't be able to go to college, boo hoo!" another guy in the back yelled.

"But then again I kinda like the fact that I don't have to do anything for this class anymore".

"Ah, class! Did you hear that? Mr. Grimes says he won't have to work at an A level anymore" Mr. B. said with a fake shocked look on his face.

"No, I wouldn't, why would I?" Grimes said.

"Everyone! That is the question of the day now, isn't it? Why not? Why wouldn't you work at an 'A' level?".

Other people were raising their hands. Mr. B pointed to Janice.

"Mr. B I see what you're getting at, and I'd love to tell you that I would still work at an 'A' level but knowing what I do about myself and the other people in this class I can assure you that everyone would eventually settle into doing the minimum that they needed to do just to get by. So no, I wouldn't do any more than 'C' work if any extra work above and beyond that went to the clowns in the back" Janice said while making a face towards the back of the room.

"Oooooo" echoed up from the gang in the back. Janice jeered at them with a forced smile.

Mr. Grimes agreed with a nod of his head.

The derelicts in the back raised their fists high in the air and booed whole heartedly while banging their hands on the desks. In the background you could hear someone yell "I'm gunna get you Janice". The whole group of them started laughing.

Mr. B. raised his hands in the air again and brought everyone to order. "How about the group of you who are doing good in this class, are you willing to give up a grade to these guys?" Mr. B. pointed toward the back of the class.

"NOOOOO!" shouted the students fearing that Mr. B was actually going to do this. They shouted with equal enthusiasm, but the violent desk banging was noticeably missing from their response.

Mr. B. opened his arms and directed his attention to the group "Do you all agree with Aaron that you wouldn't perform any higher than a C level?".

"Yes, why would we?" was the dominant response breaking through the murmur that rose from the class?".

"What?" Mr. B shouted.

"Yeah!" they shouted back with more veracity.

"Why should we!" a few of them yelled louder.

One voice rose above the others "...if it doesn't get us any farther for working harder Mr. B it wouldn't make any sense".

"Ok, Ok" Mr. B. said as he again brought the clatter to a halt. "This is the same thing that will happen and has happened in a society where the government takes from the achievers and gives to the non-achievers. It's the 'Robin Hood' syndrome". Taking from the rich and giving to the poor! This is the basic principle of a socialist form of government..." he paused to let it sink in. "By taking from the achievers I have removed the incentive for them to perform at a higher level. I have removed the reward for effort. Yes... now ask yourself, now that you have participated in this little experiment, why would you? Why would you perform any higher than a C if that's all you are going to get no matter what you do? Especially if you could do nothing at all and still get a C. Then I need you to ask yourself an even more important question- How would a concept like this effect society? Is this a good thing for society as a whole?" Again Mr. B paused for effect. "Think people. Do you feel that any of the amazing achievements and inventions of the past would have been developed within a society based on this premise?".

"Mr. B" a girl in the front row spoke up. "I think some of the achievements might still have been accomplished but I see your point. I believe operating in a society like that would have a smothering effect on its development or at least on a certain segment of the population. But isn't it a noble thing to do to give to the poor? Isn't that what's taught in the Bible?

"Yeah" was heard from the others sitting near her.

Mr. B took his time. "Now we're getting to the crux of the issue and the whole point of this lesson. We already agreed that working at an 'A' level was more apt to produce positive results in this city, in this country, in this world! We stated that this method has a better chance of getting our best and brightest 'producers' to work on solving our problems, right? You told me that it would be a benefit if you could profit from your work. Now we see that no one will want to perform at that level if we take away the incentive to do so. It's human nature, right Janice? We perform better when the potential for a greater reward is reachable, what does this policy do to our psyche? How does it affect you? Does a Socialist policy promoting the redistribution of wealth create a negative or a positive force behind society's development? Don't just think of yourself" (he directed that remark towards the back). "Think about society. Do you want the conditions of your society, of your situation, of your family to improve?" It was a great question that got everyone thinking.

Discussed at length was the negative spin against the free market. Mr. B spent a lot of time exposing what he called "The great lie of the socialist agenda". He said "There is a force out there with its whole intention designed to generate hatred among the masses to guide them into giving up their liberties. Its sole purpose is to offer a seemingly innocent answer to problems, to an emergency, that will magically dissolve by letting the Government implement the prescribed 'fix'. Liberal indoctrination has taken over the curriculum taught to our youth in many areas of the US and history has been changed and butchered into a story about how America got off track and dove into the gutter. These people have started a slow push toward socialism which was never a part of our forefather's intention. In fact, they wrote the constitution to keep that drift from happening".

Through the study of history, one can see the pitfalls. The history of previous governments shows how and why they failed the people. The morals of the stories offer valuable information about how to govern and how to avoid disaster. Our forefathers were historians. The information they gleamed from the pages of history guided them into winning arguments made against the socialist trend that governments gravitate towards.

"Governments don't produce anything; they just take from the people they control" said Mr. Bentner on multiple occasions. "They move and nudge people further into slavery with each tax levied, with each law enacted. Laws made under the guise of being a benefit to the people, but only end up as further support for the elite in power".

Mr. Bentner explained that the United States is following the same path toward socialism. One of his infamous sayings was that "Greed on Wall Street is so despised by common citizens that they begin to seek the same for themselves".

In one of his classes Bentner said "Good people have given up and those same people begin to conclude: 'If those people are getting it-then so am I'. They abandon the ranks of creators and join the throng of receivers strengthening the demand for entitlements. The whole sense of it moved into the American voter's psyche with an addictive 'What can the government do for me' attitude. Americans felt like they deserved something more, but they ended up sitting on the couch watching TV while they lost it all.

Why are the markets so choked off? How does 'government control' affect us? How does it eventually lead to economic ruin?".

Questions, conjecture, and answers were all on sale in Mr. Bentner's class. To the point where his after-school club became very popular with students who showed interest in expanding the discussion on these topics as well as getting help with their homework. A surprising number of students started to participate. Mr. B got the smart kids to work with the failing ones and many of the failing ones turned into enthusiastic participants. A lot of them started showing genuine progress. The group turned into sort of a "click". Most kids would never think of doing extracurricular schoolwork, but these were different times and some kids wanted answers. In Mr. B's class, they felt like they got them.

Over the years the group evolved. It splintered and morphed into a full-fledged gang. They even started wearing shirts and hats with the

88's emblem on them. Some even got tattoos. Students acquired the same sentiment and found that they had to bind together to survive the daily struggle of growing up in the inner city.

Mr. B taught lessons on the American Constitution and the principles of the American free market system, but he had to teach it after school, there was no room for a class on that topic in the NY public school system. He made sure students knew how unique and empowering the constitution was and how the individual was held responsible for their own success and their own failure. Mr. B always said "Success is very obtainable in America where determination and hard work will put you well above the poverty line. Desire creates ability and ability allows the manifestation of dreams. Here things can materialize unlike in any other country in the world, all due to the concept of the free market system".

It was rare to see a teacher dedicated to teaching such conservative principals. Mr. Bentner countered the constant barrage of liberal spin by the media and opened student's eyes with the truth about why our founding fathers created such a contract for the people, a contract that had never been allowed to exist between any other community and their ruler. He showed how it had created the most powerful, wealthy, and generous country of all by forming a method of government in which the people ruled. His most important point being that in this melting pot called America, people were allowed the freedom to fail as well as to succeed. It was their choice because if you worked hard, you would never stay down for long. You always had the opportunity to float back up to the top.

"It's a God given freedom! Not a 'government given' perk, it's not the governments to give in the first place. It's your unalienable human right". That was another famous line that Mr. B always said. And that's why he constantly butted heads with the school board. There was a strong push from the liberals to keep "God" out of any and all aspects of education. It was amazing that Bentner was able to operate at all. That was like many other things associated with the NY school system, people just didn't care anymore.

Mr. Bentner's comments did sometimes sound like he was preaching. He said "God gave the people the un-alienable right to be free. That is what our forefathers said and used as their guiding philosophy when they created the constitution. Liberals can't stand it; they strive to take God out of the equation and instead empower the 'government' to dole out and give people their constantly diminishing degree of declared 'freedom'. The problem is that every program the government has implemented has failed due to unanticipated negative consequences and corruption that funnels money into the pockets of the few leaving the intended beneficiaries worse off than they were before.

"You have freedom that people in a majority of the world's countries will never experience" Bentner told students in his class. He tried to guide them and mold them by using history in ways that made you think about what came before and how history has shaped our lives. He made it interesting. No, he made it relevant. And he made it crystal clear that "People who don't learn by history's mistakes are destined to repeat them". That was another one of his favorite worn-out clichés.

To get anyone to enjoy learning history was pure magic. That's why Mr. Bentner was sometimes called Merlin. He wasn't compensated for his extra time. He gave it willingly and took his reward from the appreciation expressed by students who realized the benefit of his efforts later in their lives. Occasionally, an alumni would appear at his door. There'd be a lot of hugging and dredging up of "old times", big smiles, a handshake and plenty of warm expressions of thanks from the people who took his words to heart.

Kaiden was accepted into the 88's in the beginning of ninth grade. By that time, it had evolved away from Mr. B's control. You no longer needed to participate in Mr. B's class as a prerequisite for becoming a member. It came full circle and turned into a full-fledged gang complete with colors and a hierarchy of leadership. They still engaged Mr. B as a consultant, but he became a separate entity. Many of the members still attended Mr. B's class but they gravitated toward other gang activities as well. Such were the times.

* * *

Greyhound bus #52 disembarked and was on the move. Daylight turned into darkness on the outside of the window Kaiden was looking through. Buildings passed, streetlights flickered and streaked by as the bus drove through the concrete jungle. Traces of light pierced through the glass and touched Kaiden's face. Block after block of high-rise buildings streamed by with seemingly endless rows of old store fronts at street level. Many of them were boarded up with plywood and iron bars. Only a few were still open for business, most were just vacant eye sores amongst a menagerie of old construction. It was a never-ending panoramic view of decay. All of them had different shapes and of course a different number of floors, but after a while it seemed like the only difference between them was a slightly different shade of red brick.

The bus turned onto interstate 87 and headed north into Yonkers where the scenery changed into row after row of shoe box homes. All of them stacked so close together with just a small driveway in between. After passing a couple hundred of them, the houses flew by the window and melded into looking exactly alike. Forty-five minutes later, the bus crossed the Tappan Zee Bridge and broke out into the less populated suburbs of Nyack but at 7:30 at night no one could appreciate the change in scenery. Darkness had pulled a veil down over the windows and shut off the view. The driver continued through a sea of pitch black, dotted with red taillights and white headlights on its way to the next scheduled stop- West Point, and then on to Kingston NY. But it didn't matter, Kaiden was sound asleep.

7

Yankee Go Home

Kaiden awoke abruptly to a change in speed and a sudden turn that the bus was making. The bus had made it all the way up 87 to Route 9 near the intersection of Route 6 where they were directed off the highway by a roadblock. Another delay. This would throw another stick in the spokes and add to an untimely arrival at their scheduled stop at West Point.

Here a roadblock manned by local police with a visible contingent of military support, blocked traffic and increased frustration for everyone involved. Before the terrorist attack against West Point Academy this would have been unheard of (and illegal), yet after the recent bombing with fifteen dead at the West Point Chapel these measures were accepted by the general public. No one questioned security, that was understood, but everyone hated the result.

Another terrorist plot in New York City came to fruition last May when a bomber got through and successfully blew himself up in the entrance of Grand Central Station. A terrorist named Abar Mucasta Mohammad took responsibility and is now famous in the Islamic State for succeeding to bloody the nose of the infidel. Two weeks after that a truck load of fertilizer detonated in front of the New York Stock Exchange building effectively taking out the front entrance in a Timothy McVeigh style attack. After that, new procedures were set up to insure "public safety", but which only seemed to curtail another freedom that American's had once enjoyed- mobility. Many streets in the downtown area are now closed to mobile traffic.

"We need "additional measures" to ensure the safety of all American citizens" politicians raved. So now all travelers must endure check-points like what Kaiden was about to experience. Every State passed similar measures and had them installed on all the major arteries along their borders which slowed travel and increase the cost of shipping for the whole country.

While approaching the West Point roadblock Kaiden was glued to the window. It was obvious that a handful of civilians from the Union Labor Party were part of the crew working the check point. They were easily identifiable due to the big white "ULP" letters written in bold on the back of their jackets. They walked about the place with an air of authority telling people where to go and when to stop. They were the type of people who really enjoyed their work.

Numerous military vehicles from the West Point Garrison were intentionally stationed at the side of the road at the main stopping point. By design they made quite an impression. The situation took on a more serious tone when the passengers on bus #53 looked out and witnessed a Bradley Fighting Vehicle with a fifty-caliber machine gun on top. It was manned by a soldier who stared back at them with indifference. The vehicle was painted in digital brown camouflage and was sitting there looking menacing as hell while monitoring traffic that crawled along slowly in front of it. All cars and trucks were funneled into an area with multiple lanes where they were stopped and checked by authorities. It looked exactly like a Mexican border crossing.

The bus driver's voice came over the loudspeaker "Ladies and gentlemen I apologize for this inconvenience. This is a necessary measure implemented for your safety. Please cooperate with authorities and we'll be on our way in no time".

Due to all the terrorist activity, all military bases as well as the West Point Military Academy had moved into lockdown mode. In the case of West Point, the threat of an attack forced the Academy to curtail access in the form of roadblocks that were set up on all roads leading into and out of the facility. They chose to block off Route 9 here at the Montgomery County line, but this check point wasn't manned only for the benefit of West Point. NY State Unions had banded together and formed the ULP for the sole purpose of protecting the interests of all organized labor. The group's mandate was to search for and eliminate the threat of cheap illegal labor, which was taking jobs away from union workers (they were also looking for illegal goods traveling across the border). The job market had gotten so bad that the prevailing trend for the protection of "illegals" supported by the Democrat party had fallen out of favor and evaporated due to present day circumstances. The lack of jobs in central NY forced localities to become very selective as to who was entering their region and for what purpose. At this point illegal immigrant labor laws were enforced like never before and it was now considered against the law and would not be tolerated.

An illegal immigrant was defined as anyone without legal US citizenship status who had the potential of taking work away from a legal resident or anyone who would put an additional strain on the local economy without a valid US citizenship card. It was as simple as that. The economy at this point could barely sustain the local inhabitants as it was. It had become common for large crowds of immigrant labor to gather in Home Depot parking lots across the country and after multiple incidents of riots the State moved to do something about it. People of all persuasions realized that they just couldn't afford a policy of tolerance any longer and sought to deal with it by physically picking up the illegals and sending them back to wherever they came from. What other choice was there?

The ULP was made up of personnel drawn from various local unions who would serve one day a week on the security force. It wasn't a bad deal at all. They not only got paid well for their time on the front line, but the union negotiated with the companies they worked for and secured them a full salary for the week as well as additional compensation for the hours they worked for the ULP. These were the same people that were presently flagging down Greyhound bus #53 and were now guiding them into the proper slot for boarding and inspection. Originally, they were mainly concerned with people, illegals, but success in finding valuable contraband morphed their focus into a search for illegal items that they could confiscate and then turn into a very profitable source of income for themselves. The ULP didn't like competition with smugglers.

Kaiden hadn't found the time to even acknowledge his neighbor sitting next to him other than a simple "Hey how's it going?" when the guy first sat down. Now he turned to him and said "Hey you know what's going on here?".

"Yeah, they're checkin for illegals, they've been doing it for over a year now ever since the bombing at the West Point Chapel and the one at Disney World".

"I didn't know that" Kaiden said. "I didn't think there were roadblocks except on the border in New York. How's the Disney World bombing connected to this?".

"Well, it isn't. That was just the incident they used as an excuse to start these things up on a larger scale. We got security at the Academy down pat. The Unions pitched a bitch about cheap illegal labor and got their way with the new 'search and seizure' laws that they're using to justify this shit" the Cadet said.

"By the way my name's Kaiden. Kaiden Sawyer".

"Mine's Kip... Kip Taylor". They shook hands.

"Kip, you're the first person I've met with that name. I won't forget that one. What's up with you? What are ya in for?" Kaiden asked him.

"If I don't get kicked off this bus, I'll be going back to West Point Academy. I'm a senior this year".

The young man or "adult in training" that Kaiden was talking to, looked the part of a full fledge cadet minus the uniform. You could tell, his hair was blond due to the short stubbles of a crew cut but if he wore a hat you'd never know. He was wearing his civvies, but his dress slacks and shirt still retained the same characteristics of a uniform with that permanent crease on his pant leg. The white collared shirt reminded

Kaiden of Church except for the fact that this guy sat up tall and proper with a straight spine and square shoulders like he was still emulating military etiquette. Somehow it lent him an air of authority due to a strong sense of confidence.

"Ah, you know exactly what you're in for then huh?" Kaiden asked.

"Oh, I know alright. I'm in for a whole lot of studying and a whole lot of marching. But they turn it around occasionally, so it's not too boring; we'll do a whole lot of marching and then a whole lot of studying". That drew a chuckle out of Kaiden. The Cadet continued "My brother went to the point and graduated a few years ago. My dad graduated in 1970. Now, it's my turn. Believe me, I heard it all. That's what made me want to go join in the first place".

"What? What made you want to go?" Kaiden asked.

Kip looked at Kaiden and surmised that the question was asked with enough sincerity to warrant a genuine response.

"Kaiden this world is changing". He turned and looked out at the all the cars stopped at the roadblock as proof.

"For the worse I would add" Kaiden said.

"Yeah, if I don't somehow figure out how to help my country and contribute something positive to this world before I die, I don't think I'll ever be at peace. I feel like I can obtain some kind of power here at the Academy that I can use for the benefit of my parents and my community".

"Yeah, but what can we do? To me it feels like the world goes on and on without any concern for me" Kaiden said.

"There's a force..." he looked Kaiden in the eye and said it with a subdued seriousness "That's all I can say. I feel it. I see it. There's a force that a powerful group of people are now wielding to undermine both God and country to bring the power of this government under their control. It'll be the end of the United States as it was founded if they succeed. It's a disease that's creeping into our society a little at a time. These people are now pushing for a new form of government; you can tell by the way the executive branch is making their own laws under the guise of 'executive power'.

"Yeah, I know. A good example is climate change. The president committed the United States to another treaty on global warming. I'm not sure about it though, there's evidence on both sides of that argument. How do we know who's right?" Kaiden asked.

"You can argue the merits of the issue all you want, but in actuality the point is mute. The President does not have the authority to create laws, only Congress can create a law. It's clearly stated in the Constitution- 'All legislative powers herein granted shall be vested in a Congress of the United States...' Therefore, by acting through the executive branch he has broken the law and failed to uphold the Constitution, which is something he swore to do when he took the oath of office. It's a felony to break that oath.

What we have now is a government that seeks to control using the same old tired dream of a utopian society. It's Socialism rearing its ugly head once again. Only I believe their true intent is to create a new order with themselves at the head of the class. That's the real goal of their utopian society. These schemes never work well for 'We the People', it never has throughout history".

"Wow that's got weight man" Kaiden said.

"They've already bastardized the constitution, now they're trying to get control of the money through this insane idea about a new world government".

"How would they be able to do that? It doesn't seem possible?" Kaiden asked.

"It's already happening. President Richfield is beefing up payments to the World Trade Organization. Did you know we contributed ten billion dollars last year and this year he's pledged even more? That's just one of the groups who are vying for a piece of the American pie. They'll gain power by first obtaining the funding needed to support their agenda. Wealth will be funneled into their cover organizations until they're fat enough to join together. If they get their way, and get the money, they're going to bring down the most successful form of government the world has ever known by forcing countries into this new world order crap. I'm going to fight to keep that from happening".

Kaiden looked at him for a moment realizing how serious he was.

"You sound like an old teacher of mine with that speech".

"That's one hell of a smart teacher" Kip said with a smile.

"You really think there's something we can do about it?" Kaiden asked.

"Yup, because I know one thing, if we do nothing..." he faded off as he looked toward the window. "...we're screwed".

After way too long of a wait, a member of the ULP and a uniformed policeman boarded the bus. The policeman stood next to the driver and glared back at the passengers while the ULP agent began his well-rehearsed speech.

"May I have your attention please?" He demanded in a strong voice. "There is no problem here; we're just conducting an inspection. If you give us your full cooperation I assure you, you will be on your way in no time".

He would have been totally reassuring except for one thing. The policeman behind him was holding a rifle in his hands. It turned the event into something a whole hell of a lot more serious than "no problem here". Everyone on the bus became nervous in the presence of a firearm. Not many were used to seeing one up close like that.

The ULP agent went down the aisle interviewing passengers and checking ID's one at a time. Five people were pulled off the bus for either a working permit violation or an identification problem even before he'd gotten to Kaiden and Kip. When he finally walked up to their seat, he looked the two of them over with a glare. Then he asked "Where you guys headed?"

Kip spoke up first "I'm going to the Academy sir".

"Yeah, it figures, I see you war mongering types all the time coming through here. I still need to see some ID kid.

Kip handed him a military picture ID. He looked at it and then glanced down at Kip. It must have been a match because he handed it back and turned to Kaiden.

"And you?".

Kaiden copied Kip's tone of respect and said "I'm on my way to Tenny Hill Academy sir" then he handed him his driver's license. The agent looked at Kaiden's ID more closely.

"Oh congratulations, you're one of those mush for brains students at that Hill Academy... yeah, the one over near Delhi with all the survival nuts. Ain't that a religious cult?" the agent asked.

"They do offer a bachelor's degree in theology but...".

The agent broke in "Yeah that one's on our list. Ain't nothing but a shit load of free loaders up there I tell ya". The agent stared at Kaiden with obvious contempt.

Kaiden felt the animosity but decided to let the conversation fade with silence. The agent paused but then handed back Kaiden's ID and turned to go. Before he did as an afterthought he turned back, leaned over, and advised Kip with a warning...

"You be careful who you choose as friends (and nodded towards Kaiden). Times are changing and you don't want to be caught on the wrong side of things. There're a lot of crazies out there who feel that the old way is a better way. Let me tell you, our forefathers weren't as smart as they thought they were. That's what got us into this mess in the first place. Dumb asses. We're in need of a change, a change that'll get us back on track".

Kaiden read between the lines and started to fume at this guy's attitude. The fire in his eyes built up and he was about to respond but Kip placed a firm hand on his arm to calm him down. That was enough to pull him back and succeeded in stopping the momentum before it got started.

"Another day my friend, this isn't worth it" Kip whispered to Kaiden.

Kaiden took the subtle advice and backed down from engaging in an argument that had all the makings of turning serious.

"Yes sir, but Sir..." Kip said to the agent to engage him and try to change the direction of the conversation. "I hear that a lot. But just what are these 'changes' you're talking about?".

"Why the new world order that's what".

"Yes sir, exactly what is that?".

"Don't ask me kid, I don't know how it works but it's got to be better than what we got now" he said with a glance over at Kaiden pausing for a moment to make sure there'd be no further outbursts that he'd have to deal with. He must have been satisfied because he moved on down the aisle to the next passenger leaving them to digest his answer. But of course, Kip's question brought out an obvious point that was well taken by the two of them if not for the agent himself. "How can you be for something that you know nothing about?".

The agents ended up taking a few more people off the bus. The whole event delayed the trip by about another hour and a half. Eventually the bus driver was allowed to start up and turn back onto Route 9. A policeman in a gray uniform waved them through and the bus driver took off trying to make up time by driving way under the speed limit. Everyone was just glad to be moving again. The bus driver and most of the people on the bus took it in stride like they'd been through this before, but some of the passengers were spooked by the intrusion. The people that were removed from the bus weren't let back on and no one was ever told what happened to them.

8

Ms. Drop Dead Gorgeous

The rest of the trip wasn't as boring due to a conversation with Kaiden's new acquaintance. His attitude was salvaged by the concept of this exciting new chapter in his life. Yet internal thoughts kept fading off into the wild blue unknown that was ahead of him. The bus slowed and came to a halt at the Fort Montgomery bus stop just outside of West Point. Kip had reached his destination and stood to go. Kaiden shook his hand. "It was nice meeting you Kaiden" he said. Kip dropped a card in Kaiden's lap.

"Same here" Kaiden said.

"Look me up if you ever get to visit the point".

The bus driver let Kip and a handful of others off at the bus stop. From there the driver turned the bus around and headed back south on Route 9 where once again they had to endure the same roadblock inspection. After another hour of wasted time, they were free to go. The driver turned off Route 9 onto 6 and continued West over the mountains to the Interstate. Bus #53 ended up pulling into the Kingston Greyhound terminal at 11:30 PM, if you could call it that. It was actually a small convenient store with a large enough parking lot to accommodate a bus, but it worked. It was now six and a half hours past their scheduled time of arrival.

Tenny Hill Academy Shuttle driver Emory Hill was waiting patiently at the convenient store in an older model yellow cheese colored school bus. He was there to collect students and anyone else who needed a ride up to the Academy or points in between and even to some destinations beyond the Academy. Two years before, after the government took over Greyhound, their assessors had evaluated the same "leg" of the route and designated it as "non profitable". Subsequently, it got cut from their schedule. Board members at the Academy offered to subsidize Greyhound for the endeavor but when confronted with how much Greyhound wanted, they determined that it was cheaper in the long run to buy their own bus and operate it themselves. The Academy started running the service between campus and the Kingston Greyhound terminal. They even added another leg to the route that stretched out along Route 28 all the way to SUNY College at Oneonta. It was amusing that the service turned out to be a profitable venture.

Uber was now declared illegal by the government of New York and Taxis were charging outrageous fares, so they were out of the question for the typical cash strapped student trucking back to college. Tonight, Emory's sole job was to collect students and drive them the next leg of their trip over the Catskill Mountains to campus. Now he was operating the only form of public transportation going that way. Basically, it was illegal for the Academy's bus to pick up any other paying passengers. Service was supposed to be limited to students only, but Emory always picked up anyone who needed a ride. He would never refuse a customer and leave them stranded there, especially at 11:30 at night.

Emory Hill knew the Greyhound bus schedule by heart, but he arrived at the bus stop two hours later than the stated time of arrival on the official published schedule. He was late by design. These days Greyhound was predictably behind schedule by a minimum of two hours. Today it was much more than that. Emory waited patiently until finally bus #53 pulled into the parking lot.

Yellow cheese bus driver Hill walked over to the Greyhound and even before people started to disembark, he jumped onboard the bus and loudly announced who and what he was doing. The ones who responded to his offer for a ride to THA were directed over to his waiting bus. There was no luggage storage compartment underneath the school bus, so everyone had to struggle on board pulling large suitcases down the aisle. Kaiden eased his way up near the front of the line and waited his turn to board. Seeing the need, he offered to help some of the students get their things up the steps. Instead of tickets being punched Emory just looked at them and motioned for students to "get on". Finally, Kaiden boarded the bus, paid the man, and grabbed the first isle seat he could get. He placed his duffel bag in the seat next to him. There was nothing else to do except to watch the others follow the same procedure. Curiosity got him wondering about all these people. "Who are they, where had they come from and why had they decided to embark upon this journey to Tenny Hill?".

Just a handful of people had boarded when Kaiden looked up and noticed a very attractive young lady walking down the aisle looking for a seat. Her look, her femininity, her hair and her "grab attention body" made it impossible not to stare. For an instant they locked eyes as she passed him. She smiled with a slight nod of her head and Kaiden took that as a "hello" reserved for people she didn't know. She kept on walking toward the back of the bus. In that instant a connection was made in Kaiden's mind (if nowhere else), one that he just couldn't let slip away. He shook his head and said "Woh!" like some men do when they see a woman who blows them away. The surprise was that he hadn't noticed her before, and he wondered where she had come from. He glanced back after her and absolutely adored the rear view as she strolled down the aisle to a chosen seat.

An extreme attraction triggered a spontaneous split-second decision that instantly pulled him up out of his seat. "What the hell" Kaiden said to himself. It was part of Kaiden's character, he wasn't shy about doing something like this with women. Quickly he fell in line and walked down the aisle behind her. "You only live once" he thought. "Besides, I got a few minutes before this bus gets underway, might as well introduce myself".

Miss drop dead gorgeous sat down in a seat toward the back and slid over to the window side while momentarily focusing her attention on a person outside the window. It was unexpected and the woman was startled when Kaiden plopped down in the seat next to her. It broke her out of her thoughts and caused her to turn sharply to face him.

"H..." Kaiden started to say but never got it out before...

"Smack!" The girl's hands instinctively came up into an on-guard position as she turned toward him. Her lead hand backhanded Kaiden on the side of his face with a crisp "pop".

"Oh, shit you scared me!" she said with a surprised look on her face. She quickly reverted to "I'm so sorry" when she saw who it was. "I didn't mean to hit you".

Kaiden's hand came up and grabbed the arm that had just struck him. He held it tight for a moment as if that was the cure for the sting he felt on the left side of his face. He could feel the chi in her body from the connection and noted how strong it was. A vision of a lesson in his tai chi class came to mind as he held her arm and felt it go from stiff to relaxed.

He was taken by surprise and was disappointed in himself because he had not anticipated such a reaction. And of course, he had completely failed at blocking it.

"I'm impressed" He said with raised eyebrows as he let her arm go and rubbed the sting on his cheek.

"Yeah, well you shouldn't creep up on people like that" she replied.

"That wasn't 'creep', that was pure stealth" Kaiden fired back.

"I'll give you that, maybe a little less stealth would have avoided a slap, I didn't know you were behind me, not until I saw your reflection in the glass" the girl said.

"So, if you knew I was there then why the reaction?" Kaiden asked.

Ms. DDG broke out into a smile and said "Must have been an automatic 'reflective' response to test you".

"Did I fail?" Kaiden asked.

"Not on all accounts" she said while forming a smile that implied, she at least liked what she saw. Then her face lit up and she flowed smoothly into laughter and cracked up at the fact that she had actually hit him.

"I'm so sorry" she said again while gently placing her hand on his cheek trying hard not to laugh. The gesture she offered seemed to be an attempt to somehow take back some of the pain.

A sensation of warmth came from her hand as she held it to his cheek and at that moment Kaiden could have sworn that it did take away some of the sting. He melted and was powerless to respond with anything else but… "Well, it was worth it. I got the chance to meet you" Kaiden said and then broke into a heartwarming smile of his own, a smile that moved Ciera in a way that she wasn't prepared for. It diffused the awkwardness enough to warrant the extension of her hand in a gesture of reprieve.

"Let's start again, I'm Ciera, Ciera Lowman" she said.

Kaiden took her hand and shook it savoring the connection to this lovely woman. "Mine's Kaiden, Kaiden Sawyer".

"Happy to have hit you, I mean to have met you" she said with a chuckle as their eyes met once again. Her eyes radiated a bright energy. An energy where just one sparkle pulled Kaiden in to the depths of her soul with just that glance. Kaiden was in love. Yes, it was that easy.

Then she asked "You're a freshman I assume. I've never seen you before".

Kaiden shot back "Oh that must be because you know everyone at the school, right?".

"Just about" she said with a confident toss of her long brown hair. She looked at him "I've attended THA off and on for about five years now. One year part time to…" she paused. "…re-arrange my finances" was all she would say yet that summed it up and simplified the answer without a long explanation. "I'm a Cadet. And I know a lot of people through the clubs and activities at the school".

The last person hopped on board the bus and the driver shut the door. The guy walked down the aisle with a carryon shoulder bag and stopped right next to Kaiden. Kaiden looked up and the guy smiled at both of them.

"Hi" he said to Ciera. "I see you've found someone you know already". He turned and looked at Kaiden. "She finds someone she knows everywhere we go". He said it with an emphasis on "we". The look on his face and his tone carried a slight air of annoyance. It was obvious that the strong glance was designed to convey the point that they were "together".

He looked at Kaiden, put his hand out and said "I'm Nick".

Kaiden got the hint that this was probably her boyfriend and stood up to shake hands and of course to allow Nick to sit down in the seat next to her.

"Nick. Nick...?

"Ober..." Nick tried to say his last name, but he didn't quite get it out before Emory released the brake on the TH shuttle and hit the gas. He was in a hurry and kicked the vehicle into gear without any warning.

Nick lost his balance in the middle of the handshake and started to fall towards Kaiden. Kaiden quickly stepped into a strong stance and braced himself. He pulled Nick's hand into him and touched his elbow with the other. Nick fell into him and Kaiden took the full force of his body weight. Settling into his feet he took it in allowing the force to compress his rear leg. Using a classic Tai Chi push he pressed back against the incoming force and bounced Nick off him with "spring energy". The push picked Nick up off his feet and the follow through plopped him back down a couple of feet back from his original position. He came down with a jolt as he landed somewhat off balance. A successful grab onto the back of the seat in front of him re-secured Nicks balance as the bus's momentum leveled off.

"...Oberman" Nick said finishing the pronunciation of his name with a look on his face that relayed a bit of shock at the small feat that Kaiden had just performed. After all Nick was a full two hundred twenty pounds' worth. But his amazed expression quickly turned to a frown when he saw that Ciera was looking at Kaiden with a degree of amazement too. Nick's expression turned from embarrassment into resentment in a flash.

"Nice to meet you" Kaiden said and then to convince Nick that he wasn't trying to hit on his girlfriend he turned to Ciera "and so nice to see you again Ciera. I'll look for you at the next 'Checkers and Root Beer Club' meeting. I'm running for president this year and I'm looking for anyone who would like to join. He turned and walked back to his seat.

Ciera smiled playing along with Kaiden's ruse. "Ok Kaiden" she called after him. "Maybe I'll see you there". "Oh, by the way, do you want to be on the board this year?".

Now it was Kaiden's turn to smile knowing that she was participating in the charade. He turned his head while walking away and spoke over his shoulder. "Yeah of course, I wouldn't miss it for the world".

The gorgeous views and beautiful scenery along their route over high mountains and low valleys were lost in the darkness. Many picture-perfect post card views passed by unnoticed and unappreciated while the students slept or engaged in soft chit chat in the dark. Occasional laughter floated through the air on top of playful conversation. Kaiden swore he could hear Ciera's laugh and secretly wished that he was the one sitting next to her. But it wasn't to be.

They passed a few small towns along the way where it would be easy to insert that worn-out phrase about blinking your eyes and missing it. Another hour and a half passed before they got to the town of Delhi. Yes, there were other slightly quicker ways to get to Mt. Tenny, but Delhi was one of the major stops on the buses schedule and Emory had to make it. The bus finally pulled into Delhi at about 2:30AM.

Emory announced "Coffee, food and a bathroom break" and motioned to the all-night convenience store. He waited while passengers filtered out. Minutes later they filtered back onto the bus with items they bought at the store or with just a smile on their face from being able to use the bathroom. Others had slept right through the event and didn't even realize they had stopped. In fifteen minutes, they were back underway. Emory turned south on Route 10 which was the main road that punched through the middle of the Town of Delhi. Minutes later after passing the Town of Fraser he made a left turn on a secondary road that had a small sign with an arrow that read "Tenny Hill Academy". After numerous bends and hills that forced the bus into low gear, they passed through the Town of Delancey. Yeah, if you blinked you would have missed it. After that there were more bends, more hills, and a turn onto Mt. Tenny Rd. A road that brought the weary travelers up to what you would call a long driveway to the Academy. Luckily Emory knew exactly where it was because one could have easily missed it at that time of night. Once you found it and drove in you knew exactly where you were due to the fancy gateway that read "Welcome to Mt. Tenny Academy" across the top. It was a big sign written in large carved wooden letters spaced evenly over an archway frame that stretched across the entire two-lane road. Two big telephone poles supported the sign on each side. The whole structure excluding the lettering was black from a generous coating of either tar or oil designed to preserve the wood for many years to come. Someone deemed tar to be superior to paint. It looked just like you were entering a fancy midwestern cattle ranch, but it marked the beginning of the property line of the 600-acre Academy estate.

Emory pressed on through the archway and headed down a paved road that wound its way through the forest and up the hill. The road seemed to appear quickly in front of you and instantly disappeared behind you as the bus bored through a solid canopy of trees. It took forever for the anxious students to get there but more so due to the buildup of anticipation than it was from the relatively short six-mile drive. Finally, the first set of campus buildings appeared and everyone who was awake breathed a sigh of relief. It was now just after three o'clock in the morning when the bus pulled into the parking lot and rolled up to some unknown building that was used as the shuttle's drop off point. Later Kaiden would learn it was the cafeteria.

As if on cue, passengers suddenly came alive and started to move about the bus. Some deep in dreamland had to be woken up. They all stretched, gathered their things, and started to depart. Most mingled outside the bus for a short as Emory dealt out directions to various places. One by one or in small groups, they trudged off into the night. Kaiden happened to catch Ciera's attention just before she left and when their eyes met, he gave her a warm smile and short bow of his head. She smiled back sweetly, waved, and then turned and walked into the darkness moving off towards an unknown destination with Nick at her side. Kaiden shook his head thinking "Some guys have all the luck".

Some of the students hung around chatting with Emory. He was pointing this way and that, directing people who needed guidance to the appropriate dormitory or place where they'd be staying. After hearing Emory's brief description of the campus layout which didn't sound too difficult, Kaiden shouldered his duffel bag and struck off on his own down the road in search of "Chilton Dormitory". That was the dorm the letter of acceptance told him he had been assigned to.

Kaiden found himself walking alone down the middle of a deserted road in unfamiliar surroundings. He weaved in and around the campus classroom buildings or dwellings or whatever they were. He couldn't figure out which was which. It got a little eerie and even spooky while walking down the street in the dark at this time of night when no one else was around. Kaiden kept looking over his shoulder at some unseen stalker. He decided it must be the uncertainty because this was nowhere near as dangerous as walking down a street in New York and yet he'd done that plenty of times before.

He passed a few landmarks, made a left and then another left as directed and found Chilton Hall on the right. He banged on the front door, which was locked, so he rang the buzzer to wake someone up hoping they'd let him in. One hell of a groggy RA (resident attendant) finally came to the door. With half closed eyes and a smile turned upside down he unlocked the door and let Kaiden in. This was not a happy man.

After halfhearted introductions "Raymond" the RA, conveyed his annoyance in no uncertain terms then disappeared back into his apartment. He came back with the master key, emerging from his room with a grumpy demeanor. "Follow me, you're on the second floor. Let's make this quick". He led Kaiden up the elevator to the second floor, took a left and went down the hall to the third room on the right.

"Here's yours, number 216" Raymond said. After fooling with the master key and inserting it in the lock, Raymond opened the door and walked in. Raymond thought he was being helpful by pointing out the obvious. "That's yours" he said pointing at the unoccupied bed. "The bathroom's over there. It's shared with the guy's next door in 218 so don't get spooked if you hear someone in there".

Kaiden threw his things at the base of the bed saying "Thanks". The RA didn't stick around for any small talk and left closing the door behind him.

His assumed roommate was a big lump in the bed on the other side of the room. The guy was fast asleep and never woke up. "I guess there will be no introductions tonight" Kaiden thought. He sat on the bed and found himself in a strange room, with a strange what "Shared" bathroom? And a strange roommate who he only knew was there because of the occasional sound along with movement under the blanket. He had to meditate for a while just to settle himself down and get used to the energy of the place. Then he stripped down, slipped between the covers and bam, it was lights out.

9

Home

Morning light came through an uncovered window close to Kaiden's bed. It lit up the room telling him that it was a lot later than his usual up and at 'em at five thirty in the morning. Normally he was an early riser, but today it would be a slow motion wake up routine that showed his lack of sleep and unconcern for the time. Today was his first official day of college and all he had was "Orientation" scheduled at ten o'clock. That along with a few errands was all that needed to be done. One of which was to become familiar with his new surroundings.

Kaiden rose, yawned, and immediately glanced over at his roommate's bed. The outline of a body was visible under the covers. Apparently, it was still occupied by his roommate who was still asleep. An urgent need to use the bathroom forced Kaiden to quickly assess the situation. There was no noise, so he assumed that the bathroom was empty. He went for it. With as much stealth as he could muster, he shuffled across the room without bothering to put his pants on. Thinking that everyone else was asleep he thought he could do this quick and get back under the covers without drawing any attention. Details of a large dragon tattoo on his back came into view as his naked body strut across the room. Kaiden preferred to sleep in the buff and wasn't about to change that habit just because of his new surroundings. Besides, all his things were sitting just where he threw them last night, on top of his suitcase that still lay on the floor at the base of his bed, therefore, first things first. When he got to the bathroom door, timidly he tapped on it to invoke a response from anyone who might be in there. He peaked in. A night light was on that dimly illuminated a bathroom that was considerably larger than he thought it would be. Yes, there was another door on the other side of it just like the RA said. "Shared bathroom" he thought.

All the bathrooms in the dorm were of the same type and style; one bathroom located between every other room. The whole campus had similar setups like this except for the highly sought-after corner rooms which had a private bathroom in each. The whole set up made you feel like you were living in an apartment with a bunch of connected people.

It seemed to be clear but just as he was about to walk in… the toilet flushed. The stall door opened and right in front of him, a woman walked out surprising the hell out of him in more ways than one. She was his age, vivaciously beautiful and had long black hair that draped loosely down her bare shoulders. She glanced at him without professing surprise of any kind. There was no shame or embarrassment but rather an exuded air of indifference as she looked him up and down with dark penetrating eyes. She looked up and smiled with a slow upward curve forming on her lips. It seemed like she already knew that this might happen, or it had happened many times before, one or the other.

On the other hand, Kaiden was taken back by the unexpected appearance of a pretty girl who was suddenly standing there right in front of him. It wasn't the fact that 'he' was standing there naked; the big shocker came from the fact that 'she' was standing there just as naked as he was. They locked eyes but Kaiden couldn't help it. Uncontrollably, he did a quick scan of her feminine features as they moved around each other and traded places. She was beautiful. Her round breasts blended so nicely with the curves of her youthful hourglass figure. The soft nature of her body radiated a perfect sense of femininity.

"Woh" unintentionally escaped from Kaiden's lips.

The woman held out her hand and calmly said without any concern for her condition; "Hi, you must be Kenney's new roommate. I'm Candy".

It was weird. They cordially shook hands.

"Yes, you sure are. Nice to meet you Candy" Kaiden said. "I'm Kaiden and I won't take this inappropriate moment to drum up any wise cracks about how someone very appropriately named you Candy". He couldn't help but drop his gaze down to her breasts as he emphasized her name. He looked into her eyes and raised his eyebrows. "...or the fact that it must be really cold in here".

Candy broke into a smile "OK then, I won't pussy foot around and mention that stupid joke about how 'hot' it is in here and the fact that you must really be happy to see me" she said through a curt smile and a quick dart of her eyes down to his crotch. She turned and strolled away flashing a big smile over her shoulder as she went.

Kaiden looked down and shook his head realizing that he had an uncontrollable early morning rise going on. Of course, it wasn't due to seeing her naked, but he chuckled to himself at how it must have looked. Kaiden turned and was about ready to yell something after her to that effect, but he thought better of it and stopped himself. He settled for a gorgeous rear view of her naked body in the dim morning light as she sashayed her sweet 'thang' over to the bed where his roommate was sleeping. Kaiden followed her with his eyes glued to her perfectly sculpted tush. She kneeled at the bottom of his roommate's bed and did a slow provocative crawl up and over the covers to the top while purposely accenting the view of her posterior as she went. She knew perfectly well that Kaiden was watching her every move. He gave an admiring sigh as she slipped under the covers and was gone.

After using the bathroom Kaiden sat on his bed and pulled his suitcase apart searching for a towel. A shower was next on the list but this time he wrapped the towel around himself before going in. The shower had really nice "wake up" hot water which was a great beginning. Feeling refreshed, he dried himself off, put the towel back on and walked over to his bed. Each room had a single large window in the center of the outside wall and his curiosity drew him to it. Dawn broke over campus so he could see it clearly in the early morning light. He gripped the sash and pulled it open then pressed both hands palm down on the windowsill and poked his head out into the cool morning air.

The panoramic view of Mt. Tenny's campus revealed a quaint New England style architecture in such a different light than he had experienced the night before. It was charming. His view didn't quite give it justice but at a slightly better angle it could have made for a nice picture to send to his parents. The scene was cozy and complete with a mix of new and old-style buildings with rolling hills that lined the background. The old structures were made from large blocks of dark gray stone which instilled a strong sense of history behind them. The new brick buildings looked like they were built on a budget with not much of an attempt at ambiance. They weren't really that bad looking; it's just that when you saw them right next to each other the difference was evident.

There were quite a few people walking around like you might expect on a college campus but not at this hour, it looked busy. The campus had come alive, unlike the night before during his walk-through silent darkness and empty streets at three o'clock in the morning. Out in front some people were standing in small groups and others were scurrying from one place to the other. Some classes were about to start, and people were roaming about trying to get to where they needed to go.

User friendly sidewalks snaked between and around each of the buildings, "User friendly" meaning that the sidewalks were built after the buildings were on top of paths that had been worn into the grass naturally by normal foot traffic. This allowed students to determine the best place to put them instead of an architect dictating where the sidewalks would go. The error of an architect's sidewalk placement only becomes evident when dirt paths appear next to or between existing sidewalks.

From the second story window Kaiden took in details of the place that would be his home for the next four years. With his eyes he retraced the path he took the night before. In the distance he could see the building where Emory dropped them off. Then it dawned on him that something was peculiar about what he saw. A lot of the students were carrying similar style back packs and toting this "thing" around behind them. It looked like something between a dolly and a cart and had two wheels attached to a sturdy aluminum frame that came up and merged into a pull handle.

A few of the students had the pull handle somehow connected to the bottom of the backpack they were wearing. Most of them walked with the "cart" trailing behind them. Others held onto a handle at the end of the frame and either pushed it or pulled it like a dolly. Some of them even had the handle attached to the back of their bicycle and towed it around behind them. Either way, the carts were carrying various shapes and quantities of "stuff" strapped to them. It had pouches with zippers and straps that secured the load to the frame. The whole thing was covered in what looked like the same kind of waterproof canvas material that their backpacks were made from. Kaiden assumed it kept the contents dry.

"What in the heck is that?" Kaiden said out loud.

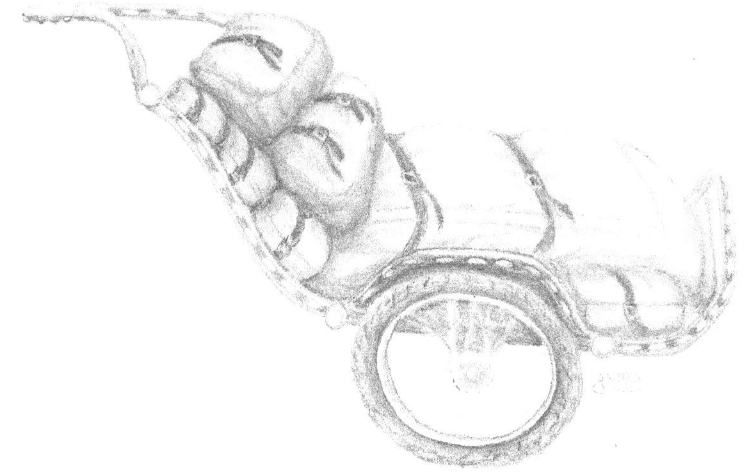

Typical "Seekers" Rat Pack

"It's a rat pack" Someone behind him spoke.

Startled, he turned around sharply to confront the voice.

"We call 'em 'RP's', that's short for Rat Pack. All the 'Seekers' got em, it holds just about everything they need to survive. Clothes, tent, cooking gear, toiletries, sleeping bag, books, and laptop. Everything, you name it. In fact, if they can't carry it in or on the "RP", you're not allowed to have it. Hey sorry for startling you like that". He stuck out his hand. "They call me Kenny Jay and no, Kenny G is not my relative although we're just a 'hi' away, that's 'h' and 'I' if you get my spin. My last name's Carlson. I'm your roommate". He held out his hand.

Kaiden looked at him kind of funny like, not quite understanding before replying "Mine's Kaiden Sawyer". They shook hands.

Kenny was thin but not frail. He had thick long black straggly hair that parted in the middle and flowed to each side of his face. His black glasses matched the color of his hair. It could be assumed that he never worked out in his life when actually it was the exact opposite. Even still you would have immediately labeled him as a "computer geek" even if he wasn't. But he was.

With a quick glance around the room Kaiden confirmed that suspicion when he eyeballed the computer setup this guy had. "Damn, nice computer" he told Kenny. Three flat screen monitors encircled a split keyboard with a cordless ball ride mouse on the right and a three-line phone on the left which he'd gotten special permission to have installed. The whole thing was awesome looking with its base being a compact unit. It contained the monitor, laser color printer, fax, CPU, modem, and server all in one. The monitor that came with it detached from the base and could be set up anywhere on the desk. In addition, Kenny had chosen to add two other monitors. Plus, the computer had the capability of projecting two more screen shots onto the white wall in between and behind the other monitors.

"And this is the guy sleeping with Candy?" Kaiden thought.

Kenny continued; "The ones lugging the RP's around, they're senior's but when they're doing time out in the bush we call 'em 'Seekers'. They live over past Emerson soccer field in Rio Linda. That's the woods on the east side of the field. It's a couple of clicks way". Kenny pointed out the window towards the east.

Kaiden had a quizzical look on his face.

"You can get to Rio Linda by heading out the 'Viking Trail'. You'll see a sign for it on the left side of the soccer field. Past that is the village of Rio Linda, the home of the seekers. Everyone who lives there lives out in the boonies in a Hogan.

Kenny kept going since Kaiden looked like he was taking it in. "A Hogan is a large tent like thing a seeker lives in. It looks just like a big, covered wagon without the wheels. It sits on a platform, and it's covered with thick canvas that holds up well in the wind and snow due to the design although sometimes you do have to sweep off the snow in the winter to lighten the load or else it will collapse.

"Seekers?" Kaiden inquired while looking back out the window toward the east.

"Yeah, this year, we have a class of about one hundred and thirty of 'em. They're all seniors who are completing their major with a minor in 'survival'. In order to graduate they must live, eat, work, and survive literally 'in the field' for two semesters. Most of them wait to do it their senior year because that year tends to be a little lighter on the curriculum than any other but there are some sophomores out there too. There're also a few crazies who have lived out there every semester since they got here. The whole thing is like their internship. Professor Jing and his wife live out there too. Now sheee's suuuch a hot number, have you seen her! No, you haven't, you just got here. You've got to check her out man. I got a picture of her. Here check this out".

Kenny moved over to his computer set up in the corner of the room and touched the mouse on the desk. All three screens came to life at once and he marveled at the two screen shots projected an image onto the wall. One of the monitors had a Google search screen; the others had a chart of some kind that Kenny was studying. On the third screen was a porn site with a picture of a very attractive naked lady showing off her perfect breasts.

"Ooops" Kenny said with a glance at Kaiden that depicted a small degree of embarrassment. He punched some keys on the keyboard and made the naked lady go away. A few more pecks on the keys produced a picture of a woman with light brown hair of about thirty years old.

"That's Mrs. Julianne Ingle" He said proudly.

On the screen was a picture of a woman who could have totally won the nomination for "down home country girl of the year". Mrs. Ingle was only twenty-seven years old but with the average age of the girls on campus being twenty... she was "an older woman".

The picture showed her standing in front of a tent with a coiled-up rope in her hand. It was rugged, yet in such a feminine way. She was wearing short cut off shorts, the kind with the classic frayed white edges, and a tight men's style tank top "T" shirt. It was immediately obvious that she wasn't wearing a bra and was doing quite well without one. The fact that she was wearing a man's T was completely lost on her. Anything she wore became totally feminine just by putting it on. The shirt was cut short and rolled up into a halter style top that just barely covered her breasts. A rip down the front formed an open "V" neck that exposed half an eyeful. One's imagination could have easily made the case that it was her breasts bursting at the seams that had ripped that shirt. It was feasible that it could have easily occurred while doing battle with the firewood that lay on the ground in front of her. One foot was propped up on the chopping block and the look on her face said that she was Queen of the forest. She was poised to swing that ax again and you could sense that she was out of breath from hard labor. Sturdy hiking boots on her feet and a nice thick wooden hiking stick resting against a tree next to her topped off a cool picture of a real "earthy" woman chopping wood in the snow.

In that pose she held her gaze at the camera. The person behind it caught her off guard and took her picture without waiting for an artificial smile. Her bare legs made your eyes linger there for a few moments before being drawn to the other features of her figure. She posed effectively projecting the image of independence and self-sufficient living. Only then did it occur to Kaiden that there was snow in the background and the irony of her dress, and the time of year became quite apparent. This view of a half-naked goddess of the woods explained why it was Kenny's favorite shot.

"Nice. I see why you wanted to show me" Kaiden said with a smile.

"Yeah, I got a few more here..." Kenny said as he started punching more keys.

Kaiden cut him off and said "No that's OK man" fearing that another naked lady would pop up on the screen. "I don't need to see anymore. Besides, I got to get going, but you mean to tell me that they live out there for two semesters even during the winter?".

"Oh, the professor and Julianne live out there all year round" a picture of Julianne hugging a bearded man appeared on the screen "That's Professor Jing. But yeah, the seekers are out there living in Rio Linda for a year at a time, winter included man! You must finish all your pre survival credits with Professor Jing or get special permission before you can do time out there".

Kaiden looked at him with a "What?" kind of look.

"We call him Professor Jing, or just Jing. He's Julianne's husband. It's short for Jim Ingle. You can call him Jing, he doesn't mind. In fact, he'll introduce himself and tell you to call him Jing".

Kaiden thought the whole concept was "kick ass". Living in the woods would be the exact opposite of anything he'd ever experienced before. He was intrigued and looked forward to the day he could get out there himself. The way Kenny talked about it and the pictures had the effect of enhancing the allure, you could tell. Kaiden's last thought was "…if there's a woman like that out there… I'm in".

There was movement in the room. Kaiden turned and caught sight of the back of Candy's naked body again as she disappeared into the bathroom embracing a pile of clothes and a pair of shoes in her arms.

Kenny smiled and said "That's my girlfriend, Candy".

"Yeah, I figured that out. We met on the way into the bathroom this morning" Kaiden replied.

"Oh yeah, she's a free spirit man ain't she"? Kenny said.

"None of it's free" Kaiden said with his own little sarcastic grin. He walked past Kenny over to his own bed.

A smile lit up on Kenny's face and he asked "Hey have you been invited to join a Cluster?" and then he answered his own question "No you couldn't have; they aren't accepting nominations yet".

Kaiden started to get dressed. "What's a Cluster?".

"It's just like a fraternity man, complete with the pledge thing and all, only we call the pledges 'cluster fucks'.

"Well, that doesn't sound too cool".

"Oh, no it is man; you gotta check into it, it's a lot of fun. That's just part of the bullshit like initiation you got to go through. I went through it and pledged the 'Pioneer Patriots'. That's the cluster you should try to get into. Man, it's the best partying one of them all".

Kenny grabbed a towel and walked over to the bathroom. He opened the door and went partially in. There was steam trailing out from the top of the door jam and you could see there was another guy in there from the other side using the sink. Candy was in the shower with the hot faucet turned way up. Steam now enveloped the place like a busy gym locker room.

Kenny started to go in but then poked his head back out and said in a loud voice to compensate for the noise of running water "Listen; there're a few tricks to getting around this place. I can help you cut out some of the bullshit that goes on around here. If you want to join a cluster, I can help. I got ties. Let me know what you're into, I'll see what I can do to help you out. We can scrounge up just about anything" He said it with a combination of a nod and a wink like a "You know what I mean".

"Oh, wait a minute..." Kaiden said while looking like he was thinking hard. "When you said you're just a 'hi' away from Kenny G. you meant the alphabet right? Your last name's "J", just an 'h' and an 'I' away from a "G" correct?

Kenny smiled and pointed his finger at Kaiden "Oh man you got potential! It normally takes people weeks to figure that one out... if ever". Then he ducked back inside the bathroom. In the haze Kaiden could see him take off his clothes then slip behind the curtain and into the shower with Candy. The ensuing giggle of a woman's voice told the story of what you could only imagine was going on.

Kaiden rolled his head, smiled and just for a second found himself wishing he was the one in the shower with Candy. But he shook it off quickly and finished getting dressed. He was gone before they got out of the shower.

First trek was over to the cafeteria. Outside there must have been fifteen of those rat pack "RPs", some parked and some being toted around by students. Kaiden walked up to one that was parked and looked at it closely. They were all lined up in rows right next to the building where normally you'd expect to see just as many parked bicycles. None of them were locked up or chained up to anything. They were just sitting there waiting for their owners to return. Kaiden walked up to one to get a closer look at it. It had a sturdy frame between the wheels which looked more like rugged mountain bike tires. This one had three wheels. Basically, it was a cart made from aluminum with wheels that made it very light and easy to handle. Large tubeless foam tiers allowed the cart to maneuver over rough terrain without the worry of ever getting a flat. The custom-made pack was strapped to the frame with clips that allowed sections of canvas pack to be removed if needed. It was obviously able to handle a heavy load because each one of them was bulging to the max with the owner's "stuff". Apparently, it was a great way for a person to tote their belongings around. Kaiden gave it an immediate thumbs up awesome.

"They sure aren't worried much about theft around here are they" He thought.

Kaiden walked to the cafeteria doors and went in passing a steady stream of students walking both in and out of the building. He wasn't hungry, but he found the coffee machine and fixed himself a hot cup amid strangers that mingled around the coffee counter. It wasn't so much for the cup of coffee as it was for the need to see the setup and to become familiar with the place where he'd be eating for the next four years.

Next stop was the administration building or "The Bunker" as Kenny had called it. It was a two-story building that really did look like a large concrete bunker. The architectural class of 2010 designed it, and it was built with a lot of student help in 2012. Students were involved in almost every aspect of this place.

Major sections of the building's first floor exterior walls were earth berm. It was unlike any other building on campus. Soil had been smoothly graded in a gradual slope right up to about two feet under the horizontal slotted windows located at the top of the first-floor walls. Grass covered the berm slope which blended nicely into the rest of the spacious yard. Juniper and holly bushes were placed strategically here and there around the base of the berm. Its smooth contour of soil broken up every so often by a concrete containment wall that held back the soil on each side of four entry points. It was set up the same way for one of the larger windows located in the middle of each side of the hexagon shaped building.

Two sets of large double doors covered each of the entry ways. The outside secondary door made of thick glass swung out on stainless steel hardware with big stainless looping door handles. It was very similar to the entrance you might see at a local mall. Huge primary doors were installed on the inside on four massive hinges. They swung to the inside and looked far from anything considered normal. More like doors to a castle only these were two-inch steel plate doors of massive weight. They were never used except during mock drills when they practiced building lock down procedures. In an emergency they could be closed and bolted with cross bolts making the entryway virtually impregnable.

Smaller slotted windows in the walls looked more like gun turrets than actual windows. They also had fold up sashes on the inside that could cover them with steel in a matter of seconds. The entire building was a fortress made of concrete including the roof which was built with the insulation concrete form method (ICF). The technique uses foam insulation with integrated steel beams as the support for the poured concrete. Result: a twelve-inch-thick concrete ceiling with two inches of foam on the outside and six inches of foam on the inside designed to help eliminate fifty percent of the heating and cooling costs of the building. The insulation offers a sound dampening bonus which can be an asset in a concrete structure.

Ten feet of the exterior perimeter of the second story roof sloped downward at an eighteen-degree angle and looked like a normal roof. The hexagon shaped center section was flat and had stairway access for use as a patio. It was ringed by a forty-four-inch parapet wall all around at the junction of the sloped flat section. Slots were installed every eight feet that made it look like balistraria ports on an old castle wall.

Kaiden walked in the south entrance of the bunker and followed the signs for the admissions office. Many students had beaten him to the punch, so he got on a long line of freshman who were there for the same reason. He patiently waited his turn. Finally, they took his information, signed him in and officially registered him as a freshman at Mt. Tenny Academy. It felt good. Then they handed him an orientation packet in a large envelope which was kind of an owner's manual for the school. It had his course schedule, tuition payment schedule, rules and regulations, a map of the school grounds, pamphlets for various activities/events around campus and even a few advertisements for some of the local businesses in neighboring Delhi. He noted that there was an advertisement there for the on-campus watering hole that was touted as the "Dug Out". It read "Last call for alcohol!" with a picture of a desert in the background and advertised beer and wine specials along with a few common items to eat like pizza and chicken wings. He looked for it on the map of the academy included in the packet of information and found it. "Wow, interesting. The Dug Out is located right in the middle of Rio Linda" he noted.

By that time, it was almost ten o'clock. Kaiden found the auditorium on the map as well and walked the distance across campus to the theater building getting there just in time for the beginning of freshman orientation. Here there were only a couple of carts parked outside on the auditorium's portico. Kaiden surmised that this was due to the large contingent of freshman attending the orientation. He imagined what it would be like when it became his turn to tote one of those things around.

As usual, a few groups of people gathered around the entrance to the auditorium waiting until the last minute before going in. A pretty woman walked up and caught the attention of the guy's milling around as she strolled over to the bicycle rack and parked her RP. There were a few "hellos" to the people she knew and a flurry of quips that welled up from a handful of admirers when she bent over and unzipped a pouch at the bottom of her cart.

Positively this girl was a "Seeker" because she walked with an RP in tow. Had to be. She unzipped and removed her things from the pack and either intentionally or unintentionally struck that tantalizing pose that tends to spur on a young man's imagination. Kaiden couldn't take his eyes off her. It made him pause at the entrance of the auditorium before going in.

Snug fitting blue genes generated a thousand thoughts about who she was. Kaiden got caught up in his own imagination. A smile crossed his face as he pictured the woman doing a spread in Hot Rod magazine modeling the latest version of the "RP". His vision morphed into her standing there in the photographer's bright lights wearing nothing but a tiny yellow bikini. She looked deliciously sexy with curves in all the right places as she professionally posed with her long brown hair that hung down and flowed softly over bare shoulders. Her 'thang' sashayed all over the RP and struck poses like it was a custom motorcycle. Then she separated her legs, arched her back and bent over while leaning on the RP's pack teasing with that famous 'rear view'. She turned and looked at him with those sultry, alluring "come and get it" eyes beckoning him to "come hither" with a gesture of her finger. She turned and started strutting towards him. Her hips swung from side to side in harmony with her step. She raised a finger to her lips, licked it wet and then motioned again for him to "come".

As the woman got closer, the bikini dissolved and was replaced by a "V neck" sweater and a pair of blue jeans. In her arms appeared books and papers and her face turned into someone Kaiden recognized. The woman of his fantasy was Ciera, Ciera Lowman, the woman he met on the bus. She was now walking up to him with a quizzical look on her face.

"Kaiden?" she said. "President of the Checkers and Root Beer Club"?

Kaiden's mind came slamming back down to reality. Ciera was standing right in front of him with a stack of books and some files in her arms.

"Ciera Lowman" Kaiden said recovering quickly. "Hey, ah, May I carry those for you" he said curtly as he did a short bow of his head in her direction.

"No, I got 'em this far, I can make it. But thanks anyway" she said with her cute signature smile. She continued around him walking toward the auditorium door.

Kaiden followed. "I was wondering if I would see you on campus" he said falling into step beside her.

"Yeah, well remember, I told you I know everyone. You'll see me alright. It'll be hard not to. Were both on the board this year, right?" she said with that kidding attitude and that same cute smile and twinkling eyes. He couldn't help but remember her comment from their first meeting on the bus; her face was seared into his mind's eye. That smile he loved; he just didn't know how to play it with her kidding around.

"Oh yeah, I'm in" Kaiden replied going along with the joke and remembering the last remark he made to her was about being on the board of the Checkers and Root Beer Club.

"You're a Seeker!" Kaiden said.

"Yes, I am. It's my turn to do the time".

"Did you sleep out in Rio Linda last night?" Kaiden inquired.

"No, I didn't have time to set up. It was too late. I ah, slept over a friend's place".

"Oh" Kaiden said as the implications of that sunk in.

"But I'll be staying in the 'Rio' from this point on".

"Wow, man that's really cool". He tried to imagine what she'd be going through living out there. They passed through the front door and walked into the auditorium lobby.

"I heard about the life of a seeker. And Ciera..." Kaiden touched her arm and made her pause as he looked into her eyes. "I really respect you for what you're doing out there in Rio Linda".

Ciera laughed "Why thank you Kaiden. But let me get out there and pass the final test first. Then I'll accept your respect".

"Deal!" Kaiden said.

Together they walked through the interior doors into the auditorium and strolled down the aisle towards the front row seats.

"The final test? What final test?" Kaiden asked after he thought about it.

Ciera turned towards him and this time she placed a hand on his arm making Kaiden pause. With a serious look and a low voice, she stared into his eyes and said "It comes in the last week of survival training, 'Go to hell week' we call it. My female partner and I will be stripped naked, blindfolded, and dropped off a hundred miles out into the boonies. We'll have seven days to make it back to the Academy alive".

With raised eyebrows Kaiden stood there picturing Ciera and her partner running naked through the woods, but the thought was punctured by the sound of a needle sliding off a record when Ciera turned, tossed her head to one side, and started laughing. Kaiden watched her long hair flow from one shoulder to the other in slow motion just like in one of those famous Breck shampoo commercials of long ago, her laugh echoing in his mind. She was thoroughly amused that Kaiden had even considered believing her and laughed knowing what he must have conjured up in his mind.

Ciera broke off the conversation by abruptly turning away and continuing down the aisle. Kaiden stood there pondering her antics. He watched as she walked down towards the front rows of the auditorium and followed, thinking he could somehow get a seat next to her. Strangely enough when he caught up to her near the front row... Ciera kept going. He stopped and stood there wondering what the heck she was doing. Amazingly, she walked right past the front section of seats and continued around to the stairs that led up onto the stage. In the center of the stage there was a podium and a continuous row of tables set up behind it in a semi-circle fashion. Behind them sat important-looking people that were evidently scheduled to conduct and speak at the orientation. Of course, there was the president of the school Chancellor Gentry who sat in the middle, next to him was the Mayor of the Town of Delhi. The others were professors and distinguished guests. Ciera walked behind the table and greeted them all.

A smile drifted across Kaiden's face as he thought how mysterious and unpredictable, she was. "Jeez, these are the kind of people she hangs out with, I can't believe it". He found himself wanting to know more about these people.

One of the speakers Kaiden recognized right off was Professor Jing. He recognized his face from the picture Kenny showed him this morning. The others at the table could be identified by reading the name plates in front of them. Kaiden made a mental note of the names and the positions they held at the school. When Ciera shook hands with, and then sat down next to Chancellor Gentry, he realized that there was one person he'd like to get to know a whole lot better... Ciera Lowman. He chuckled at who she was. The title on the large nameplate sitting on the table in front of her read "President of the senior class Miss Ciera Lowman".

"Man, you sly little sexy thing" Kaiden said out loud while folding his arms across his chest, shaking his head as he smiled to himself.

At that moment the President walked up to the podium and addressed the audience. The man spoke into the microphone with an opening statement designed to double as a test to see if the mike was on. "Alright, good morning, everyone". He tapped the microphone with a thump, thump. "This thing on? Hello, I am Chancellor Gentry".

A small portion of scattered voices replied "Good morning, Chancellor Gentry" and a slight applause came from the crowd.

Kaiden snapped out of his thoughts, turned, and looked around. It was immediately apparent that everyone else had found a seat; he was the only one still standing in the aisle. Quickly he scrambled for the first empty seat he could find. It was unlike him and a little embarrassing to be so mesmerized and caught so totally immersed in his own thoughts.

The Chancellor started the orientation by introducing Reverend Waters as the head of the Theology department and brought him up to the podium. The Reverend introduced himself.

"I'm Reverend Waters and I'm going to open this assembly with a short prayer. Please don't be offended if you're a non-believer. For even you must believe that in the beginning, something created us. We didn't just magically form, grow, and develop out of some pool of chemical slop. No matter what you attribute our creation too, this prayer is offered to that higher power that helped create us. Afterall, we came from somewhere, we were created from something, and that takes a blueprint, and it takes 'power' to build it. He commenced with a short prayer addressed to Almighty God.

After he gave a brief opening statement Chancellor Gentry came up and replaced him at the podium. Gentry spoke with authority...

"I know most of you have come to Tenny Hill Academy due to the present conditions that you and your families are now facing here in America. These are uncertain times in an ever increasingly uncertain future, a future that we all must prepare for. So, I welcome you to Tenny Hill Academy or THA as it is affectionately called. I encourage you to make 'preparation' your unrelenting goal here at the Academy. Prepare yourselves in ways you might never have thought of before, to fight the problems that we never thought we'd have to contend with in our lifetime. But those problems are here, now, at our doorstep, and I thank you, the next generation of problem solvers, for giving us the privilege of educating you.

We, meaning the organization currently managing this facility, have only been in operation for fifteen years now, but in such time have made leaps and bounds in the progress of our plan to enable you to carry on the American way and uphold our traditions and the constitutional values of the United States of America as handed down to us by our forefathers. Based on their teachings we have created a plan for the benefit of all mankind. It's a blueprint for your survival in tomorrow's world and we ask you to participate with extreme dedication. Dedicate yourself to 'get back' to our roots yet proceed with new technology which can and will once again lead us to prosperity.

THA is well funded by likeminded donors and of course by the tuition fee that each one of you pay. Yes, I know, it's not cheap. No worthwhile endeavor is cheap or even worse- free. When things are free it quickly becomes viewed as worthless, inevitably people come to consider it of 'lesser value', if not in actuality, then definitely in the mind of the recipient.

We do not accept funds from the government, especially from the 'Education Supplement Program' from which they deal out their form of 'free' education. Students on this program inevitably become puppets of the source as proven by the list of approved courses that they will allow you to take. By not accepting their syllabus, their 'common core' or their 'critical race theory' we effectively sever the strings of influence that bind a student's mind, a mind which they have no right to manipulate in the first place".

Applause rose from the audience.

"But just because you pay good hard-earned money to be here, I beg you not to consider your education as a 'right'. For it surely is a 'privilege' that you have been chosen by God to receive this knowledge. Use this concept to keep you on the path, for each one of you will earn this privilege to be here every day by your concentration and devotion to your studies. I am here to inform you that nothing else will be tolerated. People who perform below our expectations will be removed from the program and sent home".

A murmur swelled up from the crowd and students turned to look at one another surprised as if this was a foreign concept.

Chancellor Gentry continued... "I can speak for the entire faculty, the administration, and the employees here today; we are honored to have you, just as I hope that you consider it an honor to be here. I believe it's God's will that has brought myself and the people assembled here in this room together. It's for a reason and for a common goal. He has bestowed upon me the task of assembling a faculty that will teach the truth and convey the real story behind many of the events happening today. That is my job. I promise to work hard for you, and I expect the same in return. This is your chance to participate in a great opportunity!".

The president paused and the freshman class filled in with a loud round of applause that showed great solidarity with Chancellor Gentry's statements.

"But as I said, we are very well funded by outside contributions as well and therefore you are not just here for your money. We demand more from you than that. Contributors from all over the world are investing in 'you' and have faith that 'you' will be the hope for the future of our republic. The hope is that you will carry the torch of freedom and continue our fight for the republic that we call 'America'. We need you, and we need your hearts and minds!

So, what do we offer you? Tenny Hill Academy can show you how to find answers that we believe you will need to survive in the future. Information! We offer information that will give you some of the answers to your inquiry into life's questions. It is imperative that you learn it well, for it can literally mean the difference between life and death.

Your responsibility then, is to diligently seek out the truth and allow the answers you discover to form the principles that you will use to live your life. At the same time, I implore you to allow a verified, confirmed contradiction of that truth to veer you from your path. For nothing is set in stone. You will need good diligence on your part in pursuit of this knowledge. It's up to you to find it. Look to your friends, to the faculty and staff for help. If you are joining a cluster, look to your cluster leaders for support. Do not look to the government to solve your problems for you; for I can tell you right now, it will not be forth coming. Not from them, no. Not in today's world, not in this America. Our forefathers had always known; that government is not the solution; government is the problem!

The audience applauded and ninety percent of them stood up and cheered for a long moment. When they settled down Chancellor Gentry continued.

That one is a quote from Ronald Reagan but here I paraphrase a quote from one of our famous founding fathers- Benjamin Franklin: We were given a republic! Now you must ask yourself, 'Caan… weee… keep it?".

Again, the audience gave a rousing round of applause that went on for a full minute.

"So, my advice to you is to open the door of this school. Open it wide! Participate in the multifaceted aspects that this Academy can offer. We feel that we've developed a curriculum that can appropriately be applied to the next generation of trials and tribulations that are about to try your souls. You will learn a wide range of skills that are essential. You will need these skills in a big way if our country continues its present course. Take it in. Keep what you feel is useful and discard the rest but remember to keep an open mind. From here on in I want you to consider that what you thought was useful yesterday may not apply to your tomorrow. Save these lessons for when the reality of 'tomorrow' bears no resemblance to your yesterday.

Also, prepare by studying hard the lessons of the past. History... history is our heritage. Prepare for some of the possibilities because we know that history repeats itself as evidenced by our politicians who are replicating some of the same insane mistakes made by nations that have gone down the same inevitable road to eventual ruin like the once powerful Roman Empire. There are a lot of lessons there for you to consider.

You might not see something as important today, and yet someday you'll be thanking God that you learned it here. If you prepare for all scenarios, there will be a good chance that when the time comes you will be ready. If it never comes, so be it. Then let the good times roll and you will be none the worse. For you will have developed a deep ability to adapt and will have learned; how to survive!".

The whole crowd got to their feet again clapping and cheering like it was a political rally.

Chancellor Gentry broke into their exuberance "So onward to a new era for you and your loved ones because what you experience here will allow you to teach them and others how to persevere and weather the coming storm. Thank you, thank you all".

After the applause there were others that stood up and spoke as well, the Delhi town mayor, Professor Jing, and the school treasurer Mr. Clyde Bennett. Then Ciera walked up to the podium. Kaiden was amused and wondered what to expect. She took the mike and gave a short welcome speech to the incoming freshman class. She spoke surprisingly well and gave the new students a short history of the School and the School's progression toward the new curriculum. It included words of advice, points of interest and a couple of jokes that got the class snickering. She concluded with a few announcements.

"This year we are proud to have two returning class representatives on the school board representing the sophomore and junior classes;

Lisa Raven is the returning sophomore class rep, and we have Michael Murray representing the junior class. Please stand up".

The two of them were seated on stage and they both stood up and showed themselves to the audience. They got a halfhearted applause from the freshman class which was understandable because no one really knew who they were.

"Of course, our new addition to the board will be a member of your freshman class that has been appointed to represent you for the coming year. Your freshman class representative is... 'Kaiden Sawyer'. Kaiden where are you?" Ciera said as she looked out into the audience. She squinted with her hand over her forehead to shade her eyes from the light to find him.

"Kaiden Sawyer, I know you're out there. Please stand up".

Kaiden wasn't paying attention at that moment and when his name was called it blew right past him. It had familiarity but recognition did not materialize, it took a few seconds to understand what was going on. He stared blankly at the podium and everyone in the auditorium including Kaiden started looking around the room for that person to stand up.

"Kaiden A. Sawyer" Ciera said again over the loudspeaker.

Realization came to him like a punch in the face. It was his name that Ciera was calling. He turned back to the front and looked at Ciera with a shocked 'can't be' expression on his face. She found him in the audience and was now looking straight at him.

"Kaiden A. Sawyer, would you please stand up".

Very reserved and with some hesitation he slowly stood up not knowing what this was. The people around him started clapping. Then the whole auditorium erupted in applause. He felt so weird that suddenly and unexpectedly the applause was directed at him.

"Come up here and take your seat" Ciera said while swinging her arm around behind her pointing to the one unoccupied chair of board members like Vanna White on Wheel of Fortune. The nameplate in front of the chair read 'Freshman Class Representative'".

Kaiden was shocked but started his unanticipated walk up to the stage with an obvious hint of hesitation. He found the courage to put resistance aside during an impromptu internal debate. Before he reached the steps, he had decided that if this was legitimate and they would actually seat him (that this is not a joke) he would do this and serve to the best of his ability, but not for any other reason than that it would offer a perfect way to place himself inside Ciera's world.

Kaiden walked onto the stage and followed Ciera's hand motion to sit at the table. He took his seat and stole a glance at her with an 'I can't believe you did this' look on his face. She beamed a playful smile at him and turned back to the podium.

Speaking into the microphone she said "Kaiden's credentials were considered, and we found out that he was held in very high regard by the staff at PS-88 in New York City. He was also the president of the 'Checkers and Root Beer Club' right Kaiden?

A chuckle rippled through the audience and Kaiden smiled lowering his face down to the table in front of him, he shook his head back and forth with embarrassment.

Ciera turned back; looked at him and said into the microphone "You were what, president?" a smirk/smile appeared on her face after she said it.

Kaiden halfway stood up and sort of bowed saying "President, yes" and then sat back down again.

"Yes president, he was 'President' of the Checkers and Root Beer Club. Maybe Kaiden will start a Checkers and Root Beer Club for us here at Mt. Tenny".

You could hear the audience chuckle again, but the amazing part was that Kaiden heard some people start clapping and shouting "Alright! I'm in".

Board members welcomed him with applause, and even Chancellor Gentry was enthusiastically clapping and nodding his head when Kaiden looked at him. With that, Kaiden knew that this was the real deal and it all started to sink in.

Ciera went on and finished her speech wrapping it up with something about the bus route that picked up at "Center square" and dropped off in downtown Delhi...

"See the bus schedule in your information packet..." she was saying.

But Kaiden didn't hear the details, his mind was thinking about what this meant, and he wondered what exactly his duties were as freshman class rep. His thoughts went back to the streets of NY and to that day when he became a major player with the gang of 88's. This was going to be a whole lot different. On that day he had to fight his way past competition with both words and fists for the right to have a say. If they only knew his history and that he was previously top dog of a tough gang on the streets of NY, not the president of the Checkers and Root Beer Club. Would Ciera still have made the same choice? "I wonder if she knows" he thought.

After the speech Ciera sat down but not without flashing a warm smile in Kaiden's direction. A few other people got up to the podium to offer students some important bits of information that would help in the transition to living at THA. Then there was a video designed to get students familiar with various places and events around campus. Professors took turns getting up and explaining certain photos within their specific field of expertise.

There was Professor Nailor of the science department who narrated pictures of the science building, the labs and some of the projects that they were starting. He showed how they were applying new science to some of the agricultural projects on campus and he showed pictures of the before and aftereffects.

Professor Pellegrin explained the mathematics curriculum which included the computer program that was under his direction. He hinted and implied that his department was the backbone of all the other departments due to his expertise in customizing programs for each special application that the others used.

Next was Professor Jaz Monet who everyone knew as "The Major". He was one of the newer professors added to the college roster with five full years of teaching under his belt. He headed the Physical Education department along with his partner Professor Harry Coin. They split responsibilities between the two of them. Professor Coin specialized in the competitive sports aspect and the Major specialized in military training, history, tactics, and martial arts.

Major Monet was one of a handful of distinguished black men who had graduated from West Point. With over twenty-five years in service, he achieved the distinguished rank of Major in the Army. While totally looking the part, he also spoke just like you'd expect a gruff military sergeant to speak. It seemed like he was about to induct the entire freshman class into the armed forces. His people (students/Cadets) ran the rifle range and he made sure that everyone knew that he ran it 'military style' where no monkey business was tolerated. At THA it was mandatory to take two years of a martial art under the tutelage of the Major himself to graduate. Major Jaz claimed to have some of the best martial arts teachers in the country available to him and they came in regularly to teach seminars in various styles of fighting arts. It was a given that everyone at one point or another would become acquainted with the Major. He gave a speech that explained the protocol practiced at the Academy.

The Major leaned in and spoke into the microphone "Yes, we have become very serious about the education offered here at THA. We're not just a survival course on steroids. We feel that this is a superb education, as superb as you would receive at any of the major colleges with an added bonus. We are very serious about teaching you how to protect yourselves which includes extensive courses on your rights as granted by the Constitution of the United States of America. To produce well rounded individuals ready to lead this great nation, your studies will include military tactics. We are both a fully accredited College with the option of participating in a military academy style education. The founders of this school saw the need for our students to become familiar with the customary traditions of the military and concepts of the art of war. Why not, why shouldn't the public have access to the same training as the military?

It has become necessary to give you these tools to increase your chances of survival in today's world. We believe that the youth of today will need every ounce of this training to overcome. That includes knowledge of military procedures, applications, functions, and techniques. The community you live in might one day need someone with a 'Cadet' education. With this training you can become an integral part of it.

This is the ultimate form of training for survival in possible scenarios of future conflicts. It will include guerilla warfare as well as the techniques of structured modern armies. We will give you the "HBO" preview of modern weapons of today's armies so that if you are called to defend your family and your community, you will be one step ahead of the rest. Tenny Hill Academy will enable you to defend the freedom we enjoy as Americans. You will persevere and maintain our freedom for future generations as the generation before you have bequeathed to you. YOU WILL BE PREPARED TO PREVAIL!".

That last statement drew applause and cat calls that lasted over a half a minute. The audience was ripe for his style of rhetoric. The Major ended his speech with this statement; "In this endeavor, I, we..." he swung his arm pointing to the faculty behind him... "Demand the same degree of respect that would be generated in a military setting. Tenny Hill Academy has determined that learning the "Art of War" is essential for producing a well-rounded graduate and you will receive the best of this art that I can possibly offer".

Major Monet stepped off the podium ending the speech and returned to his seat among a round of applause. The room gave him a standing ovation with robust applause that expressed enthusiasm for the man and his words.

Then of course there was the Professor of Agriculture Mr. Jim Ingle otherwise known as "Jing". He looked older than the picture Kenny had shown him. He too was an enthusiastic speaker but here he touted the benefits of learning the "knowledge of the land". In his speech you could hear the undertones of a firm belief in spreading the knowledge that would once again bring people to rely on themselves to produce and bring forth sustenance from the earth.

Jing spoke dramatically; "We must be prepared for an existence in which we will need to grow our own food and gather what nature provides us for our own survival. The lessons I teach will be the ones that you're going to wish you had paid a lot more attention should you ever need them. So please do yourself a favor and in the end, do all the people who rely on you a favor, take my classes very seriously, study the material like it will make a difference between life and death because one day, it just might!" At the time Kaiden didn't know just how true that statement would be.

All the speakers gave the students information about the procedures, rules and regs that applied to each segment of study and added in their own helpful hints about how to get the best out of the courses they taught. The whole orientation ended up lasting over two hours and broke up just after twelve noon. Just in time for lunch.

The board members and faculty mingled around the stage after the students were dismissed. Ciera was talking to a small click of people that huddled around her. Kaiden walked over. He held his hands behind his back and shook his head. He didn't have to vocalize what was beaming out of the expression on his face... 'Ciera what the hell have you got me into?'

When she noticed him standing there she broke off from the group and turned to face him with that signature smile preceding her. She put it on thick in an attempt to tame him.

Ciera cringed and shrugged her shoulders "You don't mind, do you?"

"No not at all. I was going to ask you if I could be on the board". Kaiden said sarcastically.

Ciera touched his arm with her hand and looked at him with a grin.

"Really? Thanks, Kaiden. Somehow, I knew you were the right person for the job".

"You didn't tell me you were senior rep" Kaiden said.

She was relieved that he didn't immediately complain and inform her that he wasn't going to take the position.

"You didn't tell me you were president of the Checkers and Root Beer Club either" Ciera said with a big ear to ear grin like she already knew the truth about that.

"Kaiden do you really want the job? I could get someone else... if you want".

"Ciera, I'll do it. I'd love the job". Kaiden stated emphatically with a smile and a slight bow of his head.

"Great" she said. Her whole face brightened up. "Come and meet Jing". Ciera pulled on his arm and dragged him over to the Professor to introduce them.

"Professor Jing this is Kaiden Sawyer the new freshman class representative".

"Kaiden! So, you're the new freshman class rep" he shook Kaiden's hand. "It's nice to meet you. Welcome aboard. Call me Jing. Everyone else does".

"Yes sir, I've heard about you, and I can't wait to get out there in the woods" Kaiden said.

"Hey, we can arrange that, as freshman rep I could get you special permission to set up out there if you want" Jing told him.

"Well, I just might take you up on that but let me consider it. I wasn't really prepared to jump right into it my first semester. I'm just a city boy sir, with a lot of street sense yes but I'm still learning just what living in Rio Linda entails sir. Thank you for the offer. I'll let you know".

"Great, it's going to be a fantastic year like I said. We had a great show from our summer crops this year. We've canned, freeze dried and frozen enough to get us most of the way through the winter. The pictures that I showed today were of this year's crop. Next week we'll start picking pumpkins and it looks like we're going to have quite a harvest of apples too". Jing rubbed his hands together and shouted to the sky "Thank God, apple sauce is back on the menu!".

Ciera explained "Kaiden, I don't know if you knew that Jing and all the seekers who live in Rio Linda try to survive off the food that's produced here at the Academy".

"She said try..." Jing added "...because it's not a requirement, but some of the students 'try' to get along the best they can with just what we grow. Some years we don't have enough to get through and we don't make it. The diehards take it very seriously you know, but that's why I'm so excited about this year, it's looking quite good. We're getting our techniques down pat and when the weather cooperates- we do quite well".

"Glad to hear it sir, I'm interested in learning all about it. That's what I'm here for" Kaiden said.

"I want to introduce you to some others" Ciera pulled on his arm, excuse us Professor.

"Goodbye professor, Nice to meet you" Kaiden said over his shoulder.

"Jing, just Jing" he heard him say as Ciera ushered him away.

Ciera introduced him to as many of the faculty and board members as she could find that were still hanging out around the stage. Professor Jaz Monet or "Major Jaz" as he was commonly called was one of them.

Ciera escorted Kaiden over to meet him and broke into the conversation he was having with a fellow staff member.

"Major Jaz, excuse me for interrupting but I wanted to make sure I got a chance to introduce you to our new freshman class representative Mr. Kaiden Sawyer before you left".

He broke from his 'at ease' stance and faced her giving her his full undivided attention. With a warm smile he took her hand, bowed, and kissed it in typical European fashion.

"My dear Ciera, you are allowed to interrupt me anytime you want. It's great to see you; your lovely smile always warms my heart. I was hoping you'd bring him over". Ciera beamed and played along with a small curtsy of her own in response. She thoroughly enjoyed the polite attention she always got from the Major whenever they spoke. It was obvious that it warmed her heart as well by the way she reacted.

The Major turned and said “Hello Kaiden, nice to meet you. They shook hands with a strong grip.

“Are you majoring in survival training and taking courses with me?”

“Sir, it’s great to meet you too, and yes, I’m looking forward to the training. I’ve heard a lot about you (he lied). I’m taking most of my required courses up front to get them out of the way, but I will be taking the range course this semester”.

“Yes of course, but I’ll expect to see you in one of the martial arts classes’ as well, right?” Major Jaz said. “You should join now, it’s best to get started as soon as possible.

“Yes, I agree. I have a lot of experience in that department sir. I’ll be participating in as many of those classes as I can. I wouldn’t miss it even if it wasn’t required” Kaiden replied.

“Ah, an enthusiast! That’s great. Kaiden, if you have enough prior experience to pass the martial arts final exam you can skip the preliminary training and go on to AWT (Advanced Weapons Training). You can choose to study weapons and tactics or apply for the sniper program. I highly recommend the sniper program”.

“Thank you, sir, I’ll try to test out then. I’d love to see how I place and where I fit in to all of this”.

“Good show Kaiden. I also recommend pledging to one of the Clusters. Being accepted into one puts you on the path to the inner circle of operations around here. It’ll open doors for you in the future and will allow you to join the ‘Outpost’ if you want”.

“I heard the president speak of a Cluster, but I don’t know much about the Outpost”.

“A Cluster is the same thing as a fraternity or a sorority. It’s kind of a brotherhood and sisterhood combined but it’s not gender based like in other colleges. Male or female can join. As far as the Outpost is concerned you will have to learn about it from your Cluster brethren, the details are privy to members only. It’s one of our little well-kept secrets we have around here, but I highly recommend it.

“If you recommend it sir, then I’ll look into joining one” Kaiden said.

"Good. Tai Chi practice starts at 0545 outside of Chilton hall son. We're there every day except Sunday, rain or shine for at least an hour. If it's bad weather we're inside Chilton hall, otherwise we meet under the oak tree in the field next to the back parking lot. Then we have the morning run at seven. That's how we start our day. Maybe I'll see you there?" the Major said. Then he cut the conversation short by nodding to Kaiden with a slight bow. He turned to Ciera and said "I noticed your name on the roster; I understand that I'll see you at the range and in my kick boxing class this semester".

"Yes sir, you heard right; I'm looking forward to it" Ciera said.

"Until then... Good day Miss Lowman". The Major bowed slightly as he said it, but his eyes never lost contact with hers. And there was that smile he gave that you could imagine was saved exclusively for the ladies. You almost got the feeling that something was going on between them, a secret something. Then he turned sharply on his heels and walked away.

Previously Ciera would have laughed at the stiff military type personality of Major Jaz but after knowing him ever since she was a freshman, she was quite used to it and had come to cherish it. Now she saw his style as being a great influence on the boys she knew. A lot of them have started the transformation into men due in large part to his influence. Ciera would attest to that fact from firsthand experience with her present boyfriend Nick. The "before and after" effect was a welcomed addition to their relationship and was the main reason she was still with him. If nothing else, Major Jaz taught them manors such as the impromptu lesson on etiquette just like the one Kaiden had received just now.

Kaiden turned to Ciera and came to attention. "May I escort you to lunch ma'am" he said and offered her his arm. She laughed at Kaiden's imitation of the Major. But saw it as proof of the extent of the Major's influence on "the boys". She thought for a second and accepted his arm. Even though he was just mimicking the Major, it was apparent that Kaiden had gotten an "A" on his first lesson.

Ciera replied "Yes sir, you may" and smiled with delight as she hooked her arm in his. Kaiden escorted her safely down the stairs and walked her over to her RP before going to the cafeteria. The whole way there and throughout lunch they were buried in conversation about the next step in their lives and in the lives of the students at THA.

10

State Secret

Years ago, after the Health Care bill was passed in congress, every American was forced into purchasing health insurance. If they didn't, they would suffer the wrath of the IRS and pay a fine. Many couldn't afford the insurance or the fine; they simply wrote a note on their tax form saying "sorry I don't have the money". Instantly millions of people became indebted to the government and were now under the thumb of the IRS. As part of the bill, thousands of new IRS agents were hired to implement the program. They were used to collect information as well as the money and became the spearhead of the government's new campaign.

Late on the Friday before Labor Day, one of the Washington DC news stations WPBJ in their "Week in review" segment reported a story about the new two trillion-dollar environmental bill pushed through by the intense lobbying efforts of the EPA (Environmental Protection Agency). The "Environmental Sustainability Rights Act" was voted in on the eve of the Labor Day holiday upon which the originators knew would assure its passage with the least amount of attention and news coverage. But there was another story that only received a one paragraph comment during that same news cast:

"President Richfield issued an executive order this afternoon that empowered the Internal Revenue Service to hire eighty thousand more IRS agents to collect delinquent taxes more aggressively. The head of the IRS Anthony Knowles was unavailable for comment but the official White House statement concerning the order said, "It just gives the IRS greater ability to do its job and that is; to collect money rightfully due to the United States Government. We needed to put some teeth into our existing laws that govern the collection of overdue taxes. The process needs to be updated and streamlined. Many Americans are now delinquent at a time when it's imperative that the flow of funds owed to the government not be impaired in any way. America's taxes must be paid because America's debts must be paid. We are forced to expand our collection ability to stay on top of this crisis. The United States cannot afford to wait for these funds to come in at a trickle. They must be collected now rather than later".

No other WH official was available for comment.

It resounded with some degree of common sense and that's why it floated through under the radar. Most everyone would agree that taxes due to the government should be paid. And they already had the right to collect on debt so there's nothing new here. But as is the case with politics, the important part is not what is said but what isn't. The statement "This would put some teeth into the government's ability to collect..." meant that the IRS had just been issued the "Go ahead" and bequeathed a higher degree of power in the campaign for the IRS to collect due tax. Resources were allocated to form a special task force designated to confiscate property and or quote; "...such assets of the delinquent taxpayer that might satisfy the debt owed". The part that wasn't explained very well was the new streamlining power that the provision gave the IRS. This clause eliminated any obligation on the part of the IRS to offer the delinquent taxpayer terms for monthly payments or any kind of a grace period. They were given the right to go in and take full payment directly from the delinquent taxpayer's bank account "or with other assets", all without a warrant and without notice. It rendered the taxpayer powerless to legally contest any action taken against them. From now on, if you owed it, they could take it. If you couldn't pay up, they could take everything you owned as payment for your obligation without a court order; it was "by order of the IRS". With this law the court system had been usurped. The IRS was now Judge, Jury and Executioner.

The bill was snuck in like a thief in the night as all the disturbing ones are. The government was becoming desperate and needed the income now rather than later, normal channels were too slow. The formation of law and Congressional approval could take years to pass through the legislature, so they simply bypassed it and authorized it through executive law. Besides they didn't need the approval of Congress, the American people were too busy with other things to notice this small insignificant loss of due process.

* * *

Tenny Hill Academy was built on an old six-hundred-acre farm with a history that dated back before the American Revolutionary war. Some of the property had been sold off but the present property boundaries encompassed all Mt. Tenny and the rolling hills surrounding its base on all sides. Included in the school's estate was the (relatively) flat farmland and farmhouse located on the east side of Tenny Mountain. Nestled in the valley, it was used to support the agriculture program. The college campus was built on elevations among rolling hills which were not ideally suited for farming but was groomed with buildings strategically placed and tucked into positions in and around the trees and open meadows. It gave the property a charm that was often photographed and touted as one of the main attractions of the Catskill region. Pictures of beautiful landscape around campus were strategically used in brochures and advertisements to lure prospective students to this tranquil paradise. Multiple sites around the campus and of course up on top of Mt. Tenny enabled pristine views of the Catskill Mountain range. The range, as anyone who knows the Catskills will admit, is not so much renowned for the "height" of its mountains but more for its subtle picturesque views of rolling mountainous terrain with landscape checkered with patch quilt squares of farmland in the valleys. The previous owner Mrs. Daugherty donated the property to the original founders of the college in 1949 after her husband and son had both died in World War II. The entire estate was donated to beneficiaries with one restrictive covenant attached to the property deed. The covenant mandated that the property would be used specifically for the pursuit of education through the development of a teaching establishment such as a school, college, or training facility. "Facility" was further defined as-

"An institution dedicated to the endeavor of offering exceptional education in the pursuit of teaching the history of this great nation to all future generations. A designated facility devoted to studying the arts, history, and sciences of the world in order that we may learn of our past mistakes and educate the next generation in the art of avoiding them. In this way we might ensure that our nation will never fall victim to the same propaganda and the agenda of people who seek to control us. Any person(s) taking up the offer of receivership of this donated parcel of land is hereafter bound to develop the property in this manner and with that goal in mind".

The school's founders stayed true to those parameters.

* * *

Major Jazz and the Tai Chi class he taught commenced on time at five forty-five in the morning. Kaiden and about nineteen other students met behind Chilton Hall just before the crack of dawn. First the Major led them through a routine designed to wake up and stretch the body using slow motion movement mixed in with an array of breathing exercises called "Chi Gung". Chi Gung exercises combine movement with breathing patterns while placing one's concentration on various points on the body. This type of slow breathing allows for a better flow of oxygen into the blood and the movement circulates the internal energy of the body. It's composed of a simple set of movements that flow from one into another generating a positive energy flow that adds up to a stronger healthier internal body condition.

Standing at the front of the class, the Major started off with slow, soft movements building up to more strenuous stretches as the entire class swung their limbs from side to side. Imitating the Major, the whole class moved together in a synchronized pattern and continued as he switched into practicing the Tai Chi form. The form is where one experiences the essence of Tai Chi's moving meditation. It guides a practitioner from one posture into another while moving calmly from one solid stance to another. The hands perform various techniques in conjunction with the footwork looking very similar to a slow dance. Just by standing there watching you can feel peace and serenity let alone if you joined in and did the movements yourself. Early morning at dawn is considered to be the best time to practice when the energy of the night starts to change into day. This is when the "Yin" turns into "Yang" in Chinese Taoist philosophy. The whole scene was topped off by performing the routine in the presence of a beautiful old oak tree that spread its ancient branches over the group.

Loosening up the body in a subtle way without forcing the muscles is an invigorating way to wake up. For students who are able to connect and feel the energy flow, this practice quickly becomes a favorite part of their day.

"Kaiden Sawyer" Major Jaz said after the first class.

Kaiden broke away from his conversation with two other students and responded with a quick "Yes sir".

"I see that you have practiced Tai Chi before. You are no beginner".

"Yes sir, I have. I've studied martial arts since I was nine and have also had the privilege of learning Yang Style Tai Chi Chuan from Master Yin Gee How in New York City".

"Excellent. I've heard of Master Yin. Many in the New York Tai Chi inner circle hold him in high regard. How similar is your form to mine?"

"Well sir, everyone seems to teach the form a little differently but actually the way you're doing it is very close to the way I've been taught" Kaiden said.

"Great. I'd like to see your version and discuss the differences. Have you studied the applications of the movements?".

"Yes sir, but not all of them of course, that would take a lot longer than the time I've put in. I was taught the 'thirteen postures' and I have a good idea about how to use them. We practice it in a form like this...". Kaiden stood back and settled into a Tai Chi stance. His arms came up and started a routine that went through thirteen movements in a row which he named as he performed them. Split, pull, ward off, roll back, press, elbow strike, shoulder strike, deflect left, deflect right, neutral, raise up, sink down, push".

"Very nice Kaiden, would you be willing to teach that to the class?".

"I would love to Sir. I have no problem with that at all".

"Fantastic. Would you be so kind as to get together with me so I can get a preview of the movements? I'd like to know more about it myself so that when you present it, I'm not so oblivious".

"I'll look forward to it Sir".

"Thank you" Major Jazz said. Then he turned and announced to the whole group. "Those of you here for the run, let's form up. We'll be doing the west trail today". Only four out of the ten or so Tai Chi players formed up in front of him but today there were four more new arrivals that had skipped the Tai Chi class in lieu of participating in the run only.

"Ready!" The Major yelled. He looked at his watch, it was 0700 exactly. "Ho!" And with that the entire group followed the Major who took off jogging westward along the edge of the field. Kaiden fell in line and tagged along.

Kaiden's first class at the Academy was called "The evolution of American Government". Professor Mortimer Latti introduced himself saying "...not 'Late' it's 'Latti!

"This guy reminds me of Mr. Bentner" Kaiden thought. Pleasant memories and of course a few bad ones came to mind but still he smiled to himself.

Professor Latti was in the middle of a lecture on the American Constitution, Tenny Hill Academy was one of the only schools that devoted an entire course to its study.

"The constitution's brilliance is that it defined the role of government and set limits to its power. It limits the role of government as to how they can intrude in the lives of the American people. Disgruntled opponents of the document call it 'negative liberties' due precisely to the limits placed upon the government's ability to affect the lives of its people. Citizens who appreciate the limitations consider them to be 'positive' due to the inherent restrictions it places on government. Meaning that the document didn't so much tell the government what it can do, it placed boundaries upon which bureaucrats cannot cross. Thus, placing the reigns squarely in the hands of 'We The People' who dictate how society will be guided. 'We The People' gave them the authority to govern us, and "We The People" can take it away. Or at least that's how it's supposed to be. The constitution is a safeguard to make sure that it never becomes the other way around.

People, if you haven't figured it out already, our constitution is under attack by people who see it as a doctrine of negative liberties. To them it is 'in their way'. Unfortunately, there are way too many examples of abuse for us to discuss. The government has blessed themselves with the right to force the entire population to purchase a product that 'they' have deemed as necessary. Health care, electric cars, forcing us to buy energy efficient products. Banning gas stoves, outlawing the incandescent light bulb. We are no longer able to choose for ourselves. Instead of educating the public and allowing us to choose for ourselves, they made it law. And with each stroke of a pen, we lost another freedom. This is not what our government was originally designed to do. Let's start with the healthcare issue...".

"But professor" a young man in the front raised his hand. "Didn't we give the government the right to offer healthcare since we voted in the people who stated they were going to do just that?".

"Good point Mr. Benelli. Allow me to answer your question with a question. Because we elect representatives who adhere to a certain agenda, be it known or even more of a concern 'unknown', does that give them the right to circumvent the constitution?".

A murmur of voices welled up in the classroom.

"Now we see the blaring, essential point of this discussion floating right to the surface. What does the constitution allow? What does it say the government can do? Mr. Benelli does the constitution say that the government should be in the healthcare business?".

"No sir I know that it does not, at least not in those terms".

"Well, if we study the 'terms' of the constitution and understand the underlying principles that define it, and then follow the political formula that our forefathers used to create this highly successful nation, which would be more fair to say? That the government should take over and provide healthcare for the masses or that the people should be able to purchase the type of healthcare they desire freely on their own?".

"On our own!" shouted the class almost in unison.

"So, we have a problem don't we. Now let me shorten this discussion because we are running out of time". The professor pointed to Mr. Benelli "I'm sure Mr. Benelli here is dying to respond with another question".

"Yes, I am, what if they can't afford healthcare?".

"Yes, Mr. Benelli. Try to answer your own question, what if they can't afford healthcare, what would happen?"

"Well, they would die".

"Ooooo, such a grim answer. Is there no other scenario?" The professor pointed to another student who responded.

"I think if there is any help that we get from the Federal government, it should be to set the groundwork to inspire people to solve their own problems. Allow the people to flourish on their own. The best way to do that is for the government to get out of the way. When people are profitable, charities flourish in turn. We have a history that show's this is true; American's are some of the most charitable people on earth. I do have to admit that I think that this attribute is partially due to the fact that the government has declared charitable contributions to be tax deferred, but that just goes to prove my point. The government's policy should encourage people to act on their own accord, it should not force them.

I have faith in people's good nature, I think, no I know, that they would naturally step up and help other people. That's the way it should be, that's the way God intended it to be and that's the way we are. We don't need the government to take money from us and hand it out on our behalf" the student said.

Someone shouted "Wooo wooo wooo!" then the whole room erupted in noisy concurrence.

When the professor regained control of the class he said "Wow, allow the people to flourish! What a concept.

People, hear ye hear ye, the government, in this and in many other examples, has overstepped its authority as written and granted by the constitution of the United States of America. This is a serious grievance as proven by previous precedent set by governments that rule in the same manor. Let me tell you; in every example it does not end well for the people. The government has no right to force any of us to buy insurance or anything else for that matter. Their self-proclaimed ability to control commodity prices is not in the Constitution either. They are responsible for our protection, yes. Some would argue that health insurance is an effort in that direction and therefore they should be allowed to do so. But then if the government was so concerned with protection why wouldn't they require everyone to buy a gun? Isn't that the very essence of protection? I can hear the proponents now... 'Well health insurance is to protect your health, that's a noble cause. Guns injure, maim, and kill people'.

Students of THA... I'm here to tell you that our very own medical system, the one that they say is so 'noble', yes, the one forced upon each one of you by the Federal government's HR-22 health care bill... this is the very same medical system that kills an average of 225,000 people per year due to bad diagnosis, miss applied medicine, botched surgeries, complications and yes even intentionally! And all of it is due to the afore mentioned 'noble' healthcare industry. I didn't even mention or include the ones that are maimed from surgeries performed on the wrong limb or even on the wrong patient!

Does anyone know how many deaths are attributed to guns in America. I'm talking per year?".

The classroom went quiet, no one spoke up.

"Guns are responsible for, are you ready for this...on the average- 29,500 deaths per year... total" Professor Latti said. The professor paused and looked around the class. A murmur of voices expressing surprise rose from the students.

"Wow, I didn't know that" one student said out loud.

"Yes, 29,500 for guns, 225,000 for the medical industry. Sounds to me like guns might be a better thing to prescribe than our medical system now, doesn't it?".

A sobering chuckle rippled through the class.

"I suggest at least, if you're going to promote healthcare Mr. Benelli as somehow adhering to the government's role as 'protector', do not be hypocritical and then denounce gun ownership as somehow an opposite disturbing concept. For under the same analogy if you promote healthcare for its ability to save lives shouldn't you promote gun ownership due to the same inherent ability... to save lives? Fact: sixty-five percent of all gun related instances have been determined to have occurred in 'self-defense' circumstances. And who knows how many crimes have been thwarted by a gun yet unreported. Knowing what you know now, if you still adhere to the analogy that 'guns kill', shouldn't you also claim that 'healthcare kills' and seek to ban it as well? If you want to ban guns for safety reasons, wouldn't you now also want to ban healthcare for the same reason?".

"Really!" some of the students yelled out in agreement.

"Well of course I'm being facetious" the professor stated. Only those people who disregard the thousands of cases in which our healthcare system has helped or cured people would you conclude that it should be banned. That is my point. The anti-gun crowd is doing that exact misdeed when it comes to guns. They disregard thousands of cases in which someone's life has been saved by a gun. But you know..." he looked at the class and through a big grin on his face he said "Wouldn't the proponents for healthcare bitch up a storm if the government forced them to buy a gun for protection! Ha! I can hear it now. They would all yell and scream 'The government has no right to tell me to buy a gun!'. Now that would be a precious sight to see wouldn't it.

It seems our representative's idea of protection is bent in one direction and for political reasons bent in another to shun the benefit of gun ownership. The point is, is that the government shouldn't even be in this business of deciding what is best for us at all! Yet they are. From my perspective it is obvious that they are following an agenda designed to achieve a certain result. And I say the government has overstepped their bounds! You must ask yourself, why would the government want to disarm its people? We didn't give them the right to make that decision".

The professor paused and looked at the class then continued.

"I, in turn... We The People, have failed to hold true to the Constitution and have failed to use its power of restraint to reign in these out-of-control politicians".

The professor looked at his watch. "We will talk more about that and how our hands are being tied next class. You're dismissed".

* * *

Kenny Jay and fellow students were milling about the range locker room prior to class. It wasn't really the "Range" locker room, actually it was the Phys Ed building's locker room. Four years ago, after the new range was built right next to the Phys Ed building, shooters were able to share all the Phys Ed building's facilities. Ever since, the Range has enjoyed a surge in popularity, so much so that it has become one of the college's most outstanding features. Now people are calling it the Range building more than the Phys Ed building.

As well as being renowned for its "survival" curriculum, THA is also well known for its Phys Ed program too. Students can train and master such obscure arts like spear throwing, fencing, or become proficient at archery. The unique feature of the college is the re-dedication to and emphasis on, physical fitness. Unlike other private institutions that have faded away from physical education in every form, here there is mandatory participation in classes on weight training, Yoga, and martial arts classes that have never been cultivated to this degree in any other academic institution. Above and beyond other schools, they offer extensive studies on topics that many schools have dropped. Like US History, the United States Constitution, food production, tunnel building, water purification techniques, solar power, solar water heating and marksmanship. THA was the first that allowed its students the freedom to move toward and incorporate military style training into their program of study as well as to form the 'Cadet' organization.

Located on the outskirts of campus grounds, the range building and the shooting range is well situated. Not necessarily for accessibility, because many people complain about the long walk, but more for the soundproofing qualities of the location. The 25-yard indoor range was never a concern, but the 200-yard outdoor rifle range had to be situated just right to mute noise and of course to assure that no stray bullets would endanger campus personnel. With a lot of consideration, the outdoor range was nestled between the main building itself and a natural slope in the contour of the land. A rising knoll which rose sharply right up to the northeast side of the range building formed a natural sound barrier and effectively separated the shooting range from the other campus buildings. It was very rare that the thunder of booming rifles could be heard although on some occasions when the wind was right you can hear the echo of gunfire both from points around campus and in Rio Linda itself. Some grumbling by the seekers out in Rio Linda always followed. Occasionally there would be complaints about the crack of a rifle but with the outdoor range only open for practice from nine to two o'clock PM, it wasn't much of a problem.

The main building had an indoor basketball court, a huge weight training facility and a large training hall. Half of the training hall floor was padded with mats; the other half was exposed wood flooring with mirrors and ballet bars on the longest wall. The matted section was used for wrestling, martial arts, and yoga practice. The hardwood floor section was used for form practice and dance classes. Students training in any of those activities used the locker rooms downstairs to change into something appropriate or to shower afterwards. There was a strict dress code requiring students to wear the required "THA" gym uniform consisting of a T shirt and shorts or sweatpants with the Tenny Hill Academy logo on it. At the shooting range Cadets were only allowed to wear the famous blue Cadet standard issue uniform. All non-Cadets were restricted to long pants, shirt, and appropriate shoes. Meaning, no open toed sandal type footwear like flip flops for example.

Also, the range building is where Major Monet and his assistant Professor Harry Coin retained their office. It was located on the second floor and had a large internal picture window overlooking the basketball courts. From there they coordinate all the sporting activity at the school and even some outside events and competitions. After the Major came on board the shooting range classes took on new meaning. From that point on it didn't just involve picking up a gun and shooting it. There was a whole new set of exercises the Major devised and installed into the program which he used to 'pump you up' before shooting along with a series of stretches designed to 'get the kinks out'. Shooting turned into as much of a Phys Ed class as anything other. All of it was in preparation for scoring well on the famous moving & shooting obstacle course which you had to pass within the allotted time to receive the sharpshooter/marksmanship rank and be awarded the coveted patch for your jacket.

A freshman newbie sat on the locker room bench listening to Kenny Jay ramble on about the obstacle course while getting dressed. Other students were either changing or milling about the room. Kenny informed him "Dressing in uniform for range practice is required for cadet members but not for the other students who don't want to participate or who haven't joined the Cadets. Even though most of them eventually end up buying the BD's (Battle Dress) pants anyway because they're just great pants man. They're high quality and very practical to wear for any of the activities".

Kenny pulled out the dark blue uniform from his locker and stepped into the pants; he suited up and then placed the dark blue military style cap on his head while glancing in the mirror. The combination always made him feel like a member of the team.

"You should join the Cadets. You'll get a uniform, and you'll learn how to march. You'll be able to participate in the parades as well as other special training. Until then just get in the back of the line and walk out behind us. We all assemble on the tarmac (the parking lot) for exercises, then we go through some marching drills before high stepping it over to the range. But you don't have to march. Just go to the back of the line and follow us over. Pay attention though, you might want to join later".

With that Kenny grabbed an ammo belt and slung it over his shoulder. They both walked outside to the blacktop where the class was gathering. Kenny met with a few friends only briefly before the Major's "Number One" came out and blew his whistle. The guy started shouting "Form up, form up!" and all the students fell into a loose formation on the tarmac in preparation for calisthenics.

"Number one" started the class with twenty minutes of stretching and then he took them through a variety of classic exercises like pushups, sit ups and jumping jacks to warm up. When he blew the whistle again the class broke up and walked over to the exterior distribution window of the equipment room. There they picked up the equipment they'd be using for the day.

When Kenny walked up to the window, he joked with Carl who was the scheduled equipment manager for today's morning shift.

"Hey Carl, they got you dealing today huh?".

"Yeah, hey Kenny". Carl got right to the point like he was tending bar. "What'll it be Kenny, the Kel-Tec SU-16, or are you sharpening your skills on the Remi 700? I think you've already qualified on that, haven't you?

"Yeah, I have. I don't suppose you got the Barrett A1 do ya?" Kenny asked.

"No, you know it man you can only shoot that thing on Thursday between ten and noon. No one wants to be alongside someone shooting that thing, they can't stand the noise. You'll have to get here early to get online for that bad boy".

"Well alright, give me the .308 Remi, I'm still trying to match qualify at 200 with it. Oh, give me the DM (detached magazine) model will ya, I don't want to fool with single shot bolt action. I need the five-round mag.

"You got it bro; everyone needs a little work on the 700/200" Carl said. Carl pulled one off the rack and handed Kenny the Remington Model 700 BDL DM as well as a matching .308 magazine. Both the magazine and the rifle had seen better days.

When he saw Kenny examining it Carl said "Don't worry about how it looks, it'll still shoot 1 inch MOA at 100 and that's all that counts believe me. The barrel's been replaced and the trigger's set at 3 pounds. That's a damn nice rifle even with all the scuff marks".

The rifle was virtually indestructible, but it looked like someone had tried to destroy it with all the deep gouges in the stock and the many scratches on the receiver and barrel although whoever picked it as a range rifle made an excellent choice. Knowing that their firearms had to have the ability to stand up to the abuse it would receive in the hands of wave after wave of inexperienced shooters. The 700 was a great hunting rifle and was the first model that a student had to master before moving on to others.

"Or" Carl said "I can give you the first of the FN-FX-AR's we just got in. You'd be the first to shoot it".

"No, you're shittin me!" Kenny said.

Carl pulled one off the shelf and held it in his hands. "It's chambered in 308 with a chrome lined heavy barrel, pistol grip, Zeiss Conquest scope with Rapid Z reticule making this baby simple to range in. This my friend is a bee-u-tay". He pulled the slide back with a "click" as if he'd just chambered a round and aimed it at the ceiling. "It's a little heavy at nine pounds. But that keeps the kick down to no prob and you'll stay on target with that muzzle brake. It's something you'll only appreciate when you need it. Man, it's accurate as hell with a five or twenty round mag. Kenny you really need to qualify with this, I mean you can reach out to 1000 yards with this thing!"

Carl was exaggerating a bit on the 1000 yards, but he handed the FN-FX-AR to Kenny for inspection.

"Nice! It feels good. Wow, it comes in camo? What is it a hunting rifle or a sniper rifle?" Kenny said as he examined it. "What the hell is this? It says 'Winchester' on it".

"Well yeah actually it's a Winchester SX-AR but in brand name only. FN bought the Winchester name and made an exact copy of their black FNAR tactical rifle only here it is in camo, and they stamped "Winchester" on the barrel. The only difference is that this one comes without side rails; otherwise, it's the same rifle. So, I guess you could say that it's a hunting rifle with the five round and a very effective battle rifle with the twenty-round mag. It never really became popular with the masses, but I guess that's why we got a great deal on them".

Kenny accepted the clerk's assessment and looked up with a smile on his face. "Yeah, I'll take this one, gimmie a twenty-round mag" he said and signed it out.

The rifle was a hit with classmates. They were all in awe and asked the same question. "What the hell is it?" Before Kenny could get into it, the whistle blew. Everyone got in line and came to attention placing their rifle on their left shoulder or they slung over their back military style depending on which model they had checked out. When everyone was set, Number One gave the command and marched them out to the range. On the way he took them through a few maneuvers for good measure.

"Left turn march! Right turn march! Halt!" After a few remarks to people who were out of step he started them back up again yelling once again "Forward march!".

Marching practice was normally done on Saturday mornings or Tuesday nights, but it was impossible for Number One to pass up the opportunity to drill them just a bit before target practice.

People came from all around to shoot at the Tenny Hill rifle range. Its notoriety increased dramatically after it was featured in "Gun" magazine and touted as one of the nicest shooting ranges on the east coast. It's a state of the art 200-yard range that was built with a below ground service tunnel. Access ran from the shooting bench stations all the way out underground to each target pit. On duty pit managers walk out through the tunnel to tend targets while concealed behind a solid concrete wall. They can safely deal with posting new targets during hot, cold, or even wet range conditions. Up to this point no one has ever been struck by a bullet. The set up greatly increases "hot" range time and reduces down time because shooters don't have to walk out 200 yards to tend to their targets. At 50, 100 and 200 yards there's a target pit with one pit manager tending to each distance. Normally a shooter on a standard range would have to use a spotting scope or they'd have to take a long walk-in order to see how they did; here at the new range closed circuit cameras monitor each shooting station. They can be remotely focused and maneuvered onto each target by the shooter. Instantly you can see all shots on target through a small screen monitor located to the right of your shooting station. Here a spotting scope is not necessary. You can zoom in and out and take a picture of the target by pressing the camera button. A note is automatically made of the time and date. You type in the rifle model and your ammunition type. Knowing the station number, a shooter can retrieve the picture of the target from the app online at any time after the shooting session. You can even monitor the target live at any time from your computer. This enables a shooter to zero in a weapon a whole lot easier. If more serious adjustments are needed for "zeroing" a particular rifle's iron sights for example, the gunsmith can refer to the last target shot by that rifle and make the changes needed in his shop just by pulling the pictures and studying the most recent targets for that rifle.

Changing a target is as easy as pushing a button. That sends a signal to the range managers message board, he or she would then manually hoist up a new target. A manual system was chosen for ease of maintenance and lower cost over a fully automatic target scroll. The system worked well with very low overhead because the pit managers and even the gunsmiths are all students who work for credit. They are not compensated monetarily. From the Academy's viewpoint- why not use the labor at hand?

Kenny sat down at his firing station. After setting up he pointed the rifle down range and stared intently into the scope. He lined up the 200yd cross hair on the target and squeezed the trigger. Boom! The SX-AR fired a shot that traveled the 200 yards in 1/8th of a second. He glanced up at the monitor and yelled "Yeeeee haaaaaa! His first shot was just outside the edge of the target's bull's-eye.

11

On the National Front

During the first week in September, Chairman Jong Tao Wong of the Peoples Republic of China sat across from President Richfield in the living room section of the oval office. This was one of the most important meetings on Richfield's schedule. Something had to be done and today it would all come together. It was imperative that the Chinese engage with conciliatory policy that would lead to a new deal.

Chairman Jong requested this location for the meeting for three reasons. The primary one being that they of course would be a lot more comfortable sitting on a couch rather than at the thick hard oak boardroom table in the White House conference room. The high back leather seats there would have been fine, but the room just didn't have the right atmosphere for something this important to the Chinese government. The second reason was that he knew the oval office was one of the only places in the White House that wasn't bugged, and they could speak openly. The third reason was because President Jong wanted to show that he had the power to set the standards of the meeting and hold it in the location of his choosing. Exercising power over the American President in minute ways such as this allowed the Chinese to establish their dominant role in the proceedings. Chairman Jong was pleased that the requests were granted without opposition.

Initiating a "Plan for strategic recovery of Chinese assets" was the goal of the Chinese delegation. It would be consummated and put into effect today if the Chinese minister could get the full cooperation of President Richfield and his team. Its strategy was designed and developed by the Chinese over ten years ago but was only now being executed. Due to recent events its startup and implementation had become imperative. And they were waiting for the right American president to spring it on. Richfield was perfect. He was supporting an American Marxist style regime and had proven to be weak in Foreign diplomacy. He played right into their hands. It was crucial for the Chinese to start the process of recovery now without delay. Today was the day they were going to call in their chips. The issue had floated to the top of concerns many times before but due to recent events and the recent downgrading of America's credit rating it was now considered to be the most urgent demand they would present to the United States, hence the request for this meeting. Their own domestic monetary situation showed signs of stress that only the recall and receipt of major obligatory receivables could rectify. The economies of the world were shrinking like never before and a handful of them were in the process of failing at this very moment. The Chinese were feeling the drag down knock out effects on their own economy and had to start recovering their "made in America" investments before it was impossible to squeeze water out of a stone.

After the meeting things started rolling. President Richfield put together a special committee and sanctioned them with a task. The committee was called "The economic commission on monetary action" and was given the power to resolve. They met in secrecy to avoid the press and the public eye because they were considering various methods both legal and illegal to somehow tip toe around the possible crash of the American dollar. Only within the walls of those chambers was the word "crash" allowed to be used and discussed as "imminent". It was illegal to openly express that fact to any outside source.

A pressing topic in need of resolution was how to delicately dance with the Chinese Government. The Government had allowed foreign investment to build to the point where the Chinese now had the power to begin the end of the American economy as we know it... at their whim. They could make it happen tomorrow if they chose to do so. At this point the American government was in debt to the Chinese to the tune of somewhere around 10.5 trillion dollars. And now the Chinese were on the verge of bailing out on the "American dream". Or so they threatened.

The "Economic committee on monetary action" was desperate to settle foreign investors who were now threatening to sell their entire holdings of US treasury bonds. That would be catastrophic; it would create a stampede towards the exit door and send irreparable ripples through the investment community as well as start a chain of selling pressure that would only end with the American government going completely bankrupt. In the end it would leave them without the ability to borrow money but not before the cost of borrowing money climbed so high that no return on investment could ever pay the interest let alone the principle. The greed of American politicians brought the US up to this alter where they now cautiously bowed with respect. All eyes were on the USA.

It was the committee's task to stop this disaster from happening. The committee, sanctioned by the president, was made up entirely of far-left members of the president's party. They needed an "outside the box" solution to this devastating problem and couldn't afford any resistance from the right. The future career (and income) of every person on the committee as well as every politician in Washington was at stake.

Members included; two respected Senators from Illinois (Democrat Ralph Peterson and Jimmy Vail), an ex-Harvard professor of economics who now held the glorious position of chairman of the Bureau of Public Debt, Mr. Ralph Vogel president of the Export Import Bank of the U.S., Mr. Reese Burns Head of the Bureau of Economic analysis, Mr. Rail Quarters 1st administrator of the Social Security Administration along with his cohort Mr. Genus Dixon 1st administrator of the Social Security Advisory Board. It included the LAU labor action union president, an ex-secretary of state, two residing congressmen, the president of the Federal Reserve and the President's economic czar Mazzone Perez.

More representatives of various obscure agencies were also included like representatives from the Risk Management Agency, the Committee on Foreign Investments in the U.S., National Committee on Fiscal Responsibility and Reform, Financial Management Service, Domestic Policy Council, Bureau of Reclamation and quite a few others but of course it wasn't complete without the famous Mr. Gen Stevenson's-Secretary of the Dept. of Treasury. They were all authorized and given the higher directive to "take America into the next century" by setting new economic policy initiatives. The course chosen for dealing with the Chinese syndrome was just the beginning of their preparation to nudge the USA into the direction of what they considered to be the next phase of mankind's existence on this earth; the "New World Order". Most of these participants were paid back for their loyalty by assigning them to the very lucrative positions they now held. The meeting was chaired by the president's economic Czar Mr. Roy Friedman and the whole group operated outside the normal channels of congress. Recommendations by the group would be enforced by executive order.

Both the US and the Chinese administrations had the time to go over the plan between the two countries and work out the details, but each wanted to implement the plan for different reasons. The Chinese saw it as a "plan of mutual cooperation", cooperation that went a long way to help them back out of their American investments slowly with as little loss as possible. The Americans saw it as a way to keep China from bailing out and selling (dumping) billions of dollars' worth of US treasury bonds on the open market. That would have a devastating effect for world markets in general but most troublesome for the Chinese was that they would lose billions of dollars in the process. That move alone would cause other countries to sell US bonds too and the price for them would plummet in the ensuing panic. The dollar would then fizzle into nothingness and yes that would accomplish their goal for the destruction of America, but it would also harm Chinese monetary power by the huge loss of an unimaginable amount of uncollectible debt. They didn't want that. The ceremony here with both heads of state was just to put signatures to paper and to feel each other out as to the degree of commitment that each was willing to obligate their prospective countries and to apply pressure to this endeavor.

The Chinese saw the rise of Islamic rule in the Middle East as a danger to their way of life. After all, Islamic ideology promotes Sharia Law which is based on strict adherence to their religious doctrine. This is in direct conflict with the communist manifesto of government rule of the people by the elite. But if you were to believe Chairman Jong, he was quoted as saying "No, we government of people by people". Humm! Sounds good until you get down to what that statement really means. Although they do agree and have always sided with Islamic backed governments in the past, it was due to a common goal between them; to destroy America. That was considered a higher priority by the Chinese government. The free reign of Capitalism was far more detrimental to acquiring complete control of their country's population than Sharia Law. America was the major factor standing in their way to eventual world dominance.

Yes, the Chinese will eventually turn on Islam and seek to implement communist rule over them, but for now they are content with the friendship they have cultivated. First, they will help destroy the free market, the pillar of support for the "machine" behind their enemy's power, but all in due course. Today they are concentrating on gaining back as much of their investment as they can before the whole free market system collapses under the weight of American greed. Gaining back some of the billions they've invested is priority one. It would be devastating to destroy the remaining system and lose the 16 hundred billion dollars in US treasuries that they now possess. First things first.

The President and the Chairman gave a toast to the agreement and signed the paperwork to begin a new era of cooperation. But in reality, the direction the administration was about to take was a total sell out on a scale never seen before in American history. The desperation of these turbulent times was unyielding and forced the hand of those in power into this course of action. The meeting was a mere confirmation of the collaboration between the two countries to form an alliance that would eventually lead to a New World Order. They had to throw the Chinese a bone; they had to give them something- a lot of "something". This was the only thing that would suffice.

A small contingent of representatives of the insiders who created the scheme assembled in the Oval Office. Even though the program had already begun they were here for the official ceremony. They received total confidence from the true force behind the administration and won their approval to implement the remuneration process. Their ability to remain under the radar and quickly force positive results was paramount. The Chinese minister of finance was present along with his attaché who held various forms of paperwork in a large suitcase which would be needed to complete the final details. The most important of which would be the creation of a real estate company owned by an American but whose company bank accounts only needed a Chinese gentleman's signature to move funds in any direction. It was this "Chinese investor" whose identity was obscured by multiple layers of paperwork that sat next to Chairman Jong. The two previous days were spent dealing with the formalities of their highly publicized meetings where the schedule of both countries' representatives was filled with dinners, luncheons, and photo sessions.

The two parties put on a great show and performed the ceremonial signing of paperwork in front of the media. It was reported the next day in the News, the headlines read "RICHMAND MEETS WITH CHAIRMAN JONG AND SECURES NEW FINANCING TERMS". Instantly the stock market began to rally.

12

Master Nak

At a quarter to seven on a fine Saturday morning in early October a small crowd gathered outside the range building waiting for Master Bow Nak (pronounced "Knock") the renowned Yang Style Tai Chi master. This was the weekend of the long-awaited two-day seminar and Kaiden made sure he arrived early. Luckily, he remembered to bring his meditation mat. Attendees had come from as far as South Florida to participate in this class and in these times that was saying a lot. It's very hard to find good instruction on the finer points of Tai Chi outside of China Town in both New York and in California. The same could be said for the other two internal styles of martial arts called Ba Gua and Hsing Yi which was included on Master Nak's extensive list of expertise. This event was held in high regard within the internal martial arts community and the place was a buzz with over sixty-five enthusiasts attending.

Master Bow Nak was a Taoist Monk from Hubei Province in the Peoples Republic of China. He grew up in the city of Shiyan just North of Wudang Mountain where at the age of six his father enrolled him as a student in the Wudang Taoist Academy. Wudang Mountain is one of many sacred Taoist sites in China where they are famous as an academic center for the study of traditional Chinese medicine, Taoist agriculture practices, alchemy, meditation, and the martial arts. From there, along with additional programs of study, Bow Nak received a degree in herbology and had been taught the three internal arts of Tai Chi, Hsing Yi and Ba Gua according to the strict guidelines handed down from generations before. He was one of the select few who were brought into the inner circle and was taught the rare style of "Liu ha ba fa". This martial art combines all the characteristics of the three internal styles into one and has its own unique form. He studied and trained in the Taoist way of life for most of thirty-five years before moving to Argentina.

Kaiden met Master Nak in China Town N.Y. when he was fifteen years old. He had been practicing Wing Chung for over three years when his teacher recognized Kaiden's ability and his enthusiasm for the martial arts. He saw something in Kaiden, partially because of his age and partially due to his character, but definitely due to his talent. To round out Kaiden's training, his teacher recommended that he study the art of Tai Chi Chuan. It was considered an honor to receive "special training" with such a high-level Master such as Nak. Kaiden jumped at the chance. Once a week every Saturday morning Kaiden would spend an hour with Master Nak in his apartment in downtown Manhattan. It was special even for Master Nak, there just weren't that many young kids that were attracted to the art of Tai Chi at that time. Not many showed the degree of interest that Kaiden did. Tai Chi was commonly referred to as an "old fogy's martial art" by members of the more aggressive "hard" styles of Kung Fu or Karate. Soft styles like Tai Chi just didn't draw a crowd, it took too long to learn, and the slow movements bored the younger generation. One of the criticisms was "you can't fight going that slow" which always made Kaiden laugh because Master Nak was one of the quickest, skillful martial artists he'd ever seen. For Kaiden it was an honor to be chosen for this training and very rare indeed that Master Nak accepted an American as a student.

Before the seminar started students in a wide spectrum of ages were milling around outside Chilton Hall. Various groups had formed, and they all stood around talking about the latest 'What's up'. You could see them gesturing, comparing, and talking about the intricacies of some movement.

"This is one of the inconsistencies of the art" one of them was overheard saying. "Everyone does it a little different".

"Well Tai Chi is a very personal thing..." his companion said in defense of the art "...and therefore each individual practices it with emphasis on a different aspect of training. That plus a person's body shape, their degree of flexibility and even their character or personality will show through and influence their movements in different ways. Even if they learned from the same teacher there can be differences from one student to the other. It's okay though, the Tai Chi form can look different, as long as the practitioner adheres to the basic principles of the art".

"Don't forget that they are probably just plain old practicing it wrong too!" another commented with a sarcastic chuckle.

"It's understandable if you consider that each of us practice Tai Chi for different reasons. I mean it can be practiced purely for health because it is a great source of exercise and it's something that can be added to anyone's routine without the need for a gym or equipment of any kind. Or you can study Tai Chi Chuan as a martial art. After all it means 'The grand ultimate fist'. You can dig deeper into the art, and it gives you the ability to use the movements as a method of self-defense. You might imagine if a student takes the leap into studying Tai Chi for fighting then things take on an entirely different meaning. For example: a person studying Tai Chi merely as an exercise will stand in their stance and execute a movement softly by extending their arm". He did it and showed them as he was talking. "That in itself can be a strenuous exercise. Try telling someone to stand in this posture for a long period of time. Now imagine yourself extending your arm out concentrating on the thought of striking or pushing an object" he moved over to the person next to him and placed his palm on his chest. Your thoughts change the way you align your body because to push efficiently or strike effectively you must align your body for maximum results. Think about it. Imagine pushing on a heavy object without caring if it actually moves. Then push on it with the intention of making it move". He pushed on the student he was demonstrating on. "Those are two completely different actions. When you concentrate and apply 'intent' it changes the movement to an amazing degree".

Kaiden smiled at what he overheard. Some of these Tai Chi philosophers looked familiar. He recognized a few from the Major's class and yet there were others that he'd never seen before. Ciera was supposed to be here, but he couldn't find her. Over on the lawn next to the parking lot there was another group of people forming up. They lined up in three rows facing the same direction and began performing the Tai Chi form. In unison all of them mimicked the same movements in typical slow-motion fashion. Other people hanging around on the sidelines were stretching out even though there would be plenty of that during class. A few loners off in the distance were standing still performing slow moving Chi Kung exercises.

Chi Kung is similar to Tai Chi in movement except that it's mostly performed in place and the body is not overly stretched or exerted. Its movements are combined with a method of breathing where energy is visualized and circulated through the body with the mind as its guide. The goal being to "generate a healthier aura and to develop one's internal energy", energy that can be used for healing or to increase the power of a martial arts technique". The whole scene looked serene and peaceful as everyone concentrated on their internal matrix.

Kaiden greeted a few of his friends with a customary bow. That had always been a common way to greet and acknowledge a fellow martial artist ever since the beginning of his training. The bow was done with the right fist clenched and held out in front of the chest; the left open palm was placed on top of it. You gave a slight bow at the same time you gestured with your hands. The closed fist signified aggression. And the left open palm that covered it means to cease aggression or "Peace".

Since it was a cool October morning Kaiden naturally gravitated toward stretching out and warming up a little instead of standing around talking. He concentrated on loosening up his legs, did some stretches and then threw a few kicks starting low and working high. Ciera came out of nowhere and joined him. She stuck her face near his while he was in the middle of a stretch and said "Hey gorgeous". She was all smiles and uncommonly giddy for a quarter to seven in the morning.

"Wow you're in a good mood. I didn't know if I'd see you here".

"I told you I was coming; I love Tai Chi".

"Why don't I see you in the Majors Tai Chi class then?".

"That's too early in the morning, I've got too much stuff going on to make it... but I'd like too" she added when she saw a glint of rejection on Kaiden's face. "Hey, I made it to the class a lot when I lived in the dorm. Living in RL makes it a little tougher". Kaiden accepted that excuse and asked her how she was doing.

"I'm good" Ciera said while moving opposite him. She took off her jacket and started going through a stretching routine of her own. She spread her legs as far as she could, dipped down and touched the ground with the palms of both hands then swung left and then right easily touching each foot as she unintentionally proceeded to demonstrate how flexible she was. When she came back up and leaned backwards her long brown hair almost touched the ground behind her.

Kaiden couldn't help it, he kept stretching but stole glances at Ciera as she stretched. It was impossible not to. Ciera had an awesome figure. Her bright expression with the way her smile turned up at the corners of her mouth topped off an amazing body in such a feminine way. She was slim without the body fat seen on many women of all ages these days. Certainly, she did not concentrate on food. Today she was wearing sweatpants but not the loose baggy kind. They were the "stretchy" type that fit her form and clung to every curve of her body. Her shapely calves, thighs, and firm buttocks demanded attention, especially in that posture. She wore an oversized shirt that draped more loosely over her upper body for added warmth but was unbuttoned in front so you could see what she had on underneath. It all but hid the pleasing shape of her breasts while igniting Kaiden's imagination.

Most women wore a "sports bra" but not Ciera, at least not today. The black material of her bra was visible at the "V" line between her breasts and the color bled through the thin white tank top material she was wearing. The tank top was cut short "Midi" style which allowed an ample display of bare skin around her mid-section. All in all, it seemed a little too "little" for stretching out in the cold early morning. But Kaiden enjoyed her presence without complaining as she flowed from one stretch into another seemingly oblivious to his gaze.

For Kaiden "Drawn to her" would be an understatement. "How about we help each other stretch?" he asked her.

"Sure, what do you want to do?"

"Come here". Kaiden led her over to the base of the old oak tree. "Lean back against the tree and give me your leg" he told her. She followed his instructions and raised her foot. Kaiden took it and placed her heel in the palm of his hand. While supporting it from underneath he slowly raised her leg up to his chest.

"Wow you are flexible" Kaiden said. So flexible in fact that eventually (slowly) he was able to push her foot up and stretch her leg until it came up almost to head level.

"Wait, that's enough don't go any farther" she said when Kaiden had pushed her leg to the limit. Now it was almost pointing straight up in the air. She could have kissed her knee it was so close to her face. Kaiden placed her leg on top of his shoulder and let her relax a bit. Then he leaned into her and pressed his body up against hers locking her in place against the tree, all the while watching her closely while gauging her reaction. In that position he could feel her body against his and her mound against his groin as their bodies melded together.

It surprised Ciera; suddenly finding herself in such a provocative position. She too felt him, and both their eyes locked onto each other. Kaiden smiled but Ciera maintained a more serious look.

Thoughts of sex floated to the surface in Kaiden's mind. "What would it be like to make love to this woman?" he wondered. He imagined her naked in front of him.

Ciera raised her eyebrows "Wow big boy what do we have here?" She could feel all of him with only the thin cloth material between the two of them.

She could have complained, gotten embarrassed and pushed away considering how it must have looked to others standing around nearby. That's what she was about to do, but for some reason her brain never sent out the signal to rebel. Something nullified her flight response. Everything else started to melt into the background and all that was left was the feeling of his warm body pressing against hers. Surprisingly she embraced the moment and floundered in the transgression. Still, she thought "The nerve of him!" She paused yet without protest stayed there in defiance of her own indignation. Suddenly it was important that she showed him he didn't have the power to embarrass her or... was it more than that? She could sense his desire and it bathed her ego into prescribing indifference. He had clearly defined his interest by his action and wasn't ashamed to lay it all on the line. She admired him for that.

The people and everything around her faded into the background, she didn't care about them now, nothing else existed at that moment. She stared into his eyes and took him in without a battle, concentrating on where his body touched hers.

"What if he took me right here and now? She smiled enjoying the fantasy that dared to project in her mind. The true test came next when he backed off slowly, lowered her leg down and told her "Give me your other leg".

Ciera didn't object and didn't take her eyes off him. She did as he asked and lifted her other leg and put that heel in his hand. Kaiden took it, raised it in the air and slowly stretched that leg as far as he did the first. Again, he pushed it to the limit and then placed that leg on his other shoulder. They relaxed into the same position as before and he once again took advantage of the situation and pressed up against her body. Ciera felt his excitement. Kaiden didn't seem embarrassed at all, quite the contrary; he "pressed" the issue which got Ciera thinking about it to the point where the fantasy of having sex with him started to roll...

From the thought of it, a slight moan escaped from Ciera's lips. Kaiden, while pressing her leg and stretching her out a little further, heard the cute little gasp of breath that came from her mouth as he pressed up against her. Both had come out of their own little fantasies with a sense that each knew what the other was thinking. But all that mattered to Kaiden was that she had accepted him without a fight. It was a pivotal moment in which the option of upping the ante on their relationship was at stake. She liked him, he could tell. He got the answer he was looking for. Then he kissed her and parted her lips with his tongue. His tongue found hers and touched it with a tenderness that moved her.

"What am I doing letting him kiss me like that!" she thought. "Hell, I'm kissing him back and fantasizing about having sex with him!" But she didn't do anything to stop him, anything except to close her eyes and kiss him back as tenderly as he kissed her. No one had ever done this to her before. And in public no less! But his kiss was so... nice! "What's up with that fantasy?" She was never the one who dwelled in fantasies about sex. This was not like her at all. She cut him off and stopped him.

Kaiden lowered her leg and both of them looked around like they were a little embarrassed. They saw people starting to walk over and flow into the entrance of Chilton Hall for the start of the seminar. Ciera broke it off and started to gather her things. She played off their unexpected kiss like it was nothing while secretly wondering how she was going to deal with this. They walked over and fell in line behind the others, each thinking about the other in a different way.

The practice hall was a large fifty-five by thirty-five-foot space with steel I beam spanners across the ceiling that allowed architects to eliminate support columns in the center. The room filled quickly with everyone claiming a spot by laying out a mat or towel in their preferred location relative to Master Naks mat at the head of the room.

Before the event, Master Nak was standing in the back behind a reception desk in the middle of a group of people that surrounded it. Major Jaz was there too, all of them immersed in the group's conversation. Kaiden got a glimpse of Master Nak who happened to look up at that same moment. He noticed Kaiden immediately and gave a slight bow of his head in recognition. Kaiden stood still, placed his palm over his fist and returned the gesture with a deep bow. He came up smiling, clearly remembering the lessons in Master Nak's New York City apartment. It seemed like such a long time ago.

Kaiden thought back and saw himself standing in the middle of the small private studio which was really the living room of Master Nak's three-bedroom city apartment. The living room had been converted into a small practice hall or at least it was used in that way. Luckily it still retained the carpet that covered the bare wooden floor that lay underneath. That would prove to be a small luxury in the coming days when on many occasions Kaiden found himself bouncing off it.

Master Nak had Kaiden going through the Tai Chi form in the center of the room while watching from his chair in the den next to the studio. It never seemed like he could get very far past the beginning before there would be a sharp blow against his body. When he made a mistake Nak would walk over to him with his hands behind his back. Instead of showing him what he was doing wrong the teacher would fire off a kick or a punch that would land sharply on whatever limb was accused of wrongdoing.

"Pow" it stung! Immediately it brought Kaiden's attention to focus on that spot. Then Nak would say in Chinese "Shangmian" (up). If the arm didn't move up high enough "POW" another sharp pain would surge from the offending arm. Then "Crack" his thigh would receive the same punishment and he'd say "Jiao" (correct). He got smacked like that until his body conformed to the exact position he wanted. Looking back, Kaiden could see how that experience taught him to focus and concentrate on how he held his body especially when an opponent walked into his space.

"Now looking back on it, it wasn't all that bad" Kaiden thought. After he had perfected the postures to the point where he wasn't getting hit all the time, Master Nak began to teach him. "Light hands" was one of the exercises. This was an advanced training technique that soon became Kaiden's favorite. Here he got a chance to "touch hands" and go through the motions of striking and blocking with his teacher.

'Light hands' was performed in a way that came as close to actual fighting as you could get without actually fighting and without getting hurt, although getting hurt is a relative term for Master Nak. He was old school and used pain as a tool for teaching motivation. One of his famous sayings translated into something like; "A student's progress can be kicked into high gear!".

When practicing light hands, you were required to stand toe to toe with your partner while attacking and defending without moving your feet. This rule forces you to stay in contact with your opponent and to maintain your balance in the most precarious "zone" you could possibly be in during a fight- that is right in front of your opponent with your face within arm's reach. If your feet moved due to your partner's attack you were considered to have lost that exchange and you would start over. Normally practitioners don't use a lot of power and don't strike the face so that injuries are kept to a minimum. Kaiden constantly came away from these sessions bruised and battered, sometimes even dazed. It wasn't appreciated at the time but Nak's skill in striking with just enough power to drive home a point was monumental in teaching Kaiden to become an intelligent fighter. If his mother only knew she would have screamed, for when Master Nak found a weakness in Kaiden's defense or a technique that Kaiden was not blocking effectively, he'd pop him hard in that same spot constantly until Kaiden defended it proficiently enough to dissolve the master's attack. Kaiden would do his best to hide the black and blue marks from his mother but had to avoid her completely when he sported a shiner. At one point there was a question at school as to whether he was being abused by his parents. Child protective services dug into his situation on one occasion where his parents had to go down and plead their case.

Kaiden strolled over to the group his teacher was talking to with both good and bad memories pouring through his head. When they came face to face, Kaiden spoke in Chinese "Lao shi" he said and bowed. "Ni how ma?" meaning "Old teacher, how are you".

Master Nak said "Ah Kaiden, zen tong kuai, hao jiu bu jian le" (very well, I haven't seen you for a long time).

The two of them conversed in Chinese much to the amazement of Ciera and everyone else who was standing around within ear shot. No one knew that Kaiden was so versed in the Chinese language. He spoke fluently with their conversation evolving around common questions that one would ask of someone they haven't seen for a while. Answers were kept short since the seminar was about to begin but it was evident to all by the master's reaction that he was very happy to see Kaiden and that he held Kaiden in high regard. Kaiden turned to Ciera and in English introduced her to Master Nak. The Master responded to her in English saying "Mrs. Lowman, bery ni to me you. Than you fo coming".

Major Jaz walked up to the microphone at the head of the room and addressed the incoming people stating that the seminar was about to begin. He asked everyone to please find a spot on the floor and sit.

Kaiden broke off the conversation with his teacher saying "Sifu, zai ci xiang jian, tai gao xing le. Huan ying" (Teacher I am very glad to see you again. Welcome).

"Fei chang yu kuai" (I am absolutely delighted) Master Nak said. Then he raised his eyebrows and nodded over to Ciera and said "Ta hen piao liang".

Kaiden looked at her as well, smiled and said "Shi Sifu tan hen".

Kaiden bowed and joined Ciera who was standing there in amazement. "You speak Chinese! I can't believe it. Kaiden, you amaze me. What did he say?".

"Oh, we just said the normal hello, hi, how are you kind of stuff".

"You know him?".

"Yeah, he was one of my teachers in New York".

"One of them? What did he say at the end when you two looked at me?".

"He said that you are as beautiful as a jade leaf on a tree in springtime and I shouldn't let you get away".

Ciera smacked him on the shoulder "Oh he did not!".

"Well, I paraphrased but yeah he really did".

Ciera eyed him trying to figure out if he was telling the truth while Kaiden was looking around for a good place to sit.

"And what was it you said?".

"To what?".

"When Master Nak said don't let me get away".

"Oh, I told him an old Chinese saying that means; "You are a flower blossoming in the wind. No one knows which hummingbird will be allowed to roost".

Ciera looked at him dubiously but broke into a smile and then laughed. "Wow, you make such a sexist comment sound so flattering".

By that time students had already filled the room, there were only seats left towards the back so they sat where they could. The Major introduced Master Nak and he walked up and took his place on a mat at the head of the room. The microphone stand was lowered so that he could reach it and speak on the PA system and allow everyone to hear. He took it, and in broken English with a heavy Chinese accent that was hard to understand he said "It is bey impotant to wake up body slowly. Many of ou ancesto sought ansa to question 'How to live long life'. They consida dis fo many centwee. It is best to listen to dair finding and pactice what dey have luned. Let's wake up fist (first), follow me".

Master Nak proceeded to lead the class with a few minutes of sitting meditation and then moved into a stretching routine that started off with everyone lying on their backs in a prone position on the floor. That almost put everyone back to sleep but then he progressed into a sitting position and then into a standing position while striking multiple postures at each level. All were performed gently to loosen up the body slowly. Some were similar to Yoga, others were more like moving Yoga, and the rest were standard stretches that anyone would recognize.

An hour later the routine was complete, those who were sensitive enough felt a very special peaceful, relaxed kind of smile emanating from inside the body due to the way Master Nak guided them. The ones who couldn't feel it were people who had difficulty relaxing and turning their concentration from outside to inside the body.

Master Nak explained "Dis is bet way to wake up body and pepae yosef fo the day. Go from sleeping- to lying down, to sitting, to standing. All the time, nudge stess out of body with gentle mooment".

After a short break, the master continued with a quick warm up that consisted mainly of self-massage. He got everyone to spend some time massaging the major muscle groups of their own body that they could effectively get too. Next, he had them "pat" the body with soft (and then harder) slaps of the palms against the top of head, face, arms, chest, side, back, thighs, calves and the top of the feet. Then they did it in reverse. That pattern was designed to stimulate the muscles and the nervous system. Master Nak said it was good to use for "wake up".

More difficult exercises followed. Master Nak took the major movements of the Tai Chi form and practiced each one individually. Once on the right side and then showed how to smoothly flow into doing the same movement on the left. Back and forth he'd go from left to right. He did this with the thirteen major movements of the form starting in a high stance, going into a low one then back into a high stance with each one of them before switching to the next movement. Also, he varied the speed going from slow to fast and back to slow again. During the fast portion of the exercise, he showed how to add power into the movement by inserting a little "Fa Jing". Fa Jing is a Chinese term used to describe a special type of power that the body can generate under the right conditions. It starts off with softness but then he would "emit" Fa Jing sharply from his body at the right moment. It was easy to see how this could be used to add power to a strike.

Next the Master showed a few practical applications of the movements. He pulled a few people out of the audience and used them to demonstrate the technique. He went through a few partners before getting a little frustrated. Kaiden knew why. Master Nak looked around the class until he saw Kaiden in the far back and motioned for him to come up to the front. The Master called on Kaiden to come up and help with the next demonstration. The first thing Kaiden did was to stand up and bow in place acknowledging the teacher. Then he walked over and stood opposite the teacher at the head of the room and bowed to him again out of respect. After Master Nak demonstrated an application on Kaiden, Kaiden bowed saying "Xie xie Sifu" (Thank you teacher)". No one else had offered the same courtesy or given the Master proper etiquette as Kaiden had done. Master Nak had used him to teach the class how to address him. Luckily others picked up on it and from that point on everyone copied Kaiden's example.

The amazing part came in the afternoon when Master Nak went over the "light hands" exercise. He asked Kaiden to come up to demonstrate once again. After showing the class the object of the exercise and giving a few examples, Kaiden and the master performed it at full speed. It was an awesome display. Kaiden did well but he was no match for the Master. He blocked the majority of incoming strikes and Kaiden even came close to striking the teacher a few times but as good as Kaiden was he couldn't touch him. Then Nak took it to a higher level and showed the class the most amazing thing.

"Balance" he said and then asked one of the attendees to come up for a demonstration. The master faced him, told him to get into a sturdy stance and then placed his hands on the guy's arms. No matter how the student tried to maintain his balance, small movements of the teacher's body seemed to magically uproot him. The guy was thrown to the left or right seemingly at will. Ok sometimes the teacher did have to work for it and did use some larger movements to do it, but it still looked like magic. It was obvious that the Master was an expert at using the slightest degree of "off balance" against an opponent and could guide him in that direction to his downfall. The teacher allowed a handful of others to experience this phenomenon. It was the same with each of the students he touched, they very quickly found themselves thrown to the side or even down on the ground. It became comical and funny to the students watching as well as to the one being thrown around like a rag doll. The victim started to laugh at their own inability to maintain their footing or to stop their teacher from moving them at all.

Later they commented "No matter what I did, as soon as he touched me, I couldn't keep my feet underneath me. It was amazing! I felt totally unable to keep my balance. As soon as he touched my arms, I became disconnected from the ground, and I just couldn't recover".

Master Nak had everyone pair up with a partner and practice light hands. He'd walk around and help people who had questions or would descend upon a pair when he saw them doing it wrong. If it was something he felt the whole class would benefit from he'd pull Kaiden out of the crowd to help him and had the whole class watch them demonstrate the correct way. For the rest of the seminar Kaiden was further employed as Master Nak's helper both to translate certain ideas into English and to assist in teaching the finer points of the exercises.

At one-point Kaiden walked up to Ciera who was practicing with a male partner. He tapped her partner on the shoulder as if cutting in on a dance and took over. They bowed to each other and then began the light hands exercise.

Immediately Ciera noticed that Kaiden felt softer and performed his strikes and blocks with more of a light feel to his arms than her previous partners. That was the toughest concept for a martial artist to grasp; very few people ever really get it. To "let go" and become light, lose, and relaxed. It's the opposite of what most people put up as a natural reaction to aggression. Kaiden's strikes only became hard at the end just before striking a target or when he didn't want to be moved.

The last thing Master Nak taught was the "Thirteen Postures". It's an exercise that took the same thirteen postures they practiced in the morning singularly and linked them together into a short form. The difference between this and the Tai Chi form is that thirteen postures is just as the name implies, it concentrates on thirteen movements only, unlike the long form that contains one hundred and eight movements. The thirteen postures are practiced consecutively flowing from one movement into the other smoothly. It can also be performed at full speed and with power. By the time the seminar ended everyone was very impressed with the insight they received and the fine points that Master Nak taught. Students showed their appreciation by voicing a positive opinion and asking Master Nak to come back at a future date. He promised them that he would.

Towards the end of the day, it was apparent to all that Tai Chi wasn't just a wimpy slow-moving exercise; it was a full spectrum martial art. Everyone was surprised that they had been put through such a tough workout and it showed by how physically taxed they all were. During the breaks Kaiden went around and found people who complained of cramps or had any pain in their joints. There were a few people who took him up on the offer to massage the area and some who allowed Kaiden to perform some basic chiropractic manipulations to help re-balance their body.

When the students were excused Kaiden couldn't refuse a request from a friend to work on a knee that was giving him problems. Kaiden had him lie down on his mat and he bent over him looking exactly like a chiropractor giving an adjustment.

Ciera walked up to them. "Hey I'm next Kaiden. You sure are a jack of all trades, aren't you?".

"Oh, yeah well, it's just something I picked up along the way. We used to do this to each other in my Tai Chi class all the time. He turned to the patient he was working on and said "Watch your stance when you practice. Make sure you don't break the #1 rule, that is to shift your weight off the foot you are about to turn. Turn your foot and then shift your weight onto it and keep your knee aligned with your toe. This is very important, don't ever break that rule. I've seen many people get knee pain from practicing Tai Chi incorrectly. Also, you need to stretch out the hip joint more, to get it loose. You need to be able to swivel your body on it better. You're too tight. Pay attention to body alignment and stretch out more often".

Master Nak walked up to the three of them. Ciera saw him first and stood up.

"Master Nak the seminar was great I really enjoyed it" she said and shook his hand.

Master Nak took her hand in both of his and held it with reverence. He smiled at her warmly and said "It wa especially nie to me you Miss

Lowman". He held onto her and wouldn't let go of her hand as if he was feeling her internal condition through contact. It was quite a while before he let it go. Kaiden finished with his customer and started to get up.

"No, no don't get up" he said to the others. "I see you beesy, but I would like to talk to you moa befo I go Kaiden. Would you lie to met me at dinna tonight?".

Kaiden got up anyway, faced his teacher and bowed "Sifu I'd love to go to dinner with you. There's a Chinese restaurant in town called Chinese Moon, it would be very appropriate, we could go there".

"Yes, I staying in town to ni. I me you daya et seven?

"OK seven o'clock".

"Yes, yes. I meet you daya and Kaiden make sure you bing Mees Lowman with you". Master Nak turned to Ciera and bowed to her.

"Why thank you Sifu I would love to go".

"Fine, see you den". He turned and left.

Kaiden wondered how this would fit in with her boyfriend and how she'd play it after that surprise kiss this morning. "Any problem with your boyfriend on this one?" he asked her.

"Hey, I'm allowed to go out with my teacher! Aren't I?"

"Sure, and you're also allowed to kiss anyone you'd like too" Kaiden said smiling; knowing that half the details of this day would be left out of any conversation with Nick.

"Hey you kissed me! I didn't kiss you. We'll have to talk about that. I can go where I want to".

"OK we'll take the bus, but we'll have to get going".

"Oh no ya don't, you ain't getting away before you take care of me" she said smiling.

"Ciera, what's up with you? You OK?".

"I'm just dying from the workout. Tai Chi looks simple but I'm exhausted".

"That stance trainings a bitch ain't it?" Kaiden agreed.

"Yeah, I must be a little out of shape; I'm not used to standing in one position for any length of time. My thigh muscles are killing me".

Kaiden finished with his patient's leg and then pressed his knee back up to his chest and pushed down on it with the weight of his body behind it. There was a "pop" as the patient's vertebra in his lower back aligned and clicked back into place. "Got that one" Kaiden said. He performed the same technique on the other leg but didn't get the same pop as he did with the other. "Relax" he said and then tried it again. It still didn't adjust "Well the hip is the hardest joint to adjust especially if you don't relax" he smacked his patient on the leg as if scolding him. Then he turned to Ciera "Yeah Master Nak's workouts hit muscles you don't normally use, doesn't it? I'll help you. Lie down".

Ciera switched places on the mat with the previous customer and she sprawled out in front of him. He massaged her calf and thigh muscles which brought out a constant succession of "ooze" and "ahs" with an "ouch" thrown in occasionally, when Kaiden found a sore spot. Even though at a few points it actually looked painful the only thing she complained about was that the massage wasn't long enough.

Kaiden didn't get out of there for a while after the seminar ended. Several other people saw him working on Ciera and requested his assistance with their problems too. He didn't mind and did what he could with a combination of massage, minor adjustments, and advice but he made it short and offered to work on them further either after or before Major Jazz's Tai Chi class. Kaiden ran back to the dorm to shower and change and made it over to the bus stop in time for his nondate with Ciera.

The Chinese Moon restaurant looked nice on the outside and just kind of ok on the inside. It was an old, remodeled home located just off the main street that naturally developed into a business due to its proximity to the downtown area. Back in 72', the owners transformed the place into a commercial venture by running a successful sandwich shop out of it for ten years. In 1982 it was sold to an adventurous Chinese entrepreneur who converted it into a full-service restaurant. It changed hands once before the present owner took over. Mr. Kwong owned it now and successfully ran the restaurant for the last thirty-four years with the help of his family. Success came from the attraction of the pleasant 'homey' atmosphere created simply by the restaurant being located in a home. Customers who sought ambiance and wanted a more unique, maybe even more romantic place to take their date found that this filled that requirement perfectly. Of course, that alone would never have allowed it to survive through the years if it hadn't become anchored by the popularity of its tasty Cantonese cuisine. The Cantonese chicken is highly recommended by all.

The first floor had been converted into a dining area with two sections, one on the left and right. As he walked in Kaiden saw that at one time it used to be the living room and the dining room but now each section held about nine square tables of various sizes with a see-through partition separating the two dining areas. The partition contained a large built in fish tank with interesting colorful fish that swam back and forth and through the bubbles that fluttered from bottom to top. There was a short fully stocked bar along the back wall with a standard free swinging kitchen door right next to it leading into the back. It was a quaint, cute little place that doubled as their home. Mr. Kwong and his family lived on the second floor. The Mr. and Mrs. somehow lived there with their three children, two grandparents, a brother and two other relatives, all of them worked in the restaurant at some capacity or another with Mr. Kwong being the main force behind it all. It was said that even more relatives were on the way from China.

The owners lived upstairs but Kaiden noticed that they had gotten more room out of the place by eliminating the stairway going to the second floor. The families "front" entrance was now around back where a long set of wooden stairs led up to the second floor from the parking lot. The whole place was well taken care of on the outside, but it was an old home showing a bit of wear and tear, mainly due to heavy customer traffic. The trim and siding were a little shabby but at least the place was neat and clean. Certainly, it wasn't like some of the run-down Chinese restaurants Kaiden had patronized in the city, but he truly doubted that the food here would be as good as it was in China Town.

Master Nak was late, but Kaiden didn't care, he got a chance to sit down and start his nondate with Ciera. That's what he really looked forward to even more so than talking to Master Nak. He loved talking to Ciera because she offered a lot of background knowledge about the college, and she filled him in on some history as well. She also had an interesting outlook on life and Kaiden loved trying to talk to her on a higher more intellectual level.

It sounds corny Kaiden had to admit to himself; she was one of the few women he'd met that he gave a lot of credit for her brains and not just her body. And what do you know, he smiled to himself, "Ciera's got both brains and a hell of a body!".

They sat, talked, and drank plum wine while waiting for their teacher. Ciera asked Kaiden "So how did you learn so much about massage and all that Chiropractic stuff?".

"For years there was this Chiropractor in my Tai Chi class. No- correction, I'd have to call him a 'Healer' because he didn't have a license or anything. But he knew the art of Chiropractic manipulation better than any chiropractor I've ever known licensed or not. He had a special touch, in fact we called him 'Healer', that was his name. I met him right after he came back from hiking the entire 2,284 miles of the Appalachian Trail. It took him five months to hike the whole thing. I couldn't believe he did it; he was like sixty years old at the time. From that point on he went by his trail name he got while on the Appalachian Trail, that's a nickname that everyone ended up calling him. His trail name was 'Healer' so it stuck. That guy worked on us many times and sort of took me under his wing. He taught me a lot of stuff. The amazing part was that he never asked for money, at least not from me or from the people in our class. He never charged me for anything. I know he charged other people outside our group. He'd get big bucks for treating special case problems, people came to him from all around just to get a session with him. He had a high success rate and healed many of his clients, or at least made them better than they were.

I do remember him complaining once. Healer said 'Kaiden, most Americans have it in their minds when they come to me that I'm going to perform some kind of miracle on them and heal them. They believe that 'The cure' comes from outside and is administered to them by my hand to them on the inside. That's a start; don't get me wrong, getting them to believe that what I do will actually heal them is the first step. That puts the brain in the right frame of mind, without it they probably would never proceed to the next level. But what I really give them is so much more. I give them instruction... instruction on how to treat themselves. This I tell them. Some listen and take it to heart, some don't. I'm not giving you any excuses as to why some of my treatments don't work. But I am going to say that my success is totally dependent on the patient and the patient's participation in his own cure. Those who I can't convince that healing comes from within, from the inside out and not from the outside in, will not respond well to my treatments".

Healer continued "Many times religion misinterprets this and ends up putting people on the wrong path. When people are taught that 'God will provide' without any further explanation, they end up taking it literally and from that point on place the responsibility for their own lives squarely on God's shoulders. After being sold on that in their own minds they can never be held accountable for anything that happens good or bad. 'Its Gods will' they will say. Well, they're missing a major very important piece of the equation. God provides the power for you to use. The will, the gumption, and the guts to believe and to persevere come from you. God gives you the freedom to make your own choices. He doesn't force you to go in any direction. You need to go to him! Are you going to tap into that power? Are you going to use it for good or for evil? Are you going to partake in life and seek out its rewards or wait for the mountain to come to you? It's up to you. Believe me when I tell you that you will see far many more mountain tops if you start climbing the trail rather than sitting around waiting for God to pull you up there. In fact, I will take it one step farther and say that if you never start off on the path you can never reach your destination. It's up to you to place one foot in front of the other, start on the right path and focus your internal radiant energy- for good, for healing, for love... for all the right reasons'.

"That was a memorable conversation that stuck in my mind" Kaiden told Ciera.

Kaiden thought back to the previous conversation he had with Ciera on the bus they rode to Delhi for tonight's dinner. When he met her at the bus stop for their 'nondate'. It cost them five bucks apiece for the ride in, but Kaiden didn't mind, he would have paid many times that for this time with Ciera. The ride reminded Kaiden of the first time he had met her. Once again, he moseyed on over and sat down next to her with a good feeling that showed in his demeanor.

"Now don't hit me this time" he said as he sat down.

She laughed remembering the incident. "Well, you block it next time Mr. Kung Fu Man".

"Ciera" he said to get her attention and then spoke to her seriously. "I'd let you smack me again if you'd just hold my cheek and look at me the same way you did".

That got her attention. Then in a serious tone he said... "You have eyes that have the power to heal, but of course it's not your eyes, they are just the window to your soul. That moment... right after you smacked me, and you held my cheek. I looked into your eyes, and I saw the truth. It was... loving, ...caring. You shined, inside, with the very essence of your spirit. I saw it". He turned to her and faced her squarely "...you slap a lot of crap on some of the things you say to divert people from really getting to know you. But deep inside you have the power to heal my soul in the same manner that my hands have the power to soothe your body. I've known this to be true ever since meeting you. It's what attracts me to you".

Ciera looked at him wondering if he was serious or if he was going to burst out laughing at any moment. When he didn't, she gauged him as totally sincere but then responded anyway with "Nice try but you're so full of shit, that's such a line. I'm sure you got plenty of them, don't you?" She turned to the window and looked away shaking her head to disengage from the subject.

"No, that one was just for you" Kaiden said while looking away.

She heard him. And then, she heard it again and again as it reverberated against her defenses. The more she thought about it the more the comment seeped in through the cracks in a wall that started to crumble. He touched her in a way she wasn't prepared for. He kissed her in a way she wasn't prepared for. Wow, a guy (or men in general) talking about something else besides how good looking she was. Oh, the constant flattery they used was charming, but it was all an attempt to get on her good side or to try to get her to go out with them. Ha... many blatantly skipped that part and just tried valiantly to get her into bed.

"A comment about my soul? That was just too...too lame. Wasn't it?".

She turned back and looked at him, studied him for a moment. He looked a little dejected. She detected a semblance of sadness. "Could he really see my soul?".

"Kaiden" she said placing her hand on his arm. "I'm sorry. That was a very sweet thing to say. I... I'm just not used to getting so... what? I don't even know... ah... talked to or 'complimented' in that way. I do consider it a compliment though, thank you".

Kaiden looked at her with stern consideration. "Ok" he said and then smiled.

"Oh, and by the way..." she leaned over and whispered in his ear "I love your hands even more than your mind".

Kaiden cracked up laughing picking up on the ironic twist she applied to the old feminist complaint that men only appreciate women for their bodies and not their brains.

"Why Ciera, you make such a sexist comment sound so flattering".

"Touché" she said with a smirk of a smile; but then looked at him and started to think "How far am I going to let this go? What about Nick. Could I handle two boyfriends? Naw, I couldn't make that fly, probably not. Damn what am I doing then?".

The plum wine helped. Ciera was feeling a lot more comfortable, and it showed in the conversation at dinner. She was becoming more talkative, even a little giddy. Kaiden almost wished that Master Nak wouldn't show up.

Mr. Kwong's wife was playing hostess this evening and when he looked over, he saw her talking to Master Nak at the door. After a short conversation in Chinese Mrs. Kwong pointed and nodded in their direction. She escorted him over to their table with smiles and pulled his chair out for him. Both Kaiden and Ciera stood up for the usual respectful greetings. Then everyone sat down and dove into the menu.

Mr. Kwong was the chef tonight. He was a short heavy set Chinese man with graying hair who spoke English worse than Master Nak did. His wife must have told him of the master's arrival because he came out from the kitchen and greeted them all personally. He gave short greetings in English but loved the fact that he could speak Chinese to Master Nak. Instantly he took a liking to Nak and offered to "cook special" for all three of them. He kept saying "I cook special fo yu. No need fo menu, I cook special". All he wanted to know was what type of meat they wanted, and he promised he would bring out a special dish. They agreed and settled on, shrimp, chicken, and beef. The chicken arrived first; the others followed shortly after. Each dish was placed in the center of the table where everyone could reach and sample that particular plate if they wanted to. All were served a bowl full of rice which was placed in front of them looking like it was their main meal. Ciera started to reach for the serving spoon, but Kaiden put his hand on her leg and looked at her with a stern subliminal message. She got the hint and backed off from serving herself first. Out of respect they both allowed Master Nak to start serving. He used a serving spoon and placed a spoonful of the Mandarin chicken in his bowl on top of the rice.

"Ok evy one seve self" he said.

Master Nak picked up the bowl of rice in one hand and placed it next to his mouth. Using chopsticks, he scooped up rice along with a tasty morsel of chicken and shoveled it into his mouth. Ciera watched and then followed his example.

"I've never eaten Chinese food like this before" Ciera said. "I don't mean just the food itself; I mean the method. It makes so much more sense to use chopsticks this way, much better than the way I've done it in the past. I don't have to pinch my food between them and somehow get it into my mouth before it falls off. I never thought of bringing the bowl up to my mouth like that. This is great! I can get so much more in my mouth. Before I would always end up using a fork!" She pushed a large piece of the delicious chicken and rice into her mouth with the chopsticks and commented through a full mouth "Ummmm! This is great, it's sooo good".

Master Nak commented "Chinese way" and smiled.

Ciera continued with comments like that throughout dinner as she sampled each dish that came out. She sat across from her companions, ate her food and participated in conversation by asking a question here and there. The Master was very polite; he indulged her and included her by speaking English as much as possible. In fact, it became obvious that he was quite enamored with her by the amount of attention he paid her. Only when it was much easier to express an idea in Chinese did he do so and would then turn to Kaiden to have him translate.

"Master Nak…" Ciera asked "…are you going back to New York, or do you have other seminars scheduled?".

"I must tell you both that I will not be turning to New Yok. Dis is actually my last semina in de U S".

Kaiden cried "No way. This is your last! Why?".

"Things are not good in New Yok" he said in his thick Chinese accent and turned away with a grave look on his face. "I am using the money I make here to return my family to Ahentina. It has become impossible to make a living and stay safe in Ameica. I can no longer support my family hea".

"Sifu, I thought that Martial Arts would become even more important now than it was before when things were safer".

"It is Kaiden, many peopo are want to lun, but peopo cannot afford to pay nough to spoat me in me family. Many mashoo at schoo have closed. Much mo violence, yes dey need it now mo dan ever". Then the master switched to Chinese and spoke to Kaiden. After a considerable explanation, Kaiden turned to Ciera.

"He says it reminds him of the Chinese revolution. He sees similar beginnings here in America, like a movement against intellectuals, against the rich or against the idea of allowing people to make a profit either mentally or physically. It's showing itself in many ways. One being the high amount of taxes that have been imposed on everyone. He says this is like punishment for success. Then they turn around and give it to the people who don't do anything and state that this is fair, it's equity. It has generated a climate in which the rich are reluctant to operate. Government trade regulations against China have severely curtailed the Chinese restaurant industry. Some main line items are not even available anymore and the ones that are, are a lot more expensive. Restrictions designed to make it 'fair' just force customers to purchase the same product from another country that has purchased it from China. This effectively places another middleman between the producer and the consumer. Shipping plus the tax increases make it very hard to profit in the restaurant business; it's why the cost of eating out is so high. Many Chinese restaurants are closing and leaving the city.

Also, the IRS got wind of his teaching business and are now coming after him for not filing taxes on cash receipts".

"Oh no!" Ciera said to Master Nak with sympathy.

"They don't have proof that he got paid cash they're just estimating the cash that an average business of his size might have received and are now charging him past due taxes and penalties on that assumed amount. They're going back ten years and want a total of just under forty thousand dollars including fines and interest.

"Wow they're just guessing?" Ciera said, raising her eyebrows.

"Yeah, they've been clamping down for years on many self-employed businesses and are now forcing him to buy health and liability insurance for his students. He says he can't afford it. He can't afford to pay back the IRS either so he's moving out of the country. But the last thing he said was the most worrisome. He warned us. His and many families like his came here to get away from this type of obstreperous government rule, the same type we're experiencing now. He says to watch out and be warned. The American constitution is now just a piece of paper once you have given your freedoms away".

"Obstreperous? La dee da, where did you get that one from?" Ciera chided him.

Kaiden was smiling from the memory "I picked it up from an old history teacher of mine".

"So, you see Ms. Lowman, yo ha to visit may in Ahentina fo next lesson. You come stay with me. Are welcome anytime. I teach you no chage".

She turned to Kaiden and touched him on the arm "Look Kaiden we're invited to Argentina" she said joyously.

"No, not him, just you Ms. Lowman" Master Nak said it with a bright smile on his face. "He not invited".

They all laughed wholeheartedly; Ciera blushed from the obvious innuendo.

"I chage him" Nak said smiling and pointing his thumb at Kaiden. That got a second round of laughs that made Ciera giddy to the point where she was smiling and chuckling at almost everything he said for the rest of the evening. She ate it up and enjoyed the teacher's 'attention'. Kaiden had never seen her so happy and as cute as her radiant smile made her look right now. The little girl in her came out for just a little while as he sat there watching her chat with Master Nak. Of course, the wine might have played a small part.

The food was great, the wine was great, the tea was great and that's what their teacher told chef Kwong when he came over to the table to see if the dinner was to their liking. Instantly Nak and the owner jumped into conversation and started speaking rapid Chinese. Because he honored Master Nak's position as a martial art master he offered and insisted that the dinner was "on the house". But Master Nak would have none of it and paid for the entire meal anyway with cash between continuous protests registered by Chef Kwong who bowed to him profusely while trying to give him the money back out of respect.

Finally Master Nak looked at Mr. Kwong very seriously, placed his hand on the owner's arm and said something in Chinese that settled the argument. Kwong backed down and accepted the money with a bow of his head.

The trio said their goodbyes, gave their thanks to the Kwong's and then to each other as they stood outside the restaurant. They wished the Master well on his journey to Argentina. Nak honored them with some parting advice on their Tai Chi practice before he left. He said to Kaiden "Your Tai Chi good, but member the way taught and practiced by many teachers is not good for fighting. Seek development of power in movements. Concentrate on expansion and contraction of body doing whole movement. Otherwise, Tai Chi will neva ha powa. In mooment beginning, contract. In middle, expand, at end contact. You body no stay still- inside!".

He turned to Ciera "Ciera" he said and reached out and took her hands warmly. It was a soft touch and yet retained a sense of longing. "Use Tai Chi to build strength and balance. Number one: get healty body, you already have healty body..." he smiled and raised his eyebrows at her "but don't think already got healty body. Body need work. Much work for bearing child". His smile continued throughout conveying a sense of knowing, then he turned to Kaiden; "how you say 'Jixu' in English?".

Kaiden thought for a second and then said "Continue or continuously".

"Yes do 'con-tinu-ously' fo good healt. Then let Kaiden show how to put power". He squeezed her arm affectionately. "You good, keep pacticing!" He bowed to them both and they bowed in return. Ciera dispensed with the formality and gave him an enthusiastic hug. It surprised the old man. He raised his eyebrows but then smiled as he hugged her back. Then he turned and walked down the street toward his hotel. Kaiden and Ciera looked after him feeling as if it were the end of something really special, like they had just lost something dear to them both like losing a grandfather.

The two of them started walking in the opposite direction to the bus stop. "By the way, what did Master Nak say to the owner that got him to accept the money?" Ciera asked Kaiden.

"Master Nak referred to an old Chinese saying that goes something like- 'Value received deserves a valuable return'".

Kaiden was quick to place his arm around her shoulder and kid her saying "And Ciera he sure was quite taken by you now wasn't he" He squeezed her. "I think he really fancies you".

"Yeah, I was getting the impression that an invitation to his hotel room was next!" Ciera said laughing.

"I wouldn't doubt that he'd welcome you to Argentina alright! He's a dirty old man underneath all that Tai Chi".

"Hey..." Ciera said seriously stopping them in their tracks as she turned toward Kaiden. With her best seductive smile "I just might take him up on that and go down there for a visit!" She raised her eyebrows to accent the thought and then tossed her hair to the other shoulder and started walking leaving Kaiden to ponder it. It threw him off for just a second as he tried to figure out whether she was serious or not.

"Hey where would you stay?" he smiled and then darted after her.

"Oh I don't know, it sounded like he had a lot of room in his bed" she said with a laugh over her shoulder.

Kaiden just shook his head and followed her.

* * *

During the next month the situation in America grew worse. Politicians in Washington were guiding events down a path that only benefited special interest groups, donors, and themselves. For example, Health care provided to Government politicians and employees was far superior to what was offered to the general population. To sell the idea of socialized medicine to the public back in 2010 President Obama stated that "Everyone must participate and purchase health insurance for this to work. Therefore, participation in the program must be mandated by the government to include everyone". But in reality, it was being used as a tool to deal out favors. Those businesses who the president favored were able to obtain exemptions and were not required to comply with the strict rules concerning health care coverage. He also blessed those people under the coveted government program if they were of the right persuasion. It ended up the same old same old, just another ploy to generate the ability for politicians to control businesses and receive kickbacks. Indirectly the nonexempt groups paid the bill for the exempt groups. How ironic that the same companies who contributed most generously to the president's campaign were the ones who got the waivers. There are many more examples.

The government's iron fist closed with an ever-tightening grip on businesses in their rendition of an effort to force the economy into a better position. Health Care was just a trial balloon whose legal victories were used to forward the next phase of the plan to fundamentally change America. A major stumbling block to achieving their goal was the second amendment. To solidify their control, they had to somehow pull gun control restrictions over the heads of the American population and to do that they needed a way to undermine the NRA's solid political block. To the politicians it was crucial to achieve a higher degree of job security by succeeding in their efforts to curtail the opposition's ability to respond to their actions with violence. They had to get around the citizens' right to bear arms and make gun control a reality. Their plan included taking over the insurance industry and use it as leverage to accomplish something that no one else had been able to achieve in the history of the United States.

In 2012 the United States Supreme Court voted in favor of the government and gave them the right and the ability to 1) Require that its citizens purchase a Health Care insurance policy. Opponents called it "Gov luv". And 2) that it was legal for the government to offer competitive mortgage insurance and sell it on the open market effectively allowing them to go into the insurance business. That became affectionately known as "Gov cuv". Through the FHA, the Government began selling inexpensive homeowners insurance sold at first individually but then as a package deal in conjunction with a government mortgage loan. Under the guise of offering a cheaper alternative to help out poor struggling homeowners it was soon mandated that every recipient of a government mortgage loan offered by Finny Malee and Fruddle Mac mortgage company was required by law to purchase and maintain "Gov cuv" homeowner's insurance. The public perceived it as a welcomed "benefit".

At first "Gov cuv" competed with existing insurance companies fairly on the free open market. Then the government entities started receiving subsidies and the cost of the insurance they offered started dropping significantly. Even though it wasn't as good as other plans it became the number one selling policy at two thirds the cost of the competition. By making it irresistible to consumers, the government's offer quickly became the most popular way to satisfy the homeowner's insurance requirement.

The effect of Gov cuv on insurance companies was the same that echoed throughout the health care industry. As more and more people flocked to purchase the cheaper policy, competing insurance companies started to lose significant market share. The ensuing loss of cash flow meant that the remaining customer base shrank to a size too small to support their business platform. Most of them eventually dissolved and went out of business.

"Fine!" a lot of people said. "Let those greedy insurance companies go out of business, serve them right to charge so much money". But as usual they weren't adding in the consequences of the final stroke.

Government insurance had stipulations just like any other insurance company did. To be insured you had to comply and pass inspection. That's just how it is. They even had inspectors go out and take pictures to see exactly what you had and didn't have. For example, you needed to have a good roof installed up to code with the plywood nailed properly every four inches with #8 ring shank nails, tin tabs nailed every six inches with ring shank roofing nails. Storm or extreme weather shutters were required, new approved windows, metal tie down straps at the truss to wall connections, exterior equipment anchors for the air conditioner for example. There were also safety issues that needed to be addressed such as a four-foot fence around the pool if you owned one including child proof locking gates, exterior lights, safe sidewalks and driveways, entry ways with approved locks, burglar alarm system with a panic button, fire extinguishers available in all sections of the home and a local fire hydrant in close proximity of the house.

Many more requirements accumulated over the years into an extensive list that the insurance companies sought to implement to minimize their risk. Now, under pressure from the White House, major mortgage insurance companies added a policy to their requirements under the notion that it would be perceived as a major contribution towards "Public safety".

The press release concerning its implementation stated:

"In an effort to help reduce crime in America we are announcing an additional requirement to our policies that will create a much safer environment in this great country of ours. Our efforts are designed to make America a safer place to live. Therefore, from this date forward, guns will no longer be allowed to be stored in a residential home covered by Finny Melee and Fuddle Mac Mortgage Insurance Companies. If you own a policy from one of these companies, you will be required to remove the apparatus from the premises before liability coverage will be granted. Inspections will be forthcoming to verify compliance".

If an application was rejected, meaning you refused to vacate your home of weapons, you were forced to purchase from one of the few remaining insurance companies that still sold homeowners insurance. As alternative companies became fewer and fewer, the cost of coverage started to skyrocket. Private policies were now three to four times the cost of the government's plan.

Insurance companies knew who owned a firearm due to the new gun registration law that had been rammed down the public's throat by the Democrat party and their anti-gun politicians. If you owned a gun you had to show proof that you either turned your gun(s) in to the police or that you had sold every registered (and non-registered) gun you possessed. An applicant was also forced to rescind the gun permit itself. The insurance agent became responsible not only for taking pictures but also for searching the premises. Finny Melee Insurance

Co. reserved the right for their agents to look in "all possible locations" including closets and attics. Applicants were forced to open safes to prove it was clear of any deadly devices. Metal detectors were brought in in some cases to do a more meticulous search if someone was suspected of harboring an illicit item. That's when they would sweep the attic, floors, walls and even the yard looking for cache's that might have been hidden or buried. In high-risk cases a random inspection was performed at odd times of the night in which a policy holder was forced to submit. If you refused or failed the random inspection, your coverage was canceled.

Guns were not banned. There wasn't a single law against them. It just became impossible to obtain a mortgage loan from a government mortgage company if you owned one. For reasons unknown, some of the other insurance companies followed suit. Requirements effectively pried guns from the warm live hands of poor people who could no longer afford to own one. The amazing part was that these new company policies were implemented under the ruse that America still maintained their second amendment right to own a firearm.

There were a few attempts by Americans to push through a non-progressive candidate that might succeed at reversing this trend. Conservative politicians promoted change and ran vigorously on getting back to policies more closely aligned with the original intent of the founding fathers and the constitution. They spoke the words, touted the rhetoric, and sometimes the people voted for change. The discourse was typical- "I promise to stop government spending. I'll stop partisan politics and the class warfare. I'll stop the trampling of our beloved Constitution and I'll rescind the healthcare bill, turn around the decline of the dollar, set the free markets free again, abolish the IRS, shore up the dollar and balance the Federal budget. But I'm going to need your support. Vote for me in the next election and I'll fight to accomplish this".

It sounded great. And for the most part, the new Republican Party did try. The last republican administration elected on that platform started a push designed to implement those changes to reverse the downward spiral of the American dream. But when major cuts in spending were imposed on entitlement programs to cut the national debt the people most affected by it rose up and screamed bloody murder. They hollered, cussed, rioted, and threatened the politicians who were cutting off their piece of the pie. Americans wanted it fixed, but they wanted it fixed at someone else's expense and they used violence to get it. After that they voted for the other guy. Once again, the pendulum swung heavily toward the Socialist Democrat party. Americans voted for the politician who promised them the most.

Talking points directed at a society hungry for entitlements sounded good. Politicians promised new programs on top of the old ones with the intent of dispensing more food stamps to a wider range of people. There was a push to give food stamp recipients a raise along with another hike in the nationwide minimum wage, an offer of free healthcare in tangent with free education. Another push offered to anoint illegal aliens with the right to participate in the privileges of all these programs. There was new funding for Social Security and more initiatives that would in theory create more jobs. They enacted a law requiring all businesses to provide major benefits to employees. More tax relief was designated for the poor inside a new mass stimulus bill (one that will work this time). On top of that there was new funding for mass transit projects, bailouts for states that were going bankrupt, new subsidies and tax credits on top of existing ones for Solar Power. And all of it paid for by taxing the rich? No, you could take all the money from all the rich and still not generate enough money to pay for this.

Democrat politicians guided public perception with class warfare propaganda making it sound like the solution to all their problems was to increase taxation on the rich. Unbeknown by Americans who voted for these politicians was that once in office their policies ended up raising taxes not only on the rich but on the middle class as well. Progressives argued that money doesn't "trickle down" like Ronald Reagan proclaimed in 1984. Maybe, but it soon became obvious that higher taxes do! New codes taxed people earning over 200K at a whopping 70% yet the country's monetary problems continued. Then the cut off income went down to 150 K, then down again to 100K. Taxing the rich was pure politics designed to psychologically massage public discord. The annoying fact that proponents refused to believe was that if the Federal government taxed the rich at 100% and didn't let them keep any of their money the additional revenue would only be enough to run the government for nineteen days of the year. The fact that the over 200K crowd already shelled out and covered 97 percent of the total tax liability was either unknown by the uneducated voter or it just didn't matter to them. To maintain this view, they had to discard or simply disagree with the cold hard facts of the math.

Hidden taxes crept into every corner of the markets. For example: there is a mortgage fee that the government gets for giving you the privilege of being granted one, all of this while over fifty percent of the population continued paying no Federal taxes at all. Consequently, this movement ushered in an expansion of welfare that bolstered the base causes of the problems that American's faced.

Newly elected Democrat and Republican candidates both sanctioned the printing of more money to pay for programs initiated in previous administrations as well as their own. Polls showed that shutting off the flow of money wasn't a popular idea. There was constant opposition to reforming Government spending by the people empowered to spend it. The policy was strongly defended by progressive Democrats and liberal Labor Unions who both made every attempt to continue the momentum going in the spend, spend, spend direction. America was headed toward an ever increasingly more involved and powerful government that surpassed their European socialist partners.

It worked. There is a growing wave of people who believe that the well to do are the problem and all that needs to be done is to tax them more to solve the government's fiscal dilemma. "The rich can afford it" was the mantra, it was a prominent theme that bullied its way through the middle and lower classes- "They think they're better than us", "There getting away without paying their fair share", "They'll never miss it" and "those dirty rich bastards". That one was always the grand finale of remarks.

Wealthy individuals and entities ran from states like New York, New Jersey and California who exuded this attitude the strongest and taxed them and their estates at the highest rates in the world. That was alarming enough, but only when those evil profit-making corporations started running for the ports to get out from under the highest corporate tax rate in the world did anyone start to think that something was amiss. Not many considered it a problem until it was too late. Many major corporations ran into the arms of more business-friendly countries who welcomed them with a more favorable tax status and an endless supply of cheap labor. Who would have guessed?

President Richfield was a black man borne into the deep pressure of Chicago's political boiler room. For those that know Chicago Illinois well, that says it all. For those who don't, let it suffice to say that it's a powder keg about ready to blow at any minute. Richfield was ushered into office with 99% of the black vote and 72% of the Spanish vote. The white community was 50/40 against, a fact that was played up as evidence that white people are racist. But of course, the 99% black support was not, no, that was solidarity, something that everyone should have in common with this president who promises to "Take us out of the turmoil and deliver us into prosperity once again". Richfield was counting on class warfare as the centerpiece of his plan, he was going to use it to spearhead his campaign to fundamentally change America.

It was never said in any campaign speech or written in any article about the president, but deep inside, the man felt that white America had been the plantation's boss for way too long. Now it was his turn to bend the owners over the stump and use the 'cat o nine tails' to deal out the punishment they deserve. It was about time that his people rise up and take the fruit of the plane for themselves.

* * *

The price of food had been rising for quite some time but today it jumped. Revolt came stomping in right after. When people are hungry, they do desperate things. Even as Kaiden left the train station in New York for Mt. Tenny Academy, a riot in downtown Detroit left the city looking like a war zone. Some say it already was a war zone, but if you saw it now, you'd agree- it's a war zone! People can't even live in sections of the city anymore because standard services are not available. Many of the apartments and buildings are uninhabitable and burnt out beyond their ability to function except as a shelter for the homeless. Violence was becoming a viable reaction in the minds of the downtrodden.

Union organizations saw to it that violence was injected into the mix. Their cronies came into what you could call somewhat peaceful protests and inserted their own goon squad of troublemakers to nudge protesters into a more violent demeanor. Demonstrations that never would have gotten out of hand got out of hand. The demonstration at Union square in Chicago started out peaceful enough but then descended into chaos quickly with the aid of a hand full of masked demonstrators. They smashed things, lit them on fire and threw rocks at police. From heavy handed counter control measures, one protester was killed. Tens of dozens of people and police were injured in multiple protests that always seemed to turn into a battle. Ultimately guns came out in quite a disturbing number of cases. No one could believe what they were seeing on live news video feeds; People were behind barricades shooting at the police like it was the Middle East. "Is This America or the Middle East" the caption read at the bottom of the TV screen.

News broadcasts of the rallies were covered better than the elections. Every night you heard and saw something about it on the news. In one ghastly demonstration in LA crowds turned violent and were confronted by rows of riot police backed up by various models of law enforcement vehicles that looked more like military equipment. The equipment had been bought with allocated stimulus money a few years ago to beef up the police reaction force. The media called them "Riot diet vehicles". Crowds were eventually pushed back with tear gas, water cannons and rows of police with shields and batons in their hands. Hundreds of people backed down from the police and in one case a large throng of protesters retreated down a city street that unfortunately happened to house a local police station. Most of the police who manned the station were out on the riot lines, so it wasn't very difficult for the mob to outnumber the skeleton crew manning the station. The few inhabitants in the station suddenly found themselves surrounded by a raucous crowd that started to smash windows and ram the doors. Within minutes the protesters gained entrance and took over the station. They beat up the cops they caught inside, released prisoners, stole weapons, and ended up taking hostages. Ultimately those stolen weapons were used against the police themselves which contributed to the multiple police fatalities that day. Armed squatters delayed the police by setting the front of the building on fire as they exited the rear. Emergency crews responded but they were shot at and blocked by snipers. The police were blocked from retaking the station until it was too late to save the building. Hostages locked inside jail cells were left there to die. The whole place ended up burning to the ground around them. It took twenty-four hours before police took back full control of the station and the surrounding neighborhood.

***

Riots became the emergency that the Richfield administration needed to kick off the next stage in the campaign against guns and their owners. The insurance scam was a great first step. It got the public used to the idea of giving up their guns on their own accord. But just discouraging ownership wasn't enough, unfortunately there were plenty of rich gun owners who just paid the price and defied the trend to give them up. It ended up that the law only widened the gap between the classes by effectively disarming the poor and the middle class while leaving the rich with weapons in hand.

New laws passed included a ban on the sale of ammunition for semi-automatic rifles. The newly enacted "Ammunition Authorization Act" took away America's right to purchase ammunition under the guise of protecting the public from the evils of the military style semi-automatic rifle. Even the name of the bill was part of the ruse, making it sound like they were authorizing certain types of ammunition rather than banning them. Congress passed it even though it was rare that the AR style rifle was used in any of the violent crimes sighted. Documentation showed that 95 percent of all shootings involved a handgun. Yet as intended the law stymied an intense negative reaction. After all, it wasn't a ban on "guns" now, was it? The common .223 was amongst a list of calibers that were banned from use in the name of public safety. The only ones still legal were the .22. The nine-mil handgun round (for security forces only) and the .308 caliber round for hunters along with black powder and ball type ammunition in any caliber. Magazine capacity was reduced to five rounds max. These restrictions didn't go through congress; they came down directly from the President in the form of an executive order. The president was done waiting for congress to act. The legality of the move will be debated in courts for years to come.

To stem the cries of "Government control" and to appease the American hunter they allowed the sale of the full metal jacket .308 for hunting. Single shot bolt action rifles were the only one's civilians could legally use for hunting. You could use a semi-automatic, but you couldn't hunt with a multiple round magazine. Five round capacity was the max allowed for revolver style pistols and only five round magazines were legal for semi auto use. This law made the "six-gun" illegal. Americans had seen something similar back in 1994 where they were first introduced to the idea of a ban on "semi-automatic assault rifles" by the Clinton administration. It was called the "Public Safety and Recreational Firearms Use Protection Act" or AWB. With it, they banned any rifle identified as "an assault rifle" and included a list of rifles that were considered illegal. At that time the Assault rifle was defined as any rifle that fired each time the trigger was pulled. Nine named rifle models were banned outright along with any magazine over a ten-round capacity. Gun advocates called it the "scary gun law" and it lasted until 2004 when a sunset clause put an end to it. At the time of its demise there wasn't enough political pressure to reinstate the ban under the pro-gun Bush administration.

Although most of the American people hated the new ban, there was little resistance. Gun owners were already prepared for it and were somewhat complacent. Many had made up their minds long before that this wasn't an issue worth dying for. They thought "As long as they're not coming to get my gun" it would be alright. They were wrong. Yes, they are coming for your guns.

The President of the United States went on prime-time TV and very quickly blamed Republicans for the riots in Detroit. "They're defunding the welfare programs and raising taxes on the middle class" they said. Within the long-drawn-out somber speech, he announced details of the new ban on ammunition sighting the disturbing trend of riots as the basis for his decision, all the while knowing full well that most of the weapons on the streets in the Detroit riots were obtained from the police station. Oddly there was already a ban on guns in Detroit. No matter, this was a perfect catalyst and the Democrats saw their chance to finally push the gun issue over the edge. "Guns" were the problem. The issue had to be addressed.

An excerpt from the president's speech:

"We must take these steps to restrict the use of assault rifles so they may not be used against the greater good. As we have seen in these tragic events of the last few days, it is now apparent that these rifles, in the wrong hands, can create horrific damage to our Police, to our communities and to the very people who we vow to keep safe. I condemn these stone-cold acts of violence perpetuated against the very men and women who work hard for our benefit and strive to keep us safe. It is for their protection; it is for your protection, that we move to rid these types of guns and magazines from the streets. With this law we will make them unavailable to the people who seek to perpetrate these crimes".

Politicians knew that Americans were never going to give up their guns easily. They were just waiting for the right moment to force them to comply.

* * *

After the riots in Detroit and Chicago made headlines Senator Coulomb of Illinois was called in for a meeting with President Richfield. Nadd Coulomb walked into the president's office looking exactly like Morgan Freedman except with totally gray/white hair. Both were from the great state of Illinois and knew each other from serving in the State senate, from there they intermittently mingled as both successfully climbed the political ladder. Nadd considered the President a good friend as well as a colleague. His gray hair lent kindly to a presumed look of wisdom and the "Lee Haven" custom suit he wore identified him as an inside the beltway politician. He was a staunch Democrat who was recognized by the Richfield administration as a major proponent of gun control. On that issue he got along and went along with the president's agenda. But it was quite apparent that Congressman Coulomb had his own ideas about the refunding of Social Security. He was one of the few Democrats that didn't go along with the Richfield administrations plan to refund the program with another bailout package.

"Nadd, come in come in" President Richfield said as he strolled over to him and extended his hand.

"Sit down; we haven't had much of a chance for a face to face since we pushed the recovery act through last year. How are you doing?"

"Normally I'd say great Mr. President but of course you heard of the riots in Detroit. We're still recovering and we're working feverishly to avert any further breakouts".

"Yes, that was bad news Nadd, and that brings me right to my point of bringing you in today. Thank you for coming" President Richfield said. "Would you like a cigar?".

"Yes sir, I don't mind if I do".

The President took out a fine Romeo y Julieta Carlo cigar anaversario edition from an engraved wooden box on his desk. The clip is right there, I find that most people want to trim and clip their own cigars, so I'll let you do the honors".

"Yes sir, thank you" Senator Coulomb said.

He took his time and clipped the end of the cigar and then lit it himself with a wooden match from a compartment in the cigar box.

"Ummm wonderful" he said taking a few seconds to savor the moment. "Now, how can I return the flavor Mr. President?".

"Yes, yes, we'll get to that but first I need to be frank with you and get this off my chest before I get to what I really invited you here for. Nadd of course I'm aware that you've resisted my efforts to bring you in on backing the new Finny Melee Mortgage loan funding program. I just need to know your stance on the issue; I'd like to hear it from you".

"Sir with all due respect, I understand the desire of our party to offer low interest loans to stimulate the mortgage industry, it's a great feather in our cap with the American voter. But I also understand that the money for this endeavor will be funded in large part by the sale of new treasury bonds where China is once again the principal buyer".

"But Nadd we've done this a thousand times in the past it's just the way it's done". The President replied.

"Under normal circumstances sir I would agree with you, but the thirteen percent interest rate we're now promising to pay on these bonds is totally unacceptable. It's killing us Mr. President".

"Nadd, Nadd we're paying back all our obligations; America is growing and so is our debt- so what! It's nothing we can't handle".

"Yes sir, and that's why we can't be doing this anymore, we're borrowing money at thirteen percent on the front end and receiving four percent interest on the back end from low-income homeowners who default at a rate of one in four. Due to losses on deals like this, we're drowning! This is unsustainable".

"Nadd now you sound like a Republican, I need your support on this and the Chinese wouldn't lend it if they didn't think we could pay it back now, would they?" President Richfield said. He got up and paced across the floor and threw his hands apart. "One last time and I won't harp on it anymore Nadd. Can I do anything or say anything that would change your mind?".

"Maybe Mr. President, you know I need community reinvestment funds for the state of Illinois, we need it bad. We have a major problem with discrepancies in the amount of funds for the City Renovation projects. Meaning we are running out of money. If I could get some help to drive that forward... maybe, we could reach a deal. But I believe that through this Mortgage and loan bill and through various other methods, the Chinese are obtaining powerful leverage that will someday compromise the security of this nation. My constituents and I have set sail and we are bound and determined to change course on this. But let me hear what you're willing to offer".

"Whatever power you believe the Chinese are accumulating has been going on for years, for God's sake Nadd it's been transpiring for decades. This deal we're working on is just a drop in the bucket. It won't make a hill of beans in the final outcome of our relationship with the Chinese. But Ok Nadd, I got your point. Let me make mine and then I'll see what I can do for the State of Illinois. The President sat back down on the edge of the couch across from Nadd and looked him in the eyes.

"I need you for something and I know I can count on you for this. We want you to head up a campaign to promote the gun control issue. I need someone of your stature to tout the party line on this".

"Sir I always have...".

"No, this time it's different Nadd. Of course, you know that we've been successful with the insurance ban on weapons. It's time for the next step. We can't afford to treat this with just a comment here and there, we're looking for someone to champion the cause and really come out swinging".

"I would be glad to be your man on this one Mr. President. This is something I can really get behind. I've already done it for the state of Illinois I'd be happy to do it for the benefit of the country".

"Great Nadd, I knew I could count on you. See my public relations manager Mr. Gartner on the way out. He'll work with you on getting the funds you need to do this little favor of mine and kick it into full gear. And Nadd, set up the media outlets to cover this. Get out in front of them and use anyone else you can get for support. Make it look like there's a consensus on this issue. Even bring in a rock star or a rapper or something. Sell it to the youth and try to get them on our side. Make it look like everyone's behind it. Nadd, sell it to 'em with consistent coverage, keep it on their minds and keep it going for a couple of months till we make headway. If we say it enough, they'll end up believing it".

The president edged even closer to Nadd and in a more serious tone said "Nadd, this is serious. It can't get out that I've directed you to do this. This is not 'official' business. Do you understand?".

"Yes, Sir I see that you are serious about this issue and that I need to be discreet. I'll get it done Mr. President. And don't worry. I'm glad I can be of service".

"Yes, that's great Nadd I'm sure you will. In return I'll also direct Mr. Gartner to set you up with people who can help get you those re-investment funds you're looking for. Now, on a lighter note, how's the family...?".

* * *

In a classroom on the east side of campus Ciera was listening intently to her professor's lecture on agronomy. It was her last class that she needed to take to satisfy the required credits in agricultural studies and she needed this in order to graduate. All the programs instructed students on techniques used in the cultivation of various types of edible plant agronomy for either small scale home gardens all the way up to larger commercial crop production.

The professor was in the middle of a discussion on the most common detriments to growing corn. He explained "Corn has six major sources of serious detriment: birds, insect infestation, slugs, viruses, blight, and bacterial infection. Weeds are a problem but mostly because they promote one or more of the five detriments mentioned.

Insect pests include the Corn flea beetle, European corn borer, Corn ear worm, Fall army worm, Cutworms, Sap beetle, Western corn rootworm and the Flea beetle. All these need to be addressed because the degree of possible damage can be as high as 100%, especially with compounded infestations to a single field.

In situations where you are relying on these crops for your survival and adding in the possibility of 100% crop destruction, I hope you will seriously consider using pesticides. Yes, believe me I know the arguments for organic growing and I agree that it is a healthier way to grow. But if you're starving, do you care if there are chemicals in the food? Please be honest with your answer.

I will concur, that if yields can remain high with any organic technique, then I relent. It will be a much healthier product. But pesticides can make, and I will go so far as saying they will be the difference between a large yield and little to none. That word "none" will scare the hell out of you in a do or die situation. When growing food becomes imperative for your survival you will freak out while watching your crops slowly get eaten and disintegrate right in front of your eyes. I just ask you to take a softer stand on the subject, that's all. If you have pesticides, use them. Save the organic gardening for when the pesticides run out and become unavailable. And yes, we will go over some of those techniques too, but for now I want to discuss the use of pesticides.

I would like to bring your attention to Lambda cyhalothrin. If you were given a choice of pesticides and you could only bring one with you, I recommend Lambda cyhalothrin. It's a versatile pesticide that can wrestle back control of your crops and take it out of the hands of a variety of insect species. It's effective on all the insects I mentioned: The Corn flee beetle, European corn borer, Corn ear worm, fall army worm, Cut worm, Sap beetle, Western corn rootworm and the flea beetle. The pesticide "Metaldehyde" is my recommendation for controlling Slugs.

Please read chapter 2 of the 'Agro Culture Manual' tonight for homework, it will familiarize you with the mixture, doses, timing, and delivery method of lambda cyhalothrin and other pesticides which we will be discussing tomorrow.

Also make sure that you sign up for field hours. We need pumpkin pickers and apple pickers for this coming weekend. You will need to accumulate 300 credit hours in the field to graduate, so for those who are behind in hours I suggest you get started now or else you'll be on next summer's work crew for make-up".

13

Member of the Board

Kaiden attended his first board meeting on Tuesday night in the first week of September. It was held in the Bunkers' spacious conference hall that looked more like a small auditorium and was specifically designed to handle the large number of officers and board members as well as a sizeable audience. To enter he had to present his school ID to security at the door. They checked his name against a list, found it and allowed him onto the stage where the board members sat. The public was not allowed to attend but students, Cadets and faculty were welcome. Those interested enough to attend were now milling around the lobby and had started to file in and fill the seats behind the central podium.

Located at the very center of the Bunker building, the three hundred seat auditorium was a spacious hall with tall cathedral ceilings. It was plenty big enough to hold the large crowd that usually attended these important board meetings. All other rooms, offices and halls in the building are wrapped around the exterior of this central location. At the head of the room was a long semicircular desk on a raised platform with tall chairs behind a continuous desk. That effectively assigned a degree of importance to the people who sat there. As many as twenty people could be seated there at any given time, tonight all twelve board members were in attendance.

In the center of the rows of seats and up close to the front stood a smaller circular podium where guest speakers could address the board or just as easily turn around and address the audience.

Fifteen rows of comfortable cushioned chairs surrounded the podium in three left right and center sections. They were installed on an incline "movie theater style" to assure that visual presentations could be seen by all. A very large flat screen TV was located up front behind the center desk for just that purpose.

Tonight's meeting was designed to orient board members with staff, faculty, freshman through senior class representatives and the six cluster presidents. Everyone expected an update on multiple aspects of the situation affecting Tenny Hill Academy.

Again, sitting at the head table, Kaiden saw Ciera and recognized Chancellor Gentry, Major Monett, and Professor Jing. The ones he didn't know; the Dean of administration Mr. Harry Konic, Chaplin Waters, the school treasurer Mr. Bennett and school Secretary Mrs. Gates. The remaining five were listed as "the board of trustees". Kaiden assumed that they were the ones that everyone here tonight was trying to impress.

Representatives from each of the sub departments were sitting in the audience. Their names were listed in the handout he was given. Mr. Bill Sanchez, head of the ground keepers, Mrs. Rose who runs the campus infirmary and teaches first aid along with advanced paramedic training classes, Mr. McKinney was there to give an update on the status of the "outpost program", Mrs. Lacy Mars ran the stable down at the farm as well as the new corral located on campus. About fifteen other names were listed on name plates as well as his own. It was strange to see "Freshman Class Representative" written next to his.

Feeling a little unprepared and out of place, Kaiden thought that everyone else seemed to be an important part of the Academy's hierarchy or was an inner circle member that had a lot more to contribute to the meeting than he did. Tonight, there would be a whole lot more to absorb than to give. But as the new freshman class rep, he was now a part of this inner circle and privy to the information disclosed. The non-disclosure agreement he signed as freshmen class rep made it seem like he was about to receive classified information.

"The meeting will now come to order. Please rise for the pledge of allegiance". Chancellor Gentry said as he banged the gavel on the desk in front of him.

With that, all private conversations ceased, and the assembly directed their attention to the speaker. They stood up as two flags emerged out of a side door on the left of the conference room under the guidance of members of THA's Cadet honor guard. Carefully and ceremoniously, four cadets decked out in full uniform escorted the American flag to the front of the room. Accompanied on its right side was a custom designed Tenny Hill Academy flag complete with school colors and emblem. When the flags were placed in their holders on each side of the TV screen, Chancellor Gentry turned to the American flag and placed his hand on his heart.

He started it with "I pledge allegiance..." and by the time he got to "to the flag of the United States of America..." everyone around Kaiden had joined in. With their hands on their hearts, the crescendo built into a strong statement repeated wholeheartedly in unison by the entire delegation. Kaiden felt a chill go up his spine when "one nation, under God, indivisible with liberty and justice for all" was repeated in mass with more passion than he could remember ever hearing before. It moved him. From that moment on, the patriotism of these people at THA would never be in doubt.

Everyone sat down again. Chancellor Gentry took control of the floor and directed Chaplin Waters to start the meeting with a prayer. Speaking for everyone, the Chaplin expressed sincere appreciation to God and country and for the privilege of having this special place to come together.

Next Chancellor Gentry had Secretary Gates recite the important minutes of their last meeting. Secretary Gates brought everyone up to date with the previous topics and points of interest from their last board meeting. It reminded the board of the people who were assigned to present and report on special interests tonight. Understandably

Chancellor Gentry directed the Academy treasurer Mr. Bennett to present the first report of the evening.

Chancellor Gentry, the trustees, and Mr. Bennett wore dark business suits which distinguished them from the others who wore everyday attire. That is everyone but the Major who wore his uniform. The president pulled his microphone closer and from his seat among the prominent board members he spoke.

"Yes, I agree we should all know the financial condition of the Academy before discussing our future because everything else depends on what I have to report tonight... and I have good news and bad news". He glanced around the room over his thick rimmed glasses for effect making it seem like he was about to drop a bomb on them with some kind of a dire problem.

Mr. Bennett had been the treasurer of the Academy since the takeover of the first administration nineteen years ago. He was a cut and dry man of principles; it was either there or it wasn't. He spoke purposefully and presented facts and figures in a tone design to confirm that he was in the "know" with consequential information upon which all else revolved. The buck positively stopped with him.

"The bad news is that we have seen corporate financial contributions to the Academy dry up to the point where they're almost nonexistent. If it wasn't for some of the special interest corporations who have a stake in our success, the corporate contribution figure wouldn't even be worth mentioning.

For dealing with and promoting their firearms the FN Corporation, who owns the Winchester brand name, contributed the weapons we have and a $6,000 check. Secore Industries, the company that makes our rat packs, contributed $114,300. Medicore, our medical supplier, chipped in $112,900. The other twenty-five or so contributions are smaller but are certainly appreciated just as much.

The good news is that contributions from like-minded organizations and personal contributions have fared much better. The 'Minute Men', the 'Americans for Constitutional Correctness, the Sons of Liberty, and the Right to Life Organization among approximately thirteen others did a great job with total contributions of $198,076.00.

Everyone in the audience was surprised and clapped in response.

Now that's great in and by itself but that number, as you can see, is down from last year. You'll find it in the handout you received tonight on page 3 in your copy of the budget. See line item #15 vs. line #16. It's the lowest contribution total we've seen for the last eight years. If it wasn't for three very special people, we would really be hurting for funds this year. But each year it seems our private contributors come through and this year they have once again more than adequately funded the Academy's ventures.

One of our most noted contributors this year is our dear friend Mrs. Aldridtch McKinney. She passed away last January and left a significant sum of money to the Academy". He paused and directed his attention to someone in the audience front row. "I'm sorry for your loss Mr. McKinney. Some of you know her grandson Mr. Allen McKinney; he is a graduate of Tenny Hill Academy and is now working with us as a purchasing agent for the outpost program. We have the privilege of having Mr. McKinney here with us tonight, Mr. McKinney would you stand up please?".

Mr. Allen McKinney stood halfway up in his seat, took a slight bow, and then sat back down.

"Thank you for being here Mr. McKinney. Folks, Mr. McKinney came all the way from the Mountains in Arkansas to be with us tonight and later he'll give us an update on the outpost program. Now I'd like to read an interesting excerpt from the 'order to trustee' that his grandmother wrote as sort of an explanation of her actions".

Mr. Bennett read from a piece of paper in front of him...

> "To all those at THA who are deeply invested in our fight for freedom:
>
> First and foremost, I am family oriented. I'm a devout Christian, and next, I am an American. I believe in God, in the freedom of religion, the right to live

and the right to make a profit. I believe the money I make belongs to me and not to some government politician who wants to take it and tell me how it should be distributed because he knows better. The nerve of them to give it away to others who don't want to work and who don't produce anything of value.

You are not entitled to anything except as stated in the constitution, Life, Liberty, and the pursuit of happiness. All of these you work for, including your health care. So, get over it.

I have a contribution to give to the college. Only my maker knows my true intentions and is therefore the only one that can credit my spirit with homage. When the government takes it from my paycheck with promises of good intentions but hands it out to some undeserving project or funds some undeserving war that kills the undeserving on both sides, it is not the same and therefore no personal credit is obtained.

Don't get me wrong, I understand the need for a strong defense and truly appreciate our men and women in the armed forces.

I have met the good people of Tenny Hill Academy, and we are one and the same in thought and prayer. I see the path that they have endeavored to create, and I have agreed to place my grandson smack dab on it. My belief in the direction my grandson is going is so strong that I pledge this gift to fuel his and your efforts. I hope this helps him and all the others who strive alongside him. This is the best way I have found to support the type of education that can arm our youth with knowledge and the ability to determine the truth of it. I hope, and I pray, that it's not too late for me to help our country get back on track and that my grandson and I can somehow be a part of that undertaking.

Please, use this gift well. It's up to you now.

Signed

Mrs. Aldridtch McKinney

The gift his grandmother donated to the Academy wasn't just written into her will like most, luckily for us she got some good advice and did it a little differently. The gift was entrusted to a trust fund incorporated in the good state of Delaware seven years ago, about the time when Allen McKinney started school here. The trustee was directed to pay the entire content of the trust fund minus fees, plus interest, to the Academy after she died. She knew that if she lived for more than five years after the date of the fund's conception, the money would not be included as a part of her estate, and it would not be subject to the N.Y. State estate tax which is now at an unbelievable 65%. She lived for seven years after the initiation of the fund and was able to contribute a grand total of $527,000 net after all was said and done. That didn't include the rather large collection of gold and silver coins that had been contributed to the school under the table".

A murmur went through the crowd and then someone started clapping. It caught on and the whole room erupted in an applause that ended up with a standing ovation. The group of people surrounding Mr. Allen McKinney turned towards him and directed their applause in his direction. He nodded his head in appreciation and continued with his own applause in recognition of his grandmother.

When they all sat down Mr. Bennett continued. "The other two contributors would like to remain anonymous as well as the amounts that they have contributed. I can tell you that they too gave very handsomely but for various reasons I can't go into any details. And it's unfortunate because we really can't give them the appropriate 'thank you' that they deserve. But just know that there are some very prominent people out there with a vested interest in the Academy's success and it goes way beyond the average contribution.

Tuition of course is our steadfast source of income and is going strong as you might already suspect. Our attendance quota has been filled in both freshman and sophomore classes for this year. It seems that all the preppers out there are sending their kids to us. We did have a few dropouts in the junior and senior classes but that is typical and quite normal. Expenditures have gone up, see line #32 this year as compared to last, but we have kept tuition at the same pace as inflation and so we have been able to head off any shortfall. All in all, without boring you to death with more details, we are in the black and looking good for this year. Please see the Academy's budget in the handout you have, you will notice that many of the items are funded at the same level as last year, but I am happy to report that a few have been increased much to the chagrin of the agricultural department and the outpost program. Each year we have increased our investment in the farm and according to Professor Jing we have been producing a rather productive return for our efforts.

Let me bounce this back to Chancellor Gentry, if you have any questions see the school web site or my email address is listed in your handout, thank you".

Chancellor Gentry took the floor again and introduced the next department. He did that one after the next until they each presented their yearly report. Then he called on a representative from each of the classes for an update. Finally, it was Kaiden's turn to speak for the freshman class. Kaiden walked up to the podium and addressed the board members and the audience. When he got nervous, Kaiden reverted to a thick New York accent.

"Foist off I'd like to thank the powers that be that landed me this ere job. It was kinda unexpected you know, but now that oim ere oim very appy to be soyvin".

People could be heard giggling. Kaiden recognized right away that he was leaning on his accent a little too hard, so he switched up and did his best to tone it down.

I would like to report the results of a short survey I took among the freshman class and relay the response to its main question- 'how can we improve your experience here at the Academy?' The response wasn't what I imagined it would be. I totally expected we'd get a lot of negative feedback; I'm used to getting negative feedback (more giggles). Oh, yes, I did hear the common complaint about the long walk to the range complex. Otherwise, I heard a lot about what's great about being here". Kaiden turned around and looked at the audience without losing contact with the microphone and smiled. "Maybe they just haven't been here long enough, yet I don't know".

A murmur of chuckles fluttered through the audience with even a few board members showing a smirk of a grin.

"The policy of boarding a freshman with an upper classman is working well. What freshman need most is information, information that will take the mystery out of the modus operandi around heea. To live with someone with experience enables the newbies to get answers to questions and guidance as to the best way to get her done. It's a whole lot better than havin to go to the guidance counselor every time you need somethin. The food's not drawing any fire, yet, and the ice machine in front of the cafeteria's workin, so I'm here to report that the freshman class is doin pretty good so far with very few complaints. As I ear more bitchin and complainin from my constituents I'll let cha know".

It was the New York accent in conjunction with his straightforward comments that got the crowd laughing and clapping. They were pleasantly amused with Kaiden's short and to the point assessment. He sat back down feeling good about getting that over with.

There was some interesting news in the ground keepers report. The head grounds keeper: Mr. Billy Sanchez, stood up and took the microphone.

"My crew this past summer along with a hand full of students working for field hour credits finished building our two new trails, the "farm trail" and the last new section of the horse trail. I'd like to report that they are now usable. The farm trail makes it possible for a hiker to walk directly from the Academy down to Stockman's Farm. I still tend to use that name, it stuck for many years after the Stockman's sold it to the Academy but there's a push by students now to re-name it 'Mt. Tenny Farm'. Anyway, it's a beautiful trail that begins in the wooded forest behind the range complex. The new section runs up from there to connect into the existing trail we know as "Tenny trail" which originates behind Rio Linda villages and eventually leads a hiker to the top of Tenny Mountain. Since the entire mountain is part of Mt. Tenny's estate we are now able to make better use of it. As you know that trail is used frequently by adventurous students and Cadets for an afternoon hike or overnight campouts, and it too has been upgraded. We also worked on the shelter and set up our clean water source by installing a pipe in the slow flowing stream where you can now just stick your canteen underneath it and fill it up from a continuous flow of water. It's the little things that really help out there.

The camp site has been there for a long time but just recently it's been upgraded with a privy. After the privy was installed at the shelter, we've seen a lot more traffic going up there. It's become a favorite destination for students and even for other hikers from outside the Academy. You can see people sunning themselves on "bald ledge" in the middle of the afternoon from campus. It's now quite an attraction to hike up there on a clear day. I recommend the hike to all of you. There's a beautiful panoramic view of the Catskill mountain range that can't be beat. Sometimes you can hear a group of hikers up there combining their voices and yelling down at the students on campus. And then there's a group of students who get together down here and try to yell back up to them. You might imagine some of the witty conversations that take place.

We used a part of the 'old' section of Tenny trail to take a hiker over to the Northern slopes of the mountain. Instead of climbing and continuing on over the old trail, the new trail branches off to follow around the contour of the mountain with just a modest descent over to the far east side. From there it branches off again with one leg descending sharply down the slopes into the valley and the other continuing on around the mountain to eventually head south. The section leading down to Mt. Tenny Farm was a little steep, but switchbacks were installed in the trail at the steepest section which made the climb or descent a lot easier. My department is responsible for maintaining the shelter as well as the trails. Another project that had been completed last spring was the new underground food storage locker behind the cafeteria…".

There were a few other projects Billy Sanchez said his department was working on and he gave the group an idea of their progress and the possible timeline for completion.

Chancellor Gentry accepted the grounds keepers report with a thank you and moved on.

"At this time, it would be appropriate to hear from Mrs. Lacy Mars. She'll give us an update on our equestrian program".

Mrs. Mars walked up to the podium and spoke into the microphone "Yes Chancellor Gentry, thank you. I am a very happy lady since given the go ahead to expand our equestrian holdings along with the construction of the new campus corral. I'm pleased to announce the addition of five new 'Quarter' horses bringing the total we now have to twelve.

I thank you Mr. Sanchez for not taking the wind out of my sail and allowing me to give the details on the new horse trail. It's an extension of the existing trail we've had for years with the new section connecting the campus to the old logging road. Signs at various points show its direction and designate it as a horse trail and they politely ask hikers to keep off. It's best to separate the hikers from the riders you know so they aren't in each other's way.

As you know the old trail begins at the stables located next to Mt. Tenny farm and it starts going up the base of Mt. Tenny on its east side. It soon connects into the old logging road that runs north and south at that point. It's somewhat overgrown but in most places it's a nice combination of trail and dirt road that's a lot wider than a normal hiking trail. Perfect for horses. To get to the campus you take the logging road north and follow it for about three miles, which takes you around the base of the mountain on the north side. The ride is very pretty in through there and it winds its way around with casual inclines and declines that make it a real relaxed trip. From there the logging road heads north down to Tenny Mt. Rd., that's the point where the new trail breaks off to the West and brings a rider over to campus conveniently exiting the woods right out behind the new campus corral. Look for it on the new campus map between the range building and Seaton hall.

Students now have the ability to board a horse on campus overnight and then ride down to the farm for class or field work the next day. This will be a nice feature for those involved in the equestrian program. They can constantly be involved with the horses.

Please see the schedule for our overnight rides and special equestrian events. Thank you, that's all".

Before she stepped away from the mike Mr. Gentry asked. "Mrs. Mars, before you go, I would just like to know how many horses the new campus corral can accommodate?".

"Oh, yes, it has ten stalls so ten comfortably, but we could hold twenty horses or more on a rotation basis between the stalls and the two pens".

"Thank you, Mrs. Mars. Now we'll hear from Mr. Allen McKinney".

Mr. McKinney moved to the podium in the center of the auditorium and addressed the board. "For those who don't know me my name is Allen McKinney. I graduated from the Academy two years ago and have stayed on to work with the Cadet organization out of a desire to further its success. I'm now the head of the Outpost projects and I'm here as a spokesman for the outpost program. Thank you on behalf of my Grandmother for the warm appreciation that I felt in this room tonight. I can speak for her; that applause alone would have made it all worthwhile. I love my Grandmother and her gift will go a long way to help us achieve our goals.

All six of the outpost reps have submitted similar situational reports so my comments will reflect the status of all of them.

Because we don't publish details on these projects as a rule, please take us at our word that the outpost program is coming along very well. Each year the Academy produces a great group of people to work on the sites. All the sponsoring campus clusters have been able to fulfill quotas for the work crews, so we're never shy of help ever since breaking ground on the post projects. We have some very motivated people, and I can't thank those on the work details enough, both past and present. They are the backbone of our success as well as people like my Grandmother who contributed so generously to make it all happen.

All six of the outposts are at various stages of completion. Three have come "on line" and are very capable of supporting a cluster of thirty to one hundred people or more at various degrees of comfort. We have the capability of expanding if needed. By 'on line' I mean the main building is complete, or at least dried in, but the exterior villages might not be fully set up just yet. Of course, they all have at least one fully functioning and operating village that houses the work crew.

Planning and design have paid off, we are now putting the sites through some of their paces and the feedback from the crew is positive. We have experienced a few minor supply problems that seem to crop up and plague projects of this type. But we see improvements and success at all the locations. We are working out the bugs. I put a heavy reliance on suggestions that our crew members make. After all they're living it, and they are giving us valuable information as to the validity of our techniques and design.

Outpost number one was of course our first outpost and has been in operation for just over eight years now. Number two and three have been up and running for five and we are just beginning trial runs at outpost four and five. Work crews on number six will finish the main building this spring. That site will be occupied with its first village at that time.

My job is to obtain the monetary means to carry on and deliver the supplies needed to support the effort. That's why I'm here tonight. Each of the cluster reps will submit a budget to the board for approval, obtain funds and then get back to work. Luckily, it's as simple as that, we don't want it any more complicated. Thank you".

There was a round of applause as Mr. McKinney sat down.

"Thank you, Mr. McKinney" Chancellor Gentry said without pressing him for more details. I'd like to introduce the next speaker; the backbone behind this organization- Major Jazz Monett. The Major unlike the other board members got up and walked out from behind the semi-circle desk and walked up to the central podium and spoke into the microphone.

"Good Evening" he said to the board members and then turned and addressed the audience as well. "Good evening. First before I forget, I'd like to notify everyone about some scheduling changes and inform you about an upcoming seminar. Also, I am proud to inform you that we had a very successful Tai Chi seminar with Master Bow Nak last Saturday. It was a very interesting look into the inner workings of the Tai Chi Chuan style of martial arts. I hope you took the opportunity to participate, it was truly a wonderful event. If not, please look on the calendar for upcoming events and try to catch the next one. We have various professional speakers scheduled as well. Note the topics and dates on the calendar; a copy is included in the handout you received tonight. Guest speakers will cover topics like bow hunting, concealed carry, bullet making/reloading and we've even scheduled the appearance of an ex-navy seal who is going to talk about his experience in the failed attempt to take out the Iranian dissident Mahmoud Demahana Shosun.

Oh yes, our first down range event will be in the first week of October. Again, always check the schedule or see me for more details.

I'll start right in by stating that the range facility was officially completed last spring, I guess except for a few odds and ends that need to be tied up. The major expense of the building and the range is now behind us. Allocated funds that Mr. Bennett has eluded too have been put to good use upgrading all our equipment. We made a purchase of some new rifles and a few used ones because I was offered a deal we just couldn't refuse. Of course, there was a matching purchase of ammunition, mostly target rounds for the range, but we have accumulated a year's supply of hunting rounds as well. Believe it or not, hunting becomes much more humane when the correct weapon and bullet are matched to the type of animal being hunted. You might agree that a kill would be preferred over wounding and the subsequent suffering of an animal. Some combinations work well, and some do not. These are the lessons we teach in 'Hunting 101', then we hone them in the practical excursions we take. Our 'Advanced Hunting Techniques' class taught by Mr. Shots is an important class that you won't want to miss. His expertise becomes apparent, and your time will be well spent under his tutelage.

Unfortunately, I must inform you of two serious matters. One is that we still have an informant among us who is reporting our activities to... let's just say, various agencies.

A murmur rolled through the audience.

Now folks, everyone here knows that the path this school decided to embark upon would not be void of controversy. Although the number one risk was 'If we offer it; will they come?', I'm talking about students. There was also an unknown reaction to our curriculum by the community at large, the government and even the religious sector. In 2010 we changed our name from Mt. Tenny College to Tenny Hill Academy and since then we have made it our mission to navigate through uncharted waters and bring together a variety of arts for a comprehensive style of education that has never been offered by an accredited academic facility in NY before. The reason for our success is that these "times" have funneled a new wave of people our way. People who have reached the same conclusion that we have; that the education we offer here is an asset that will help our communities endure in tomorrow's world, a world that is changing before our very eyes to the point where people perceive these arts as imperative for the survival of, if not only themselves, but for loved ones and for this American way of life.

Most certainly, everybody does not share our enthusiasm for this endeavor. And I am here to take some of the blame. The military training that I have brought into the curriculum of this school has drawn some harsh criticism. As you might know we have gotten a lot of negative publicity from the press. Someone is feeding them information about our activities. They seem to know everything we're doing. Last spring, they called us a terrorist training camp. Since then, I've been contacted by the Department of Interior, the FBI and a few other agencies who are constantly drilling me trying to find out what and why we do what we do. They want to know exactly what our intentions are and what our 'training' consists of. The guy on the phone always ends up referring to us in a negative light no matter how I describe our intentions in our defense. The FBI ended the conversation trying to impress upon me that they believe that what we are doing here is illegal. I try to tell the ying yang's on the other end of the phone that we are not a threat to the government in any way and in fact we are both on the same side. It's evident that my explanation and my assurances go unheeded and only bolster their mistrust.

This whole series of events leads me to a conclusion that I never thought I would come to..." his voice got more emotional and louder. "...anyone who would think that we, with all the good that has been accomplished here, are subverting the government and their plans... those people... ARE AN ENEMY OF WE THE PEOPLE, THE CONSTITUTION, THE BILL OF RIGHTS, AND OF THE UNITED STATES OF AMERICA!".

The auditorium exploded with applause. Major Monett had to wait for it to die down.

"I need to relay a story to all of you, so we are clear on this point. I took over the department in 2010, the same year the name of the college was changed to Tenny Hill Academy. I'm sure you can imagine that I, by design and by direction from above..." The Major glanced over at the board of trusties and slightly bowed his head to them "...as well as decisions from the board... brought in a military structure along with the values and attitudes that go along with it. Due to my background of serving the army for twenty-five years, I live it and breathe it. That's the reason I'm here.

Back then, in the beginning, I would meet the range students every day in the old Craig Center locker room and deal out rifles, ammunition and any other piece of equipment required before walking the class out to the old outdoor range. It was located near where the new range building is now for those of you who don't know. I donned my range uniform every morning which I alone wore on my own accord. I used the uniform and my strict attitude to distinguish myself as the instructor. And I walked the half mile over to the range with the students every day for practice.

Yes, I asserted myself as someone who set the rules in no uncertain terms and was the one who was going to be obeyed come hell or high water in this relatively dangerous business of dealing with firearms. As any career military officer might, I marched in military style typical of a sergeant taking out his column. At no time, 'AT NO TIME!' was any student required to dress like me, march like me or act like me. They are not required to address me as sir or fall into any kind of military protocol when they do. All they had to do was make sure the gun was in 'safe' and pointed in the right direction; away from me!" Laughter bubbled up from the audience.

"Some mimicked and joked about my mannerisms. I took it as lighthearted feedback. Some followed along nonchalantly like it was a walk in the park. Still others, which soon became the majority, became serious and copied my mannerisms and fell in line and marched behind me in the same way.

One day in the middle of my third year, I got the surprise of my life. I waited outside for the class to emerge from the doorway of the old Craig Center locker room. They were late and I was about to go in and kick some ass, but my number one came out and assured me that they would be out any minute. He even said "Please wait sir" because he knew that I was about ready to bust in there.

Ladies and Gentlemen, picture my surprise when I heard the whistle and the whole class came out of the Craig Center, but not from the doors of the locker room. No. They marched out from the main entrance and formed up in perfect four by four formations with the

American flag and school colors flying up front. Each of them wore a uniform. They shouldered their rifles and began marching in perfect step as if it was my old company from Fort Brag. When they were abreast of my position, the acting drill sergeant called the column to a halt. My number one who was standing next to me took off his coat revealing a uniform just like the rest. He marched up to the acting drill sergeant, relieved him and took command of the company. I can still hear him in my mind. 'COLORS MARCH!' His flag detail marched forward out of the way. 'COLORS HALT!' The detail stopped. 'COLUMN ABOUT FACE! COLUMN MARCH! RIGHT FLANK MARCH! LEFT FLANK MARCH!' My number one took that column through various commands and then marched them in excellent form back around and right up behind the colors again. They joined ranks and then marched past me on the way to the range. I fell in line and marched next to them with tears in my eyes. I've never been so proud.

Somehow, they had gotten someone from West Point to come up here once a week and teach them how to march. I know his name I just don't want to disclose it. They held secret practice sessions in the auditorium once or twice a week until they got it right. All of them had paid for their own uniforms and boots.

They formed their own 'club' and from that point on they called themselves the "Cadets". To this day they are not required by me or by this school to dress in uniform, march or play soldier. Let me repeat that because no one seems to believe me. And yes, this is for the snitch we have among us. My students are not required to march or participate in the Cadet program! They are not required to wear uniforms. It is their choice! I do not teach the Cadets, but I have advised them on certain issues. Yes, it has turned into what you would call a 'militia' or a militia type of an organization over the years, but their right to exist is clearly written into the constitution and made room for in the charter of this school. They come complete with an oath to protect the citizens of the United States with their lives if need be.

But now I see, there are people who have a problem with that. Therefore, I HAVE A PROBLEM WITH THOSE PEOPLE!".

The completely silent audience broke into applause with some students and Cadet representatives going absolutely nuts. They stood up and clapped until their hands were red. For Kaiden that speech and the crowds' reaction to it was the highlight of the evening. The Major had a few more things to say but Kaiden was immersed in his own thoughts so they only superficially registered. The whole concept was so intriguing that it left him with a strong feeling that he wanted to become a part of it. It was something very important that he hadn't seen before. He couldn't help but feel that this was going to lead to bigger and better things, and it gave him a sense of hope for the future. For the first time he saw himself as one of them and that yes, that this was his calling. These people were serious and now more than ever, he wanted to be a part of this movement.

The rest of the meeting went on with the remainder of reps standing up and speaking about other aspects of the school's operation such as Adrian Phillips who was the head of campus security. He is also third in command of the Cadets. His building, complete with a weapons room, two jail cells, offices and a holding room are located in the rear of the Security building and house the commander as well as his six-man security team.

Phillips talked about the "State of the Academy" mostly as it pertained to security and went on about a few other things before giving up the podium to the Arleen's.

Dell Arleen and his wife Judy stood up and spoke in length about Stockman's farm. "Some call it Stockman's farm because that's who owned it for a century before the Academy bought it, but students now call it Mt. Tenny farm. Currently we are the live in caretakers. We manage all farm affairs including coordinating its functions with the school faculty. Every one of the students at Tenny Hill Academy will deal with us at one point or another…". They continued giving an evaluation of the farm and its present status of operation which included a profitability report.

Their assessment also included a significant statement of affairs that Kaiden had heard before, but its degree of significance escaped him.

"We have seen a change in the community recently. In the past we have been the ones seeking out, buying, and stocking up on various consumer items that we need to operate this facility successfully and we've done well. Mt. Tenny farm went from small scale to large where it is now capable of lending major support not only to the Academy but to the community as well. We buy in bulk, and what we don't grow or can grow better at different locations we do so by leasing the field or in one case the orchard. But we have a problem that is growing into a major hindrance. In the last year and a half to two years we have seen members of the community coming to us to buy certain items ranging from farm supplies to produce. It's become a lot more difficult and expensive to deal with commerce outside the State or to be exact, even outside an approximate fifteen-hundred-mile radius.

The Governments price freeze has brought on similar results to what price fixing has always produced- shortages. This is a prime example of trying to do the same fix expecting different results. It now costs more to produce beef than you are allowed to sell it for. Therefore, people are just producing what they can eat. Why operate at a loss?

People are looking for cheaper sources and are complaining about shortages. We've felt this too. The cost of shipping is outrageous and I'm sure you've heard about the armed truck hijackings in which the driver was killed. It's happening all across the country. Just last summer one of our own shipments of fertilizer was hijacked. It never made it here. They found the cab with the driver tied up, but the container and its contents were long gone. The same has happened to numerous gas tanker trucks and even trucks carrying shipments of tires. They're really in demand and I'm sure the fact that the price of tires has doubled over the last two years has something to do with it. But that's not all they're after, nowadays just about anything that moves has been indiscriminately targeted. It seems that the criminal element has determined this to be a very profitable way to derive an income.

All this has made trucking a very dangerous business. Now transportation companies are adding in the additional cost of security for these shipments and it's making the purchase of these goods skyrocket.

We can't afford the goods these days let alone having to pay an outside party for security. People in the community have come to me asking for help and we are in a unique position to offer our services to help solve this dilemma. A possible answer is that we could supply a Cadet escort, at a reasonable price, to accompany shipments bound for this college or even to this community to insure their delivery. This would reduce losses and therefore reduce the cost to an acceptable level, and we can make up for some of the added expense by selling our services as well as certain overstocked items to the community. This could be a profitable venture and open a less expensive source of supply".

Dell went on to voice some other concerns, but the looming shortfall was the main gist of his report. On a micro level it was a simplified explanation about how their county was struggling. On a macro level it gave an indication of how the world was changing. Americans operated in a world where it was hard to imagine shortages of anything let alone becoming unavailable. Not here in America. Yes, there had been times when common items had become scarce but the thought of them becoming "unavailable" never entered the realm of possibility.

Between it all Kaiden heard more details about the inner workings of the school's operation than the average student would ever know. But the main thing he wanted to know more about was the Outpost. That concept intrigued him.

Milling around after the meeting, Kaiden found Ciera and tried to hit her up for more information. But it seemed like she, along with everyone else, was in a big hurry to get out of there. Board members disappeared quickly. He had to run after Ciera to catch up with her.

"Hey Ciera, wow, so that's how you run the Academy is it?".

"Yeah, me all by my lonesome" Ciera kidded.

"From what I see in you, I believe you could do it" Kaiden said in an obvious attempt to flatter her.

"Why thank you Kaiden, I'll make sure to bump my ego up a notch with that one".

"I read in the handout... wow; I didn't know that you're also the Cadet's company supply manager on top of being senior class rep".

"Yeah, I like to sit up front" she said.

"Why haven't I seen you in uniform? Kaiden asked".

"I don't know Kaiden. Why haven't you? Got a thing for woman in uniform?" she said raising her eyebrows. "No, you're right, I don't wear it much, they don't require me to and besides I don't think I look good in it".

"Ciera, you've got to be kidding, you'd look good wrapped in a just a bed sheet. Well maybe if it was my bed sheet" he said with as much of a seductive voice as he could muster.

She raised her eyebrows "Yeah right, that's because all you'd be thinking about was how naked I was underneath".

Kaiden combined his smile with a laugh. "Hey you know Allen McKinney?".

"Kaiden remember? I know everyone. Why? Do you want to meet him?".

"Now I believe you, you do know everyone. Yeah, I'd like to meet him".

"Then come to the RL party tonight. That's 'Rio Linda' for you outsiders. The Seekers are putting it on in conjunction with Cluster House Kappa, everyone will be there. It'll be kick ass. That's where everyone's going".

"OK, I'll be there, but where in Rio Linda?".

"Oh, don't worry, just walk towards it, you'll know". She turned and took off leaving him there to think about it.

14

Party Central

Kaiden ripped the map of Tenny Hill Academy out of the college brochure he had and took it with him just in case. Utilizing campus sidewalks, he made it to the soccer field without a wrong turn but there he asked someone for directions just to make sure.

"Hey where's the turn off for Rio Linda?" The guy pointed out a sign that directed you to a path leading into the woods on the left side of the field. It said "Rio Linda" with an arrow. Ciera was right, the path wasn't hard to find. He followed the path making his way through the woods until he could hear the beckoning din of distant drumming. It started low and then got louder as he walked. Eventually it sounded like a major event going on up ahead somewhere in the woods beneath Tenny Mountain. It took a while, a lot longer than he thought to walk the distance. The walk turned into a hike.

"I can't believe that students complain about the walk to the range, this is even more of a bitch!" Kaiden thought to himself.

Rio Linda was located off the beaten path and well into the forest on the southeast side of the mountain. It was positively "off campus". The seekers who lived here always ended any discussion about it with "Yeah, well you get used to it".

Kaiden followed the worn path until he came to an intersection with two other trails. More signs were there to designate direction. One arrow pointed left saying "Tenny Mountain", another to the right that said "Farmhouse". The one pointing straight ahead said "Village A and B".

"Well, Ok, next stop Rio Linda" Kaiden said out loud and he took the path towards the farmhouse. A few steps farther and the path dipped into a heavily wooded forest that cut out most of the available moonlight. It would have been a little scary if it weren't for some party goers that he saw walking ahead of him and a few behind him on the same path. Kaiden hadn't the foresight to bring a flashlight, but he could see the fluttering beams of other people's flashlights up ahead.

As he got closer the drumbeat grew louder. Ciera's face and her comment "Don't worry, you'll find it" made him smile. He picked his way through the woods with rocks and tree roots continually tripping him up. Eventually he caught up with the people ahead of him who had a flashlight. "How in the hell am I going to make it back out of here without one" was the thought going through his head.

His group came across another intersection where they all stopped to read the sign. It said "Village B and Village F with an arrow pointing both left and right respectively. It also had "Club Gitmo" with an arrow pointing straight ahead. The drumbeat came from that way, so that's the way they went. After a short walk on a trail that wound its way through the trees the trail opened into a big meadow with the drumbeat reaching a crescendo as they entered the open space. In front of Kaiden, in the center of the meadow, was a large fire pit full of lively flames emanating from a big pile of wood at its core. It was bigger than any bonfire that Kaiden had ever seen. The pit had a knee-high rock wall surrounding an eight-foot flame that blazed away inside the protective perimeter. Flames from the fire threw dancing light across the meadow accenting the trees at its edge with intermittent shadows that fluttered in cadence with the wisps of yellow flame. At the far end of the meadow was a rather large old-looking house with a really nice looking covered wooden porch that seemed to wrap all the way around it. Between it all a multitude of people filled up the meadow and meandered around like it was an outdoor Woodstock concert. Some centered their attention toward the fire pit where off to the side a group of people sat or stood in a circle. About eight of them held a drum of one type or another in their arms or between their legs. The rhythm that emerged from their bongos, congas, and the djembe, was an orgy of sounds reminiscent of an African native beat that reverberated in a repeating cadence. The sound was totally pure, amplified only by the number of instruments present. It was catchy and the partiers around them moved to the pulse of the music.

"Wow it's Woodstock all over again" Kaiden said out loud.

It sure looked like it. Off to the side there were tables with kegs of beer out of which people were filling their Solo cups. Occasionally you could smell the unmistakable scent of marijuana and burning CBD oil that punctuated the air between the smoky wood and the delicious smell of food cooking on a grill. Kaiden selected a path through the crowd and scanned the many faces for someone he knew. Independent circles of girls and guys had formed near the fire pit with people frolicking around dancing to the beat of the music. Some couples were hand in hand, some just stood on the side watching. Passing them he smiled at a large group of girls who danced with each other making provocative movements that attracted onlookers by design. The guys formed their own little mosh pit right next to them with each one trying to butt the other out of its center without spilling the beer in their hands. Some contenders were successful in maintaining their position and valiantly fought off an adversary but never were any of them able to succeed in keeping from spilling their beer.

Eventually Kaiden made his way through the crowd and up to the front porch of the farmhouse. He climbed the wooden front steps onto its wide wooden deck happy to have made it through the crowd to his destination. A look back over the throng of people and the noise confirmed that this was the largest outdoor party he'd ever been to. A glance through the front door of the old house told him he wasn't going in there. People were standing wall to wall, and it was obvious that he would have needed those mosh pit skills to make it through. He opted for a left turn on the spacious less crowded side of the porch that wrapped around the exterior of the house. Old antique chairs, swinging rockers and wooden stools lined the porch wall much to the delight of the patrons who put them to good use. In places the chairs were pulled into circles that seated a group of people engaged in chit chat.

"So, this is the famous 'Club Gitmo'" Kaiden said.

A lot of things in RL were named after or had some connection with the late great Rush Limbaugh. After he died and ever since his show was forced off the air by the Truth and Fairness Act, he had become something of an icon.

Gitmo was the only hard top standing structure in RL, not counting the privies between each village and the community shower. The house was an old two-story farmhouse with "country" written all over it. Natural weathering made it look old, more so because it was built during the depression in 1928 rather than because of its need of a new coat of paint. Students didn't have to worry about beating up on the place; it looked like they had been doing a good job of that for years. But it was far from a dump, quite the contrary. It was just worn, well used, and well lived in. Actually, it was constructed rather well with good craftsmanship. Caretakers had done it justice and taken good care of the place over the years. Especially with the wrap around porch, that as well as the entire house had a new roof and the porch floor looked like it had recently been rebuilt. It felt solid and sturdy. Hell, it had to be to hold the weight of this crowd. It truly looked like a great place to hang out.

Club Gitmo was the old homestead of the Daugherty family who originally donated the home and the property to the school and started this whole venture going back many years ago. Now it was used as a sanctuary by all the seekers and served as a cafeteria, a meeting hall, restaurant & lounge, library, study hall and refuge during really bad weather. But tonight... it was used for what it was most famous for- party central!

On the far side of the long porch, over and around groups of people, Kaiden saw the first person he recognized... Ciera Lowman. She was talking with two other guys dressed in Cadet uniforms, one of whom Kaiden recognized as Ciera's boyfriend Nick Oberman. Kaiden started to thread his way through the crowd over to where she stood but by the time he got there, Ciera and the two guys were gone. Looking deeper into the crowd, he saw the trio walking off the porch in the back and down a long set of wooden stairs. He followed.

Ciera and her companions walked around to the back of Club Gitmo where there were a lot of men and women in uniforms milling around near a rear entrance. Kaiden assumed it was the basement entrance because the concrete stairwell led down to a door leading to a lower level underneath the home. The sign above the door ended the mystery; it said "Welcome, You Are Entering The Trench Underground".

Ciera and her escorts walked up to the two Cadets who were what "guarding" the entrance? They had on the full Cadet uniform, complete with an arm band insignia that had the big letters 'CS' (Cadet Security) written on it. Kaiden instantly took note of the Beretta side arm holstered on the guy's hip in plain sight. Ciera walked up to one of them and said "hi". She touched the guy on the elbow and smiled making a passing comment like she knew him. He let them in ahead of everyone else and Ciera along with her two companions walked down the concrete steps. Kaiden got there just after and looked down into the stairwell just as they disappeared through the basement door. Cadets had formed a line and were filing past security one at a time. Kaiden stood out because he was the only one out of uniform. He tried to walk right in and follow Ciera but one of the security dudes put his hand out and stopped him. The guard said sternly "Sorry guy, this is a private meeting for Cadets only".

"Oh, I didn't know" Kaiden said and backed off moving to the side. He tried to think of how else he might be able to get in. "Maybe there's another entrance" he thought when suddenly a male voice behind him called out his name.

"Kaiden Alvin Sawyer".

He turned around and saw a man in civilian clothes standing there.

Kaiden pointed to him and was somehow able to pull the guy's name out of memory. "Mr. Allen McKinney" Kaiden said. If he hadn't just seen him and heard his speech tonight at the board meeting, he certainly would never have known his name.

"You got it" McKinney said. "I saw you at the meeting tonight".

"Yes sir, I saw you too. I was hoping to meet you afterward, but I guess everyone was in a hurry to get out of there".

Mr. McKinney waved his hands to each side and with a smile looked around and said "Well I guess they had a party to go to!".

Kaiden smiled along with him "Yeah what a party. I've never been to one like this before but there are a lot of things I'm doing now that I've never done before".

Mr. McKinney nodded his head. "I see you're having trouble getting past security".

"Yeah..." Kaiden started to say.

"Well, it's a member's only meeting but I think I can help".

Mr. McKinney walked Kaiden back up to the head of the line and spoke to the same security guy who had just barred Kaiden from entering.

"Jim" McKinney said to him. "This is Kaiden Sawyer; he's the new freshman class rep. It's Ok, let him in for me would ya?".

Jim came to attention and gave Mr. McKinney a military style salute "Yes sir" he said. Then he turned to Kaiden "Sir I apologize, I didn't know, we must be careful who we let in. It's good to meet you" and held out his hand.

Kaiden shook it saying "Don't worry about it, I'm just getting used to being class rep myself".

They were allowed to pass and both he and McKinney walked down the concrete steps to the bottom of the stairwell. Kaiden turned to him and said "Mr. McKinney".

"Yes Kaiden".

"Ok. Ah let me ask you. You let me in, and thanks, but how do you know that I'm not the informant?".

"First of all, call me Allen or McKinney like everyone else does. And..." he glanced down and then back up looking him straight in the eye "I read your file". He paused, letting that sink in as they stared at each other. "...And in addition, I happen to know someone who has a lot of faith in you".

Kaiden looked back at him absorbing what he had said, slowly coming to the realization that somewhere out there... there was a file on him and that a certain someone was talking about him. The first point overshadowed the reference to Ciera and the fact that the two of them must have had a conversation about him.

"Oh" is all Kaiden mustered in response.

Allen gestured with his arm toward the basement door. "Shall we?".

They both walked through into the basement.

Stepping through the threshold of that basement door immediately sent you back in time, you could feel the change. The place smelled like you might imagine a musty farmhouse basement would smell with that damp musky odor, but it was mild, not pungent, so it was bearable. It lent to your first impression and added character to the place. The noise and voices of the party outside faded into the background and was replaced by the mumbling of people that gathered for this event. Kaiden looked around and smiled. The decor immediately caught his attention. The place had been turned into a World War I theme bar.

"We call the house above us 'Club Gitmo', but now we are in 'The Trenches' as they say. This is our community bar; we affectionately call it the 'Trench'" McKinney said. "You'll come to love this place".

The 'Trench' came complete with sandbag walls that made it look like you were entering a WWI trench. Upon entering the first room there were more sandbag dividers that separated the tables, and they also lined the entire interior wall. The ceiling was low throughout with dim lighting run off spools of old cloth covered wiring that was strung across the rafters. Over each booth the wire connected to one of those real old looking light fixtures with an exposed clear glass bulb. The whole thing looked as it might have in an underground WWI bunker complete with the dim yellow light that those bulbs gave off. Every so often, over speakers placed in strategic places, came the rumble of what sounded like a bomb going off in the distance. It seemed coincidental at first, but then obvious that the sound was somehow connected to the lighting because the light flickered when you heard the deep rumble of an explosion in the background. The only thing missing was the vibration and the dust floating down from the ceiling.

Somehow the whole scene set the tone for quite a cozy atmosphere. WWI (and World War II) memorabilia hung all over the place, lanterns, army helmets, boots. Old Garand style rifles were pinned to the walls. In one corner underneath a silk parachute pinned to the ceiling was a setup of a real looking antique M1917A1 Browning machine gun. The whole thing was set up in re-creation style depicting a scene of a British machine gun nest as it might have looked back in WWI. It had sandbags surrounding two very realistic looking soldiers dressed in the British combat uniform of the day. One guy had his hands on the trigger of the gun that was mounted on top of a tripod. The barrel of the gun pointed out from a dip in the sandbag wall and aimed out at the patrons in the room. It looked like the soldier was poised to shoot with the help of his realistic looking partner who lay prone next to him. With a determined look on the guy's face, he was pulling an old cloth ammo belt from an old steel ammo can and was in the process of feeding it into the machineguns' breach. You got the willies walking by it when for a moment that machine gun was pointed directly at you. You couldn't help but imagine it firing away.

For Kaiden it easily achieved the creator's desired effect; he looked at the gun and thought to himself "I'm dead". Besides that, the bar looked like a really cool place to party. Someone had done a great job of it. But that machine gun nest was a little over the top.

With only a few exceptions all the people in the room wore a uniform. The officers or members of rank wore their stylish dark blue slacks and light blue collared shirts which differentiated them from everyone else. Some wore the full dark blue Cadet "swat" team jumpsuit. All of them ushered in filling the room to capacity and stood around waiting for the event to start. Kaiden was dying to find out what this was all about. The basement was large enough to hold a hundred and twenty-five people comfortably but it seemed like there were about two hundred already in there. The two of them squeezed through the crowd and found a place to stand next to one of the thick steel posts that supported a massive beam that held up the upper floor. Everyone had to duck their heads a little to pass underneath it.

A countertop bar ran half the length of one of the basement walls right up to the wooden stairs that came down from above. It wasn't a "stocked" bar but stacked against the wall behind the bar was a large rack of glass beer mugs available to patrons. That invoked a classier image of the place with a far superior method of drinking beer over the alternative plastic cup. Tonight, they had a couple of kegs on tap and sold beer along with a limited menu of chips, wings, and microwave pizza. Additional edibles were brought in on an "as needed" and "as available" basis for special events such as this. Tonight, apple cider and pumpkin pie were the special of the evening. Waiters and waitresses were busy running drinks and food to the booths and the large wire spool tables that were set up in the center of the room. There were chairs all around and every seat in the house was occupied. The place quickly filled until even standing room was taken up. Congestion slowed the service down to a crawl, but it didn't matter, at that moment people weren't there for the food. The meeting was about to start.

Many of the Cadets recognized Mr. McKinney. They all said "Good evening, Sir" with a slight bow of their head when they saw him.

"Allen..." Kaiden said with hesitation since all the Cadets had just addressed him as "sir". "I was going to ask you about the outposts. Where are they? You didn't give much information about the program at the board meeting".

"Kaiden, that's intentional, you see, details about the outposts are kept real hush hush. We don't want anyone except Cluster members who have proven themselves worthy to know much about them, especially their location. Even a Cluster graduate moving into the outpost program will be blindfolded, driven to one of the locations and dropped off. If he makes it as a productive member, he will then be given the privilege of knowing its location. Details about the setup, what goes on there, who's in charge or anything else is unknown until you earn the right to know it".

"Oh, you mean there's a 'file' on them too" Kaiden said sarcastically.

Alan smiled. "But actually, no there isn't a file on them. It wouldn't be prudent to leave a trail and let people who don't like what we're doing to compromise these projects in any way. They're too important".

"I see, I guess that's the part that surprises me the most, this secrecy thing. I mean no one knows where they are going? Wow man. And why are the Cadets calling you sir?".

"Well, out of respect. Let's just say that I held a position of high regard. All I can tell you is that it's something like the Peace Corps and let's leave it at that. But Kaiden, I will tell you that this is something very worthwhile. Have faith and please believe me when I tell you that what we are doing here is for the greater good. We're not the bad guys. We're just trying to ensure that Americans have the tools and knowledge to carry on into the next century and can better deal with whatever that brings us".

"I believe that already sir. I wouldn't be here if I thought otherwise".

"You're a good man Kaiden. I'm glad you're on board". Allen said it as he gave Kaiden a pat on the shoulder. "I don't give this out to too many people and therefore I must ask that you don't give it out either, but I want to give you my number. Give me your beeper".

Kaiden pulled his beeper off his belt and handed it to him. Allen added his beeper number to Kaiden's address book and gave it back. "My number is under the name 'Peace Corps'. If you ever need anything don't hesitate".

"I won't sir, thank you" Kaiden said.

Coming from the upper floor, three men dressed in officer's uniforms walked down the thick wooden staircase at the end of the bar. They stopped and stood on the last step which widened out sufficiently enough to form what they used as a small stage for live entertainment. It placed them only slightly higher than the rest of the room, but it was enough. When people recognized that one of them was Major Monett everyone in the room stood up and came to attention. The whole place quieted down and someone handed the Major a microphone.

"At ease Cadets" the Major said into the mike. Everyone at a table sat down. "Good evening". His voice could be heard clearly throughout the room via the same speaker system. The intermittent sound of bomb noises suddenly ceased.

"Good evening, Sir" the crowd responded.

"Thank you for coming, I wouldn't have called this meeting if it wasn't important. And don't worry; this won't take long. We got a party to go to right!

"Yeah!" everyone shouted back enthusiastically.

Certain things have come to light and a few recent events have been the catalyst for a slight change in priority.

First, I want to announce that the board has given their approval for this year's budget which includes a larger piece of the pie going to the Cadet program. You will be awarded a grant that will fund your operations at the requested level, so all is a "go" on project "Fortify". But please proceed with caution, try to be as invisible as possible, maintain a covert status and try to plug any leaks we might have. There are forces at work against you and they are making themselves known.

As you know I have had a "hands off" policy when it comes to the Cadet organization. I did advise you, but it was all your show, you dictated the direction and I applaud you for your insight, your patriotism, and your courage to build this organization into what it is today. You've done a great job and your leaders deserve recognition. So, let's hear it for one of them- Captain Allen McKinney. Where are you, Captain?

Clapping roared from every pair of hands in the room. Kaiden looked at him and said "Captain?" Allen looked back with a smile and walked away towards the front of the room. The crowd parted as he made his way up to the Major. When he got there Major Monett put one arm around his shoulders and gave him a good old boy hug. Kaiden was a little taken back by who the man he had just befriended really was.

"Captain McKinney has done an excellent job as the head of the Cadet Organization but will now be stepping down to head up the Outpost projects. They have gotten a little more complicated and need an overseer to keep things on the up and up. He'll be out of town a lot and will not be attending Cadet functions as he would like. Captain..." the Major handed him the mike.

"Thank you, Major Monett, and to men and women of the corps, it's been quite a ride. But yes, it's time to move on so I can accomplish something in other areas where I can achieve even greater results. We are still going to work together you and I, for you will become even more of an integral part of the outpost program than we originally thought. That's why I was chosen for this job, to be able to help with coordinating the two organizations. My knowledge of one will help the other and vice versa. Don't think I won't be back around now and again so stay on top of your game; I'll be checking on your progress and expecting some major improvements in your skill as a team. I'm very proud of what you have accomplished so far. Good luck in the coming year. Thank you".

The Major took back the microphone "Captain McKinney, ladies and gentlemen!" he said into it.

After a noisy applause the Major yelled "Cadets!" and the room quieted down... "I love how the word "Cadets" covers both men and women because you are all one and you are all part of a special team.

"Hoo ya!" the crowd yelled.

"You seniors are well aware of the resistance we've run into in keeping this organization afloat and like I told the board at the meeting this evening, I'm getting more and more flak from outsiders about the Cadet program. They are blaming me for your existence and I'm not even responsible for the program. The training you all are receiving has been controversial to say the least and they want to shut you down.

"Boo... boooo" deep voices surged from the crowd and the sentiment echoed off the basement walls.

Now wait, wait... I must inform you that this resistance includes a surprise response from an area where I didn't think we'd get any flack.

A well-known religious organization has weighed in and it's not good. You see these are good people who believe that preparing to defend yourself is like an act of war against your adversary".

"No way" someone in the crowd shouted.

McKinney continued "They don't want war so therefore by default they don't want to prepare to defend themselves. That's how they think and unfortunately, there are some who don't trust people who own guns or people like yourselves who train with them for worst case scenarios. They don't know you like I do and in their minds any 'preparation' leads to the possibility of a violent response against the evil that wants to take this all away from us. They say "violence would do irreversible harm to our movement" and I agree. It would give the opposition the ammunition they need to bolster public opinion against us.

I say thank God for those people! The ones battling with love in their hearts and who use 'peace' as their rudder. Negotiations for the future direction of this country cannot be obtained in a better way. Let us pray that they will win the hearts and minds of the people of this great country and take it back peacefully from those who wish to dominate under the guise of social equality. A moment of silence please. Let us pray".

The Major paused, bowed his head, and started to recite a prayer. Then he allowed a pause in which there was complete silence in that room for over a minute. The silence was broken when he finally said "Amen" Then he continued "The good people are right about one thing. If we stray from our principles, we will lose the support of the people we have sworn to protect. We will become outcasts, so we must never let that happen. Besides we are one and the same. What's our motto?

The crowd yelled (almost in unison) "Peacefully working to prepare for the future of America".

"Damn right! That says it all. The only difference between us and those good people is that we will not just lie down and let someone take our liberty from us. Before it comes to that, we will fight!

"Damn right!", "All right!", "Yeah!" the crowd shouted between the whelping and the high fives that spread throughout.

The Major continued "There is no negotiation; this is not something we will allow to be taken from us on an assumption or a promise that if we'll be good boys and girls that someday they'll get around to giving our freedom back. No. We will strive to learn how to defend and keep our rights so help me God!".

The cheering was immediate. The crowd ate it up.

"For the reasons mentioned I have decided to take a more active role in your training. If I'm going to get blamed for it anyway, I might as well be in the thick of it. I'd like to announce that I have agreed to take the position of leader of this great organization. I will retain my rank as Major, and I am going to support you with all the resources at my disposal". The room came alive with cheers, but the Major stepped over it. "We're going to step up the training and work to a new level. I mean when it comes to the point that an organization sworn to uphold the Constitution of the United States of America is told to cease and desist, then IT'S TIME FOR ME TO GET MORE INVOLVED!" he yelled.

The crowd went nuts. There was strong applause and screams that clearly expressed their heart felt approval. "Woo...woo...woo" they shouted. The exuberance went on for a while until the Major again spoke over them.

"I have contacts that I would like to bring to the table that can help us achieve our goals. I can promise a step up in training that we are really excited about and I'm sure you will be too. I'll have access to new equipment that we will need to branch off into some more specialized training, one of which being our snipers' program. That's all I can say about that right now. But I'm here tonight to tell you how excited I am and to ask you to stick with me during the coming year. I'm going to ask a little more of you but I'm also going to promise you that you'll be a far better person and therefore a far better 'team' for your effort. It's all good, and someday you might really appreciate the things you learn at this academy, but to tell you the truth ladies and gentlemen, I hope you never have to use them. I pray to God that you never find out how good of a warrior you really are".

"Here, here!" someone shouted.

"There's one more thing on the agenda tonight. I have the honor of announcing Captain McKinney's successor. We have thought long and hard about this and have decided on one of many deserving individuals. All the ones considered have shown great skill in leadership so please if you're not chosen, do not take this as an insult. Your time will come. But we had to pick one... will Cadet Nick Oberman please come up".

Nick stood up from one of the tables amid his friends who stood up with him and were cheering and patting him on the back. That's when Kaiden saw Ciera sitting next to him; she stood up and expressed her approval with applause and had an ecstatic look of joy as he made his way up to the front. All the Cadets gave him a round of applause that followed him the whole way. When he stood next to Major Monett, he came to attention.

"Nick Oberman" the Major addressed him "Will you accept the promotion to Captain of the Cadet organization and devote yourself to the principles laid out in the Cadet charter?"

"Yes sir, ah... I do?" Everyone chuckled.

And will you act incessantly upon the responsibilities that go with the position of Captain and guide this organization forward with discipline and integrity?".

More seriously he said "Yes sir I will".

Captain Oberman saluted and then shook hands with the Major who then presented him with Captain's bars. The Major pinned it on his uniform- it was official. He turned and among the enthusiastic cheers from his friends he pumped his fist in the air a few times along with a big broad smile on his face. That generated more clapping and cheering especially from Ciera's table, all of them hooted and hollered at their new captain. Captain Oberman was given the microphone and he addressed the audience.

"I am honored to be your captain and look forward to the coming year because I know what we are capable of. All the indications show that if we train with serious intent, we can and will be able to make a difference in the safety of this nation. Together, this year! We will go out and make a difference!".

Acceptance from the crowd showed with the wave of applause that followed. It was obvious that Oberman already held a degree of respect among the Cadets. The Major took the microphone from him and dismissed him.

In his final remarks the Major said "Now we're ready for the coming year. Let's get our minds focused and our actions precise so that mistakes are minimized, and results are maximized. Let's show the nation that the only mistake being made here is any lingering doubt about the integrity of this organization and the adherence to American values. And a note to my adversaries; you have unleashed the wrath of Major Jaz Monett. And as my students know, you should never, ever, razz the Jaz!".

The Cadets loved him and poured out a standing ovation and cat calls that showered the Major with an endorsement of tonight's message and sealed the acceptance of the change in command.

15

The Militia Wants You!

The meeting broke up shortly after without any fanfare. Many blue uniforms left the bar and were replaced by more and more people wearing standard clothes who were now allowed in. All the tables were full, and the horde of thirsty patron's ran the waiters and waitresses ragged. Captain Oberman was sitting at a crowded table in the center of the room. His table was full of officers who held rank in the Cadet organization, among them now was Allen McKinney. They all stuck around and bought their new Captain beers while celebrating his promotion. That's when Kaiden walked up to the table. He stood in front of the man of honor who was in the middle of a discussion concerning Nick's possible first move as Captain.

"Captain Oberman Sir" Kaiden said successfully getting his attention.

"Kaiden hello. Yes, I heard your report at the board meeting tonight and I remembered you from the bus. I understand that you're our new freshman class rep".

"Yes Sir, I am. I was also at the meeting here tonight and I wanted to come over and congratulate you on your new promotion to Captain..." Kaiden raised the beer mug he held in his hand. The rest of the table became quiet and listened. Kaiden suddenly found himself at the center of attention giving an impromptu toast so he winged it and began "...I'm going to do what to some might feel is insignificant. It is a small gesture on my part. But I'm going to drink this beer in your honor Sir". Kaiden held it up and studied his mug of beer for a moment before looking back at the group. "I come from a place where I have learned that small is not necessarily insignificant. Not when one's words are genuine and true. For when someone puts attitude behind the words, the gesture becomes paramount. What I have learned about the Cadet organization makes me proud enough to join, it makes me proud that there are people like all of you..." he swung his mug around toward everyone sitting at the table "... and Captain Oberman here who has dedicated himself to protecting the very principles that this country stands for. I hope and I pray that somehow you and this organization can truly 'make a difference".

Kaiden nodded his head and paused for effect "...a toast to Captain Oberman".

"Here, here!" The cadets at the table chimed in and raised their glasses.

Kaiden took the beer in his hand and chugged it. He didn't stop for breath until he raised the bottom of the mug to the ceiling and poured the last of it down his throat. Right after; he swung the glass down and slammed it on the table in front of the Captain with a loud glass against wood "Crack!" putting significant emphasis behind the gesture.

Captain Oberman stood up and grabbed his beer in response and started chugging it just like Kaiden did. The rest of the men at the table jumped up and yelled "Yeah!" and started chugging their beers along with their Captain. The whole bar heard the distinctive "crack, smack, bam" as eight mugs slammed down against the table with zeal. Then they all laughed and high five'd each other as well as Kaiden.

Kaiden turned and happened to catch the attention of a waitress. He smiled at her and said "Darling were going to need another round here".

The Captain was impressed. Previously he had seen Kaiden as kind of a threat to his relationship with Ciera, it seemed like he was always flirting with her, and Ciera had recently started speaking very highly of him on more than one occasion. A little too high in his mind, it was inevitable that a little disdain dripped out along the edges when confronting Kaiden. But now, after that speech he was curious. Oberman pulled up a chair and said "Have a seat Kaiden". Ciera was sitting on the other side of him and Kaiden smiled with the thought that he had succeded at wiggling his way into her company. Now he could speak to her on her level.

"Hi Ciera, you look very nice tonight. Thanks for the invite I'm glad I came".

Captain Oberman took note of the fact that Ciera was the one who invited him and reacted subconsciously by putting his arm around Ciera. He hugged her with a big smile on his face as he stared at Kaiden. The subliminal message was clear; 'she's mine'.

"Thanks that's nice of you to say" Ciera said. "Yes… ah Kaiden by the way, how did you get into the Trenches tonight?".

"Allen and I, ah…" he looked over at Allen. "…I mean Captain McKinney" he said with a smile. "We met outside; he must have thought that I was an acceptable risk because he let me in".

"What do you mean 'acceptable risk'?" Captain Oberman asked.

"Well with all the scuttlebutt about an informant that I've been hearing about… you know it's starting to sound like a mystery movie complete with spies and all".

Captain Oberman responded with a laugh "Well we've always had a problem with negative publicity, but it might not necessarily be an informant who's spilling the beans, it could be just a negative reaction to our own advertisement about the school and the Cadets. You see, we don't hide the fact that we exist, not like other militias do. We even call ourselves "Glorious Boy Scouts" on the school website. That's part of the attraction to this Academy. The people who receive a degree here can go on to become officers in the armed forces or a private citizen group anywhere in the USA. They could start a Cadet type organization or work with an existing one, or they are well suited to simply work on community committees to help set up emergency plans for various scenarios. They'd be able to teach the finer points of running a military organization. But I do have to admit the media does seem to know a lot more of the details than we would like. I'm worried that the suspicion of an informant might cause a wave of distrust. That's not good for the organization. We need a strong sense of camaraderie".

"I can relate to that. I belonged to a group back home and it fell apart in the end due to mistrust and backstabbing" Kaiden said.

"Yes, we know..." Ciera said. Lowering her head, she raised her eyebrows and looked at him like Kaiden's mother did when she already knew who took the cookies from the cookie jar. "...and it wasn't the Checkers and Root Beer Club now, was it?".

"Ah, no. It wasn't. I see you've read my file" Kaiden countered.

Ciera cocked her head and raised her eyebrows showing a little surprise that he knew there was a file on him.

"Where are you from Kaiden?" Oberman asked.

"New York" he answered.

"And how's it going down there in the big city these days?".

"Not so good. I think it's falling apart, both literally and figuratively. It's so hard to do business these days, it's so stifled. I feel I'm worlds apart from it up here. This is all so different. It took me a while to feel it but now I know that this is where I want to be. I feel I belong here, and I want to be a part of it".

"Oh yeah, you mentioned that you were proud enough to join. Do you want to join the Cadets Kaiden?".

"Yes, I do, I decided that tonight".

Oberman abruptly stood up and addressed everyone at the table as well as anyone at the other tables who cared to listen. "Ladies and gentlemen, may I have your attention please? We were just talking about my first order of business as Captain of the Cadet Organization, and I just figured out what that will be". He turned to Kaiden and said "Follow me".

Kaiden looked at Ciera with a "what's up" look on his face but she just shrugged her shoulders. He fell in line behind Oberman who led him up to the same small stage where he had received his Captain's bars. On the way he grabbed the microphone that was still sitting on a stool and turned it on. With it he addressed all the patrons in the bar.

"Ladies and gentlemen, may I have your attention please. May I have your attention". When the bar quieted down, he continued. "For those of you who don't know, as of tonight I am now Captain Oberman of the Cadet Organization". Some of the crowd started to applaud but Nick cut them off.

"Thank you, but I'm not up here to seek recognition for myself. Tonight, I have the opportunity to accomplish my first order of business- the induction of a new member into the Cadet organization" he waved his arm in Kaiden's direction and said to the crowd. "Don't worry it won't take but a moment of your time. Whenever someone joins us it's a very special occasion and I only request that you witness this ceremony for the record.

You might think that a candidate up for admission to the Cadets is going to bore you by the applicant standing here repeating some kind of pledge that describes his duty to the organization. No, I assure you, it's quite the opposite. In a swearing-in ceremony such as this- WE, all the Cadets here tonight who represent all Cadets everywhere, are going to pledge our dedication to this candidate- Mr. Kaiden Sawyer. Everyone in uniform please rise". Oberman turned to Kaiden, who quickly came to attention. They looked each other in the eyes. At the same moment all the Cadets in the room stood up and came to attention. Oberman started to recite the Cadet Pledge and as he did, every Cadet in the place joined in and spoke the words along with him.

I, a soldier in the Cadet Organization do promise and solemnly swear to uphold your Constitutional rights and liberties as granted to you in the Bill of Rights and embodied in the Constitution of the United States of America. I will obey my commanders and pledge to strive for your survival as you do for mine. Never will I betray you or the principles by which we stand. Always, I will pledge to uphold your right to the fruits of this land and to your pursuit of happiness.

Guided by intelligent example I offer my service to you and to our countrymen and hold in reserve the force of arms to guarantee our right to freedom. To you, to God and to my Country, I pledge my life to this endeavor. I do this of my own free will, so help me God.

"Mr. Sawyer" Captain Oberman said "You are not required to repeat this oath at this time to become a member. You have never heard it before and haven't committed it to memory... yet. But after you join the Cadet organization you will. You will be required to state this oath and swear this oath to the next joining member and to all Americans each time you attend a swearing in ceremony. Whether you swear an allegiance to an organization is immaterial, we swear our allegiance to each other.

Kaiden Sawyer- will you say this oath and swear your allegiance to your fellow Cadet and the people of America and give every ounce of your being to uphold the God given rights of your fellow citizens?".

"Yes sir, I will".

Captain Oberman reached over to the flap on the pocket of his own shirt and unpinned the first-year pin that every Cadet receives at their initiation ceremony upon entrance into the organization. It was the same one that he had received when he joined the Cadets and became a private three long years ago. He took it off, reached over, and pinned it on Kaiden's shirt pocket then stood back and saluted.

Kaiden returned the salute and they both locked eyes for one highly significant moment. That ended with a sharp crisp snap of the hand off the brow. Then the Captain smacked him on the chest with a closed fist right on the pin.

"Kaiden Sawyer, you are now a Cadet serving in the New York State Cadet Organization. Remain at attention" he said to Kaiden and then spoke into the microphone "Just the Cadets from my table for this please so that we don't bore the patrons any more than we have too". With that all the Cadets at the Captain's table got up and walked over to where Kaiden was standing on the stage and formed a line in front of him.

Unknown to Kaiden at the time the first man in line who now stood in front of him was Lieutenant Chester Fairmond second in command of the New York Cadet corps. Previously he had just been introduced as Chester Fairmond. He stepped up to Kaiden, saluted and popped Kaiden on the pin with a closed fist just like the Captain had done. Next was the company supply Sergeant Carl Roughett, then platoon "C" First Lieutenant Earl McKafree, Cell Sergeant Manny Stern, Cell Sergeant Seal Hutchison, and Lieutenant Irene Stalouti of platoon "B" who was one of three female officers in the Company. Allen McKinney saluted him next. They all stepped in front of Kaiden, looked him in the eyes and repeated the same procedure with a salute and then a strike to the pin with various degrees of intensity.

Ciera was the last one on line. She took her place in front of him and with a calm relaxed demeanor along with that killer smile, stood there and looked into his eyes. They both repeated the salutation. Then she raised her arm and gently placed her palm on his chest. It covered the pin and lingered there for just a moment, a moment where Kaiden felt so much more than just the warmth of her hand. It reminded him of the bus when she placed her hand on his cheek after smacking him. It meant more to him than words could ever portray.

That little event was way too meaningful for Captain Oberman too; he noticed and scoured inside but smiled with the knowledge that Kaiden had just placed himself under his control. Now he was Kaiden's Captain and that made him feel like he held an edge over his competition. Mission accomplished.

Kaiden was invited to sit at the captain's table. It was an honor that no Cadet would have refused. A beer appeared in front of him and for the next half hour he partied with his newfound brothers and sisters. The Oath, the ceremony and the beer eventually got to him. He contemplated this new beginning and couldn't help but glance over at Ciera and wish that things were different. Seeing her with Nick started feelings that weighed heavily on his mind; his life had just become so much more serious with what he was getting into. A wave had been building inside him ever since he'd gotten to the school, it wasn't just tonight, but after talking with the other officers at the table, it came crashing down on him. After all, swearing your allegiance and offering your life to a just cause is something a hell of a lot more serious than just joining the boy scouts. It built to the point where he knew it was time to go. He couldn't stand watching Ciera and his Captain as a couple anymore. The pangs of jealousy showed themselves and created a restlessness inside. Then it came to him with sudden clarity...

Kaiden stood up, thanked his Captain, and shook his hand. He said goodnight to the other officers at the table, then he said goodnight to Ciera. There were so many more things he wanted to say to her, to ask her and to do with her. When he said "good night" he realized that in a way he was saying goodbye to her. Goodbye to a certain direction in which he envisioned the two of them going.

He was welcome at their table, and he could have stayed and partied with the upper echelon of the Cadet organization all night. Anyone else would have said it was crazy to have given up a place at that table. But now he was a member of the Cadets and Nick was his Captain. Yes, things sure had changed.

Up to this point he fantasized way too much about Ciera playing a major part in his life. He was determined to try his best to take the relationship to the next level. Never had he wanted to impress a woman as much as he had with her. And never had he concerned himself so much with the boyfriends of a women he was after. Boyfriends were immaterial, they were irrelevant. In the past, if he did his job right, his woman would take care of that problem for him. Now, the pledge he had just made while staring Nick in the eyes on that stage became a barrier. A barrier to what he truly desired. When he said goodbye to her, he felt it. It was like that technique in the movies where the camera focuses on someone and then the distance between starts to elongate with a turn of the lens. He looked at her and she faded off into the distance out of reach.

Kaiden walked out of the Trenches, this time using the wooden stairs that took him up to the first floor and into the center of Club

Gitmo. The air changed as he walked into the hallway leaving the musky basement behind. There was no other way to move through the crowd he encountered except to pardon and excuse himself while weaving between all the people who were packed into the rooms and hallways. Now he knew why the support beams in the "Underground Trench" ceiling were so massive. They had to be to support the tremendous weight of a packed house. The adjacent room on the right was a library, on the left a large room had been turned into an office. The hallway opened into the living room that blended into a kitchen with a cafeteria style serving counter between. People were everywhere, most with food and drink in hand. All of them were chattering and laughing creating a crescendo of voices. Kaiden didn't recognize any of them.

Making his way back out onto the front porch he was relieved again by a slight breeze that blew fresh air across his face. The noise of the party outside in the meadow returned with the sound of the rhythmic drum beat still coming from the center of the field. Once again it intruded as a dominant factor, the beat had changed but it came across with no less intensity than before. The drummers themselves had also changed. Those who got tired gave up their instrument to others who carried on the anthem. Kaiden was walking to the porch steps wondering how he was going to get back to the dorm without a flashlight when a voice broke above his own thoughts.

"Kaiden! Kaiden Sawyer! Over here!".

Kaiden looked over at where the voice was coming from and just barely saw his roommate in between the flow of people. He was sitting on one of the porch swing chairs with Candy at his side. She was clutching his arm with one bare leg thrown over his lap. Kenny was wearing his Cadet uniform and sat amongst a circle of friends who wore the same. He was desperately trying to get Kaiden's attention without getting up and frantically waved at him to come over. Kaiden smiled, threaded his way through the crowd and walked over.

"Hey everybody this is Kaiden Sawyer my long-lost roommate. I haven't seen him much since the semester started. Hey Buddy! How's it going?" Kaiden walked over and they butted fists in greeting.

"Hey Kenny. This is great, I was hoping I'd see someone I knew at this party. Hi Candy" Kaiden said nodding his head in her direction.

"Hi Kaiden" she replied.

"Dude I would have told you about it but it's so rare that we see each other these days, you're a busy man. You must be outa there by what five thirty every morning. Hey someone get this man a beer".

"Yeah, I have Tai Chi practice and then an eight o'clock. It keeps me going alright".

Someone in Kenny's circle of friends said "Oh you take Tai Chi with the Major? I heard about it, I always wanted to go to that but it's way too early man".

"Kaiden this is Shane" Kenny said. They shook hands. "That's Ivan. We call this man here 'Pico' for some reason".

They all laughed, one of them punched Pico's arm in jest.

"This is Shelly and Ricky; they're a couple so don't hit on Shelly Ok Kaiden".

Again, there was laughter.

...and that's Gore and Brute and ...oh man there's some more over there" Kenny waved his hand at some other friends that were standing on the other side of the porch.

"Hey Kaiden, glad to meet you" Brute reached over and shook Kaiden's hand.

"...and this, this is Shiloh". Kenny reached over Candy and smacked the woman sitting on the other side of them on her leg. You have my permission to hit on her".

"Hey!" Shiloh's arm flung out smacking Kenny on the arm before he could pull it back.

"Hi Kaiden" Shiloh said. "Don't mind him he's in rare form tonight".

"Shiloh" Kaiden repeated. "I love your name".

"Oh thanks. Wow no one has ever 'loved' my name before".

"Yeah, everyone just loves you, Shiloh! One of the onlookers yelled". The others started laughing.

"Was that bad? Do I hit him?" Shiloh said looking at Candy and Kenny for help. "Hey someone hit him for me!" she yelled faking being mad.

"Dude! You joined the Cadets!" Kenny yelled. He pushed Candy's leg off him and stood up staring in amazement at the pin on Kaiden's shirt pocket. "I can't believe it". He raised both hands in a double high five gesture with a big, surprised look on his face. They smacked hands and you could see the newfound sense of pride in Kenny's manner as he absorbed it and studied the pin with curiosity. "How did you join and how the hell did you get that pin? We haven't had a swearing in ceremony yet for new recruits?"

"Oh, I… I was just sworn in tonight by Captain Oberman…" Kaiden started to explain.

"What! No way man!" Kenny was incredulous. You were at the meeting tonight?

"Yeah, I was…".

"I was there I didn't see you man; I wish I knew. How'd you get in?" Kenny asked.

"Allen McKinney allowed me…".

"Holy shit! You know Captain McKinney? Dude, you have been busy!" Kenny reached out for another high five with a big smile on his face that showed a newfound respect for his unsung roommate.

"But there's been no swearing in ceremony. How did you join up?" Kenny asked.

"It was kind of an impromptu thing to say the least. Captain Oberman swore me in…".

"You gotta be shittin me man. I don't believe you; Captain Oberman swore you in!" Kenny shouted, which got the attention of more blue uniforms. They started a circle around him with Kaiden at the center of the conversation.

"Yeah, he was just promoted tonight" someone in the circle said to the other. "I was there I saw it".

"But how in hell did you manage to get sworn in?" Kenny asked Kaiden.

"Well... after the meeting ended, I went over to congratulate our new Captain and he asked me if I wanted to join. I told him I did, and he dragged me up on stage and swore me in right then and there. It was an awesome experience".

Kenny looked at him almost not believing it. His focus on the story was contagious. The same Cadet next to him said "Yeah- every uniform in the Trenches stood up and swore him in, then all of 'em at the Captain's table lined up and sealed his pin".

"No shit. But how did you get the pin?" Kenny asked.

"Captain Oberman gave it to me".

The same Cadet spoke up again "Man you should have seen it; the Captain gave him the pin right off his own uniform".

"You mean to tell me... that is Captain Oberman's pin?" Kenny's hand went to the pin on Kaiden's shirt, and he looked at it for just a second before looking around at his buddies almost as if asking for more confirmation.

"Yeah Lieutenant Fairmond, McKinney and Lieutenant Stalouti, all of them, they sanctioned him man, even Sergeant Hutchison and Ciera too".

"Man how in hell did you swing that bro? You know Ciera! You've definitely been holding out on me man".

"It just kinda happened" Kaiden said.

Seeking to be included, Candy and Shiloh wiggled their way into the circle of Cadets surrounding Kaiden and pushed a cold unopened can of beer into Kenny's hands. Kenny took the beer, popped the tab and handed it to his roommate. With a major slap on the back and a manly hug Kenny teased him "I love this guy" he said. "You told me you were class rep; but not about all your connections dude".

Kaiden found himself surrounded by blue uniforms; they all looked at him with expectation.

Someone asked him "If you're class rep then you were at the board meeting tonight, weren't you?".

"Yes, I was there" Kaiden said.

"What's goin on, any news?".

"Yeah, there is. We were briefed on the financial situation of the Academy, and I'm not allowed to mention details, but I can tell you that the school's doing Ok monetarily. Surprisingly well actually, we're in the black and in these times, I thought I'd be hearing about shortfalls in that department. The economy is the number one concern. It's causing a lot of problems in other areas; things are really getting tight out there. They informed us that we have a situation developing with supply; it's getting difficult to obtain certain items and some of them are common food stuff. They're getting hard to find and even if we can find them, transporting them is hard to stomach due to the cost. Recent events have added the cost of "security" onto the price tag. We've all heard about the increase in theft and truck hijackings. There was a double murder just last week in Nyack where a double duce convoy was hit; both drivers were killed execution style. We're kicking around the feasibility of sending out Cadet Escorts to accompany shipments to and from the school".

"Wow, bad news good news" a Cadet spoke out from the other side of the circle. "On one hand we got work, on the other- It's getting a whole lot more dangerous. How on earth can things be getting scarce here in America; we don't run out of shit man, what the hell's happening out there?".

"Our system is failing" another Cadet offered.

"Oh no, here we go again" the Cadet next to him complained.

But the Cadet kept talking "Make no mistake; be aware that our system is only as good as the people running it. The politicians we've elected haven't had the integrity to run the country the way our forefathers intended. They had the foresight to create this country... gambling that future leaders would themselves be guided by a moral compass held true by the teachings of Jesus. You must know the will of God and live within the guidelines of his expectations. When you lose that connection, you lose the bonds that hold you to those ideals...".

"Also..." Kaiden broke in. "Before you get going on a religious rant and before I forget. Major Monett has invested in new equipment at the range for you guy's, I mean 'us' guys" Kaiden corrected with a smile. He held up his beer gesturing a toast to his new comrades.

They laughed and picked up on the toast idea and held their beers up yelling "Hoo ya".

"I don't know what the 'new equipment' is, but…" Kaiden said.

"I know one thing" Kenny interrupted "I just shot the Winchester SX-AR .308 yesterday. They got a bunch of them in. It's quite a 'hunting rifle' he said with a wink putting emphasis on hunting. "I love it. It's almost shooting 1" moa's out at two hundred yards!".

"You mean you are almost shooting one moa's" Gore kidded. Everyone laughed.

"Hey! You don't even know what MOA stands for you SOB so shut up". Kenny threw a kick at Gore which Gore blocked. They stood there for a moment in a mock boxing stance pretending they were about to go at it, then Kenny relaxed and said "No, real deal man, it's got this scope, this Zeiss scope with a "Rapid Z" reticule. The reticule's got cross hairs at ranges from 100 to 1000 yards!" Kenny was almost whispering it like it was top secret information. "Just range your target and then line up the correct cross hair and BANG! You're in there. It's got windage marks to each side for correction and man it makes it so easy without having to lug around calculators to chomp through formulas or any of that shit. No batteries, that's a key advantage unless you're shooting at night and using the illuminated reticule of course. The rifle's got Mossy Oak camouflage, perfect for a sniper. It is a little heavy though, but that keeps the kick down to reasonable and allows you to stay on target better. I love it man. Semi-automatic is better than bolt action".

"Wow, I'd like to take it out to the long-distance range and test it at 800" said one of his friends.

"You will. They want everyone in the sniper program to qualify on it, Gore that means you. I heard that straight from Sergeant Roughett".

"Yeah, I gotta see that, don't normally use a semi as a sniper weapon. That's where you'll see the flaws".

That was the first time Kaiden had heard of the existence of a long-distance range and the first mention of sniper training too. He got plugged into all sorts of new information tonight just by listening in to some intriguing conversations that followed throughout the rest of the evening. Kaiden got a better grip on why these people were operating at such high intensity. They were extremely well informed about politics and what was happening all across America. The topic always seemed to get back to that. They all had the sense that something was going to break sooner rather than later. They blamed it on pressure from the progressive socialist party, their members were ratcheting up to the point where everyone felt that it was a direct threat to America's grip on the Constitution itself. They labeled the current situation as "Serious". Most everyone felt strongly about the possibility of having to put the material taught here at THA to use if or when the shit hit the fan. In their minds they were gearing up and digging in somewhere around A3 (Alert status 3) with a few of them already at A2, all of them were seriously contemplating an A1 scenario as a real possibility.

Kaiden was dying to know so he threw out a question to Kenny. "Why are you here at Tenny Hill instead of in the military?".

"Because I wanted to go to college..." Kenny said. "And also, I believe that nowadays the enemy is within. Our destruction is occurring from within like what happened with the Roman Empire. If I joined the military, I'd get sent overseas to the Iranian Russian conflict and I don't want that. I feel that I can protect myself and my family, either present or future, with a more rounded education that includes some kind of survival training mixed in with some military style training. This is a perfect place to get both of 'em for the same price".

Another Cadet spoke up "Yeah, I agree; the threat we're facing is internal. The police and even the military are too busy to help us. They aren't going to be there when we need them. I want to be right here man!".

"Yeah, I agree" Gore cut in. "Becoming a Cadet was a way for me to participate in playing Boy Scout without the prospect of signing up for a six-year stint overseas. It's not that I don't want to go and fight;

I just feel that the fight is here. This survival shit? Well, I don't know. It just kinda goes along with it. I'm here more for getting a degree and shootin guns man".

"Boy's" Kenny jumped in with a big smile "I'm here for one reason-the pussy!" he said it and then turned to Candy standing next to him and wrapped his arms around her shoulders with a big broad grin. He picked her up with a bear hug and spun her around making her scream. She didn't seem to mind the sexist comment and just laughed along with him. She even allowed him to kiss her dramatically on the lips after he put her down. But then she turned to the group and got him back.

"Boy's, I just came to college for the dick! 'Dick head' that is" she said pointing her thumb in Kenny's direction.

"OHHHHHH!" the guys all screamed as if they just saw Kenny get kicked in the balls. Everyone laughed at the two of them. Kenny held his heart like he was just stabbed there and pretended to faint while falling backwards into Kaiden's arms. Luckily Kaiden caught him before he fell on the floor.

Kenny popped back up, turned around and looked Kaiden in the eyes. In a serious tone he said "You see that? I trust you man". Then he pounded his fist onto the pin on Kaiden's chest saying "Congratulations, you're one of us!". They slapped each other's hand and bumped arms in salute.

The conversation moved on to lighter subjects and Kaiden was eventually able to work his way into a one-on-one conversation with Shiloh. It was hard to get her alone; she stayed close to Candy mirroring her movements all night long like two stuck slices of cheese. Kaiden almost got the impression that something was going on between the two of them. But he pushed that thought out of his mind. It only took a few minutes of conversation to decide that he liked her. Somehow the conversation got onto the topic of horses which Kaiden knew nothing about. Kenny and Candy disappeared, probably on purpose, and left the two of them standing there by one of the farmhouse windows.

"I'm a senior living in RL" Shiloh told him. She was a true southern bell from Greenville Mississippi. She had thin long black hair with bangs cut straight across her forehead just above her eyebrows. It was naturally straight, and she was the envy of all women lugging around a straightening iron. Of course, she was the one who complained and wished she had naturally curly hair. She was cute, especially with her girlish manner that came out here and there when she talked. It was her giddy kind of personality accompanied by a bright smile that Kaiden liked. Shiloh was just a bit on the smaller side of the coin but not frail. "Light boned" would be a better way to describe her. Although her physique made her a little light in the chest department Kaiden never considered it a deciding factor. That kind of thing didn't matter to him like it did with some guys, besides, she fit into those blue jean shorts and blouse real nice! Kaiden was impressed.

To hear her talk with a southern drawl was heaven to a hard-core city boy. Shiloh had the sweetest accent. He found out that both she and Candy lived in the same Village in RL; Village "E". She lived in the Hogan right next to Candy's. Individual Hogan's were occupied by either all male or all female occupants, but the villages were a mixture of both male and female. This way they avoided the panty raids and the silliness that occurs when the sexes are separated.

"What do you do if you want to be alone out there with a special someone?" Kaiden asked her.

"Oh, we can tent if we want to".

"Tent?".

"Yes…" she said with a shy smile "…we set up a tent, there's a couple of good tent sites just off Mt. Tenny trail. That's the trail that you passed on the way in here, it heads up into the woods right next to the village... goes all the way up to the top of Mt. Tenny".

"Oh" Kaiden said with a smile. He liked the way she said "we".

Just like Kaiden did, Ciera walked out of the Trenches and into the crowd swarming around the inside of Club Gitmo. She had enough of the chatter at her table and gave an excuse about the bathroom. It enabled her to get up and walk around a bit. Now she was standing among the throng of people looking for something, or for someone. Occasionally, she saw a friend or an acquaintance and would wave and say "Hi" along with an added comment or two. But she moved on, eventually making it to the front door and then out onto the front porch. While wading through the crowd of people, every so often the crowd would part in such a way that for a short moment of time she happened to have a clear view across the porch. Over by the front living room window of the house she saw the person she was looking for; Kaiden Sawyer. It seemed to lift her spirits and she looked up and started off in that direction. Then she noticed that he wasn't alone, and it stopped her in her tracks. He was talking to a girl; it made her pause and switch gears. Disappointment showed in her demeanor.

Kaiden and Shiloh were both leaning up against the wall talking and laughing. Kaiden leaned in close to her as if they were a little more intimate than just two colleagues having a beer. By the smile on his face, it looked like he was really enjoying her company. She found herself staring and wishing that she was the one Kaiden was talking to, but she didn't want to bust in on him. After all, who was she to interfere? "I got my own thing going right?" she thought.

A twinge of jealousy was something Ciera didn't expect. "Where the hell did that come from?" she thought, and then "Well after all he's a good-looking guy". She couldn't help but feel an attraction toward him "But I can't let that happen" she told herself. "I'm not in a position to offer him any more support than I already have". The surprise was that she was standing there wishing she could. Her relationship with Nick, "Oh Captain now", wasn't going in the direction she wanted. It hadn't been for quite some time. That's why Kaiden was a breath of fresh air when he kissed her by the oak tree the other day. It seemed so innocent and sincere. "And he's so damn cute!" There was hope, but now that's gone. The disappointment showed on her face.

During a pause in their conversation, Kaiden looked up and out into the throng of people crowding the porch. For a split second he saw the silhouette of a woman in the crowd that looked exactly like Ciera.

She was looking right at him. The crowd moved and people walked in front of her obscuring the view for just a moment. When they passed and he could once again see clearly, there was no one standing in the spot where he thought he saw her. Shiloh was talking to him saying something about her old high school, but Kaiden didn't hear a word; he was preoccupied with thoughts of Ciera. When his mind came back on track, he realized that he didn't know what Shiloh had been saying.

"Ah… Shiloh" he broke in.

"Yeah, what is it?" She followed his gaze and looked out into the crowd in the same direction where he had been staring.

"Oh nothing, I just thought I saw someone. Hey, do you think we could get out of here? Could you show me you're Village? I've never been to a Village before. What's that thing called you stay in, a hoagie?

"No, a Hogan".

"That's it. I've never seen one".

She looked at him with a suspicious glare "Sure, you're Hogan or mine huh? I've heard that one before" Shiloh said lowering her eyebrows and putting a mock frown on her face.

Kaiden grabbed her hand, held it tenderly and looked into her eyes. He said in a serious way "Shiloh, believe me when I tell you that you're safer with me around than without me. I would never disrespect you. You ever heard of the cliché 'I would fight and die for you'?

"Yeah. Oh, you're so sweet" she replied.

"Well, no, it's not like that with me".

"What?".

"It's more like; I would fight and make the other guy die for you".

"Oh". She cocked her head and grinned almost laughing in her beer which she tried to sip to stop herself. It was a morbid thought.

"No, what I mean is that I really like you Shiloh and yes, I would love to jump your bones but that's not why I'd like you to show me around. Honestly, I haven't seen a Village before, and I'm really interested in you and how you live".

She liked his style, but more importantly she believed that he meant what he said. It only took a second to come to a decision. "Ok, let's go, I'm in Village "E", I'll give you the tour".

Everyone had a flashlight except Kaiden. Shiloh lent him hers and put him in charge of getting them there without stumbling over roots and rocks. He took her hand and led the way down the trail. There were a few people ahead and a couple walking behind them on the same trail. They all had a single beam of light that flickered and danced along as they walked. Sometimes the beam of light shot out way ahead then it snapped back to illuminate the trail around their feet. All the flashlights followed that same pattern the whole way out.

They passed the biffy just past the wood pile on the right of the trail. At least that's what Shiloh called it. "Everyone around here calls the bathroom a "biffy" she explained. "Don't ask me why". The "biffy" in RL was a communal outhouse with four toilets, four sinks and the luxury of hot and cold running water. Kaiden took the opportunity to stop and use the toilet and was surprised when Shiloh followed him in and used the stall right next to his. That was weird. "I've never used a bathroom alongside a woman before" he thought. Yet for Shiloh it was just "the way it is".

The biffy was located just off the main trail right before a path that broke off leading to Village E. A carved wooden sign marked the entrance if you could call it an entrance. They took that path and after a short hike they walked into a semi cleared area with a fire pit in the center. The spot was loosely encircled by eight "Hogan" shelters that were positioned randomly around this center common area. Yes, the Hogan's looked just like a covered wagon alright, only they were a lot larger than the old west version and these Hogan's were sitting on the ground with no wheels attached to them.

On one side of the common area there was a long metal trough sink standing on legs off to the side. It had running water with multiple spigots and was used for brushing teeth and cleaning up. Towards the center of the common area was a fire pit where a few people were hanging out around a lively campfire. The smell of burning wood made it all seem so earthy. On the outside of the rocks that encircled the fire there were various items you could sit on. One was a large log, and there were two big boulders and a few smaller ones that someone had placed in the right spot for sitting. Two folding chairs were set up where there was room and that completed the set of outdoor furniture. Now, a group of people sat and stood around the fire, all of them engrossed in conversation with a few just sitting there staring at the flames. You could hear the chit chat accompanied by an occasional loud voice and then laughter.

Shiloh led Kaiden up to them and greeted her friends. She introduced Kaiden to all the ones she knew but had to ask for introductions from a few new faces. They both stayed for a while and contributed to the light-hearted chit chat but then Shiloh pulled Kaiden by the hand and said "Common, I'll show you my Hogan".

Smaller paths of various lengths broke off from the common area and led up to the door of each of the surrounding Hogan's. Shiloh chose a path that led away from the common area and traveled up a slight incline before leading to the front door of her Hogan a short distance away. This one was tucked into the woods so that you could barely see it. Supposedly there were eight Hogan's in village E but only five of them were plainly visible from the common area. All of them were spaced appropriately enough apart and tucked into the forest so that when living out here you really got a sense that you were living in seclusion.

Shiloh led Kaiden to the front door of her Hogan and climbed up three wooden steps that led to the raised wooden deck of her home. Thick waterproof canvas covered the roof and sides supported by arched wooden ribs that made up the skeletal frame. The frame was attached to a three-foot-high wooden wall that enclosed the platform on the left, right and rear side. Its front flaps rolled up and were tied off to each side of the doorway. A screen covered the opening to inhibit the bugs and allow adequate ventilation. It was pulled over the opening even though bugs were not a big problem at this time of year. The back of the Hogan had canvas flaps that were tied shut. They too could be opened with a screen pulled down to help with bugs and ventilation. In fact, the canvas covering the Hogan could be rolled up on its frame on both sides and tied off creating the effect of having open windows. In the summer it was common to see them all open on those hot stagnant days where just a little more airflow made it a whole lot more comfortable. Shiloh parted the screen door and entered.

To Kaiden it looked like the old west. Inside the covered wagon was a sturdy wooden floor with four cots, one in each corner. Next to each one was a large trunk or in one case, a chest. In the center of the room was a small old Sears circa 1900 iron potbellied stove. It sat on a concrete pad with its stove pipe extending straight up through the ceiling. The age of the thing made the place look rustic. Obviously, that was the Hogan's source of heat. An adornment of pots and pans hanging on it made it evident that it was used for cooking too.

"Wow this is nice and cozy" Kaiden said. "I envisioned that you guys were living out of a little tent.

"No, a big tent" Shiloh smiled. "This one's mine" She patted the bed on the left. "It took a little getting used to, but now it's home sweet home and I wouldn't have it any other way".

"Oh yeah. How about in the wintertime? It must get really cold around here".

"Yeah, the weather's starting to remind me that we're getting to that time of year. We've already had a few chilly nights where we cranked up the stove; might even need it tonight. Yeah, it's a little tough during the winter. But this stove does a great job of keeping us warm. We winterize the place which just means that we plug and seal every crack against the cold air and with just a small fire or when we cook a meal this place gets nice and toasty. In fact, sometimes it gets too hot. It's kinda hard to regulate the temperature with the stove and the vents; you gotta work it just right".

"And you cook meals here too? Well, you sure have enough wood up at that wood pile" Kaiden said. "Somebody's been busy".

"Yeah, we go through a lot of firewood, seems like we're always working on that pile" Shiloh walked over to the stove. "If we run out of wood or are just too lazy to go get some, the stove has a propane backup burner. That's a little easier to use, and it's not so smoky, the tanks out back. It works pretty well. That makes it a little easier to regulate the temperature too. We try to keep it off though to save money. It's expensive to get it filled and a pain in the ass to switch out the tanks and haul it out here".

Kaiden sat down on Shiloh's bed and looked around. "I like it; I could live here. He tried to picture himself living in a Hogan. This would be drab man!".

"Drab? Oh, as in the opposite?".

"Yeah of course man this is 'revel'". ("Revel" was the latest word used to describe "cool".

"Oh, you'll get your chance" Shiloh said "You'll be livin out here whether you like it or not".

"Close those flaps please" Shiloh asked with a point to the front door of the Hogan. She stood in front of the stove and started the process of lighting it. Kaiden closed the flaps and then watched her fiddle with the stove. His eyes were drawn to her curvaceous figure as she stood there messing with it. He sat back on the bed and lay back against the pillow while he studied her. Her body held his attention, and her face was cute in a pleasing natural 'country' kinda way. Out here in the woods women didn't pay a whole lot of attention to makeup. Shiloh's long hair fell across her face when she looked down and then she'd look up and toss her head to the side to get it out of the way. She was so delightful when she allowed her feminine features to emerge out from behind those wisps of hair. It made him smile. She'd look at him and grin, triggering a warm feeling that soothed him. He couldn't help but feel at home here and just fell in love with Shiloh and the whole concept of Rio Linda. Yeah, he would have been ashamed to admit that it was that easy. He really liked her; she reminded him of Ciera. He thought about how different country girls are compared to city girls. In her own right she was just as attractive as any he'd ever seen. Somehow the girls who flaunt their stuff so blatantly with all the bare skin they could muster couldn't hold a candle to the one standing in front of him fully clothed. He couldn't figure out why. Was it the allure of not knowing, not seeing? Or was it just his macho 'love the one you're with' attitude showing through no matter what? No, it wasn't that. He shook his head; it was something a whole lot more. These days, everything seemed to mean a whole lot more.

Shiloh put a pot of water on the back burner. Kaiden did the same with his thoughts about Ciera. Ciera was out of reach and here right in front of him was someone who he felt was at least open to the prospect. He decided to find out. Kaiden got up and walked over to her.

She turned to him and said "Would you like some tea?".

He ignored her question, took her hand softly in his and pulled it until she turned and faced him. Another slight pull and their bodies came together. They touched. The first test; his other hand went to the small of her back and he pulled her into him. Her body melted into his with a discernable surrender. She pressed her hips into him until he could feel the warmth of her mound against his thigh. She leaned her head back and he looked into her eyes and lowered his lips to hers. Both their eyes closed, and they kissed tenderly. Shiloh kissed him back with a softness that offered warmth and a volume of information in return. He had his answer.

They drank hot tea on the front steps of her Hogan and talked way into the night. Kaiden met two of her Hogan mates when they returned from the festivities. They all spent some time talking outside before Kaiden had to break away and make the trek back to the dorm. Shiloh walked him down the trail just out beyond the edge of the village to make sure he got on the right path back to campus. There was another kiss like the one before that sent him away with a smile. He kept thinking about her, her smell, and the taste of her lips. He was happy, even giddy. He felt... in love? No. He knew it was just infatuation; maybe someday it would be love... "What the hell is this, I'm thinking about love?" he thought.

Alone and at two thirty in the morning, walking through the dark forest accentuated one's thoughts and amplified noises. It seemed like it was a lot darker on the way back even with the flashlight he borrowed from Shiloh. That was because the light ruined his night vision and turned the darkness even darker. At least this time he made his way out smoothly without stumbling around so much.

16

In The Groove

It was official. Kaiden was now a member of the New York State Cadet Militia. After the paperwork was taken care of, he was fitted with a uniform and picked up three different sets: standard blue dress and camouflage in both summer green and winter grey. He also purchased the coveted Cadets "Standard Issue Kit". The kit contained all the basic supplies that a Cadet would need for the various activities they would be participating in. It all came packed inside a backpack that would become one of his most important possessions.

Saturday morning rolled around and Kaiden participated in his first set of training exercises. Right up front was a crash course in the fine art of marching. Kaiden now blended in perfectly with his new uniform. For the first time he looked, marched, practiced and exercised as one with all the others. Then his superiors put him through the Academy's obstacle course to test him and see where he stood physically. It was all new to him and running it felt awkward. On his first attempt Kaiden timed in at 3.05min. That was just over the required three-minute time limit, so he failed which surprised him. "I thought I would do better than that" he told a classmate. "Hey, that's not bad Kaiden" the classmate said. "Only about three percent of new recruits ever pass it on the first try". That somewhat pacified his disappointment and after analyzing it more, he attributed his poor score to messing up on a few of the obstacles. He vowed to shave that score down to serious competition level and run with the best of them.

The Cadet organization was just shy of "Company" strength with six participating platoons totaling 249 men and women listed on this year's roster. Each platoon contained four squads consisting of eight members each plus a sergeant unless they were short a man, if so, the Sergeant became the eighth man. To designate themselves each squad chose an Indian tribal name as their call sign. There were many to choose from, but most took native New York Indian tribe names for their own. Cadet squads were known as the Shinnecock or the Poospatuck. Others had similar cool names like Munsee, Abenaki, Saponi, Onandaga, Mohawk, Algonquin and Cayuga. Once upon a time all of these except for the Algonquin's (they were a Canadian tribe) inhabited a section of New York State. For example, a platoon would be designated as the "First Poospatuck" or the Third Cayuga and so on. Kaiden was assigned to the second platoon and was in the Algonquin squad designated simply as the "Second Algonquin". The other names in his platoon were the Mohawk, Iroquois, and Seneca's. Although the "Iroquois" wasn't a tribe, it was a confederacy that encompassed many tribes, but it was still allowed. This gave them a sense of identity and made for interesting competitions and rivalries between the squads with each trying to outdo the other.

The complete list of active Company personnel was comprised of participating members working out of the local area as well. There were more Cadets listed as members, but they had either graduated or subsequently moved out of participating range. Some of those had started their own Cadet Organization in other parts of the U.S. and returned occasionally for special events or just a spontaneous visit to maintain contact. Every graduate was always considered a member and was welcomed back at any time, they're just listed as non-active. In theory if a call was sent out to mobilize, the organization could pull together over a battalion (four companies) of members if everyone showed up.

The Cadets were very serious about modeling their training after the military. It's what Mt. Tenny Academy was known for. Training was akin to Marine Corps exercises, the Major saw to that. During workouts you could see an eight-person squad pick up a log and run with it over a distance and then hand it off to another squad. That squad would do the same to the next until it came back to its starting place. The first log to come back won. It was like a relay race with one hell of a heavy baton. Individual squad members had to work together to pick it up. Then they had to figure out the best way to hand it off and work with that squad to pass it off smoothly. And so on.

Then there was the Rifle Range which was an intricate part of Cadet training. The school offered classes in standard target practice for students or walk-ins. If you were involved with the Cadet program, you were eligible to take it to another level with what they called the "Rock & Roll" firing range. That was a course set up where shooters ran through several obstacles and fired at targets on the move. Some of the targets were moving targets as well, making this type of training much more realistic and fun as all participants would tell you.

Last semester Major Monett completed the construction of a small unfinished two story on campus house and added "Urban Warfare" tactics into the training schedule. It was affectionately nicknamed "Grandma's house". Students and Cadets could now experiment with "take and hold" techniques as well as teach them how to clear a building. This offered them a great chance to practice taking over an actual structure and the best way for a squad to set up and hold the location. The upper story rooms were used to teach snipers how to set up urban "hides" from which they could deal out their deadly art.

Kaiden started calling his training "serious shit" because the degree to which they played war surprised him. The instructors not only taught the 'how to' of it, but they also incorporated physical exercise in almost every aspect. For example, only on occasion did they carry real guns during these maneuvers, most of the time they carried the steel bar which the Cadets affectionately called the "Iron Maiden". It was a 'Z' shaped curl bar which weighed about twelve to fifteen pounds each. Weights could be attached to them to make them even heavier. Sometimes the Sergeant would burden a Cadet with more weight as a punishment for some infraction against the rules. The school had collected over thirty bars over the years and now stored them in a line up against the wall in one of the rooms in Grandma's house. Somewhere in the yard or field, was this pile of cement weights of various sizes and denominations (the piles location always changed). Most of them were the "cement" type of barbell weights, chosen because they didn't rust. Instructors would give the Cadets various scenarios and directed them to attack and secure the objective using the heavy bar as a substitute for a rifle. After successfully securing Grandma's house or an area outside the house, they'd be directed to move the pile of weights from its present position to some new location, most of the time from either inside the house to the outside or from outside into one of the rooms inside the house. Each Cadet would be required to go to the pile of weights, attach as many of them as he could to his Iron Maiden and move them to the new designated location. This training was derived from a famous saying that the instructors constantly drilled into the Cadets "If you can't carry it, you can't use it". This technique got them really acquainted with 'carrying it'.

Part two of this drill was that squad #1 was tasked with the job of attacking and clearing the house with squad #2 practicing retreat maneuvers. They would rotate and switch back and forth. The attacking squad would have to remove the pile of weights back out into the field after securing the premises and so on.

Along those same lines, hiking became a very popular tool with the instructors. They took the Cadets on a multitude of day and overnight hikes and had them carry various types of equipment (sometimes with the Iron Maiden) along with ammunition and occasionally a real weapon. On a typical overnight hike up to Bald Ledge they carried seventy pounds or more on their backs.

To head off inevitable complaints about "heavy pack" syndrome, a squad leader would perform what's called a "shake down" on one of the new Cadets. They'd take his pack apart and pull out one item at a time and discuss the value of the item with the group. In most cases, after going through the pack more than half the gadgets and equipment a Cadet considered "can't do without" were now sitting in the reject pile.

On the first Saturday in October both the Mohawks and Kaiden's Algonquin's set out on their first overnight hike up Tenny Mountain. True to form, it became a race between the two squads from the start. The Mohawks got a slight lead on the Algonquin's due to some equipment trouble that hampered the Algonquin's progress. Mohawks took to the trail first giving them a major advantage. The Algonquins were hard pressed to catch up with them, plus it was highly unlikely that the Mohawks would allow the Algonquins to pass them on the trail even if they had caught up.

Kaiden's SL (Squad Leader) Brute Witiker took the challenge seriously and plotted a detour that would give the Algonquins their only chance to snatch victory out from under their totally confident rivals. Taking a vote, everyone agreed to the alternative course. Thus, they turned off the trail and set on a more direct route yet much more difficult climb straight up the mountain. The move would bypass the zigzagging trail the Mohawks were on and in theory could get them there faster if the steep climb didn't significantly slow them down. This forced them to utilize a method called "bushwhacking" which is basically creating your own trail as you go. Now the squad was on a trek straight up the mountain side to bald ledge without the luxury of a trail. The Mohawks kept looking over their shoulders but never saw their rival at any point making them confident that victory was in the bag.

Hiking was something Kaiden had never considered doing before, now for the first time he was standing with his buddy Brute on top of Bald Ledge after a long arduous trek straight up the roughest side of Tenny mountain. The rest of the exhausted members of the squad were falling to their knees and panting for breath behind the two of them. SL Witiker had become one of Kaiden's best friends during the last few weeks. He said honestly to Kaiden (and anyone else who was listening) "You never know how difficult this shit is until you do it. But if I never did it… man look at what I'd be missing".

Kaiden stood next to Brute on the ledge and looked out over the cliff to the mountains and valleys below taking in the breathtaking view. One by one the rest of the Algonquin squad stepped out onto the rock ledge and found a spot to sit and rest. It was more like they collapsed down on the ground under the heavy weight of their packs, sweating and out of breath. Some leaned on their equipment seeking to recover from the climb before they could even consider the view. Eventually Brute and Kaiden were joined by others, and they all stood there overlooking the Academy and the countryside below.

The setting sun had just started painting crazy designs on the horizon and the shadow of distant mountain's etched their dark design into the landscape. Shadows crept and cut across the campus in front of them. They saw the bunker in the center, and the cafeteria. They could pick out and were able to identify the various school buildings. Following the road, it was easy to find the rifle range and then Rio Linda right below them at the base of the mountain. Rio Linda was already engulfed in shadow by this time of day. The whole experience could only be described as beautiful. Kaiden fell in love with it. The difficulty of the hike and then… this. It gave him his hard-won reward. Standing on top of a mountain made him feel like he was closer to God. The scene snuggled into his heart as one of the most inspiring moments of his life.

"Wow" Kaiden said "To stand here and look out over Gods creation… it's like I'm feeling him".

"You don't get a chance to see something like this every day now do ya? This is INSPIRATION!" Brute yelled it out trying to get an echo.

The Mohawks arrived a short minute later bewildered as to how in the world they had been beaten to the ledge. They spread out too, with most of them collapsing onto their packs while getting a round of chastisement from the Algonquin's for coming in second. By winning, the Algonquins got first dibs on the camp site. Witiker ordered the

Algonquins to vacate the ledge and to allow the Mohawks to gawk at the scene as they had done. They gathered their packs and walked the short distance farther up the path to the shelter. Witiker made the decision not to camp there but to pass through it and set up camp in the woods on the east side of the brook away from the shelter. That was different and it angered some of the crew.

"Hey what the hell? Witiker! Why are we giving up the shelter? We won the right to take it!" one of the squad members said in protest. "Let's take advantage of our hard-won dibs on the shelter. It's got a fire pit and a biffy".

The new site Witiker led them to was more 'uncomfortable' and more difficult to find a good place to set up a tent.

"We're going to give up the easy and practice for worst case. It's what we might encounter in a real-life scenario. And… I have my reasons. It's not for you to question private" Witiker rebuffed in a commanding tone.

Witiker took charge and barked out orders. "Ok guys let's set up here and get socked down before dark. I want everyone to tighten up as quickly as possible, cooking dinner in the dark is unacceptable". He posted the order of the guard and then rallied the others to start cooking.

Lookouts were set up and stationed around their position. The Algonquins found out that Witiker took these over nights seriously insisting that his men follow protocol and secure the perimeter. Three people were assigned guard duty for the first shift of the night. Protocol stated that a guard served a two-hour shift and would man a predetermined post on all four sides of the encampment (only three sides tonight due to the steep mountain behind them). Guards were entrusted with the safety of the squad and were expected to remain alert and sound the alarm if prodded by the enemy, namely the Mohawks, but it could also come from any one of the instructors at the school too. They were known for such devious excursions where they beat on sleeping Cadets with sticks in the middle of the night.

Not all the Cadets in Kaiden's squad understood why Witiker passed over the best camping site on the mountain, giving it up to the Mohawks who gladly took it while verbally abusing the Algonquin's for being so stupid. The spot Witiker picked proved to be more than uncomfortable. Only at one point during the middle of the night did Kaiden and the rest of the squad smile with understanding when the sound of shouting voices came from the Mohawk's campsite at the shelter. Someone was shouting at the top of their lungs "You fucking idiots..." Whack! Whack! Whack! "If I was the enemy..." Whack! Whack! Whack! "...you'd be fucking dead!".

Three Cadet officers shouted such obscenities for fifteen minutes straight as they ambushed what they thought were the sleeping Mohawks and Algonquin squads camped together at the shelter. While they were noisily beating sleeping bags with sticks and yelling, Witiker and his guys quietly surrounded the shelter and, on his command, rushed out and pounced on the officers from behind. Completely taken by surprise, the Algonquins took the officers prisoner and tied them up. Later Witiker got in trouble for shouting at the officers "You idiots, if I was the enemy, you'd be fucking dead!".

During the many hikes they made and around numerous campfires, Witiker gave them fictitious scenarios and talked about how they might attack or defend their position. It became a game to pick apart the landscape and then discuss the art of war. Due to this type of training Kaiden now assessed everything from a defensive standpoint and was becoming able to assign priority to the equipment that he needed to carry in the field. Practicality and quality vs. weight took precedent. The very first question asked when buying boots, clothes, camping gear, sleeping bags or even a water filter was "How much does it weigh?" He also started looking at his surroundings in a much different way; constantly he and the members of his squad would discuss how to defend their position. Lessons learned from excursions like the one tonight taught Kaiden the rudiments of both survival and military tactics.

* * *

College courses were a lot harder, math being the worst which Kaiden had never done well in. Now he was in real trouble because he was way behind. To turn it around, he started sitting up in the front row and he paid a lot more attention than he ever had before. He was trying to listen and comprehend the material with a newfound desire. That really helped along with multiple trips to the library and a constant drive for answers. Kenny had warned him that other courses such as physics and some of the math in his architectural classes were based on it, so he had to get the basics to do well in future classes. Kenny also advised him "Do the homework right after class if possible, that way the material is fresh in your mind and the pieces all fall together a whole lot easier". Kaiden tried it, and it seemed to work. It was also extremely helpful to hang out with friends and study at the library (Kaiden refused to call them study groups). That way when a question came up it was possible to get an answer from another classmate right then and there. He started comprehending the material a lot better and actually started doing well. Surprisingly enough, he even became good friends with some of the nerds at the library.

* * *

It was already early October and apples were ripe for picking. Applesauce with a smaller consideration towards apple butter was the latest endeavor in the Academy's Natural Cooking & Canning classes. Candy and Shiloh took the same course this semester and found themselves busy at work in a special kitchen that doubled as a classroom and a fully functioning large scale canning facility. The set up was capable of canning runs of various seasonal farm commodities as they became available. Lessons at various times of the year would focus on the culmination of the featured crop and were mostly centered around crops that were grown right here on Mt. Tenny farm. Between dealing with their own products, it was not uncommon to purchase various bulk items from other local farmers or even from local vendors if the price was right.

In early September the agriculture class finished a production run of carrots. Before that it was strawberries and raspberries. Before that they ran a batch of lima beans and green peas. Mid to late summer was devoted to sweet corn and squash. But now for the next few weeks Candy and her classmates would live, breathe, and eat "apples". Work crews rotated in shifts. One crew concentrated on picking, another on making batches of applesauce and still another on jarring it. Then they would rotate with each crew getting experience with every phase of the process. That way it never got overwhelming or boring.

For Candy the change from summer crops to "apples" was a relief; even as short lived as the season was, over the summer she had gotten stuck with a crew doing the same process over and over. She participated in the Natural Cooking & Canning class and was so sick of canning squash and sweet corn that she was singing while bustling around the kitchen moving buckets of apples from storage over into a huge pot of boiling water in the center of the kitchen. Change was good and any change was better than the monotony that can settle if stuck doing the same thing over and over.

* * *

Professor Margaret Hayer had just started her lecture on the crucial subject of clean potable water. She turned to her students and said rather dramatically "No water, no life! It is very important that you get your priorities straight. Believe me when I tell you that "drinking water" should be at the top of your list of priorities when you find yourself in a survival situation. If you ever do, remember this class, and commit this priority to memory" the professor pointed to the large banner pinned up above the chalk board which read #1- SECURE A SOURCE OF CLEAN WATER!". And remember if you don't have it, you will be forced to get it. That goes for your competitors as well, meaning anyone else living nearby. In a survival situation they will become your competition.

The best scenario is to quickly move and get access to a clean moving stream. That will go a long way to ease the intensity of your situation mainly because efficient filtration devices might not be necessary. Although I'm going to make it a rule so that you can never blame it on me, here it is- No matter how clear the stream is and depending on how good your filter is, you will still have to at least filter your drinking water and preferably boil it too. Boil it for at least ten minutes to kill any bacteria. I admit, with the right stream you won't have to do that. Look for small run offs, like brooks that seem to spring out of the side of a mountain without any upstream exposure. Those are the best, the ones that dispense nature's own purified mountain run off. You'll never taste such good cold clean water in your life. Those streams are found halfway up mountains where contamination is minimal. Once you get down into the valley all bets are off. Brooks and streams must be considered contaminated, and you must go through every technique you know to ensure safe drinking water.

Today we're going to begin our discussion about water filters by analyzing the most rudimentary device and then moving all the way up the chain to larger commercial water treatment facilities. I'm going to start by teaching you how to make a water filter out of some basic materials commonly found for filtration.

The first step is the hardest; finding the material you will need to generate clean water. If boiling water is a necessity, then your first task will be to find a suitable pot to boil it in and then to store your clean water. This sounds so simple to us today when we have ample access to items of our choice and supply is not a problem. But I am fifty-nine years old, and I can tell you that today it is not as easy to obtain some of the wares that have been so plentiful in the past. Many businesses have gone under, and their products are no longer available. For example, recently I found it very difficult to find a source for palm fiber, especially here in New York. Palm fiber is a great filtration material when available.

I pose this question to you. What if you couldn't run down to the store and buy a pot? What if there was no store? We take this for granted, don't we? If you're out in the woods fighting for your life, something as simple as a pot to boil water in can become the biggest hindrance to your survival. You'll also need to obtain a canister of some sort that can work for making a water filter. Or even a piece of plastic sheet or a large plastic bag. If you do not have access to these few key filtration ingredients such as we have here..." she waved her hand at the bins standing in front of the class containing various items. "...you are at a major disadvantage because you'll really have to work hard at getting substitutes. You'll also have to wash the sand and gravel before it can be used. Then you'll need to accumulate filtration material in large enough quantities that will be sufficient enough to work well in filtering out particles, all of this of course while you are dying of thirst.

Ok, let's be honest, you won't bother with filtering the water because it will be too difficult at that point but... you should. Why? Why go through all the trouble? Well class I'm going to state the obvious, it's as simple as this; drinking bad water will make you sick. Whole armies have been disbanded and battles lost because of diseases stemming from the lack of clean water. It will show itself instantly in the form of diarrhea or dysentery. Diarrhea is a major problem for the body, and worms don't do the body much good either! We lose our ability to absorb nutrients in this condition. With that, even if you can find food, anything you eat will not sustain you, it'll blow right through you. You will become weak and then... you will die". She paused to let that sink in.

"Therefore, let's get back and concentrate on the first step- finding various filtration materials. Your job is to accumulate the following" she stood next to each barrel looked in and rattled off the name of its contents: activated charcoal, sponge, clean fine sand, gravel, palm fiber, chlorine pellets, alum, fine gravel, and a canister of your choice to place these items in. You could use regular charcoal from a fireplace, that'll work in place of the activated charcoal, but it won't have anywhere near the same efficiency, and it will color the water. The reason lies in how activated charcoal is made. It's a special process where various materials are burned at over four hundred degrees in a pressure oven with all the oxygen removed. Basically, this forces the material to expand like popcorn to form a material that has five hundred times more surface area than regular charcoal. You can imagine that the absorption capability of this product would be greatly enhanced by this technique.

Please read chapter three on filtration, that will give you the basics on how to layer the components and put your filter together. Your homework is to make a filter with the materials we have available here. Use your imagination; let's see who can make the best one".

* * *

In a classroom on the first floor of the range building, Major Monett was standing at the head of the class addressing an assembled group of sixteen Cadets. His assistant Mr. Harry Coin was at his side. "Thank you for accepting an invitation to sign up for the "Mortar Crew" this is going to be a very interesting class". The Major held his hands behind his back and rocked back and forth on his heels. "All eighteen of you were picked because we thought that you would be well suited for this type of training both mentally and physically. You have made the cut out of seventy-five Cadets who applied for crew member positions, and you will form the first of the Academy's new Mortar Crew. This is specialized training that we've never been able to offer before, not before we acquired the appropriate equipment. I can't tell you how I got it, let's just say that I pulled a few strings". The Major turned and directed the group's attention to the corner of the room where a new looking M224 60mm mortar launcher with all its components was set up. The kit contained the TA-1 telephone, field communication radios, ammo carrying cans, binoculars, M2 compass, fire control equipment, ballistics computer with plotting board, the M7 and M8 base plates and a bore sighting device.

Classes like this were not new; another had started two years ago with a different weapon that the Major had dug up and dragged in; a working M1917A1 Browning machine gun. It was the same model as the one on display in the farmhouse 'Underground Trench'. There were plenty of rumors going around about a ghost machine gun squad that haunted the woods. The rumors were augmented occasionally, by the sound of machine gun fire that came from various locations around the school at odd times of the day or even in the middle of the night. The mystery could have easily been dispelled if participating students were allowed to talk about the special squad that occasionally went on secret hikes to train and fire the weapon. But no one said a word.

"This is an inert practice round, the M3". On cue, Mr. Coin handed the Major one of the rounds that were sitting on his desk and the Major held it up. "It doesn't explode, this one is just for practice. Eventually you'll do an actual fire with a live training round like this. Mr. Coin handed him the next round. "The M766 SRTR which stands for short range target round. This one has the propellant and a spotting charge but no fragmentation charge. Sorry you won't be shooting and blowing things up!

The whole class gave out a disappointing moan. Quickly the Major backtracked and with a sinister smile he said "Well we might be able to dig up a live round for graduation".

"Yeah!" the class yelled almost in unison. They high five'd each other with enthusiastic slaps of the hand.

Then we'll move to the M769 TP and set you up on the long-distance range and see what you can do. That one has a range from 77 to 3877 yards depending on the round. There are color coded marking rounds and even white phosphorus rounds, but we will only be dealing with the fragmentation round because it's the only one we could get. The target round can be re-used over again until it's too banged up to go on. You'll be taught how to replace the propellant charge and how to load it with a spotting charge. So, study hard, there's a lot to learn and your final grade will be determined by how well you can place a round. There will be a target set up where the bull's eye will be worth "50" the second ring "20" and the third ring "10". Your team will have four shots to score, and your score will determine fifty percent of your grade. The other fifty percent will be scored on your teamwork and efficiency in setting up. I even heard there's a case of beer in the wings for the winner". There were smiles all around and another cheer rose from the group.

"We'll divide you up into three squads of six even though only three people are required to fire the weapon; you'll pick a squad leader, a Section sergeant, two gunners and two ammo bearers. You will all trade off and cross train, so everyone knows the others job. The SL and the Sergeant are responsible for security so they will carry a rifle. Everyone else will normally carry a side arm but in training we are going to dispense with that protocol. Remaining members are responsible for carrying the mortar tube, plate, tripod, and the ammo. It weighs 47 pounds total and breaks down into three sections. I think the plate weighs about fourteen and a half pounds, Mr. Coin?"

"Yes, fourteen point four to be exact. We have the M8 plate also which is lighter than that and can be used with the handheld model if needed".

There was a murmur from the Cadets as they contemplated the difficulty of lugging around all that equipment. By itself it wasn't that bad but then you throw on the standard supplies you need for extended missions like food, water, rifle ammo, pistol ammo and waterproofing tarps- it becomes significant.

"Thank you, Mr. Coin. It's really not all that bad; this version is positively a lot lighter than previous models of the modern mortar. Hey, be glad, the 81mm mortar we lugged around in WWII weighed 136 pounds. That base plate was a bitch'in 45 pounds. The plate alone weighed almost as much as the total weight of the 224.

Gore raised his hand.

"Yes Mr. Tillman".

"Sir I take it eventually you're going to have us hike up Tenny Mountain with this set up on some overnights, am I correct?".

The Major smiled "Mr. Tillman, if you were in charge of a mortar team what would you recommend for a training exercise?".

"Sir I would want my team to be fluent with the equipment. The only way to achieve that would be a lot of set up and tear down exercises in different conditions. As a leader I would want to know how mobile my team is and how long it might take to get them and the equipment from point A to point B. And of course, how tired they will be when they get there.

"Fluent Mr. Tillman? I like that, and I agree with your assessment".

"Well sir if I may" Gore continued "I saw some students the other day hiking up Tenny Mt. using a Rat Pack to haul their stuff".

"Yeah, the beer!" someone yelled out. The people around him chuckled.

"I was just thinking" Gore paused and then went on... "If we could modify a Rat Pack for heavy duty use, we could move the 224 and its ammo a whole lot quicker and easier on the trail".

"Hmm, interesting idea Mr. Tillman. What do you mean by modify?"

"Well right off the bat I think the wheels would have to be switched out with a wider more durable tire. It'd have to be able to take more of a beating and yet allow a smooth ride". Gore seemed to be thinking to himself and talking out loud. "Probably a soft foam tire that eliminates the possibility of ever going flat, yet something that's not too stiff. If the tires could adjust and possibly collapse closer to each other, that would make it easier to maneuver on foot trails. It would need a heavy-duty axle as well. Wow, maybe even convertible to a one-wheel barrel type setup...".

The Major turned around and looked at the blackboard while Gore was talking and then turned back to his student. "Mr. Tillman, excellent idea. I'm going to appoint you as the first leader of the 1st mortar squad. I give you permission to go ahead and design a prototype of the cart you envision. I'll supply the rat pack and any parts you might need to make this happen. See me after class".

Now I'm going to leave you in the very capable hands of Mr. Coin. You'll be put through classroom training first. He'll be responsible for teaching you target acquisition where you'll learn all about deflection, elevation, and transverse movement. Yes Mr. Tillman is right, the most important thing is to learn how to move this equipment, set it up and aim it accurately all in the shortest time possible. Working together as a team to accomplish this will be the most important aspect. Let's see some hard work in acquiring these skills. It'll be interesting to see how well you can do. All in all, I know you're going to have a lot of fun with this. Good luck, I'll see you out on the range in about two weeks".

There was a sense of excitement from the expectation of shooting this new piece of equipment. None of them ever expected to be involved in a mortar crew and they felt honored to be picked for this special training. The class settled down and listened to Professor Coin's first lecture on the M224.

17

Big Brother

In the city of Reston Virginia, located in the northern quadrant of the state, Mr. and Mrs. Walsh sat at home enjoying a quiet evening. Reston is a twenty-minute train ride on the "B" line just West of Washington DC but well within the range of the IRS ART (Asset Reclamation Team) working out of DC. The home was a full thirty-nine hundred square foot Tudor style residence on an acre of cleared land spotted with a few ancient trees that rained leaves down on a gradual sloping grass covered yard.

The Walsh's were able to afford the place when they were both working. But now James and Leigha were without jobs and found themselves at home most of the time. Leigha couldn't work because of a leg injury and James had folded the doors to his architectural firm three years ago. They both thought that it wouldn't be that hard-to-find other work, after all everyone always said that DC was spared the rod and the bulk of the recession due to all the military contracts that kept the place moving. But the trend ended, and the results came home to roost for businesses in this area.

Washington DC was never going to change. It's fueled by pure agenda, but due to recent events the controlling progressive party was forced to implement a few selective budget cuts due to the barrage of intense anti-spending rhetoric that not only sprang forth from the conservative party but resonated from the general population as well. Our beloved politicians put on a show attempting to give the impression that something was being done about it. Yes, they could now say that they had finally made cuts to the budget. Yet for every cut they approved they spent three times that on additional spending elsewhere. Trying even harder to look as if they were implementing spending cuts, they once again went for the juggler of the US military. It was always a wonder to see, even in times like these the government was hell bent and hard at work trying to maintain all the other special interest expenditures and yet ended up cutting back on the one thing (some might say the only thing) that government is truly responsible for; the protection of its people.

The budget for the United States military had been cut by thirty-five percent just over three years ago. Many said that the reduction was a good thing, a good trend, and used the reasoning that we should stay out of wars and not get involved in any of the foreign conflicts that are helping to drive up the deficit. The rhetoric and talking points coming out of DC reeked of innuendo and were spun as if the military was where all the money was going. "Wars are expensive!" politicians yelled. What wasn't mentioned was the fact that the United States budget for all Military expenditures had already been cut from its earlier 2025 level. Politicians rode the increasing wave of anti-spending sentiment and used it to hack away at the budget- again. They were fulfilling a basic step in their goal which depended heavily on reducing the workforce that was dedicated to the Armed forces. Progressives perceived the military as a threat and wanted to replace it with a large workforce dedicated to Washington DC from which all jobs flowed.

James Walsh and his architectural firm had been losing money for a few years before he finally closed the doors. New business had evaporated. Towards the end, he and his wife had to prioritize to make ends meet. James felt he had no choice; to survive he had fudged the figures in his favor on the company's tax returns to look less profitable to the IRS. He saved thousands in taxes by under reporting his personal income to the point that it seemed impossible for a man at his level to be able to support the home and the cars that he owned with his income. The IRS red flagged his tax return and performed an audit last year. They recalculated his taxes for the last seven years, guessed at what he truly owed and sent letters demanding repayment of $290,000 in back taxes. There was a fine and interest on the unpaid amount which they claimed brought the total due to $410,000. James immediately hired a lawyer.

It was eight o'clock on a Saturday morning; James was watching the news in the family room when Leigha came in from the kitchen with a frightened look on her face. It was the kind of look that instantly portrayed the seriousness of some event that was about to transpire.

"Jim! There's a man walking around our back yard!". She called him Jim when she was upset.

James jumped up out of his chair and walked briskly over to the kitchen doorway. He could see over the counter and out through the kitchen window and sure enough caught a glimpse of a man in a dark suit with dark sunglasses walking around the outskirts of the patio. No sooner had he confirmed what his wife said than the doorbell rang.

"Lock the back door, Leigha!" he shouted while moving to look out the front window before going to the door. There was a police car and two other unmarked cars on the street in front of his house. He was both relieved and yet worried at a new set of concerns. *"At least I know it's not robbers but then... who is it? Why is someone walking around my back yard?"* he thought.

James noticed that the local policemen standing out front were unarmed. A night stick in a holster replaced the pistol they normally carried. The scary part was the men in black who accompanied them with an AR-15 cradled in their arms. This was evidence of another trend that filtered into Democrat run cities all across America. The intense riots and the violent response by police created many examples of brutality committed against what the opposition called 'helpless citizens. Special police squads were formed to deal with what they called terrorists.

Extreme animosity towards the police was picked up and used by Democrat politicians who turned it into a way to galvanize their political posture with the far left. They turned their attention not to the burning, looting, and shooting instigated by rioters, but used their power to restrict the ability of the local Police to respond in a forceful way. They saw this as an opportunity. An opportunity they weren't going to pass up.

Democrat politicians issued executive orders forcing the police to stand down and refrain from confronting rioters. Subsequent legislation passed by progressive city council members defunded and disarmed the police to make them a more politically friendly entity. Members of the Police couldn't be trusted to do their bidding and go along with the master plan. Their power had to be replaced by something more acquiesce. Hence the growing power and size of the IRS-ART (Asset Reclamation Team). The police were only there to lend a degree of legitimacy to their action.

James met his wife in the hallway. "It's the police" he told her. Both walked to the front door and opened it.

A Police officer greeted them. "Mr. and Mrs. Walsh?".

"Yes".

"I'm officer Mayers and this is special agent Atkinson".

Roy Atkinson was a company man who gained position by disregarding concern for legal fallout in many of his previous assignments. For these assignments he was told that his team was sanctioned by the president and that he would oversee a new effort to enforce existing laws already on the books. Laws concerning the collection of monies due to the government. It would require fieldwork and he would head up a new task force of special service IRS agents who would be responsible for physically collecting past due accounts.

Atkinson was on the ground floor of the newly formed ART which just recently became a fully sanctioned branch of the IRS. He had no problem pulling goods out from under the feet of nonpaying customers. He was good at it. Being overwhelming in appearance helped him quite a bit on many occasions both psychologically as well as physically when he was forced to use his solid heavy boned two hundred and sixty-five pounds of persuasion to get the job done. His intimidation factor ranked high, and he was good at wielding it to his advantage. It got him what he wanted but more important, it got him what his bosses wanted, which worked well and allowed him to inch his way up the chain in the repossession business. He was a repo man through and through and he was good at it. His reputation and his left-wing stance got him an invitation to head up the IRS-ART.

This gig differed from others the IRS offered, mainly in job skill requirement. You didn't need four years of college or an accounting degree. No, for this you only needed experience in debt collection, repossession in either the mortgage industry or banking industry and of course a kick ass attitude. Atkinson had it all. A list of previous jobs on his resume included work with the "Bank of the United States". Working for them full-time for five years gave him plenty of experience with repossessing all different types of assets and he went about his job with calculated precision. Consistent success earned him the reputation of being one of the best. He wore no emotional baggage on his sleeve, and none ever came back to haunt him. He looked forward to this new job with eager anticipation.

"No warrants" he repeated to himself with a smile. That smile appeared on his face every time he thought about it.

It took serious consideration by the IRS upper echelon to settle on how they were going to operate this campaign. Agent Atkinson worked with his superiors to iron out procedures and to develop the basis of operation for the ART. It took two months to work out the techniques and to hire the right personnel. The team was put through training and four weeks later the first class of ART members graduated and went to work.

Since no warrants were necessary it saved them an immeasurable amount of time, paperwork and countless man hours devoted to judges and lawyers. Roy had to constantly fight the paperwork when he worked for the banks. He thought about the warrants and smiled again; he just couldn't believe his luck. But still he was going to have to count on the cooperation of the local police force. By directive there was to be a minimum of two local police deputies involved in each transaction. That gave them the legitimacy they needed to get in the door, although the police didn't really have a role in this. Atkinson was comfortable, another smile came across his face when he thought about the firepower his men were allowed to bring to the party. In this state the police were only allowed to carry nightsticks. That was considered by the left to be all that was needed if things took a violent turn.

If they did run into trouble, the police would get the publicity, not the IRS. That was an overriding theme that came down from his superiors "Avoid negative news coverage at all costs. Refrain from actions that could rile up public opinion against our operations". They made that perfectly clear.

Previously, agent Atkinson had everyone in position when he got off the phone with the cab company. The door to his unmarked Ford sedan opened and Atkinson stepped out and walked up the front sidewalk of the Walsh residence. Two agents met him at the top of the steps. They took their place behind Atkinson and Atkinson fell in line behind two policemen who continued up the porch to the front door and rang the doorbell. Procedure directed that two more agents move around the back of the home at the same time, to witness anyone exiting the rear of the home. They weren't mandated to stop anyone from leaving, on the contrary, they were only tasked with preventing someone from re-entering. After all, that's what they were here for, to get them to leave the premises.

Mr. Walsh cautiously opened the door; his wife was standing right behind him. "What's this all about?" he asked without offering any pleasantries.

"Mr. or Mrs. Walsh?" the policeman asked again for confirmation.

"Yes I'm Mr. Walsh".

"May we come in and discuss a very important matter with you".

"Yeah, I guess so, come in" Mr. Walsh said.

When they walked into the hallway, Mrs. Walsh asked them "Can I get you gentleman something to drink".

The same policeman turned to her and said "No thank you Ma'am, we're here on official business" and then directed his next statement to Mr. Walsh. "We have some bad news for you. We're here to enforce an eviction order". He unfolded a piece of paper and handed it to him. "All personnel must leave the premises, and this means... right now".

Mrs. Walsh felt flushed when she heard it. She gasped and held her hand to her mouth.

"Agent Atkinson is here from the IRS; he will explain" the policeman said.

At that moment agent Atkinson entered the front door and all eyes turned toward him.

"Mr. and Mrs. Walsh I am Agent Atkinson from the ART which is a division of the IRS recovery task force. I'm sure you've received the letters concerning the account discrepancy?".

"Well yeah, but I have a lawyer who is working on that for me..." Mr. Walsh started to say.

None of that matters at this point Mr. Walsh, by the powers invested in me by the Bureau of Internal Revenue Service I hereby notify you that you are evicted from these premises as of..." he looked at his watch then looked up and handed Mr. Walsh an official eviction notification pamphlet "...nine thirty-five on the morning of October fifth. All property in the home as well as the cars in the driveway will be confiscated as payment for the debt obligation. You will be allowed fifteen minutes each to pack a small bag and leave".

Mrs. Walsh exclaimed "Oh my God! Jim they can't do this!" She looked at the policeman for help.

"Ma'am, unfortunately it's the law" the cop told her. "They have federal authority and it's perfectly legal. I'm sorry".

Agent Atkinson continued "You may take your wallet, ID's, credit cards and all that stuff. We're not interested in shutting off your credit. We're just here to confiscate property that can effectively pay off the debt you owe to the IRS. Please, you must listen to me carefully and follow my instructions. You can't take anything of value off the property. Agent Simpson and Whiles here will escort the both of you to your room or wherever you need to go to pack a bag. They will see to it that nothing illegal goes into your bags. Do you understand? I have a cab waiting outside for you. If you cooperate it will all go very smoothly".

"I'm going to call my lawyer...".

"Sir you don't have time to call your lawyer, by the time you do your fifteen minutes will be up and the two deputies here will be escorting you out of the house. I suggest that you take advantage of the time you have to collect some of your things while you can. You can call your lawyer from the cab".

Mr. Walsh looked at the policeman with his mouth open but didn't say anything.

Anticipating a negative response, the policeman said "Mr. Walsh I suggest you do as he says. We will be escorting you out in fifteen minutes".

"And what if I refuse?".

"Then we will forcibly remove you from the premises" the officer said.

"On a stretcher if we have too" agent Atkinson rudely added to speed up this man's degree of comprehension.

Mrs. Walsh gasped and started to speak out "Well I've never heard of such a thing... Jim they can't do this".

"Sir you have fourteen minutes".

"Let's go Leigha. We can call Silverstein from the cab. Let's get our things".

"Agent Mayers, go with Mr. Walsh and agent Whiles, go with the Mrs".

The two agents followed the couple up the stairs and into their bedrooms. Mr. and Mrs. Walsh grabbed a small bag each from the closet and started to throw some things in them. Mrs. Walsh was crying. The agents were there watching to make sure that no money, gold, silver, or any jewelry were dropped into their bags. When Jim tried to throw in a watch, agent Simpson stopped him, took it out and threw it back on the counter. He even made Mr. Walsh take the Rolex off his wrist and lay it on the counter.

"Fifteen minutes is up" agent Simpson yelled. "It's time to go". Mr. and Mrs. Walsh were escorted out amidst complaints about not having enough time to get everything.

"Anything else you need can be purchased with your credit cards" agent Simpson said.

When they came down, two agents were busy searching the first floor, another two were in the basement. When Mr. and Mrs. Walsh came down, they were appalled that strange men were going through their things. Agent Atkinson met them at the bottom of the stairs.

"Mr. Walsh is there any other personnel in the home that we should know about?".

"No, no one else lives here but us" he said in a defeated tone.

"Do you have any guns in the house?".

"No".

"Do you have a safe in the house?".

Mr. Walsh Hesitated.

"It's just that if we find a safe, we are going to get a lock smith to drill it open. It would go a lot better for you if you cooperated and told us where it is and gave us the combination".

Nothing was offered.

"I'm just thinking that if you ever get the house back and by the way, that is possible (he lied), you will have an operating safe instead of one with holes drilled in it. I'm just saying…".

James closed his eyes and lowered his head. "Ok, ok, the safes in the bedroom closet behind the shoe rack. The combination is 12L-06R-49L".

Atkinson wrote that down. "Thank you, Mr. Walsh," he said with a big 'I just won the lottery' smile. "I'll make sure that goes in your file so the review board sees that you're cooperating. OK guys, they're good to go" he said to his men. The two of them escorted Mr. and Mrs. Walsh out to a waiting cab.

Agent Simpson approached Atkinson and commented "Can they really get the house back boss?".

"Not in a million years Simpson" he said while staring out after the Walsh's who were now getting into the cab, his mind was off somewhere else. Then he snapped back "Don't tape off the place like we did on the last one, the neighbors see it and know something's up. I'm going upstairs to start inventory on the second floor, you do the first floor and have Whiles write up the basement. Agent Atkinson turned and walked slowly up the stairs feeling like it was Christmas morning.

The shoe rack was on hinges, it pulled away from the wall like a cabinet door. On the wall was a built-in safe. Atkinson rubbed his hands together for effect and went to work on the safe's dial. It took him three tries but then a smile broke through the concern that started to form on his face. The tumbler clicked and the door opened. Inside were four shelves with a Jewelry tray on the top, gold and silver coins on the second, two stacks of cash on the third and ammunition sitting beside a handgun on the fourth.

Not a word or a screech of jubilation came out of his mouth. He kept his demeanor stoic, yet his brain was in calculating mode behind that sparkle in his eyes. It wasn't just from the reflection off the jewelry he held in his hands. He turned to look and made sure no one was watching him and then placed the bracelet and the diamond rings in his pocket. Half the cash followed. He didn't' care about the coins or the pistol and left the rest for the record keepers figuring that he needed to leave something of significant value for his boss, further rationalizing that this was just his well-deserved ten percent off the top.

18

Guns R Us

Senator Nadd Coulomb started to see some success in the campaign against gun ownership. It took two months for his staff to beef up the pressure but now they were getting some good results. From a long nationwide tour that he was just now finishing the Senator concluded that he had achieved his goal in helping to solidify some real solid support. The intensive anti-gun campaign was in full bloom from other angles as well coming in especially hard from the left-wing press. It was easy to get the media spin masters on board to help fuel the fire. Just a small donation or a commitment to purchase airtime went a long way. The liberal media was committed to the same agenda and saw to it that hunting season on guns had commenced. They continuously got memos and spun the latest propaganda with newfound zeal.

Somehow four years ago the majority liberal legislature got enough votes to pass the equal fairness doctrine, the same one that eventually shut down the Rush Limbaugh show that lived on even after his death. It ushered in another round of "fairness" that required radio stations to air the opposing political viewpoint with equal time. The conservative viewpoint was dampened with liberal radio segments spewing out their anti-gun rhetoric. Icing on the spin was a full blast of TV advertisements headlining the famous rapper ZD. Through his lyrics they injected a little class warfare by insinuating that gun laws would help to disarm the upper white class who were using them to kill blacks. The campaign was a little over the top but highly effective. It rallied hard against the right's hardline stance on the individual's right to bear arms and... it was working. By emphasizing the protests against guns and ignoring the pro-gun movement they gave the impression that public opinion had turned and was well behind a gun ban. They succeeded in building a strong voice in the community that agreed with the government's push to start taking weapons out of the hands of law-abiding citizens. Americans came to believe that they would be safer if guns were illegal. Even a "made for campaign" rap song became a catchy hit tune due to the hot half naked chick in the video's background shaking her thang and implying that she'd do it if "You don't got no gun".

> "Oh yeah come on, come on, come on,
> It's time to git white'ie off a da gun
> Ya know I sho like ta start do'in dis one.
> Like taken diss girl fo some big time fun,
> but I can't if her fatha's packin one.
> No I can't if he won't be slackin none.
> Damn if she packin one I can't git me some.
> When she talkin gun it ain't da real one
> cause when she say I'm packin
> brotha now you know I ain't jackin.
> Now she says I ain't gunna be da one.
> Dat I only kin git it wit out duh gun, huh!
> Ya kin only git it wit out duh gun, huh!
> Huh! What she say...?
> Ya kin only git it wit out dat gun!"
> Cum on dalin baby lets go have some fun
> But she kep sayin
> ya kin only git it wit out duh gun!
> ya kin only git it wit out duh gun!"

Overwhelmingly, blacks accepted the concept of gun control. Convinced by an intense, powerful media barrage aimed against the hyped-up white supremacy movement. They didn't realize that the people most hurt by the loss of the right to bear arms would be themselves. From the proposed legislation (legislation that would make guns too expensive to own for the lower class) the people who most needed protection would be the ones who would lose the ability to defend themselves. Yet even in the face of that fact, most black folk were convinced and ultimately relished the idea that they would be delivering a blow to their rich white oppressors (the ones who could still afford to own a firearm) and that somehow by voting for the legislation they would be taking a step toward making their neighborhood safe for the children. Ninety-three percent of them voted in favor of gun control.

That video was surprisingly effective in swaying public opinion against the second amendment. It went on about gangsters and "poppin" but was really just a backdrop to the visual argument with various clips of protesters shown marching with signs that flashed between sporadic images of violent crimes and murders. At the end, a gorgeous Native American Indian woman wearing an Indian string leather bikini with feathers in her hair stood in a dilapidated ghetto in "somewhere" downtrodden USA (probably Detroit). She turned and surveyed the nasty scene and the camera zoomed in to see a big tear roll off her pretty cheek. It was oh so reminiscent of an old ancient very effective commercial against pollution back in the 70's where an old Indian man turned in the same manor with a big tear that dropped off his cheek as he observed all the garbage strewn about 'his' landscape. Of course, the insinuation was that "white people" were doing this to the land that once belonged to him.

Back then the spot was very effective and helped to sway public sentiment against "polluters" yet the whole thing was disgustingly ironic to people who knew about a few examples of Indian behavior as it applied to "garbage". One would have had to drive onto a few select reservations (not all) in order to witness the phenomena. Upon entering the reservation, you would instantly notice a ton of trash on the side of the road; it was such an eye sore and stood out as "such a shame". Bottles and cans were everywhere, so much worse than on any other road outside the reservation. The reason it was strewn with garbage was simple. Outside the reservation it was illegal to have an open alcohol beverage container in a car. So before crossing the reservation's border many of the Indians simply threw their cans and bottles out the window.

19

Checking In

A man was roughly pulled out from the back of a Lincoln and "escorted" into the rear entrance of the Ramadoor Hotel in Kansas City. Four nonsense guys surrounded him with two of them holding one of his arms in each hand to keep him up and to keep him moving forward. He didn't have a choice but to stumble in the direction they guided him. Purposely avoiding the crowd of people that gathered near and around the front entrance of the hotel, they brought him in the back service entrance and then over to the freight elevator to avoid the crowd.

For some reason the main security camera overlooking the back parking lot was not working. Men walked with handheld anti-gun signs in front of the precession and as they passed through the hotel's rear door, they held them up in front of the security cameras as the main body passed by. These cameras were working; they had been inspected for proper operation that same morning, but a problem with any one of them wouldn't immediately be noticed for at least twenty-four hours. The hotel, to save money, had reduced security personnel and eliminated live monitoring. They figured that they didn't need to pay anyone to sit there and watch. If something happened, they would go back and review the video recordings. No one would know that this group had entered the hotel until well after the event.

It was a perfect day; there were no parties or events scheduled for the banquet rooms and the hotel itself was at seventy percent capacity. It meant there would be a minimum number of hotel employees on premises. The Hotel was located on 1642 Vine Street and the high-rise building had a commanding view of the whole area. It was ironic, a small sign outside the front lobby on the main entrance read "NO GUNS ALLOWED".

A significant crowd gathered on the corner of Irving Street and Vine in front of 'City Book Store' which was just across the street from the eight-story hotel. It was 7:00PM and people were clamoring to see the senator and to voice their opinion in the town meeting/book signing. The crowd had overflowed out onto Irving Street and was now strangling normal traffic patterns. The commotion was looking like it was about to spill into the streets where a slew of policemen were attempting to contain the crowd.

The four serious men manhandled the man through the hotel lobby. The guy seemed to be drugged or something. His eyes were halfway shut, and he could hardly stand up on his own without help from the two men who held him. They forced his arm forward when they got to the back door of the hotel and made him push on the door handle with his palm to open it. Through the door and across the hall was a short twenty yards. Just past that they turned left and moved the inebriated man right up to the elevator door. This time they used his finger to push the call button. No one spoke, yet it seemed like they knew exactly what to do. The elevator bell sounded, the doors slid to each side and the lead men entered and immediately raised their signs up in front of the elevator camera. The group followed right behind uniformly entering the elevator as one. and everyone filed in and took a corner. The doors closed behind them.

Elevator doors opened on the fourth floor and the entourage moved out like a synchronized swim team. They knew exactly where they were going and quickly navigated the hallways making a left, then a right until they were staring at door number 342. It was a corner room on the third floor that overlooked the intersection of Irving and Vine.

They pushed the sleepy man up to the front and pressed his body against the door. The leader forcibly took his hand and placed it on the doorknob pressing it around the brass to insure the imprint of a good set of prints. A crisp knock on the door got it to open and then the group dragged the guy inside. The door closed behind them but not before one of the men glanced around to make sure that no one saw anything. Satisfied, he ducked inside and closed the door.

Inside the Hotel room, another man was waiting by the half open living room window. He was holding a small pair of binoculars with both his hands covered by white latex gloves. From behind the thick hotel curtains, he peered out the window. The newly arrived team of men forced the drugged man into a chair in the middle of the living room and threw him into it. He didn't have the strength to resist if he wanted to. Then they stood back and waited.

Somewhere within the next hour the man with the binoculars saw what he was looking for. He calmly turned and gave the signal to the others and handed his optics to his partner. All of them had latex gloves on. His partner took it and placed the binoculars in the hands of the man who was now asleep in the chair.

The man behind the curtains bent down and picked up a Danial Defense DD5 AR-10 rifle equipped with a more common lower end Leopold scope. It was nothing fancy, but it was a popular selling brand of AR rifles on the market with sales of this model reaching over six thousand a year at the height of its popularity. The looming ban on semi-automatic weapons guided their choice of weapon making sure this deed was done by an AR style rifle. It wasn't a rifle that a sophisticated sniper would use, no, far from it. It was just a rifle that thousands of Joe blows out there had in their possession. But no matter what kind of rifle it actually was (hunting or whatever) it would now be called "That nasty black AR rifle" by the media.

Down at street level on Vine, Senator Coulomb exited the bookstore with a small contingent of armed security guards around him. News reporters were waiting outside, and fans trailed behind as he left the store. He paused on the street to address a quick question posed by a news reporter. "Senator Coulomb, you're on the record as an ardent anti-gun sponsor but it is a well-known fact that your security force carries guns to protect you. How do you justify that? After rattling off the question the reporter quickly shoved the microphone in the Senator's direction. Senator Coulomb couldn't resist the temptation to respond on camera.

"Well now my very young naive man" (the reporter was very young looking) "...at this point, it is legal for security forces to carry guns. We aren't breaking any laws. As soon as I get guns out of the hands of criminals my security force won't need to carry them now will they". It was obvious that the Senator was disappointed in the question due to the tone in the guy's voice. The Senator brushed off the reporter and moved on to a smiling pretty young lady who looked a whole lot friendlier.

The curtain behind the window on the fourth floor moved and the sniper behind it adjusted the angle and shouldered the rifle. He set the rifle's barrel down on the window ledge for support and laid his right cheek on the stock of the gun. His right eye settled on the scope lens that he adjusted until the cross hairs were clear in front of a focused background. Taking aim, the cross hairs floated across a view of many nameless faces and bodies of people in the crowd outside City Book Store until the center point found its intended target- Senator Nadd Coulomb. The impact point settled on the middle of his neck. If the shot was high the bullet would strike his head, if it hit low, it would be a deadly shot to the heart. A shot anywhere between and the sniper would be just as pleased, it would surely strike the spinal cord and separate the scull from the torso causing instant death.

Nadd Coulomb chatted warmly with the attractive lady for a bit longer than he should have. He gave her more time than the average taxpayer. The bad gun acquired its target and then shook with a crack. The senator was hit square in the neck with a 30'06 hollow point magnum bullet. From the front it just looked like he got punched- hard.

He crumpled to the ground with his mouth open and a calm expression on his face indicating that he had no clue as to what was happening or why he couldn't control any part of his body. Without suffering, he died just seconds later.

The sniper at the window quickly walked over to the chair in the center of the room and dropped the rifle in the lap of the man sitting there. The guy semi woke up and looked at his captors. The killer manipulated the man's hands to hold the rifle as if he had just shot the gun, effectively putting his fingerprints on the rifle in all the right places. Next, he pulled out a nine-millimeter Colt pistol and manipulated the slide back and then sharply forward. There was no talking between any of this as the killer worked, just the famous "cha ching" of the pistol as the man chambered a round. Disturbed by the sound, the drugged guy became somewhat more fully awake. His eyes bugged out wide open with realization when he saw the rifle in one hand and a pistol in the other with the barrel of the pistol pointed at his head. The scene was set and without hesitation the sniper pulled the trigger.

Blood and brain matter splattered all over the apartment just after the pistols crack of death. The man's head snapped back against the chair and bounced off the backrest. Then his body slumped forward over the rifle in his lap. Quickly the sniper made sure the pistol's safety was in the "on" position then pushed the man's body back up in the chair and pulled one of the dead man's hands off the rifle and placed it on the pistol. Once again, he molded his fingers around the plastic molding pressing them into the gun and his palm into the handle and fingers on the trigger to assure good prints. Then he switched the pistols safety back to "off" and let the hand and gun drop naturally to his side.

All three of the men moved to the door looking back making sure they didn't miss anything. The sniper with the latex gloves on was the only one to touch the doorknob on the way out. As they scurried out the rear door of the Hotel, Police entered the front door with guns drawn.

20

Nasty Black Rifle

News hit the street about Senator Coulomb's assassination and there was an immediate uproar by the media and by all politicians. A call for the government to do something about automatic rifles was instantaneous. And now that the attack had been against a sitting senator the executive branch was quick to respond.

The main obstacle in the crosshair was not the Senator; it was the second amendment and the people's right to bear arms. Guns were in the way so therefore guns had to go. The elite knew it was imperative to disarm the population to ensure a smooth transition into the next phase of transforming America. The president was told to make this happen. No amount of uproar from pro-gun organizations including the now impotent NRA could sway the opinion of the political class who were now bound and determined to change the political landscape. This issue just happened to coincide with the UN's "Treaty on small arms gun sales" which passed by a large majority just last month.

The President gave a speech within minutes of the shooting. After saying a bunch of nonsense, he got down to it.

"...by executive order EO-129-52A I hereby institute a ban on all Automatic rifles and others, as described herein.

Last month the United Nations passed the "Treaty on small arms gun sales" and its high time we follow world opinion and abide by the

UN mandate. The whole world is behind us on this issue and it's time for America to join them. Laws that the World Organization deems as imperative for the future of a peaceful planet ride parallel to ours. What message would we send if we rejected world peace? This is the direction the world is going. We heard all the arguments; the debate is over. In memory of Senator Nadd Coulomb and by executive order, I hereby ban any and all AR-15 style rifles, period. This weapon is only designed to kill human beings! In no way does a law-abiding citizen need to be in possession of one of these military style weapons. From now on we will place our confidence in our police who are perfectly capable of protecting the citizens they serve. That's their job, let's leave it to them to do it.

Also included in the ban are any semi-automatic rifles or pistols with large capacity magazines of over five rounds or more. This is fair and still leaves the hunters among us with plenty of options.

It's a shame that guns are used with such malice and ill intent. I feel for the family of Nadd Coulomb. In an effort to curb their abuse and to save the lives of common citizens, I feel that this is an important step to do what's right in order to win the battle over this growing atrocity. We can't allow fear to permeate into the lives of our congressmen. They too have a job to do and none of them should have to worry about guns! We will no longer tolerate their misuse! Guns take people out permanently! Now we must take guns out- permanently! It's time. No more! We're going to make it safe for our children to live in the United States of America!".

In the week that followed, more details of executive order EO-129-52A dribbled out. There were two major differences between the 1994 ban and the new one. Politicians noticed that there wasn't a violent reaction to Clinton's weapons ban in 1994, probably because it only scratched the surface by banning about ten of what they called "military style" rifles. It didn't piss enough people off to have any kind of adverse reaction. In the new EO-129-52A the inferred list of banned weapons was ten times as long as it was before and now included in the ban was the common .223 caliber bullet which all AR-15 style rifles use. EO-129-52A didn't bother to list what was illegal; it just gave a short list of the few models of .308 hunting rifles and 9mm handguns that were legal. Anyone desiring to purchase one of these models along with all existing owners who wished to keep them were now required to apply for an owner's license and to pay a yearly fee for each gun they owned.

Gun ownership was narrowed to where a citizen was only allowed to own a single shot bolt action hunting rifle or a single- or double-barreled shotgun. period. The second difference was the clincher; confiscation. It was now not only illegal to buy a military style weapon it was illegal to own one. The ban would be phased in over a three-month grace period and within that time an owner was required to voluntarily turn in their weapons by dropping them off at the nearest police station. There would be no penalty if done so within the allotted time. If you possessed an illegal firearm past the effective date the weapon would be confiscated, and you would be arrested for possession and charged with a felony. From that point on, as a felon, you wouldn't be allowed to own any type of firearm for the rest of your life.

Immediately the government launched a campaign to sequester all weapons in possession at gun stores and also their records of sale. They also put out a request for all records on private owner gun sales too. They had to act quickly because gun stores all over America were going out of business or more likely going underground fast. Of course, going out of business was the preferred result of the law. Within days gun store owners received notices demanding the voluntary surrender of all banned items along with all applicable sales records. The letter demanded that they be given up to local police under the threat of jail time if they failed to obey the order. And to top it off, there was no provision to provide compensation for anything anyone turned in. Businesses and private owners alike had to turn in their entire cache of illegal arms so that they could be destroyed (or sold to deserving foreign countries).

There was an instant uproar and major resistance from every sector in complying with the order. Hatred toward the government brewed in the minds of people who still cherished the Constitution and their second amendment rights. "This is an outright breach of American law" they shouted. But it fell on deaf ears. The government's campaign was a blatant attempt to start that steam roller rolling and sell the idea that the Constitution was an old, outdated document that needed to be modified to reflect modern times and that any clause contained therein should not be immune from being "tweaked". Of course, the obvious difference was that the government was doing the tweaking, not "We the People" which was clearly the original intent installed into the process by the founding fathers.

The White House press secretary stated "Anyone who believes that the second amendment and the right to bear arms is still relevant today is living in the past".

Most of the population got mad, really mad. The media reported that poles showed that over half the population sided with the president even though statistics coming from the NRA showed the exact opposite. Lines were being drawn and people began to stand on one side or the other. Suddenly, those same gun owners who always referred to Charlton Hesston's famous quote "They'll have to pry my gun out of my cold dead fingers" had to make a choice and either give it up, go to jail or die.

It took gun owners a while to respond. Many didn't know what could be done. They had to dig deep and needed time to think. All of them were stunned when they realized that if they defy this order, suddenly every one of them would become a criminal, a felon! Everyone had to conclude and figure out how they were going to fight this. Most of them waited to see if political pressure could be applied effectively against the administration to get them to back down. And they waited to see how the government planned to enforce the law.

Multiple incidents of antigovernment protests began to rear up from the throngs of angry citizens, sponsored heavily by pro Constitutional rights groups. They tried to push back against the federal government's latest decision to alter the Constitution. This topic above all else split America down the middle exactly like the issue of States rights did before the Civil War. One was either passionately for or vehemently against the government's push to increase its power and bolster its control over "We the People". Once more a freedom that Americans had enjoyed for over two hundred years evaporated under the thumb of executive action.

The deadline for voluntary surrender of illegal weapons came and went. A report from the ATF estimated that only about fourteen percent of gun owners had participated and had turned in illegal firearms. Note: The ATF is now called the BATFE. Bureau of Alcohol, Tobacco, Firearms and Explosives but it is still commonly referred to as the ATF. It was immediately apparent that a more formidable method of persuasion would be needed to achieve a higher success rate and the ATF was assigned the task of implementing the initiative. They switched into offensive mode and would now use their manpower to execute result-oriented missions that would procure the maximum amount of product. The head of the agency Mr. Lyle Koneham was under a lot of pressure from his peers to speed up the plan and, as quietly as possible, disarm the American public.

To obtain the desired results, the ATF organized their task force and first planned multiple shock raids on the largest Gun stores located in the Border States with Mexico. They knew they'd have to act fast to confiscate weapons before the word (and the weapons) got out. If they didn't, guns as well as paperwork would start to disappear and go underground or filter into bordering countries.

* * *

It was a big surprise to the clerk when the large black GMC box van with no lettering written on the side pulled up in front of "Firearm Sales Inc" in Dallas Texas. Mr. Al Sack's suspicion flared immediately. He was tending to a customer at the counter who was inquiring about the price of a Heckler & Koch P2000SK pistol when the commotion outside the window caught his attention. He glanced over the customer's shoulder and focused on a team of men in black deploying out of the back of the van. Initial reaction shot his blood pressure up to 140/100 before he was able to read 'A.T.F.' written in large yellow letters on the back of one of their uniforms.

Quickly assessing that it wasn't a robbery, Al was able to control himself and contain the flight response that surged through his body. Besides, the store had one of those locked iron bar cages at the front door where he had total control over who entered. They wouldn't be able to get through that quickly if at all. That gave him solace but the thought process froze him in place. Just to be on the safe side he decided to go for the gun under the counter. That's when the customer in front of him pulled his badge and flashed a gold shield at him. "I wouldn't do that if I were you" the guy said and then declared in a loud voice "I'm a Federal agent. Don't do anything foolish".

Al looked out the window and saw the ATF team deploying behind cars and walls for protection one by one pointing their rifles at his store. One of the uniformed men continued and walked calmly up to the front door, opened it and walked into the iron bar cage on the inside of the store. He stood there and waited, staring at the clerk.

It wasn't much of a standoff. Al just had a commonsense decision to make.

"We're just here to check inventory" the agent standing in front of him said. "What's it gunna be?".

At that moment another clerk came out of the back with a shotgun in his arms. Luckily, he wasn't in full defensive mode, the barrel was pointing up to the ceiling.

"Stand down Amos, stand down. I'm going to buzz them in" Al said to his partner. He reached under the counter and pressed a button. The buzzer sounded and the door lock on the cage clicked. The agent opened the iron door and held it open for the other members as they ushered in.

The three major newspapers still in business didn't run the story. This headline along with others like it only appeared on the internet blogs and news sites as the information trickled in from relatives of the people who were arrested.

"ILLEGAL GUN STORES RAIDED BY THE ATF"

At that time, it was almost guaranteed that the ATF would find something illegal. Store owners didn't just get rid of the items (or turn them in), they tried their best to sell them quickly to get rid of them. It sickened them to have to throw that much inventory down the drain. Every store that was raided got caught with some sort of left-over illegal inventory and their owners were arrested and sent to jail. Conspiracy theorists theorized that this was the main intent of the law, to document who they were and to put these pro second amendment people away.

News of the government initiative got around and spread quickly throughout the states. In conjunction with the stories zooming around the underground internet about swat teams, there was a smaller article of no less significance describing another government atrocity.

"IRS Gears Up For Recovery"

"As if the intrusion on our right to bear arms is not enough there are also reports circulating of a new push by the IRS to confiscate the property of private citizens. The reasons for this change of policy is unknown, the IRS has refused comment, but our sources report that teams of IRS agents are performing missions in which they surround and forcefully enter the homes of common citizens. They claim the victim owes the government large sums of money and are there to collect the debt through the process of procurement. In a pamphlet left with the victims the IRS site article IV in the "Reclamation Act" that gives them the

> power to do this. They state that the IRS has always had the right to satisfy debt through "confiscation" and now they are just exercising that right. They then proceed to execute these orders without civil warrants of any kind. The result is that the homeowner loses their home".

Two weeks passed and reports came in about a dramatic rise in arson related fires. The media added an obvious slant to stoke the controversy between certain segments of the population. It was like the North against the South all over again along with the left playing the race card between blacks and whites and fanning the flames of the poor against the rich. One TV news segment aired like this...

"An overwhelming number of fires are afflicting gun store establishments all across the south" (In the background were scenes of a large-scale fire showing emergency vehicles, fireman and police dealing with the burning of a commercial building. The camera eventually got around to the storefront sign that designated the establishment as the Century Gun Shop).

"I have interviewed the owner of this gun store" the reporter said. "He has refused to come on camera, but he claims, and I quote that 'This is the work of anti-gun protesters with the help and support of the Federal Government who is vying for the destruction of gun dealers all across America'.

Yes, it is true that in most cases the buildings were burnt to the ground effectively putting the dealers out of business, but in every case, suspicion permeated the scene because all the computers and therefore all accounting records were conveniently destroyed in the fire. Now the Government has no way to trace the history of the owners of illegal firearms sold at this location. By design? It looks pretty obvious to this reporter".

The camera switched to a shot of the Chief of Police himself standing at the crime scene with an ATF member at his side. Bunton Texas police Chief Allen Wex was being interviewed and he had this to say "We believe the fire was not the criminal act of an anti-gun protester. We feel the fire was started by the owner and that this is a blatant attempt to divert blame onto the anti-gun segment while at the same time it's an effective way to destroy the records of hundreds of illegal owners so they can no longer be identified" (The scene switched to the aftermath of the fire showing the smoking ruins of the store and the burnt-out shell). The reporter continued "At the very least we can be glad that some illegal firearms were also destroyed along with the building. It's worthy to note that the conservative movement has been identified as a common factor in the identity of people involved in the arsons and in the increase of violent Klu Klux Klan type protests that have sprung up all across the South. The South is once again picking up its flag 'old glory' ..." (new footage showing protestors holding up and marching with the Confederate flag are mixed in with images of blacks getting beat up by a gang of whites). "...they're resurrecting one hundred-year-old wounds by arguing states' rights while at the same time trying to rekindle isolationist immigration policies designed to cut off immigration into the US. We are even hearing the same old rhetoric about seceding from the Union! Batten down the hatch's folks; here we go again- one more time. Those rebels will never learn".

21

IRS A.R.T.

"Going smooth" was how the IRS-ART program was described during the early morning briefing at IRS headquarters in Arlington Virginia. All the main players in the operation had gathered for a private meeting to assess their progress. Eight of the officials involved became quite optimistic after reading the initial results. Tallies had been laid out in a black and white report that sat in front of each one of them on the conference table. Inside was a spread sheet showing totals from the first month of operation. The figures divulged remarkable numbers and upon hearing more details about the mechanics of the operation all the members were impressed.

"Opposition to the recovery program is almost nil" explained the head of the IRS Mr. Anthony Knowles. "We have also been successful at controlling the media and getting them to ignore the initiative. Our main objective (resources) are flowing in as planned and I give high praise to the head of our recovery department, Special Agent Roy Atkinson. The routine he has developed is working flawlessly and has integrated well with the various local police agencies that we have to deal with. The report details some of the early feedback we have gotten but we have Agent Atkinson here to report to us in person".

Atkinson didn't bother to stand up, he just began speaking from his seat. He was quick to comment on resistance to his efforts. "When or if we encounter any resistance from local police, I just repeat my favorite line- Sir you don't want to mess with the IRS. That got a slight chuckle from the board members. "I stare into their eyes for just a second until that statement sinks in. When the offending official thinks more seriously about the possible repercussions, all resistance melts away. It's magic. Every one of the twenty-seven re-possessions we have made so far went without a hitch".

Atkinson's boss Mr. Knowles and his superior Mr. Fletcher along with Mr. Shi Fong were all very pleased. They praised his work after reading the final figure at the bottom of the "Total Monetary Value of Assets Recovered" column.

Atkinson continued, "Oblivious targets were consistently unprepared for the appearance of my team and in most instances, they caught a lot of valuable assets on the property due to well-timed surprise visits. If we can keep the lawyers from shutting this down, I can assure you, the Agency's going to recover a highly significant amount of assets. Once we get ramped up with teams operating in every major local you can multiply that total by three hundred or more".

Mr. Shi Fong raised his eyebrows. Then he directed his Chinese partners to the figure that Agent Atkinson was talking about and spoke to his partners in Chinese. "All of this I consider very promising" he told them. "This will indeed transfer a consistent flow of money back into the hands of our partners". They all nodded their heads in approval.

Mr. Fletcher read the results and agreed silently calculating that from his share he'd be a rich man before the year was out. It showed in all their faces. The members of the board were ready to proceed with the next phase.

When a property was confiscated by the IRS, an "in their pocket" Judge immediately transferred the property deed into the name of Allied Real Estate Company. The capital generated by the sale of the property registered on the books as "payment on account" by the US government. Mr. Fong then transferred the money or the physical property itself to a prioritized list of parties pre-determined by his boss's directives. The contents or valuables in the home or building were sent to the Allied auction house and put up for sale. Proceeds for the sale of these items were treated the same way. Mr. Fletcher was the representative to the IRS who was listed as the owner of the ARE company and Mr. Shi Fong was named as the treasurer who oversaw the transfer of funds. The plan was working to the satisfaction of all entities involved.

Orders came down from the board to proceed with the escalation of the asset reclamation effort. Roy was promoted to Commander and authorized to head up the creation of additional teams modeled after his own. He wasted no time in using the budget and the resources at his disposal to expand the operation. Within two months he had twenty-five teams up and operating in five states with many more to follow. They all started to perform smoothly with similar bottom line results. Combined, they produced approximately two hundred twenty-five million dollars in the first month in which all the teams were active. Even that was considered just a drop in the bucket compared to what was owed to the investors involved but the Chinese Government used the returns from the project to placate some of their more loyal comrades. Either they were paid off monetarily or they were offered ownership of a "summer home" in the USA. Surprisingly enough, many of them took the summer home option.

All went amazingly well with success showing up as an ever-increasing number on the monthly reports bottom line. But there was one sign of trouble on the horizon. It showed up in a few sentences at the end of the report that referred to a noticeable upsurge in instances of resistance. Violence had been reported during a few recent ART missions. It surmised that informed tax cheats were becoming more resistant to their efforts. Word was getting around and some victims were becoming increasingly reluctant to give up their property. In one case even the Police escort was given a hard time in entering the property. An actual fist fight broke out when the owners figured out what was about to go down. Rumors were running rampant all over the internet; citizens were warned about government swat teams that were going around confiscating property and kicking out the owners.

Opposition had to be expected, agents gave their victims their best song and dance to get them to comply and go peacefully. It worked most of the time but in an ever-increasing number of cases the criminals had to be subdued and taken away in handcuffs, not by a taxi. The second type of resistance came from an unexpected source; the police themselves. Increasingly, in certain districts more than others, the police were bucking the program and were expressing disdain for the ART's methods.

Newly appointed ART Texas Division section leader Dean Minolta wasn't happy about it. His boss Roy Atkinson was coming to meet him to discuss the problem with the police. Dean oversaw the Texas division and had been active with his team for about four weeks now. Everything was going smoothly until they started running into major problems in getting cooperation from certain segments of the police, not to mention that he had personally been assaulted twice by the owners of confiscated property. There was also the attempted murder of a team member when he was hit and almost run over by a fleeing vehicle. Dean was bound and determined to minimize his personal risk and attempted to get more police protection for these jobs, but his request was turned down. The Chief of police in some precincts gave various excuses that started with "We have limited resources and we're short on funds, short on warrant personnel, we're not set up for that or it's not our job. It always ended with some kind of statement about how Minolta was lucky to get what he got.

It was the Monday before Thanksgiving; Agent Minolta was assisting in the morning's early raid. His men followed the only two available Houston Texas warrant officers up the stairs to the front of the Claymore residence. They were in standard formation with two of his men walking in front of him and two men who broke off and worked their way around back just as they had been taught. It was 6:35 in the morning and it was just now getting light out. Prior experience had determined that this was the best time to perform recovery raids and had the best chance of catching the owners at home.

AIC Minolta (Agent in Charge) looked at his watch hoping to get his repo team set up and running early so his men could handle the details and he'd be done and on his way. That would leave him free for his lunch date with his boss Roy Atkinson who would be arriving that morning. He couldn't be late for this one and it would be a feather in his cap to have this raid go down smoothly so that he could show Roy how efficiently he and his team were working. This was important; he had to keep this job. Tonight, he planned to have a discussion with his wife about how they were going to pay for their son's college education. He just couldn't screw this up.

Agent Minolta turned around and saw that the taxi had arrived on time and was now waiting outside the target property. He sat in his Chevy suburban parked in the street outside the home as per SOP (standard operating procedure) everything was a go. The Claymore's were an old couple, their file said 72 and 74 years old so he wasn't worried about an energetic response to their re-claim. He turned back and nodded to his warrant officer giving him the signal to proceed.

A knock on the door produced a small child of about eight who opened it and stood there looking at the policeman. "Son is this the Claymore residence?".

The child nodded his head.

"Could you get your mommy or daddy and tell them it's the police and that we need to talk to them".

The boy didn't respond, he just left the door open, turned around and walked back down the hallway. The officer took it as an invitation, pulled the screen door open and walked into the residence. The kid disappeared down the hallway and turned into one of the back rooms. An entourage of men came in and settled into the front hallway with an eye out for the parents. "Police!" one of the officers yelled as he entered.

* * *

Minolta's boss Roy Atkinson was pissed. Atkinson took a cab direct from LaGuardia airport to the scene at the Claymore Residence, where Minolta's Texas AR team ran into heavy resistance, he was at the house within an hour after getting the call. It just so happened he was on Jet Blue's 915 out of Washington on his way to Texas to meet with Agent Minolta and his group at the time of the incident. He had to get out of his cab a half block away and make his way through the traffic jam of police, ambulance, and detective vehicles to get to the crime scene. He showed his badge two times along the way to placate a couple of cowboy cops. They let him through.

"Damn them for not knowing who I am" Atkinson thought. Again, he showed his badge to a uniform cop at the barricades in front of the house as he whisked by the guy without explanation. It was disenchanting "I have IRS ART written on my jacket. That should be enough. Can't you read you fucking idiots. These letters don't carry much weight around here- BUT THEY WILL!" he promised, swearing to himself that in the ensuing days he'd change all that.

Atkinson walked up to the cordoned off area and ducked underneath the thick yellow tape to get to the front door. On the steps just off the porch was a body, he had to maneuver around it. A member of the forensics team was hunched over the lifeless man looking for evidence, another was taking pictures. There was a pool of blood that had dripped and meandered its way down the steps. Atkinson paused and shook his head; he could tell it was one of his men. Not a pretty sight and it wasn't a good way to start the day. He asked one of the policemen stationed at the front door "Detective Sanchez?" and the guy motioned toward the house. Inside he found the guy talking to two crime scene specialists and a member of the coroner's office. They were in the middle of the living room analyzing the scene when Agent Atkinson walked up.

Sanchez looked up as Atkinson approached and immediately assumed that he was the main man from the IRS AR team who he had just spoken with on the phone. He turned back to the coroner and said "I'll sign the release for this one, you can take him. I'm not done with the others yet". Then he broke off from the conversation to address the agent. "Agent Atkinson?".

"Yes, Detective Sanchez?"

"We spoke on the phone" Sanchez said.

"What the hell went on here?" Atkinson asked right off.

"Look agent Atkinson, I'll give you a brief description of what I've been able to piece together here and then you've gotta go, we're a little busy right now and only internal agency personnel are allowed on the crime scene at this stage. You can see we're just now clearing out the bodies".

"Detective, that's all I need, and I'll be gone".

Sanchez led him over to where he believed it all began. He explained: "The Claymore boy let our men in, police entered the residence through the front door and met an old lady here who came out from that room down the hall; I heard she slowly hobbled up to the men and greeted them with a noticeable limp in her stride. That's why they weren't too worried about her... she seemed innocent enough. Atkinson pictured the scene in his mind.

"Yes? What is this about and why are you in my house?" The old lady stared at the police and the strange men who were now unexpectedly standing in her front hallway. She scrutinized them with squinty eyes and a frown that became permanently affixed to her face. The frown deepened when she saw the IRS ART patch on the agent's jacket.

"Ma'am I'm officer Kinzick from Metro Police and this is IRS Agent Minolta. May we speak with you and your husband? Is he home?".

"Blank" was how she stared at them, seemingly without comprehension. The grimace never left her face. "I'm not the owner, I'll call him" she said and pulled out a cell phone. Quickly she speed dialed a number and whispered into the phone as she turned around "Harry there's IRS agents in the hallway!" She harmlessly hobbled slowly down the hallway and yelled over her shoulder "He'll be down in a minute". One of the agents called after her "Ah Ma'am, don't leave, come back please".

But the old lady quickly disappeared back into the same back room she had just come from. One of the men followed.

"Our men fanned out on the first floor" Sanchez said to Atkinson as he pointed in three directions down the hallway. "One agent went down the hall, one scoped out the living room and the other moved toward the stairs". Sanchez looked up the stairwell to the second floor and thought about how it must have gone down...

The old man appeared at the top of the stairs and one of the agents at the bottom yelled up to him "Sir, can you come down here please we need to talk to you?" The old man responded by pulling out a shotgun from behind his back. With amazing agility, he caught the agent totally off guard. The man was quite the opposite of the old lady they had just met. In a split second, the barrel of that shotgun pointed squarely at the agent. The blast sent a deafening roar throughout the house. Everyone else jumped and cringed. It was so loud that it instantly impaired the hearing of everyone in the hall; that is everyone but the old man, it didn't affect him a bit because he was already hard of hearing which gave him a distinct advantage, he didn't freeze up or flinch at all which made him that much quicker than the intruders. The old man continued pumping the action of the shotgun with amazing speed pulling the trigger again and again while he blasted his way down the stairs.

The first blast struck the agent square in the chest and blew him backwards against a large picture on the wall behind him. Its frame fell on the ground with the glass shattering into splinters as it hit the floor; the agent followed and slumped to the ground against the fractured picture. A second blast tore into his body as he hit the floor. Everyone in the hallway instinctively ducked and tried to get out of the way of the next shot. The cops pulled their weapons and had them in their hands as they sought cover all the while looking around for the source of the threat. The most likely direction of the threat was from the second floor, so their attention was drawn to the stairwell.

Agent Minolta saw two legs and a shotgun barrel through the stairway banister. He quickly decided he wanted nothing more to do with the situation and ran towards the front door. At the same time the cops pointed their guns up the stairs the old lady appeared from out of that back room down the hall and raised her stainless steel 357 Ruger with a crooked look of determination on her face. Everyone who had a weapon fired at the same time. The old lady walked down the hallway firing shot after shot and the old man did the same as he walked down the stairs toward the intruders. The cops and the agents returned fire but were caught in the crossfire.

Agent Minolta ran out crashing through the front screen door without even trying to open it. He ran all out until his legs went numb and crumpled underneath him. His face turned into a bugged-out expression with his eyes and mouth wide open as he fell flat and sprawled out over the concrete porch. Momentum made his body slide another foot across the terrace until his upper body slumped halfway over the first step on the walkway. It looked like he might tumble down the stairs but instead his body came to a stop near the top. Looking closer there was a bullet hole in his back where a small red spot started to expand as he bled. Minolta couldn't move a muscle; the bullet had severed his spine and then pierced the right ventricle of his heart. A few moments later, he died with his eyes wide open.

Looking at the house from the street, you could see flashes of light flicker from every window and the open doorway like the kid was playing with the light switch, only each flicker was matched to the sound of a gunshot as the people inside continued to blast away at each other. Then it stopped, and there was dead silence.

Who got the worst of it was the question on Agent Hopkins mind as he crawled cautiously in a low squat from the back to the front of the house with his gun drawn. He was the first to come upon agent Minolta's body lying outside at the top of the stairs and was appalled. Hopkins crouched over the body with his gun aimed at the front door, one hand checked for a pulse with his eyes looking frantically around for the shooter. Another gunshot echoed loudly from the back of the house. Seconds later the sound of a car engine roared to life and the screeching of tires was heard. Hopkins stood up and watched a blue

Chevy Challenger hall ass out from the garage at the back of the driveway behind the house. It was the old man. He drove violently steering around obstacles, as well as the police car, which stood in his way at the entrance of the driveway. He hit a curb, bounced, barely missed a tree, ran over a bush and scraped off a ton of metal sparks as it slammed down on street pavement at full throttle.

Officer Kinzick, the only one still alive in the house ran out the front door at full speed running parallel to the escaping vehicle as it sped down the driveway. Kinzick was one hell of a lucky agent; Hopkins recognized him and didn't shoot. He was covered in blood clutching his chest with his left arm and ran out into the street behind the fleeing car. He had to settle for staring at the rear of the getaway car as it fishtailed and screeched its tires in front of him. He raised his good right arm and aimed a badly shaking Glock pistol at the vehicle. A small boy's head popped up in the rear window of the car and stared back at him with wide eyes as the car started to speed off down the street. Kinzick fired and then fell to his knees, his gun sinking to the pavement in defeat. The car disappeared into the distance as the officer blacked out and fell the rest of the way to the ground.

Detective Sanchez walked over and motioned to the body on the floor in the hallway and then looked out the front door at the covered body of agent Minolta lying on the sidewalk outside. "That's your man out on the porch" Sanchez said to Atkinson as he squat down on the floor to look at officer Shelton's body.

Atkinson looked out the front door, closed his eyes for a second and shook his head as he visualized the events and pictured how they died.

"One of ours, we think officer Kinzick here got off a shot and took out Mrs. Claymore over there" Sanchez motioned to the body of a lady in the hallway. "Damn it! The old man must have had more than a five-shot capacity in that shotgun of his. Shelton was killed where he stood. Kinzick took a 12 gauge to the left arm and chest and fell there. He was knocked down and out from the blast but was still alive". The detective pointed to a blood trail on the floor in the center of the hallway.

"Mr. Claymore made it down the stairs and ran down the hall to the back of the house bypassing Kinzick thinking he was dead. Either that or he just didn't care. Probably shocked to see the body of his wife". Detective Sanchez walked past Mrs. Claymore's body and down the hall. Agent Atkinson followed. They walked through the kitchen and out the back door of the home.

"Mr. Claymore must have grabbed the kid who was still somewhere in the back here and high tailed it out the back door. Your agent Newton there..." the detective pointed to agent Newton's body lying on the sidewalk going to the detached garage. "...confronted the shooter on his way out, unfortunately- it wasn't agent Newton's lucky day. Mr. Claymore had at least one shot left and put one in his chest at point blank range. We figure it happened right in front of his grandson whom he took with him. They got into a late model Chevy Charger and took off out of here like a bat outa hell". Detective Sanchez walked Agent Atkinson out the back and up the driveway to the front of the house.

"We know this because your agent Lawson did a duck and cover in the living room. He came out of it unscathed and was able to give us a limited account of events from his perspective. At that point, wounded Officer Kinzick had gotten up and saw the car taking off from that living room window. He ran out the front door and even in his condition chased the car into the street. He saw the boy in the back seat of the car just before he passed out in the street. He's at Belleview right now in critical. This was confirmed by your Agent Hopkins, who was out back when he heard the shots and then came running up here to witness the tail end of everything. He's being questioned now.

Detective Sanchez had effectively escorted Agent Atkinson back off the property to the front of the driveway while telling the story and now pointed down the street. "He got away. And that's that. Now if you don't mind, I've got to get back to work".

"Thank you for your time detective. Please call me when the crime scene is cleared. We still have our job to finish".

"Ah yes, your job. Just a word of advice Agent Atkinson, things just got a little more complicated around here and a hell of a lot more dangerous, I doubt if we are going to be able to assist you in the same capacity as before or should I say I doubt if anyone is going to want to assist you if you know what I mean".

"Thank you, Detective, I appreciate your candor and after seeing that..." Agent Atkinson paused and glanced back at the house "...I can't say as I'd blame them. No worry, I'm already making changes as we speak". Agent Atkinson turned and walked away already deep in thought contemplating his options. He was oblivious to his surroundings and appeared at his waiting taxi down the block without remembering the walk. "The Agency will be transformed and kicked up to a whole new level" he said to himself. "I'll see to that".

It was a whole new ball game now and Atkinson envisioned himself not as the coach or the star player, in his mind he had become one of the elites.

* * *

When asked, life at Tenny Hill Academy was never described as easy, but most students responded with "It's great". Kaiden said the same thing to his father on the phone when his dad asked how things were going. "Dad it's not easy but over all I'm doing just great. I've met a lot of friends here and I'm learning things that I never thought I'd be interested in. It's like I'm a whole different person up here and people are interested in me for what I am, not for what I can get them".

His father said, "Living in the country is a lot different than living in the City huh son".

"Yeah, I feel that all that time there was this veil over my head keeping me down, keeping me from seeing what's truly out there. By coming here, I popped my head up and looked around for the first time. The things I see as important have changed. I mean I used to think that I just had to have those silver mirror finished Nike sneakers, remember? Damn I paid 275 bucks for them. I haven't even thought about sneakers since I've been up here. Now a good pair of hiking boots seem like a hell of a lot better deal, and they cost less than the sneakers! Can you imagine that?

"Son this is music to my ears, I thought you might resent your mother and I for sending you there. We didn't know how it would turn out. I'm glad it's working out for you. It sounds fantastic".

"Dad" Kaiden said in a more solemn tone. "I would never resent you or mom, heaven knows you had good reason for sending me here. I was worried I'd hate it too; thought it was going to be a jail term. Hell, I even had plans to take off and get at a hea. But don't worry about that now; I'm seeing things a lot differently. There are things here that I want to do Dad. I know now that there's something that I want to accomplish with my life".

"Oh? Like what?".

"I don't quite know yet. It's something I feel. All I can tell you is that I see a purpose and I want to contribute, and I want to somehow make a difference. All my life I've wondered who I am and what I'm going to become. Here I finally feel like I'm on the path, the path to whatever that will be... That's all I can say".

"Wow, what are they teaching you up there?".

Kaiden laughed. "What are they teaching me? Well, I'm learning about the world in ways that I never thought of before. It's like I'm understanding the other side of the argument and it's all starting to make sense. I'll have to admit Dad that I've heard some of it before-you know the old Liberal Vs Conservative arguments, but it never really meant that much to me, I just didn't care back then. From what I heard; I just didn't like all the restraints that the conservative ideology put on people. As you might already know I preferred the freedom of a more liberal lifestyle. You know like 'if it feels good do it' modus operandi. Now I see the results of living with that kind of thinking. I never listened and now I'm seeing how all this stuff affects my life, your life, and moms, and in such a profound way. I never realized it before. Dad, I know what socialism is now. I had to sit myself down and figure out what I was, a Liberal or a Conservative. I took it topic by topic and defined how I really felt. And what do ya know, it ends up I'm a

Conservative. Now I know what direction I want to go, and even what direction I want the world to go..."

His father had tears in his eyes as he sat there on the phone listening to his son, now sounding so grown-up. The scattered visions of an adolescent had given way to the mature thoughts of a young man. He quietly thanked God that his son's connection to his gang along with ties to inner city life had been broken and hopefully left behind for good. He thought how it didn't take much for this rising star to transform himself into something positive. And to think that it almost went the other way. It just took a little push and a whole lot of help from above! A side request in his father's prayers was that Kaiden would also leave his old high maintenance girlfriend behind too. And then even that prayer was answered...

"Dad, I met this girl, her name is Shiloh, Shiloh Mead".

22

It Begins

Chancellor Gentry spoke into the intercom sitting on his desk "Send him in Mary".

Just before his guest entered, he let out a reluctant sigh and leaned back in his chair. A feeling bubbled to the surface telling him that this wasn't going to be a palatable experience due to the letter that was sitting on the desk in front of him. If it wasn't for that he would have made his guest a lot more comfortable, maybe held the meeting over lunch, but this exchange was better served in his office where he could end it on his own terms.

The letter prepared the Chancellor for the nature of the visit, but he never imagined the full ramifications of what would transpire. It sat there in front of him growing in significance as he looked at it. He suddenly realized that this was it; this was the bane that always threatened to rear its ugly head. This was the moment where proof that America had lost its way was literally waiting right outside his door. The freedom that we all took for granted had now begun to break down just like what was about to happen to the door that separated him from his guest. The door opened and the reaper entered.

Gentry looked up from his desk and watched the man walk into his office. He said to himself "So this is how it begins" and then thought about how this must have been what it was like when the Nazi Party rose to power in Germany before World War II. He glanced down at the letter in front of him.

From the Bureau of Alcohol, Tobacco, Firearms & Explosives.
To:
Chancellor Gentry
Tenny Hill Academy
1469 Mt. Tenny Rd.
New York, NY 10604

It has come to our attention that your facility is in possession of firearms that are deemed illegal pursuant to executive order in effect EO-129-52A. Our records show that you have not complied with the voluntary surrender order and that you are still in possession of these weapons.

The office of the ATF will be sending an agency representative to inventory the weapons in your possession and will determine their legal status. Please have all the items in question readily available for inspection. Any illegal weapons forthcoming at this time will be treated as in compliance and will not be dealt with harshly. Be warned that the hoarding of illegal items is considered a breach of federal law and violators will be fully punished. Any individuals involved in false testimony or conspiring to deceive the ATF will be arrested and prosecuted.

We require your utmost cooperation in this matter and your degree of cooperation will be duly noted.

Scheduled date of inspection: December 2.
Special Agent in Charge
Mallory Hicks

Agent Mallory Hicks walked into the Chancellors office with an air of importance trailing in his wake. They both went through the customary handshake but did it quickly, as if to get it over with. Hicks sat down, pulled out a file from his briefcase and started to flip through it. The file was clearly the result of someone's extensive research and contained the history and other records concerning THA.

Agent Hicks had sent out his application to all the Federal agencies, his efforts ended up landing him this job with the ATF. It wasn't his first choice, but he didn't hesitate, he jumped at the offer. "ATF Agent Hicks" I like the sound of that he said to his wife with a smile. Now, just a year later, he had lost the smile and most of his patience but not his determination to maintain a good reputation with the agency. He wanted a quick resolution to this case so he could be done with it and add another accomplishment to his record. Hicks had worked for the ATF for less than a year now but had come to love his job even more than he loved being a cop. His stint on the force in Frampton Pennsylvania made him aware that each successful arrest or high-speed chase that ended in the capture of a bad guy got him one step closer to his goal which was to become a prominent figure in one of the agencies. It didn't matter which one, the FBI, Secret Service, Federal Marshal, Homeland Security. Any of them would have sufficed. Once getting in the door he would move up the chain of command. His worse fear was to wallow around for years in Frampton Pa. as a common civil servant. "Someday…" he always said to himself, his wife, partner, or anyone else who would listen "I'll be the one giving the orders".

Hicks looked up at Chancellor Gentry and stated "Chancellor I'm here on serious business so I'll get right to the point. I've read your file and I see why this school is quite a concern to my boss.

The Chancellor raised his eyebrows "Really Mr. Hicks, and why would that be?".

"We have multiple complaints that have been registered against the Academy's admission board for one thing. Complaints that need to be addressed. It has been alleged that you have broken the Equal Opportunity Admission Law, more specifically by rejecting prospective black students who adhere to a certain political persuasion".

"Oh, and what persuasion would that be?" Gentry asked.

Agent Hicks lowered his head and raised his eyebrows while staring at the chancellor. "You know exactly what I'm talking about Mr. Gentry; let's just say anyone with a progressive liberal lean to the left or a member of the Progressive Liberation Party to be more precise. We have quite a few cases listed here of people who were denied enrolment. Can you explain that?"

"No, I can't, we don't even know a student's political interests until after they arrive here. There's no question on the application that requests that type of information, at least not that I'm aware of".

"I think it can be gleamed by reading between the lines, like when a student lists their extracurricular activities as being a part of a political debate group for example or when they list hunting as one of their favorite past times or the fact that they were president of the "PITA" organization for example. You get my drift".

"I do, and I can only say that this school doesn't hide what we are. We advertise that we are a military style Academy which in and of itself filters out a lot of the liberal mind set wouldn't you agree?".

"Oh, so you're saying that all people with a liberal mindset aren't interested in a military style career. Watch out Mr. Gentry your bias is showing".

"No, what I am saying is that many find out that they are not interested in investing their money in this style of education. I'll have to admit that we are on the higher end of the spectrum when it comes to tuition fees".

"And what is this about not accepting government subsidized students namely from the Higher Education Subsidy Program" Hicks asked him. "Its sole purpose is to allow students living below the poverty line to receive the same level of education that the rich get. Isn't that fair Mr. Gentry?"

"'Fair' doesn't enter the picture when considering accepting or rejecting an applicant Mr. Hicks. It's all determined on an applicant's eligibility, their IQ, and of course on their ability to pay".

"You mean their credit score? I think that's a form of discrimination right there, isn't it?".

Gentry avoided going down that path and stayed on topic. "I guess that's where we differ. We consider it 'natural selection', a process that happens naturally all on its own in a free capitalist society. But let me assure you, our decisions are not determined by a discriminating set of guidelines. Decisions are made on an individual basis. Yes, we positively select the ones best suited for this environment. That is our right as an independent business entity. That is why we don't accept money from the government; we do not want to be attached to or indebted to the government in any way. When the government throws money at something Mr. Hicks, they will then exercise a perceived right to control it. We want to keep outside influence on a student or on our curriculum to a minimum. Besides, we do accept people from all walks of life; it's just that the ones that find themselves outside the parameters of this school's philosophy tend to filter themselves out of the program either before or shortly after they arrive- it's their decision".

Hicks moved on to the next issue like he wasn't even listening. "We are also aware that you operate a 'militia' type organization out of this facility, called (he looked at the file and read from it) the New York State Cadet Organization, chartered by Tenny Hill Academy".

"The Cadets" The Chancellor corrected. "It's no secret Mr. Hicks, we are an Academy. By the way, why do you attach such a negative connotation to the word 'militia'. The Cadet organization does fulfill that requisite, but we don't believe it should be perceived in such a negative way, not in today's society. As an Academy, we are unique in that respect, a student here has the option of participating in a full military style education if they so desire. On the other hand, we are a fully accredited institute where one can participate in what you might call a 'standard' college education".

"Well not quite so standard Chancellor, I see from a list of your available classes; Government for the People, Survival 101, Caning for the future, Primitive living, Marksmanship, Fitness for survival, Military Combat 101, Man tracking, Martial for the Artist, Stellar stallions, Basic Military Maneuvers, Bartering basics and Mr. Chancellor… Safe Tunnel building?"

"Yes, well you never know when you might need a good tunnel" Gentry said with a lingering smile. But it faded quickly when Hicks didn't laugh. Then he added "Did I mention that we are unique? However, I might add sir; no more 'odd' than say; the University of Rochester who I understand is offering a course in "Alien Sex". In comparison I think we are well within normal boundaries wouldn't you agree?".

Agent Hicks leaned forward without cracking a smile and looked at the Chancellor. He spoke his words seriously with as much weight as he could muster "Mr. Gentry, we feel that it's best to leave military training to the military and we've determined that the Cadet Militia you're training at this college is an illegal organization. It has not been called upon or called to order by the State of New York and therefore has not been sanctioned as a legal entity. Let me read this to you;" Agent Hicks again referred to his file, flipped a few pages and then started to read with heightened emphasis on certain words and phrases…

"Article 1, Section 8 of the Constitution of the United States of America provides that: "The Congress shall have the power… to provide for calling forth the militia to execute the laws of the Union, suppress insurrections and repel invasions… To provide for organizing, arming, and disciplining the militia, and for governing such part of them as may be employed in the service of the United States, reserving to the states respectively, the appointment of officers and the authority of training the militia according to the discipline prescribed by Congress".

Hicks paused before going on. "Mr. Gentry. Let me head you off. I know you're going to rattle off the rest of the second amendment right here and try to use it for your defense. Please, allow me to finish reading it… again I quote from the constitution '…a well-regulated militia being necessary for a Free State, the right of the people to keep and bear arms shall not be infringed' end quote. You see, taken in its entirety without reading just that one last sentence clearly shows that the Constitution itself demonstrates that militias are a creation of the State, subject to being called forth by the government 'to execute the laws of the Union...' it reserves to the States 'the appointment of officers and the authority of training a militia...' You sir are not an authorized appointee of the State of New York government and are therefore not allowed to call up and appoint officers in your so-called 'State Militia'. The charter you have with the Cadet organization is illegal and the ATF herby issues you an order to cease and desist".

Hicks slid a paper onto the desk referring the Chancellor to the C&D order and then sat back in his chair quite pleased with himself and his delivery. He had presented it just as they had taught him to do.

Gentry noted that the confrontation was living up to his prediction, but he didn't like the way this was going. He said aloud, "It's funny that you, of all people should come in here and use the constitution to back up an organization that doesn't believe in its premise agent Hicks. The nerve of them to believe they have the right to confiscate firearms and then go even farther and demand to disband the Cadet organization". To himself he said "and above all they sent this errand boy to deliver such a serious ultimatum". He stood up after glancing at the order placed in front of him and faced the window. After a moment of contemplation, he turned to Agent Hicks and said with restraint and in very measured words...

"First of all, Mr. Hicks, you miss quoted the Second Amendment".

"Oh, I did? No, here you can read it...".

"Oh yes, I know what it says, but you did misread it. I quote: 'A well-regulated militia being necessary 'to the security of' a Free State, the right of the people to keep and bear arms shall not be infringed". The Chancellor started to copy his opponent and put his own emphasis on certain words like 'to the security of' as he spoke. Unlike agent Hicks though, Gentry recited the verse word for word from memory and looked like he almost came to attention as he said it.

"Please quote it correctly because each word is very important as I'm sure you would agree, right Mr. Hicks?

"Yes, it sure is" the agent replied with full confidence that every word was on his side for this argument. He beamed at the Chancellor and said "That's why you're in violation; it's all here in black and white".

The Chancellor smiled at him. He turned and began to pace back and forth behind his desk with his hands clasped behind his back. "Yes, but Article 1 Section 8 of the Constitution actually says, and I quote 'Congress shall have the power to provide for calling forth the militia...' 'Provide' means to 'make available' which doesn't sound like it means that they will do it themselves. By specifically using the word 'provide' the founding fathers meant that the State would furnish the resources, to 'provide for'. For example, like allocating money for an appointee to be able to accomplish the task. 'Call forth' means they will 'call out' or 'call up' or 'call over'. It means exactly what it says Mr. Hicks, to 'call forth' the Militia. "To 'provide support for' and to 'call it forth'" the Chancellor re-stated with a wave of his hand for emphasis. Hicks was looking down trying to follow while reading the same line the Chancellor was reciting.

"In the next sentence it clarifies and supports this, it says '...and reserves to the States the authority to appoint officers and to train the Militia'. That infers that authority is given to the States, yes, I agree. But even more important to note is that you are correct; it infers that the 'State' has the right to 'deal with the Militia', and I take it that you and your boss are taking the position that only the State has the right to call up the militia, right Mr. Hicks?"

"Yes exactly Mr. Gentry, that's what it says clearly, I concur" Hicks said with a smile through an air of buoyant self-assurance.

"Yes, and I see that you and the people who put you up to this, like to go exactly by what the Constitution says".

"Yes, we do" Hicks said.

"Well then, let me ask you, how can the Congress or the State call up a militia if it does not exist?" The Chancellor paused, turned, and glanced back at agent Hicks.

Taken back for a moment and contemplating what the Chancellor just said, Hicks looked up from his copy of the second amendment and said "Come on Chancellor they call up people like it says 'between the ages of 17 and 45 to form a militia' that's pretty 'obvious' now isn't it?" Hicks said it with a sneer directed at the Chancellor while placing emphasis on the word obvious.

Gentry replied "But you just said you're going strictly by what the Constitution says. Well, it doesn't say to call up the 'people' and turn them into a Militia, it says to call up 'the Militia'. 'Militia' is defined in Webster's dictionary as, and I quote '...an organization of men enrolled and trained as military reserves. Mr. Hicks, if you really thought about this, I'm sure you wouldn't want the State to call up individual untrained unorganized ordinary 'people'. To be most effective you would want a trained body of men. That clause in the constitution clearly states 'to call up' yes, but they are referring to an 'existing' organization of trained individuals which are called the 'Militia'; they used that term specifically.

Training these men is the service that this Academy performs for the State. We hold available- a Militia, a body of trained men and women ready and available for the State to 'call up' during times of need. Don't you agree? Don't you think that this would be a valuable way to assist in the defense of the State in a time of need? To assist the people in a time of need?".

Agent Hicks looked at the Chancellor for a long moment before answering. "Mr. Hicks?" Gentry prodded.

"Uh, no. I don't. It... ah... it states that..." Hicks shuffled through his paperwork. "...only the state can appoint officers and has the authority to train the militia..."

"Well, yes, that is... when... and if... the State ever wants to or needs to 'call them up' and consequently 'provide' for their training as described. Meaning to compensate them as well as to 'provide' for the expense of supplies and equipment. Then and only then do they deserve, and I would be glad to give them the appropriate inherent right to 'appoint officers and prescribe discipline'. I would gladly hand over my organization and give them that right to deal with a just cause such as defending this nation. That becomes the 'obvious' part now doesn't it Mr. Hicks?" The Chancellor said it with major emphasis on the word 'obvious' just like his opponent did.

Hicks sat there dumfounded searching for something to say. He thought he had a well thought out undeniable argument that he had memorized and repeated just like he was taught. The Chancellor had just blown it away with logic and said something that made sense. He never thought of it in that way before.

"You see Mr. Hicks; we are on your side... aren't we? This whole set up is designed to help the government. Remember this, for what I am about to say is very, very important; there's one thing you must understand about our forefathers. When they spoke of the 'State' back in 1776, they meant 'the people of the State' not the 'government of the State', this stems from the fact that in America the 'people' hold the power, not the government. You can look it up if you wish, but this should sound logical to you. It's looking like this is a fact that you and your associates have conveniently left out".

Hicks stood up acting like he was insulted by the remark. Gentry stared him down and added in a boisterous tone... "When they referred to 'the government' they used language like 'Legislature of the State' as they do in Article 1, Section 8, Paragraph 17. The people are the government of the State, Mr. Hicks! They decide what power, if any, to delegate to their state governments, especially concerning Militias, not the other way around. Militias are created for the protection 'of the people' against tyrannical governments that might try to take away their rights just like you and your cohorts are trying to do right now. If you see us as the enemy..." Gentry's voice rose to formulate a stern conclusion "...consider what that tells you about your employer, for it is obvious by their contempt for this organization that they see something designed to 'protect the people' as something that is in their way!".

Instead of returning a logical argument of his own Hicks snapped back at the Chancellor "Yes but that's not how it is nowadays is it, Gentry. I think people are idiots who think like that". He gathered his papers, stuffed them into his briefcase and stood up. "I'm here to do my job not to argue the intricacies of what our stupid forefathers did. I need to see your cache of weapons so that I can complete my inspection. I know your Cadets are in possession of the Kel Tec SU 16 and they also use the Colt AR-15. These are considered 'military style weapons' and are now illegal to own by nonmilitary personnel. I have a truck waiting outside to confiscate them and any other illegal weapons that I may find. If you voluntarily hand them over now there will be no repercussions, I give you my word. If you don't, then you will suffer the consequences".

"Why that would be illegal!" Chancellor Gentry exclaimed.

"No, I assure you that we are acting within our rights to enforce executive order EO-129".

"No, I mean it would be illegal for us to still have the rifles you mentioned in our possession Mr. Hicks. We sold them to a gun dealer as soon as we got word of the change in the law. Here's the bill of sale and name of the dealer involved".

Agent Hicks looked at Mr. Gentry with a frown and glared at him like this was going to spoil his day if it were true. He reached out and grabbed the piece of paper from the Chancellor and read it with angst, then he looked up.

"We'll need to verify this" Hicks said with a look that conveyed exactly whose side he was on. "I still need to see the storeroom and inspect your firearms".

"Yes of course you do". The Chancellor looked back at the ATF agent and returned the same glare the agent gave him. They both stood there glaring at each other for a long uncomfortable moment.

"I see you've made your choice" Gentry said. "The side you've chosen is evident. It's understandable, they pay your bills. But you were sworn to uphold the Constitution against all enemies both foreign and domestic, weren't you Mr. Hicks? I would think that with the truth that I have just presented to you and the revelation about the real intentions of the founding fathers, that this newfound contradiction would shed new light on your stance and change your position if it were true.

"If it were true!" Hicks shot back. "And that would be if you believe that the founding fathers knew what the hell they were doing in the first place. Now that's the real question, isn't it?".

"No not really, we've already proven that they knew exactly what they were doing by how well they shaped and guided the 'American experiment'. The mere success of the United States has proven that beyond a doubt".

"I doubt that. It's not looking very successful to me. I think that the constitution is old poetry that doesn't apply to today's world. It needs to be updated and changed" Hicks said.

"I could have guessed that is what you'd say about the most brilliant document ever written. But remember, the transformation of the system and our constitution began many years ago. It's been happening for quite some time. What you are seeing now is the negative effects of the dissolution of that document. Our lack of 'success' today is the direct result of the actions of our present state of government and the very people you now work for. I know that they are part of that transformation and that you are just a pawn in their effort to spearhead a campaign to facilitate the end of the American experiment. They're turning our country into the same socialist mess that's been tearing other countries down for decades. Look at Grease, Italy, Spain, Germany, and Brittan even, they're all broke! They have seen the fall of the Euro by the same policies that are now dragging our dollar down into extinction. It's not even a question anymore, we're doomed. I pray that you seek out the truth before it's too late. Don't take this lightly; many other countries have fallen to this disease. My argument can be verified by history, can yours?

"Yes, my argument can" Hicks said.

"What!" Now Gentry was getting mad. He got up and walked toward him aggressively. "I can tell you sir... you don't know what the hell you're talking about. A frustrated tone bubbled to the surface. Gentry faced his adversary- "Your argument has been handed down to you by your superiors, you haven't even fact checked it, you're conveniently leaving out truths that blow gaping holes in their position and obscure the repercussions of their actions. A little advice Mr. Hicks; think for yourself man! Seek out the truth! Your conclusion on this matter will have grave consequences for this country especially if we continue down the path we're on".

For a split second the agent pondered the message and turned it over in his mind but then responded plainly "I need to see the storage room. There is no reason why you or anyone else needs a semi-automatic military style weapon. That wasn't a right given to you in your precious constitution. I can prove that. You're so fond of explaining the intent behind what the forefathers wrote, well I am certain when they wrote the second amendment they were talking about the 'black powder single shot rifle', a hunting rifle Gentry, not modern weapons of war that are designed to kill people with each pull of the trigger".

"You're kidding me, right? You believe that when they ratified the second amendment in 1791 that they were referring to the technology of the time and that by giving citizens the right to bear arms in 1776 the intent was to restrict citizens to the technology of the time which was black powder hunting rifles?".

"Of course, how could they be referring to anything else? That's just common sense" Hicks told him.

"Alright Hicks. In 1776 our forefathers also declared that god gave American citizens the right to freedom. In court cases argued since, as in 'Shapiro Vs. Thompson and other supporting decisions, it has been ruled that the state of 'freedom' is construed to include the right of a citizen to travel freely within a state and across borders inside the US... According to your own definition that means they were referring only to the technology of transportation 'at their time' which in 1776 was a frickin HORSE AND BUGGY! With your logic, today, everyone would be forced to ride a horse and sail around on wooden ships! Hicks you're an idiot".

Hicks got mad. No logical thinking was forthcoming. Without considering the merits of what Gentry was saying Hicks yelled "That's it! No more of your bullshit! Show me your storerooms or I'm placing you under arrest for resisting the execution of a warrant".

Gentry backed down and moved back to his desk. Speaking into the intercom he said "Mary please send in Security". The Chancellor and agent Hicks didn't move to shake hands, this meeting was over. A smirk appeared on the agent's face expressing the belief that he had won over his opponent as he knew he would. After all, he held the rein of power.

The door opened and Cadet Sergeant Seal Hutchison walked in. He walked sharply and looked the spitting image of authority in his Cadet uniform. He was carrying a side arm in a black holster, which immediately caught the eye of agent Hicks.

"Sergeant, take Mr. Hicks to the range and give him complete access to the armory storage room. Give him your total cooperation; he has my permission to take any illegal weapons he may find.

The agent chuckled to himself and then said to the Chancellor "How absurd it is for you to think that the ATF needs your permission to inspect and confiscate weapons. I assure you that in the future we will be showing up un-announced and we will take anything we want with or without your permission". He turned to the Sergeant and gave a nod to the gun on his hip. "You got a permit to carry that?".

"Yes sir, I do".

"Open carry is illegal Sergeant. May I see it?" Hicks said.

Hutchison started to unholster his pistol and said to Hicks "Sir, in Delaware County, which is where we reside, open carry is legal with a permit and besides…" he added as a side note… "We are on our way to the range Sir. Delaware County law states that you can legally carry a weapon to the gun range even without a permit". The Sergeant pulled the semi auto pistol out of the holster, flipped it around and handed it to the agent butt first. Then unclipped a magazine from his belt and gave him that as well.

"It's a nine mil Beretta 92FS" he said proudly. "Four round magazine".

Agent Hicks took the weapon and the magazine and examined them. He unlocked the slide and cocked it back to see if it was loaded totally prepared to arrest the man right then and there for carrying a loaded gun. But the chamber was empty, and the clip was on the Sergeants belt was separate from the gun. "OK it's unloaded, but Sergeant..." Hicks looked at him with a serious look "...I happen to know that this is a pre ban magazine with a fourteen-round capacity. Sergeant, this is illegal".

"Sir you would be correct if that actually was a fourteen-round mag, but it isn't. Beretta has only now started manufacturing a five round magazine that conforms to the ban but it's on backorder at this time. As soon as the ban went into effect, we had our technicians convert all our magazines to four round max".

"Oh yeah? The ban states you can have five rounds why would you only set it up for four?" Hicks said with a bit of skepticism.

"Well, the wording in EO-129-52A is unclear sir. It states that the capacity of a 'gun and its magazine' cannot exceed five rounds. We figured we'd cover our ass by including the round in the chamber as the total capacity of the gun in question. Then there would be no confusion and no gray area that might give someone like yourself the impression that this gun is anything but legal".

Agent Hicks cocked his head and looked at him with a skeptical sideward glance. "How do you 'convert' a magazine sergeant?".

"We take 'em apart, place a wood block of the proper size in the bottom as a spacer, shorten the spring, re-assemble and wah la, we're in compliance".

Sure enough, Hicks looked into the peep holes drilled along one side of the magazine, which allowed for visual inspection of its contents. Through them, a shooter can quickly determine how many bullets are in the magazine. He saw that a major portion of the indicator ports were blocked off inside by what could have been a wood block. The bottom section of the magazine was clear, so Hicks popped out one bullet at a time with his thumb. He counted four and then looked up at the Sergeant. Satisfied, he slid the mag back into the gun until it clicked and locked into standard position. He stared at it and paused for a moment as if trying hard to find something else wrong with it. Reluctantly he handed the gun back but, in an attempt to save face and exert authority over the situation he defiantly put the bullets in his pocket. "I'll keep these", he said.

The gun went back into its holster and the Sergeant swung his arm motioning Hicks toward the door. He complied and was escorted out. When the door closed behind them, Chancellor Gentry breathed a sigh of relief and stared at the floor for a moment. He crossed his arms over his chest and shook his head in utter disbelief. "So, this is how it begins" he said to an empty room.

Sergeant Hutchison offered to take agent Hicks over to the range in an electric cart, but Hicks declined preferring to ride over in his own black Chevy Suburban. Hicks jumped in his car and briefed his partner on how the meeting went giving the guy the impression that he "kicked ass in there".

"The son of a bitch claims they sold the guns. They think they got their asses covered" Hicks said it as he slammed his fist on the dashboard. "I don't believe them. They're here, somewhere, damn it I just know it".

A large empty Econoline bus with two additional agents followed the SUV to the range. It was obvious that they were prepared to haul out quite a load of illegal items. Sergeant Hutchison and Hicks walked into the range building with three other agents, they were led to the basement where the equipment room was located. Supply clerk Carl Roughett was on duty and came to a respectful attentive posture when addressed by the Sergeant.

"Yes sir" he said after hearing the request. Carl unlocked the door and allowed the agents to enter the supply room. They walked in with an attitude and stood just inside the spacious twenty-five by thirty-five-foot room looking around at the contents. There was a whole line of rifles, must have been thirty or more, stored in a long continuous rack up against the adjacent wall along with four other empty racks of similar style positioned in the center of the room. There was an aisle on each side of them leading to the back where various guns and parts strewn about a workbench that stretched across the entire length of the far wall. Those were being repaired or cleaned or upgraded and were in various stages of disassembly.

Agent Hicks looked at the type of rifle sitting in the rack. He quickly assessed the situation and became visibly upset. Cursing, he turned around and abruptly pushed past the other two agents behind him. They looked at each other and then followed him out.

Sergeant Hutchison was standing at ease in the hallway, just outside the door with a smile on his face. Agent Hicks walked swiftly past him but then, as an afterthought stopped, swung back, and walked up to him and got in his face. "You won't get away with this," he said with fire in his eyes and a pointing finger. Then he turned and stomped off down the hallway with his cronies in tow.

Carl came out of the supply room into the hallway and watched the agents leave. He turned to the Sergeant and they both smiled with a devilish grin. All the hunting rifles on the rack were various models of the single shot Remington 700 with a few of the 504 models mixed in. There were also about thirty Ruger 22's lined up at the far end. Hicks couldn't tell the caliber of any of the rifles on the rack, but it didn't matter, he wasn't looking for some insignificant caliber infraction, he was looking for something a lot more incriminating to pin on the Academy. He totally expected to see a cache of illegal semi-automatic rifles. Intel had reported that the Academy had them in their possession. The new law would have allowed him to confiscate the lot of them and jail the Chancellor on the spot. It would have been so satisfying to go back to that man's office and charge him with the infractions especially after that disaster of a meeting. All the rifles on the rack were single shot bolt-action hunting or target rifles, which were still completely legal. Instantly the satisfaction and the image of the Chancellor being taken away in handcuffs faded.

23

In The Market

Ciera rose in the ranks to the position of Cadet Secretary Treasurer and subsequently was now in charge of supply for the organization. That involved working closely with the school's purchasing agent because their needs overlapped with the Cadets in quite a few areas. Over the years they found it much more cost effective to coordinate purchases that could benefit multiple parties. Ciera excelled at her job and became famous as the "go to person" for anything the organization needed and sometimes even for what the Academy needed. She was familiar with the process and the problems on a small scale and was a natural to head up the committee assigned to investigate the growing supply problem.

The main grocery store in Delhi had noticeable gaps between various products on the shelves. Ciera Lowman walked the aisles with a notebook in her hands and the manager of Pantry Plus grocery store trailing right behind her. "Mr. Mead..." she asked.

"Oh please, call me Curtis, Mrs. Lowman" he said with a flirtatious smile. It wasn't every day that he had the privilege of escorting a pretty young lady around his store. Especially one that was so interested in the current problems associated with his business.

"Ok… Curtis, I'm trying to determine which items we might be able to purchase in bulk that would be attractive to you and other retail outlets such as yours. I need to know; what are the most popular items you sell and of those, which ones are you finding hard to get?".

"Well, I'll have to differentiate here Mrs. Lowman; there are two categories of scarce products nowadays. There are products I am no longer stocking because of the increased cost and products that I am not stocking because they are hard to come by or simply not available anymore. The first category I can get, but they've become so expensive that my customers are doing without them. "Water" for example, I used to sell a hundred or so cases a month at nine bucks a pop. Now, for what they're charging me, I would have to sell a case for eighteen dollars". He turned and looked at Ciera "Customers are simply going back to drinking filtered tap water. So, you see, I would be interested in adding that to your list but only if I could get them at a much better price. I have a feeling that getting a better price will be very hard to do Mrs. Lowman, even when buying in bulk".

"You might be right Curtis, but have you thought about selling low-cost water filters?".

"Hmm" Curtis mumbled as he thought about it. That's a pretty good idea, I never thought about that. Filtering tap water would be popular if it helped to lower the TDS level (total dissolved solids) but we don't need water treatment to make it taste better, the water around here is pretty good right out of the tap".

"Then a simple charcoal filter would do. Ok what else Curtis?".

"Well, the soup here…" Curtis stopped in front of the soup section and pointed to shelves that were more than half-empty now. "…it sells very well these days when and if I can get it. Minestrone and pea soup are my best sellers I might add" he said it like he was trying to sell them to her.

"Hey that's unfair Curtis, I like the Italian style wedding soup the best".

"Nah, the meat balls taste like dog food!" he kidded.

"Well, I guess that's a matter of opinion" she offered to settle the dispute.

"I'm just kidding" Curtis said. "I like the wedding soup too, but the minestrone and pea move very quickly".

"Ok" Ciera said "What else?".

"Yeast, flower, sugar, salt, all the common stuff for making bread is very popular now since my bread shipments have become sporadic due to delivery problems. I heard that my last order left the bakery yesterday, but it hasn't arrived yet. Very strange, they don't know where it is, the truck or the driver. Spaghetti sauce! I could really use twenty cases of spaghetti sauce, but I would want it accompanied by a shipment of noodles too. It's a complementary purchase and would sell a lot better together. Vegetables are hard to come by in the winter months. They need to be shipped in from the southern states and lately the cost has negated demand. Because of the price they sit around too long, a lot more of it spoils which adds more to the cost as well".

Curtis Mead was kind enough to spend an hour and a half with her discussing various products. The more Ciera dug into it the more difficult the endeavor became. Certain items were time sensitive for delivery and others needed refrigeration.

Before going back to her office, Ciera had two more stops. First, she visited Mt. Tenny farm and spoke to Judy Arleen asking the same questions that she put to the merchants in Delhi. "What are you finding hard to get these days?" Her last stop was the school cafeteria to speak to the manager, and then she was done. She spent the entire day going from one merchant to the next gathering as much information as she could until there were three lists of sought-after items that had become difficult to get. She listened carefully and wrote down everything no matter how insignificant or small and found that there certainly was a distinction between hard to "afford" and hard to "find". It was very enlightening; in one day she got a glimpse of the present state of the US markets and a rundown of the communities' problems directly from the local business owners. But the most shocking thing of all was the cost of all the items on her list; Gasoline- $13.19 per gallon, milk $14.25 a gallon, orange juice- $18.40 per gallon, a pound of flour $22.60, ten-pound bag of rice $34.90.

Here at the Security Building on campus Ciera had been graced with her own office that came with all the trimmings, everything except for her own personal secretary. Except for that, she had everything she needed. All the personnel in the building shared the use of the front desk clerk who doubled as a helper for anyone working there. The clerk wasn't called a 'secretary' because he or she was a member of the security team who just happened to pull desk duty for that day or night shift. Ciera found it to be a great place to work as well as to do her homework. She thanked God daily that she was lucky enough to have gotten this position; it was so much more convenient than trying to do homework in her Hogan as other seekers did. Even though most seekers living in RL didn't do a lot of schoolwork in their Hogans anyway, preferring instead to use either the school or farmhouse library for that. Still Ciera felt lucky to have a place to go where it was quiet, on occasion she even slept there.

In the comfort of her office, Ciera reviewed the results of today's survey and combined the three lists of most needed items from the community to an existing list of materials needed by the Cadet organization. After cross-referencing, she compiled a list of common items requested by multiple end users. To get as much help as she could she sent out a shotgun BeepX message to the members of the supply committee with instructions for them to look for sources for the items listed. Their homework was to scour the entire countryside for the best deal with the intent of purchasing in bulk. "The Committee" consisted of Supply Sergeant Carl Roughett and Outpost Purchasing Agent Allen McKinney, who was out of town but present courtesy of long-distance broadband conferencing. There was Mrs. Lea, who was the school treasurer/purchasing agent, Mr. Clyde Bennett the school's accountant and Mrs. Julianne Ingle (Professor Ingle's Wife). In addition, Mr. Dell Arleen was on board representing Mt. Tenny Farms. He had expressed an interest in addressing the supply problem that had recently floated to the top of his list of major concerns.

The first meeting of the six member "Supply Committee" commenced on time at seven o'clock the following Tuesday night.

"Let's bring the meeting to order and get started" Ciera said and then spoke to the laptop computer sitting next to her on the table. "Are you with us Mr. McKinney?".

A tinny sounding "Present" was heard from the computers built in speaker. If you were sitting at the right angle, you could see a matching picture of Allen's face and upper body that went with the voice.

"I can hear you fine, I just wish I was there in person, sorry for my mode of travel".

"For the record- all are present. OK, I have sent everyone pertinent information gleaned from a very interesting survey I took of merchants throughout our region and gave you all some homework. Did you have any luck in finding sources? In addition, let's please discuss any ideas on the best way to go about obtaining them. Julianne, would you go first and give us your report".

"Well, I've discussed this project with a few people on this board as well as others and we debated the possibilities. I noticed that much of the discussion turned into 'We can do this, and we can do that'. I quickly realized that I was hearing the word 'we' way too much, meaning; it's starting to look like the only way to get a grip on this is to take hold of it ourselves and to play a more active role. It keeps coming up as the cheapest way to operate. We concluded that the only way to do this is to form our own trading company and provide our own security for shipments to guarantee their survival and timely arrival".

Ciera broke in "Clyde, Do you have the figures on transportation costs if we used Tri County Transportation out of Albany to make our runs"?

"Yes, I do". He fumbled through the papers in front of him, picked one out and studied it for a second before handing it to her. "First, with Mrs. Ingle's help, I got together estimates from various carrier services and the company 'Tri County' was the lowest. Those figures are for shipping a container and half container size load of maximum weight at present day costs.

"OK" she said after studying the page. "Now how does that compare to plan 'B'?".

Julianne answered enthusiastically "The alternate plan is for us to do it ourselves. We rent or eventually buy a truck and use Cadet Security as an escort. We did a cost comparison on operating a single freight truck on a north south route from here to Florida".

"Why to Florida?".

"Well from your email we took the list of items you we're looking for, researched all the possible purchase points and then searched for a simple circuitous route in which a dedicated convoy could travel and pick up a large percentage of the products requested. We would need to go as far as Florida for the citrus. We found that by using our own truck and doing the pickup and deliveries ourselves we could shave approximately forty-five percent off the cost of hiring Tri County Transportation to do the same job. We suspect that this is because of Tri County's overhead. To pull off the same number of deliveries, they would be using multiple trucks and drivers compared to our one. The issue of security has thrown in another layer of added problems and expense for both them and us. However, in each of the categories for us to consider; Security, Shipping, and the Bulk Purchase of goods- we came out far ahead of the competition. We have a cheap source of security personnel to pull from thanks to the Cadets. Shipping costs are cheaper as stated and the fact that we can purchase in bulk quantities allows us access to last column pricing in most cases. We are having some problems in obtaining suppliers who want to work with us or who are even allowed to sell to us, but we're working on that.

Julianne concluded "After adding up the savings in each of the three categories, I have concluded that it would be very profitable for us to go into the shipping business. I highly recommend it".

Clyde was quick to jump in and shoot down everyone's hope of making any money on the project.

"Wait, wait, wait, let's not get ahead of ourselves and get too excited here. I haven't had a chance to discuss the requirements for starting an adventure such as this. We just might have to forgo the profit idea if we are to operate legally; after looking into the legal ramifications of providing this service it gets a little... complicated. The regulations require that we obtain two different types of liability insurance, a state license, a local business license, inner state transportation license and a national transportation license. Yes, in effect we would have to become a mini 'shipping' company to operate as a legal entity here in the glorious state of New York. First, it would involve the startup costs associated with creating a company. That alone can be around three thousand dollars just in legal fees. Then, we have the Security guard license and gun permit fees associated with it and additional federally mandated gun liability insurance as well. There is also the 'Import tax' imposed on companies shipping across New York State borders. This tax is designed to stop people from doing the exact thing we are contemplating by making it cheaper to buy from local suppliers. Of course, all it has done is make imports that much more expensive and hence that's why we are here trying to figure out how to circumvent the system.

Speaking of 'expense', the total cost of starting up a legal company such as this is alarming, it would be quite an investment. We would have to operate for several years just to break even. Of course, that depends on a few unknown factors like the quantity of tons shipped. With that in mind, the only other options are to operate illegally or to operate as a non-profit organization. I don't advise operating illegally and damn it! The 'nonprofit' status sure takes the wind out of my sail. The whole venture would become just an exercise in 'securing what we need'. Profit? I think you can forget about it".

Everyone around the table looked around like their trip to Disney world had just been canceled. Internally they were all searching for a solution.

It was Allen McKinney who spoke first, "The requirements you quoted Clyde are for a commercial shipping company, if we do this for ourselves then I don't think all those legalities apply. We'll have to consider the nonprofit route. I got an idea. How about we investigate the possibility of attaching our operation to Reverend Water's non-profit organization? If he's willing, we could use his license or more importantly his charitable tax-exempt status with the State and operate under the radar".

There was a pause where everyone considered the idea.

"I think that could be a great idea if all parties are willing Allen". Ciera said.

"I agree but I'd advise us to be a little discreet. I don't think we should be too open about our intentions or offer a lot of information about some of the items we're picking up, namely ammunition. I mean, don't lie to him, just don't make it a point. It's important that we make a run and swing through Pennsylvania ASAP to pick up a shipment. I'm in the process of setting it up right now. This might be the only chance we get. You're not allowed to ship it in the mail these days', and I have a dealer who's dying to get rid of a load of various calibers that we need. He will sell it to me, but we'll have to pick it up. This is a priority, and we need to secure this transaction ASAP. The ban on ammunition is taking its toll. It's becoming really hard to get".

"I see where this is going" Clyde said. "Any further progress on doing this semi legally revolves around our ability to create a relationship with Reverend Waters or someone of that stature. Anyone here have a good rapport with the Reverend?".

Mr. Arleen raised his hand.

"You do Dell?".

"Yeah, I know Reverend Waters well. He's with the Methodist Church and the nonprofit organization you're talking about is called the 'Humanitarian Relief Organization' we call it the HRO".

"Really. What kind of service is that?" Ciera asked.

"As far as I know it's a service where they accept contributions of all kinds of stuff like furniture, used appliances, cars, and the like. They wheel and deal, swap it out, give it away to the needy and hold garbage sales, I mean garage sales occasionally. They got this flea market thing going on in the church parking lot".

"Ok Dell, you're in charge of contacting Reverend Waters, check out the possibilities. He might want to come on board if we can convince him we are helping the community with our efforts".

Dell told her "Ciera, that won't be difficult to do when it's the truth. This campaign's underlying principle took root from a desire to help the community, that's why I'm here. The fact that it helps Mr. McKinney's self-interest is just a small part of the scope of this project. I hope it will help everybody out. Everyone will have a stake in it with the driving force being their own necessity, but out of that, many people will benefit from the effort if we succeed. Mr. McKinney here will just be one of countless satisfied customers. Don't worry the Minister's goals and ours are one and the same, I can tell you that".

"Well put" Ciera said. Ok, get back with me on this tomorrow, will you? In the meantime, I need everyone to seek out connections and possible points of purchase. Keep in mind it looks like the first run will be up and down the east coast. I also need to know the best possible routes that will take us past the known State roadblocks or any construction that might be going on. See what you can find out".

"I can help with that" Carl volunteered. "My father's in the TSA. I think he'll know what's going on out there".

"Ok great Carl, get the rundown on that and get back to me. I'm curious about what's going on out there on the roads myself. Sounds like a great inside connection. Anything else?" There was only silence. "Meeting adjourned!".

Market conditions pushed the project to the forefront out of necessity. In successive meetings, board members debated over a list of products and then made decisions concerning what items their new-found venture would deal with. Their decisions were based on two factors; degree of necessity and the ability to produce a profit. Degree of risk was also considered but it was determined that their own skill and effective management heavily influenced the risk factor. For example, to pull off dealing with a shipment of oranges or any item with a shelf life, completely relied on their own ability to pick up and drop off in a specific timeframe due to the spoilage issue. Also, there was a "handling" factor that came into play; even if they picked up and dropped off in a timely manner any form of product wear and tear from mishandling the load could make the product unattractive to the end user rendering it unprofitable. This was a major concern because at this point, they really didn't know what their own strengths and weaknesses were.

One thing was certain; junk food items that showed up on the list of requests were discarded in lieu of more substantial food. The final draft of Ciera's product list included; Vegetable seeds of various varieties, potatoes, fertilizer (fish emulsion and cow manure), feed corn, apple juice, orange juice, ammunition of various calibers, mason jars, granulated carbon, Jerry cans, gasoline, coffee, olive oil, canned soup, flour, sugar, salt (including salt licks for cattle), yeast, toilet paper, water filters/purifiers, dry beans and dry split pea, peanut butter and peanuts and various seasonal food items such as oranges, grape fruit, avocados and the like. Of course, some items would only be available at certain times of the year. There were more but these were considered the most popular sought-after items that people would want to purchase on a regular basis.

After Dell brought up the issue of security at the board meeting, the school board mulled it over with Major Jaz and agreed that Mr. Arleen had offered a viable solution to what was becoming a major problem. They knew he was right; the Cadets were in a unique position to help. Dell also informed the members that there had been occasions where they had sold some of the surplus generated on the farm to local establishments at a profit and that these transactions could be expanded and pursued to a larger degree. Apple juice and apple sauce for example. He reminded them that the farm leased an apple orchard where apples, applesauce and apple juice could be produced at higher levels just by leasing more acreage. In season, there would be plenty of apple produce that could then be sold. It was decided to pursue both matters further.

Reverend Waters was contacted the very next day and after explaining the benefits of the campaign to all parties involved the Reverend became enthusiastic and was totally on board with the idea. He agreed to operate the business under the umbrella of his existing non-profit "Humanitarian Relief Organization" which was conveniently already set up and running. They have been dealing with the transfer of various merchandise and produce to people in need for years now; operating on a larger scale would be a simple matter of expanding the effort. Without any further thought, the Reverend sanctioned the joint effort.

24

Baby Cart

All agreed that the formation of the TSD (Transportation Security Department) would be a welcome addition to the venture. The plan was to fill the positions with either Cadet Members or their trained equivalent. Their job would be to escort incoming and outgoing shipments of merchandise to and from the school and church as well as to offer their services to any other business entity that required it. It was decided that the TS would become a branch of the existing campus Security cell commanded by Adrian Joe Phillips. Commander Phillips and Major Monett put together existing shipment security techniques and adapted them to their needs. They copied other security operations and formulated their own set of "rules of operation". Security employees would be taught the intricacies of driving transportation security in a one-week crash course.

One Chief Security Officer would be pulled from the campus security force to head the squad. That job went to Sergeant Lee Pointer. Pointer was campus security team leader and was one of the security cell Cadets that was on the payroll. The Academy had four paid security members with a small contingent of volunteers who were trained and ready to go for special events. They were waiting in the wings and biting at the bit for a chance at an actual job opening such as this. The Academy would add a four-man transport squad to the payroll, it was justified by the summation that the venture would pay for itself, and the revenue gained would pay for any added expense. They also decided to up the pay scale for qualified Cadet Members who joined the security team. The news about the rise in cargo theft across the country was well known and the pay would help overcome the fact that this type of work had become a lot more dangerous. They were banking on the possibility that their services could be offered to other paying customers and envisioned that this would become a profitable venture. An ad for recruits ran in the campus Journal the next week:

Immediate Job Opening- Needed: a Transportation Security guard. Part time or full time. Travel and get paid for it. Great chance to get ahead, great pay $$$. Clean driver's license required. NY State gun permit holders preferred but not required.

It took the help, effort, and concentration of all the board members to seek out and make contacts to obtain sources for the products they were looking for. Deals were made with every method of payment considered including bartering and accepting payment in silver or gold. It was decided that "Bit Coin" would not even be considered as a viable payment method because in any type of calamity the money could become difficult to get to and would quite possibly disappear into some inaccessible internet cloud. A decision was made, after much discussion, to make it a priority to seek out and promote gold and silver as the preferred tangible method of payment for any services rendered or products sold especially in bartering situations where they envisioned the need for some form of monetary compensation to balance out the sale. Many people had invested in gold and silver coins and bullion in the last decade due to the fear that an economic meltdown scenario was becoming inevitable. Tenny Hill Academy was no exception.

Six Cadet Candidates were accepted and put through the one-week TS short course. Two members out of the six were chosen for the first team, with the others held on standby or for 'fill in' if one of the chosen could not work that particular job. Commander Phillips solidified his plan for the team's operation and made sure that each member would adhere to the strict rules of procedure. The class taught them what to expect and how to react to different situations that they might encounter.

For their first mission, the TS team would man two escort vehicles with two Cadets in each. One vehicle would ride in front and one at the rear. In their first assignment, the team would rendezvous with the driver of a rented eighteen-wheeler in Northern Florida and were tasked with the job of escorting the truck back along a preplanned route. They would act as scouts and inform the truck driver of any concerns through CB radio contact. Hopefully well in advance of any problems they might encounter. Along the way, they'd stop off at various points to pick up prearranged orders of prepackaged products that would fit into the truck as well as fit into the tight schedule of the run. That was the tricky part. It took a lot of thought to calculate the timing as well as the available space. Would everything fit? The square foot of each product had to be determined and it had to pack into the ever-dwindling available space after each load was picked up. It was well known to the engineers of the run that any screw-ups would cost them time and money, possibly turning the whole affair into a wasted effort.

As it worked out, they were forced to hire a union truck driver with a valid CDL (Commercial Driver's License) to make the first run. Due to the cost of the driver they hired, it was immediately apparent that in the future it would be cheaper to have one of their own team members apply for a CDL license of their own. They could pay a Cadet half the salary of the union driver, which was perfectly acceptable to any Cadet in need of a paying job. Even if the school picked up the application fee of $2,992 and paid the fee for the truckers training course of $1,900, they could recover their investment with just a few runs. It was a no brainer and was now "in process".

Today they were going to proceed with a trial run with just one escort vehicle to test the waters. TS members Candon and Riley climbed into the white Toyota Tacoma four-cylinder truck marked with the

THA campus security logo on the side. Riley took shotgun and grabbed the mike to the CB radio and spoke into it "Breaker one nine this is Flight Leader and Wing Man, we're on the go and 10/10 on the side".

Candon told Riley "We'll make a run down 87 to I 95, then head south. Hope this thing makes it". It was really the only vehicle available, but it happened to fit their needs or at least that's what the board members thought (they didn't have to sit in those uncomfortable seats for an untold number of hours). Since it was already equipped with a CB radio, it was good to go and being a four cylinder, it was better on gas. The truck was set up with four five-gallon jerry cans of fuel in the back as a backup in case gasoline became an issue. Cruising down to Melbourne Florida was as hectic as they were warned it would be. At one point, they had to use some of the spare gas because they couldn't find an open gas station.

On the CB radio Candon used "Flight Leader" as his handle. Forty-two hours later they met their truck driver in Melbourne who went by the handle "Mother Load". The Cadets decided that the drivers handle gave out an impression of the value of the load they were transporting. So as not to attract any unwanted attention, and for the purposes of this run only, they asked him to designate his truck as "Baby Cart" after the classic movie "Baby Cart I- Sword of Vengeance" starring Tomi Saburo Wakayama. It wasn't difficult to get the truck driver to use the handle; he was a fan of martial arts movies and knew that Master Swordsman "Itto Ogami" was the main character in that movie. He even said he owned the old DVD of the second movie in the series- "Baby Cart II- The River Styx". The truck driver thought it was cool; he said he could relate their own mission to the theme of the movie. In the movie, the main character Itto Ogami was "escorting" his infant son all over Japan in a baby carriage that he guarded with his sword.

Flight leader briefed Baby Cart before they got started- "On the way down we went through four major check points and three minor ones, the worst being in Southern Pennsylvania on I-83 just north of the Maryland border. One of our Cadets (Carl Roughett) got us a report on road conditions from his father who works at the TSA. However, there was no warning about that one. They were lucky though; having the Academy official campus security logo on the side of our truck came in handy, it lent some credibility".

"Yeah, Flight Leader played it up and got us through a hell of a lot quicker than we would have" Riley told the story. "After sitting there for two hours in traffic, a man in uniform came up to the truck and directed us to pull over. He had a clipboard in his hand and proceeded to scrutinize our truck. Flight Leader say's to him 'Good morning officer, hey what should we be looking for, convicts or contraband?' Ha, it was brilliant man; it sort of put us on the same page as him. The inspector checked our designation as security and immediately lightened up. He didn't' take the time to search us like the other vehicles, he just walked up to the driver's side window and briefly looked around.

'We're looking for both, mostly for illegals on the way north and illegal contraband going both ways he told us. I asked him why the roadblock? Why don't we just pull suspects over and search them randomly? The guy said 'Hell don't ya know? This is great for business son. We should have done this a long time ago. A lot of 'em try to get around all this shit. Goin around takes 'em through the back roads and through the smaller towns and cities. Business is way up because of it, they say York is doing a whole lot better since we started this. Hell, the locals hate it and love it at the same time. We do have a problem with illegals though, haven't ya heard? The Feds are down on the Mexican border with the National Guard…".

"Enforcing immigration law?" Flight leader asked.

"Nope, they're making sure it stays open. Can ya beat that? There's even been a clash between the State police and the Feds. Those damn wet backs are being escorted over by the hundreds and are still comin up here out a Baltimore. Heaven only knows why? There ain't no jobs here. Bet all those riots got 'em on the move, got 'em comin up here looking to take our jobs, bringing their drugs, whores, babies, diseases, and all that shit with em. Pennsylvania's got the balls to try to put a stop to it. We gotta protect our own ya know'.

"I told the inspector that we'll be on the lookout for illegals and turn em' in if we find any. He said 'Thank ya for that boys. We could use all the help we' kin git'. All he did, other than that, was to ask us about weapons. I told him we weren't carrying any".

'No contraband, no drugs, right?' the guy asks.

"Nope, not even a wet back sir!" I told him.

"The inspector laughed then he nodded, stepped back and sort of escorted us back into the through lane sparing us a full search of the vehicle. He waved us on past two more uniformed men who looked at us like they would have loved to have had any excuse to search us. The fact that there was a roadblock was surprising enough but when we saw that officials were searching trucks for contraband it became worrisome".

"Yeah, that sent up a red flag" Candon interjected. "I'm wondering if they're going to label any of the items we're picking up as contraband".

The truck driver stated "That's gunna affect our time if they're gunna search my truck at every roadblock. I heard bad stories about them blocks". He walked to his truck, climbed in the cab, and turned on his CB radio to check conditions. Riley and Candon could hear him shout out. After hearing back from a few contacts, the driver came out and told them "The word on the street is that they're mostly looking for weapons, ammunition, cigarettes, and alcohol as far as contraband goes. All those items have been reported to have been confiscated".

Candon tried to get a hold of the Academy on his phone. Contact by phone these days is sporadic at best. There are many large sections of dead zones, where reception is impossible. That was quite daunting to a team that relied on the phone to call police when and if they got into trouble. But Candon was relieved when he finally got through. He advised Captain Phillips of the situation and got instructions to "Be discreet and cover your tracks".

By design, Cadet TST members weren't supposed to carry a weapon. Connor only now informed Riley that he had his Beretta stashed behind the passenger seat. Riley yelled at him for not mentioning it earlier.

"Holy shit you could have gotten us both sent up the river!" Riley said.

"Sorry. I heard all those reports about armed hijackings. It seemed like the right thing to do at the time" Connor said.

Now they had to worry about the gun as well as the cargo. The Board had been cautious and decided that the team would go unarmed because of the possible reaction from law enforcement. Ramifications of the new ban on firearms were unknown. Nowadays there is a lot of negative attitudes toward concealed carry and no one knew how the Feds, or the police were going to act. Even security agents might be scrutinized and treated adversely. That would have jeopardized the mission and might have left the freight truck unguarded if the security team was delayed in any way; therefore, carrying a weapon was kicked out of the equation. Supposedly, security personnel were exempt from the ban on concealed carry if their paperwork was up to date, but who knew. Detainment is to be avoided at all costs.

Flight Leader and Wing Man continuously monitored the CB radio seeking any information, fact or rumor concerning reported locations of roadblocks. As they drove, they made detailed notes on suspected locations of each for future reference hoping that they might be able to drive around them.

First stop along the route was to pick up oranges, orange juice and sugar in Clewiston Florida. They loaded up about a quarter of the truck with crates on top of crates of oranges filling the truck with the smell of citrus. The engineers of the run gambled that they would be traveling back up into colder weather, which would help keep the juice from spoiling. The drawback to that plan was that if they got laid up and didn't travel fast enough through freezing weather both orange juice and oranges could freeze which was just as bad of a scenario. Although they prepared for that by carrying a propane heater that could be turned on to help maintain an above freezing temperature in the rig if needed.

From the same location in Clewiston, they picked up "fifty" forty-pound bags of sugar that came in heavy fiber reinforced plastic bags.

After loading them inside the truck, it looked like they had closed off the oranges with a sandbag wall.

Reilly and Connor led the truck back onto I-95 and they both drove up the Florida coast. It was smooth sailing and clear all the way up past the Georgia borderline where they detoured over to Douglas Georgia to pick up thirty crates of raw peanuts. From there they jumped back on I-95 and continued north attempting to stay on I-95 as much as possible. Only once did they have to drive the back roads around Savanna after hearing scuttlebutt about heavy police activity on I-95.

It got dicey while driving off the interstate through local municipalities where they had to maneuver around areas where the local inhabitants paid a lot of attention to "who" and "what" was traveling through their town. Another stop on the run was a pesticide manufacturer in Marietta, a fertilizer plant in South Carolina, a mason jar distributor in Virginia along with a REI camping equipment supplier that offered a great deal on a quantity of Camelback hydration packs. There they also picked up seventy pairs of hiking boots and hiking poles that looked more like ski poles.

Hearing about some major problems around Washington DC forced Flight Leader to detour and guide Baby Cart along back roads and alternative routes all the way into New Jersey. There they picked up one hundred and fifty cases of Progresso soup and then trucked back into Pennsylvania to the city of Apollo to pick up fifty cases of tomato sauce, salsa, and tomato paste.

Luckily, the maps they had were detailed and accurate; the GPS on their phone was only as useful as their sporadic phone service. At times it became a pain in the ass game of cat and mouse, one that they were able to play well enough by using the CB to confirm and find back roads around obstacles when they had too. Skillfully they meandered up the East Coast without getting stopped, searched, or robbed, especially at the rest area at 2:00 in the morning when Baby Cart forced them all to take a nap. After making every scheduled pickup as planned, the last leg of their journey ended up being a long seven-hour drive to the Academy. Finally, they made it back and pulled into Mt. Tenny's parking lot totally exhausted about 138 hours after they left.

Officially, the load was signed over to Ciera. She paid the truck driver and immediately shifted into distribution mode. Calls had already been made and products had already been promised to local venders. Vendors came and picked up their order right out of the back of the truck. The remainder was delivered to a booth at the HRO flea market the following Friday. Already Ciera had another convoy scheduled for the Monday after with many more to follow on the heels of their first successful run. Reverend Water's "Humanitarian Relief Organization" was open for business!

* * *

Tenny Hill Academy turned a nice profit from the venture, which fueled the administration's enthusiasm to support and continue the effort. Surprisingly the request to be paid in gold or silver was popular with several customers. Many it seems had the foresight to have made a substantial investment in precious metals over the years and now found it convenient to use it for purchases. Especially purchases that needed to be kept 'off the books' and away from the prying eyes of the government. Thus, the directive to deal in precious metal coins fulfilled the Academy's directive to accumulate gold and silver instead of the devalued US paper dollar. The HRO itself was run strictly by the books so as not to arouse the IRS, and because the Reverend would have it no other way. The Academy's TS department was paid a fee for their security services and Reverend Waters sold the merchandise (that he dealt with) at cost plus 5% to cover his expenses. This way, they were assured their "nonprofit" status. The overwhelming success of the association was due in part to the TS team who was instrumental in getting the loads through without incident. It boosted their ability to deliver products safely and was the driving force behind the operation. Without them, it wouldn't have been worth taking the risk. At this early stage, losing just one shipment would have put them in the hole and made continuing the venture very unattractive. In addition, the association with the HRO allowed them to circumvent third parties and avoid double and triple dip taxation. That made both buyer and seller smile at the bottom line.

Ciera and other board members from the Academy also used the association to purchase "specialty items" needed by the school. Hard to find items or sometimes even illegal items such as gunpowder and ammunition were occasionally up for sale, although those items were only offered to certain trusted local venders through confidential channels. Availability and very attractive "way below retail" pricing drew interested buyers from all around. The Academy did virtually no advertisement, yet the products and service were highly sought after by merchants who were "in the know". To the locals it became known as the "underground flee market".

25

War Games

There was no snow on the ground, yet, but the cold crisp air of a typical December day made it certain that if bad weather rolled in it quite possibly could be snow. The white wisp of Kaiden's breath was the only thing that moved as he stared intently towards the meadow up ahead from behind the protection of a tree. There was something out there that he and the members of his patrol were staring at. Both Kaiden and his buddies could hardly be seen dressed in their white/gray camouflage uniforms. They were spread out along a perimeter in standard formation as taught to them by their teacher Sergeant Shots. Their call sign was "Alpha Babe" or as some of the other squads kidded them "Baby Alpha". The patrol paused in place. Kaiden's patrol leader Dale Coonrod examined the situation ahead with binoculars.

Two days before, the entire Platoon set out on extended practice maneuvers, which just meant that the students would be out in the woods for the weekend instead of the standard four hours of class time they had during the week. They weren't a full platoon yet with only forty-seven participants, but they still described themselves as a "Platoon". This exercise was in its second day where the students were now on the verge of nailing the hunting party they had been tracking. It took a combination of all the hunting, camping and tactical skills they had learned in class to get to this point. Their quarry was somewhere just up ahead.

Most of the students looked and dressed like regular military in complete winter camouflage uniforms, although there were a few students who didn't bother. They just dressed for warmth. It seemed to be a distinguishing factor in determining who was serious about this class and who wasn't. It was obvious that a handful thought it was just a game by their actions and lagged behind the others with indifference as to what was going on. That group was following nonchalantly down the trail about a hundred yards behind the main patrol. Occasionally, Kaiden could hear them horsing around and yelling "Hey what's going on? Where are we?".

The teacher, Sergeant Shots, allowed them to do so. It was their prerogative. Students could either involve themselves in the course and take what they've learned in class seriously and put it to use in the field- or not. It was totally up to them. Subsequently their grades would coincide with their enthusiasm. Besides Sergeant Shots was only interested in the ones who were serious, the rest could do whatever they wanted, except get lost or make too much noise. That was against the rules.

Yes, it was a game, but Kaiden and his teammates took it seriously. On the way up the ridge the patrol had practiced military tactics using various formations and flanking maneuvers while adapting their technique to the immediate terrain. All the while the patrol stalked an unseen prey they called "The Fox" while looking quite the part of a military unit down to the rifle each one cradled in their arms. This was the first exercise where they were without their Kel Tec SU16 rifles. Ever since the ban went into effect, they had to give them up and carry the single shot bolt action Remington 700 hunting rifle. Kaiden considered it a major "downgrade". All of them aimed their rifle menacingly forward at an unseen enemy as if they were about to spring an ambush. Then they jumped up and moved fast leapfrogging from one concealed position to another communicating with sign language as they went. Each one attempted to gain a better position without making any noise. But now, here, they moved forward more slowly using stealth while focusing intently on the terrain ahead. With the same caution as men at war, Coonrod signaled his men to halt and once again pulled out binoculars to survey the meadow at the base of a rolling hill that stood before them. He gave the signal; the enemy was nearby.

The whole idea for the exercise had been crafted back in 2009 after a student handed in a unique term paper entitled "The Effectiveness of Militia Training Tactics". At the time his assignment counted as fifty percent of a student's grade for the required "Military History" class. Rightfully so this frequently referred to paper got a well-deserved "A". The professor thought so highly of the student and his ideas that he brought it to the attention of the administration. Within the pages the author made several recommendations, one of which was to combine the practical applications of two courses, hunting and military tactics, into one. It was a simple suggestion designed to install some fun and realism into the standard training which up to that point had been considered- well let's just say a little "Ho hum". After studying the report, board members concurred and deemed many of the highlighted recommendations as worthwhile. They implemented many of them and the resultant effort morphed into these popular weekend retreats. It became a very effective way to teach multiple aspects of these two disciplines.

Somewhere up ahead of Kaiden's squad there was a three-man hunting party consisting of the teacher and two students. Kaiden's team tracked them to the meadow about two hundred yards to their twelve o'clock. The hunting party was called the "Fox" and the team members called themselves "The hound dogs".

The fox knew the hound dogs were right behind them, but the three of them continued to accomplish their mission. Just an hour before they had seen deer tracks that led them to this meadow and were now getting into position to hopefully catch it feeding out in the open. In this exercise they were the only ones allowed to have live ammunition and the only ones allowed to use it.

They had permission from the combined owners of this 300-acre remote section of the Catskill Mountains to freely roam, hunt, and perform their maneuvers. It was a perfect choice because it had plenty of examples of various types of terrain that they could get lost in. Multiple running streams crisscrossed the land and game was plentiful most of the year round. The rules were simple. The "Hound dogs" allowed the "Fox" a three-hour head start from base camp and then they would start their pursuit. In their attempt to find and capture the Fox the patrol was to treat them as an evading enemy patrol and use all standard military procedure, tactics and intelligence learned in class to locate and capture them. The twists and turns that took place within the confines of this exercise taught the Cadets a variety of valuable lessons.

Sometimes the Hound Dogs lost the trail of the Fox and searched blindly from that point on. Other times patrols would simply stumble upon their prey, surround them and take the hunters into custody. If they had time, they were then let go and given another two-hour head start before the patrol would resume searching for them (after they were interrogated and tortured of course). Or, if the hunters were successful in their hunt and made a kill, it then became the patrols responsibility to overtake the hunting party and help dress the deer and transport the carcass back to base camp.

If the party was successful in their hunt, it was a lot sweeter on the last day of the event because everyone participated in a feast that featured their kill. Thus, it came "full circle" in learning how to hunt from "A" to "plate".

One of the lessons learned was "how to transport a wounded man out of the forest". In this case it would be a dead deer if they got one, but it nicely paralleled the chore of moving a "body". Everyone understood it doubled as a lesson on how to remove the wounded as well as a dead body from an isolated area. The hunting party practiced their skill at evading capture as well as how to track an animal which of course parallels tracking human prey. If the Fox was captured, they would switch off and replace the students with two more to give others the experience of becoming the hunted.

Hunters will tell you that this is not the best way or the preferred method to hunt. You make way too much noise with a bunch of guys moving and following an animal. Most hunters sit in a blind or on a stand in a tree and wait for their prey with dawn and dusk being prime time for a kill. This exercise was a perfect way to teach the fine points of "ambush", and this was exactly what the Master Hunter was teaching his students now, somewhere right up ahead in front of Kaiden's patrol. Not more than two hundred yards out was a grass covered meadow. The Fox had circled around and descended upon it at a perfect angle and at the best time of day- dusk.

Most Cadets had covered themselves with branches and common foliage of the area for added camouflage. When they hunkered down and became still, they were a lot harder to detect. Using tactics as prescribed by their teacher Sergeant Shots, Coonrod gave the signal for the main patrol to move forward. The forest came alive with about twenty Cadets who emerged out of concealment and ran forward to another position. It was amazing. When the patrol stopped, they once again disappeared into the natural surroundings as if they weren't even there. When Coonrod was satisfied, he motioned with the same signal and the second group ran forward leapfrogging over the others into a position in front of them. They were using the clover leaf leapfrog technique and appeared and disappeared on command as the platoon assailed their objective. The squad spread out at about ten-foot intervals and moved in a sweeping formation toward the meadow.

Coonrod gave the signal and Kaiden's detachment split off to the left to form a flanking maneuver. Kaiden had orders to swing his group around in a sweeping maneuver to catch their prey between the two forces. Kaiden kept in contact and coordinated with his patrol leader by radio. At all times Master Sergeant Hutchison was in contact with all parties through the same radio network. Each of them had one, including the Fox. But they all couldn't hear what was being said. It was a great feature of the Midland GTX radio; you could use the group mode and assign a code to each radio. Then you could call direct to one or the other without everyone hearing the message. He was able to communicate and command the entire exercise.

A single rifle shot rang out from up a head. The "crack" came from somewhere near the meadow that they were about to envelope. Everyone froze and hit the dirt.

"Papa John to Alpha Babe".

"Papa John go".

"Confirm shots fired, have you got eyes on?".

"No sir. It must be the Fox, he's real close".

"Ok, use caution on your approach. Do not, I repeat, do not inadvertently get mistaken for prey, maybe some 'not so stealthy' maneuvering would be appropriate right about now over".

"Roger that Papa John. Will advise over".

Erin Stotts was the teacher's real name, but everyone called him "Sergeant Shots". The man practically lived and breathed firearms, if you ever needed him for anything you could always find him at the Range. Many thought that Shots was his real name. He was a short, stocky, burly man who loved hunting and felt honored to be able to get paid to teach it. For the last twenty-five years the man had been a renowned hunter in the hills and valleys of this region, but his military background is what inevitably landed him the job. He was a sniper in the Middle East war where he experienced the reality of many of the lessons he was now teaching. Shots held a zeal for these games that even he would admit went a little overboard at times.

"It's just that I take these games very seriously and expect my students to do the same" he would say in his defense. The degree of effort that he made to evade and avoid being captured was admirable. Camo was his dress code, and he easily held the imagination of the Cadets for hours over a campfire with the stories he told. Many of them detailed events such as the one that was unfolding right now.

Sergeant Shots was lying prone next to a log with his two students lying next to him. He had a spotting scope glued to his eye and his students had two Remington 700 rifles pointing at some unseen object on the other side of the meadow. All three of them had settled in next to a downed tree in a small natural depression in the earth at the edge of the meadow. About an hour before, they had started the slow crawl downwind toward their objective, hopefully undetected. Now they hunkered down to wait. It was a perfect trap and a perfect time in the evening to spring it. Five o'clock was approaching fast and a nearby mountain shadow had already pulled a dark gray shade over the meadow. The meadow offered an open space in the middle of a tangle of forest where earlier in the day they had found fresh deer tracks along the opposite side. Now they just had to wait for the deer to come out to feed in the open.

They had chosen their "hide" well and were camouflaged to an even higher degree than the members of the patrol that followed them. Shots saw to that. He never played around and was dead serious about every aspect of this hunt. All of them wore ghillie suits that were made of strips of material attached to a jacket type of a coverall that allowed them to cover their bodies and heads to hide their features. It worked well and allowed them to blend in with their surroundings. Each one of them looked just like a large clump of grass on the edge of the meadow. The only problem was that hiking around in the heat made the wearer sweat which wasn't so bad for the first "hunter" but if they were caught and the suit passed on to the next unlucky person, he or she inherited something that resembled a smelly wet mop.

"Bam!" the bullet was sent, but even after the shot the three of them lay there without moving a muscle. "A hit. Good shot" Shots said softly from under the spotting scope. Joe had just fired at a deer that had ventured out into the open; they had watched it meander around the edge on the opposite side of the meadow and glassed it with the rifle's scope until a clear shot was acquired. "One hundred and twenty yards away" his partner said. Joe used the hash marks on his scope to zero in; there was zero wind, so he didn't have to allow for it.

Smoke trickled up out of the muzzle of Joe Herring's rifle. Joe happened to have been the next in line to acquire the job of "hunter/ sniper" and now reeled from the excitement of a possible kill. But no congratulatory cheering or high fives were given even though the deer was visibly hit. It leaped into the air after the crack of the rifle. As soon as its hoofs hit the ground and gained traction it leaped again and disappeared into the forest behind it with amazing speed. There was no reaction because the Fox knew how close the Hound Dogs were. Sure enough, out of the forest on each side of the meadow appeared their counterparts, the flanking patrol on their left and the main patrol on their right. Their pursuers had almost stumbled out right on top of them.

A point man from Alpha Babe happened to have spotted the deer a few seconds before the shot rang out. He witnessed the deer jump into the air yet couldn't nail down exactly where the shot came from. After, the point man linked up with the main force and reported in, Coonrod sent Kaiden's group over to reconnoiter the area where the deer had fled into the woods. But Coonrod was even more interested in the other side of the meadow where the shot had most likely come from; he searched it now with his binoculars. Back and forth his eyes scanned the wood line and then once more. Nothing. He sighed and then turned to one of his men.

"Sergeant, send a five-man scouting team to quickly scout the perimeter before it gets dark. We'll hold over here for the night, have the rest of the platoon start setting up camp. I doubt we're going to find the Fox tonight. We'll pick up their trail in the morning" Coonrod told him.

Out of the woods on the adjacent side of the meadow came four students who had been following behind the fast-moving patrol. At this point they all lacked a single stitch of enthusiasm. None of them had a uniform on, one of them was using his rifle as a crutch and the others were carrying them haphazardly as if they were a burden. These were the small number of students who took the course but weren't really interested in learning anything. They didn't' participate in the maneuvers, they just kind of tagged along for the ride. You could hear their voices as they yapped back and forth at each other without a concern for stealth and could tell that they were quite agitated with their plight by the dialog between them. Complaints permeated the conversation and ran the full spectrum from "This is getting really heavy" to "Why do we have to carry this damn rifle anyway?" They sounded so childish that you'd expect to hear "Are we there yet?" at any moment. Then the next thing one of them said was "Are we there yet?".

The lead student of the four of them stopped on the edge of the meadow and stared out into the open field before him. He saw the platoon sprawled out on the other side and noted that they were starting to set up camp. He put up his hand in a weak attempt at sign language and stopped the others from walking out.

One of the stragglers came up and said "Hey look! We found the patrol man. It looks like we're camping here tonight".

Another one said while inching forward "Yeah there's Jackson starting to set up the tent".

Stifling their enthusiasm, the lead student stopped them "Wait, I got a better idea". "If we hang here for a few they'll already have the tents set up and dinner cooking before we even get there".

"Yeah..." another one said realizing the implication "...and they'll have already sent someone out to dig the latrine!".

"Now you're thinking". They all smiled at each other and tapped their fists together in salute, then went and sat down on a log while flinging their rifles and packs off their backs. The other two happily went along with their buddies, un-slung their rifles and threw them carelessly to the ground with a clatter. Their packs followed with a thud looking like they were just dying to get rid of them.

"Man, my feet are killing me" the one on the log said. He placed one foot on his knee and took his boot and sock off. "I think I got a blister". But before he was able to examine his foot there was movement just in front of them in the meadow. It was getting dark fast, so it was becoming more difficult to see. When they focused on the object, two Cadets were standing there just inside the meadow with rifles pointing at them.

"Damn Harvey! You jackass" the Cadet with the rifle yelled. "I could have blown your stupid heads off!".

"Randy you ain't got no fucking bullets in 'em and you ain't gunna shoot shit!" Harvey yelled back.

Three other Cadets from the search party came up beside the two with their rifles pointing seriously at the group but when they realized who they were they all relaxed and lowered them.

"What the hell are you guys doin?" Randy asked. You should be over with the patrol settin up".

"We were..." Harvey lied "...they told us to come over here and jerk off".

"Ass hole" one of the Cadets behind Randy said, disgusted by their indifference.

"Ass hole!" Harvey yelled back at him.

"Just a bunch of ass holes" the Cadets in the scout team mumbled to each other. "Come on let's go, we gotta search the perimeter before it gets dark". The scouts took off in the same direction they originally headed.

Before Randy turned to leave, he said "Harvey you could at least help out a little, Jesus. Have you seen anything, any sign of the Fox?" he nodded his head towards the woods where he assumed they had just come from.

"Nope, all day long all I've seen is the fucking trees" he said flashing him the finger and a forced smile.

"Harvey, shut it up and get all your asses over to the patrol and help set up camp, you're lucky I don't report you to the Sergeant. Make yourselves useful for once will ya? This would all go a lot easier if you'd just chip in and carry your weight". The Cadet turned and followed the other scouts along the perimeter of the meadow.

"Yeah, I've been carrying my weight alright!" he stood up, turned around, dropped his pants and mooned him as he walked away. His cohorts fell to the ground laughing. When Harvey turned back Randy was already moving off shaking his head in disgust. Harvey yelled after him "That's the whole problem with you guys!" He pulled his pants up and kicked his pack with his bare foot.

"Ouch. Ouch! God damn it that hurt!" Harvey yelled. He hopped on one foot and then sat back down on the log and rubbed it with his hands with a cringe forming on his face.

"Harvey, it's getting late" his buddy said to him. "I don't want to set my tent up in the dark. Let's get the hell ata here. Deal with your foot later".

Harvey already came to the same conclusion and started to put his boot back on. The others saddled up their gear more quickly and walked out of the woods into the meadow. They left Harvey sitting on the log mumbling up a storm and left him there alone with his insults and complaints. Harvey got his boot on and slung his pack over his back and then moved out after the others. As soon as he was out of range, three large clumps of grass lying right behind the log Harvey was sitting on started to move. Magically they slid away from the meadow back into the safety of the woods behind them.

Kaiden and his patrol found a blood trail going off into the woods along with tracks that gave evidence of a wounded deer. It had leaped in bounds and ran down the thin animal trail that they were now following. Tony Cransen was placed in charge of the four-member crew by Sergeant Hutchison and given two live rounds of ammunition so that he could finish off the deer if necessary. His search party was assigned the task of locating it. His squad considered their options in a brief huddle before moving out. When all the excuses were thrown out, they concluded that it was imperative that they find the deer tonight. To wait till morning could invite certain desecration of the carcass by other animals during the night. The meat would be ruined and that forced them into acting quickly. There was just enough light left to track the animal for another fifteen to thirty minutes or so, after that his squad would be roaming around the woods in the dark. Kaiden wasn't looking forward to it, but he accepted the mission.

"Let's do this" he said to Carson. They all moved off down the trail in pursuit.

Hopefully the animal was mortally wounded and had fallen just a short way down the trail. Yet recent experience with other kills showed that they were probably in for a hunt before the deer was found. The bullet or more to point the type they were allowed to use by law just wasn't as lethal as other types. Too many times they would wound without facilitating immediate death. Quite often the deer would run until it bled out before falling over. If that happened, it could take hours to find it. This was a direct result of the ban imposed on higher caliber ammunition and bullet types like "hollow point" and other better engineered hunting rounds (as well as simply having bad aim).

To see the fallacy of the ban you'd have to understand the difference between different types of bullets. Basically, the now illegal tipped and hollow point bullets create more damage and therefore facilitate "death" more quickly. The legal FMJ bullets (Full Metal Jacket) had a higher risk of wounding without killing. Some brilliant politicians thought that was a good thing. The .308 FMJ bullets that the ban forces hunters to use is actually a target round which is a slight bit inadequate to use for hunting deer and you can forget about hunting bears with it. The fact that it's more likely to wound made it illegal to use on deer in some states before the ban. But now hunters had no other choice, it's the only caliber and bullet type allowed on the market. You'd have to shoot a deer just right and exactly on target to get a clean kill and that is hard to do especially with an amateur marksman. Hence deer are destined to suffer a more painful slow death. How ironic is it that the law intended to lessen the ability of man to kill just made the act of killing perfectly and appallingly inhumane.

Of course, the elite behind the gun ban are simply pursuing their own hidden agenda. An agenda disguised in the fallacy of acting "for the safety of the people". In their rhetoric they site the goal of becoming more humane and that they are just limiting man's ability to kill, all the while keeping the ability to kill for themselves. Their own security guards are required to carry guns and they are certainly armed with hollow point bullets. They fear for their own safety and assuredly protect it yet seek to limit the ability of others to protect themselves.

Since Tony didn't know how accurate the shooter was, he didn't know what to expect as he followed an overgrown animal trail into the forest. But one thing that made him suspect that he had a long night ahead of him was that there was only one shot that echoed from the meadow. The hunting team had two members in it for the express purpose of enabling the team to shoot twice at the same target if needed, all to increase the odds of a kill whenever possible. Of course, it was not always possible. The window of opportunity hardly presents itself to a single hunter let alone trying to coordinate two hunters to shoot the same target at the same time. Even still, they did have some good results from utilizing this technique on a few other occasions, but not today.

The Alpha Babe team didn't know it at the time, but the flanking patrol had spooked the deer in their attempt to sneak up on the meadow. The hunting party only had a split second to take their shot. That might be why the deer was only wounded. Now Kaiden's search party had their work cut out for themselves. It was tough going getting through the brush they were in. But after an hour of searching and after losing the trail twice, with flashlights in hand they zeroed in on the deer's location. It was a buck and it had crawled into a thicket of bushes which must have been one of its "hides". A small opening led to the interior that was just large enough to crawl through. It was dead. It had given up from loss of blood or lack of energy or both. Tony was relieved that he didn't have to go in and shoot it again.

The death of the animal was dealt with by performing "the ceremony" over the body after the kill. They recited a heartfelt prayer of thanks to God that their lives would be nourished and sustained by the sacrifice of this animal. Next, they had to drag the deer out from the bushes, which was a chore they all dreaded. Wider access had to be hacked out of the brush before the body of the animal could be removed. There was also the possibility that the meat would be less than ideal because the deer had been frightened to the core after being shot.

"That doesn't do justice to the quality of the meat" Tony said. "Lactic acid has a chance to build up in the animal's muscle and can turn the meat into dog food if he lives for longer than ten minutes. Hopefully the deer died quickly".

Either way they went through the motions, did their job, and brought the carcass out just like they were taught to do. A hunter is responsible for his kill and the process had to be carried out to the end. They dressed the deer right there in the field, cut the carcass up into sections, buried the entrails and carried the meat out on a deer sled. "You eat what you kill" was the motto drilled into them. If it turns out that it's dog food, then that's what you're having for dinner.

On the last afternoon of the last day of the exercise the Cadets had their feast. It looked like a boy scout Jamboree with all the uniforms milling around multiple campfires. When the hunting party emerged from the woods, they were relieved and converged on the base camp in a better mood. It looked like a nicely kept park but would have looked a whole lot nicer if it was midsummer and the grass was green, and the foliage was thick. As it was, the landscape was gray and barren on a cloudy overcast winter day. Everyone found a fire and stood around it with their hands in their pockets looking like they were cold and trying to warm up. Of course, that's when stories of the hunt and the hunted flowed one into the other as observers and participants described their role in the events of past and present. There was a large central tent set up near the middle of it all where white smoke emanated from a super-sized grill. It had its own vent system that purged the smoke and heat from the tent without burning the canvas overhead. The kill of the weekend could be seen broiling, smoking, and turning on a spit set up over the flame. There were also slabs of meat cooking on the black grill which the cook and his assistants were flipping like hamburgers and handing out at the right moment to a line of people that stood in front of them. You could see the anticipation on their faces as they fumbled with an empty paper plate in their hands.

There were a few women who participated in the event, but they were rare. This event generally attracted male participants. Kaiden didn't mind though, he thought the platoon performed a lot better when women weren't in the mix. There was evidence that a lot more attention was paid to the job at hand minus the showing off and bravado that occurs for the woman's sake. But looking around he noticed that a lot of women had showed up for the after party. They hung around and seemed to be listening and laughing while pretending to be interested in the hunting stories being told. More than likely, they were just there for a special someone rather than any genuine interest in the event itself. It couldn't have been just for the beer- could it?

One of Kaiden's buddies was standing around the fire with a fine-looking woman, obviously his girlfriend. They were hugging, kissing, and looking at each other with sincere happiness in their eyes. Occasionally, they would smile and then laugh at each other. True honest affection showed through between the two. Kaiden was happy for them. It made him think of... Ciera.

Why Ciera entered Kaiden's thoughts became apparent just seconds later when he looked up. It must have been her energy. There she was standing not ten yards away with her hands buried deep in the pockets of her winter jacket and the hood pulled up over her head. She was looking at him with a smile on her face, happy to see him. It was a smile that looked as true on her as it did on the woman he was just observing.

"Hey there gorgeous" Kaiden said with a calm serious tone and a twinkle in his eye. They hadn't seen much of each other since he joined the Cadets at the Club Gitmo party. It seemed like ages ago, but it was really only three months.

"Hey handsome" she said with a shy smile.

Kaiden stood up and walked towards her, she met him in the middle, and they hugged warmly.

"Wow, where've you been, I haven't seen you at all lately. Not even in Tai Chi class".

"Yeah, I haven't seen much of you either" She said with that joking smile of hers.

Kaiden lowered his head down and shot her a glance over his eyebrows "You haven't been avoiding me, have you?"

She looked down at the ground for a second and then back up "No, it's not like that, I've been busy".

"Oh, yeah, I know, I know you're a busy woman. Ciera…" he drew inward and took his turn to look down at the ground. "…I've got to apologize" he looked back up and into her eyes. "I came on kinda strong back there and I shouldn't have. It was…"

"Hey, don't worry about it, there's no need to apologize. Kaiden, really, it's OK" she said. "I liked the kiss".

"Ok" he smiled and almost laughed feeling like the ice had been broken. "But Ciera…" then he got serious and again looked her in the eyes "…I want you to know, I need you to know, that there's someone else out there who really cares about you. It sounds kinda weird since I haven't seen you for a while I know, but I've thought about all the people I've met at Tenny Hill and you're one of the ones that I feel really connected to. Maybe we could get together more often, I mean bring what's his name too…"

"Nick? Your commanding officer?".

"Yeah, that lucky shit head" Kaiden said and then smiled. Ciera laughed at him. "And when you hear this, it might sound… well insincere, but here it goes. If you ever need anyone or anything, let me know. I'll be there for you".

Ciera cocked her head to the side, smiled and crunched her shoulders. "Thank you Kaiden. That's nice to know". She took his arm and turned him to face the main tent. "Let's go get some hot chocolate, what do ya say? Tell me all about the hunt".

He looked at her and smiled. "You really want to know? Well, all right".

"By the way…" she said teasingly "…who is this someone else that cares about me?".

Kaiden turned out of her hold on his arm and playfully pushed her away as they both cracked up laughing.

Two seats were open at a picnic table near the tent, so they sat down with their cups of hot chocolate. Both used the cup to help keep their hands warm. "I saw you at the last board meeting and heard your report. I believe you when you say you're busy. I don't know how you do it".

Ciera rolled her eyes in agreement. "I'll say".

You must be having quite a time with that what... 'Humanitarian aid' thing you got going.

"Humanitarian Relief Organization" she corrected him.

"That's it. How's it going? Your report was encouraging".

"Actually, the Relief Organization is Reverend Water's baby, well sort of, in name anyway. At least that's the way we want it to be. But at this point we're basically running it all. And yes, it's a lot more work than I thought but that's because it's been such a tremendous success" she reached out and touched him on the arm and beamed with a smile as she bobbed her head back and forth in a self-congratulatory gesture.

"That must mean that you were successful in finding buyers for the stuff you brought in huh.

"That part ended up being easier than obtaining it" she told him.

"Congratulations! I remember that was your main concern at the board meeting".

"Yeah, if we couldn't sell it, the whole idea would have abruptly ended right then and there. The key is to get a great deal and give a great deal so that it's impossible for customers to pass it up. Oh, and to stick with items that are in high demand, which is the cornerstone of the whole project".

"Wow sounds like you've created a great service to the community".

"Ah, it's just a great example of how capitalism seeks a path of least resistance".

"Yeah, but how do you make a profit then? Isn't profit the guiding force behind capitalism and if your organization is a 'nonprofit' then where's the incentive?".

"That's a good question and I'll answer it by saying that we do make a profit but that's not the crucial point. In today's economic environment I see that 'need' or 'necessity' would be better words to use to describe the 'drive' behind our effort. Forgive the pun because we sure are 'driving' all over God's creation just to put this together! Necessity has become the primary force, almost replacing the need for profit. But yes, we are making a profit on it".

Kaiden chuckled at her.

"Need my friend, can be a powerful incentive" Kaiden said. "But then how do you make a profit?".

"Well, there's the security department that's now moved from the 'Red' into the 'Black'. They're even getting hired out by other companies and other runners too. You should think about joining Kaiden, you could make some money doing that".

"Hey, is that a job offer?".

"Damn right it is. I could put in a good word for you and get you on".

"Thanks Ciera, I always felt like you were on my side".

"And don't you ever forget it!" she said with a playful grin and a finger pointing at him. "But don't thank me, it's dangerous work. I'll warn you now".

"I didn't think I'd qualify for the position; my roommate told me they were looking for people with a gun permit".

"They are. Have you applied for yours?".

"Yes, but they say it'll take about six months to a year to get it".

"Don't worry, I can still get you on, they decided not to let the escorts carry guns. That requirement is just for the Jobs that require armed personnel".

"Thanks, I'll think about it. I could use the extra money".

Kaiden flashed her a thank you smile but he also felt like she was evading his main question. "OK but how 'do' you make a profit then. I mean, is that it? The security department wins from all your effort?"

She looked at him more seriously as if he'd picked up on it way too quickly. "Well, we make something off the top".

"Really. How do you do that with a nonprofit organization?"

Her eyebrows rose slightly, and she said with a straight face "There is a little more 'incentive' that we get from the sale of 'some' of the items. Since the Humanitarian Relief Organization can't show a profit on paper, we request a 'donation' to the school from our customers. It's almost like they bid on the product with a donation. The highest bidder wins the product".

Kaiden cracked a big grin "Now we're getting down to it! A donation? How much?".

"Ok, I'll tell you but please don't let it get around. It's something we don't want advertised. We ask them for a ten percent donation and a two percent discount if they pay in silver or gold".

"Ask them? And if they don't pay?".

"Well so far, we haven't had a problem with that. Even with the ten percent 'donation'... she said it with her two little fingers going up to make the "quotation" gesture... Customers are happy with the purchase price which of course includes the ten percent. Believe me Kaiden, the prices we are offering are that good compared to what's out there. I've seen savings of forty to fifty percent. If they don't want to contribute, then we would either require it before doing business with them again or just plain old cease doing business with them altogether. It's their choice".

"Wow a kickback. It sounds like you're running a black market-market".

"Cute Kaiden. It's a flea market. We run it out of the Church parking lot every Friday through Sunday. It's quite popular; a lot of other venders show up as well. Tough times require tough measures. It's just a subtle way to get around the system or really if you want to get down to it, it's the system forcing us to do business in an unorthodox way. It's a matter of survival and it just so happens that we're really good at it".

"Damn right" Kaiden said. He looked off into the distance "I'm learning about a whole lot of things I never thought I'd have to deal with. I feel empowered though, I feel like I have a better chance of... of living".

Ciera looked pleased with Kaiden's conclusion and smiled. She stood up abruptly and said "Let's get on line for some grub and go find us a warm fire".

26

Return of The King

A convoy approached the Academy without any warning or notification. One hundred yards in front of it flying above the trees was a sniffer drone operated by an agent in the leading SUV. He saw what it saw on a monitor built into the console of the vehicle. A succession of vehicles drove through the campus entrance with purpose. Traveling way above the posted 20 mph speed limit, they raced up the road looking like they were in a big hurry to get somewhere. Seven black SUVs with dark tinted windows blew through the campus on the way to a predetermined site. Two of them peeled off from the convoy and turned into the administration building's parking lot. Both came to an abrupt halt one right behind the other in front of the "No Parking" sign posted on both sides of the curb. Three state trooper vehicles, a bus and a cargo van pulled up behind them moments later.

ATF agent Mallory Hicks stepped out of the second SUV. He took off his sunglasses and looked at the Administration building as if he was General Macarthur returning to the Philippians. He had been dying to do this ever since his first meeting with the Chancellor and looked forward to this day with a vengeance. His men, dressed in the same black suit and dark sunglasses, assembled on both sides of him. The whole group moved briskly down the walk and up to the entrance of the administration building with Hicks in the lead.

It startled Mary sitting at her desk; their brisk entrance and a sudden demand to see the Chancellor. They didn't wait for an answer and ignored her protests as the whole entourage walked past her and through the door into the Chancellor's office. Gentry was just as surprised as his secretary when Hicks burst in. He strolled up to the large oak desk and slapped a folded piece of paper down in front of him.

"I have a search warrant that I'm executing on this campus which allows me to search all buildings I feel necessary- I'm starting with this one. I want access to all storerooms and basements of the buildings on this list. He handed another piece of paper to the Chancellor as well. Get your maintenance man up here or someone who has a set of master keys, I'm not interested in being escorted around by security. Not this time. I will escort your personnel around with my security. Got it?".

The Chancellor didn't have to use the phone; Mary was at the door with a flustered look on her face. He glanced at her and waved her back. "Mary it's OK, get Bill in here ASAP".

She turned and almost ran into three State troopers who came up right behind her. "Oh my" she said with her hand covering her mouth. She shuffled past them with an expanding look of alarm.

State trooper Lieutenant Sergeant Henry Welch walked into the Chancellors office; his two deputies were right behind but they stayed at the door. Gentry looked up and stared at him with a serious look on his face. He acknowledged the trooper's presence with a nod of his head. "Henry" he said as if he knew him.

"Oh yes it seems you already know Officer Welch here, They're my backup team" Hicks said giving the Chancellor a winning smile. He waved his arm towards the Troopers as if he owned them.

"Hello Rodger" Welch said. "Yes, it's legit. They have a warrant. I wasn't allowed to contact you". His eyes trailed off and glanced at agent Hicks.

"It's Ok Henry..." Gentry said. It was obvious that they knew each other well. "We have nothing to hide here". He stood up and turned to agent Hicks "You'll get my full cooperation Mr. Hicks. Search any building you like".

The five remaining SUV's and the sniffer drone raced on through campus on their way to five other targets. One of them peeled off from the convoy and descended on their assigned building- the Range. It drove into the parking lot and came to a screeching halt at the front entrance. Six agents got out and ran in. Monett along with all the occupants in and around his office were taken back by the appearance of men in black with badges and holstered guns that were intentionally on display. The phone call from Chancellor Gentry to Major Monett wasn't in time to stave off the surprise, which is exactly how the ATF planned it. The Chancellor advised the Major to cooperate and give them everything they needed to complete their search including blueprints for each of the buildings. The same scene repeated itself throughout the campus at each of the locations the SUV's had targeted. Their job was to secure the premises quickly, by surprise, and to detain the personnel in charge of the building so that nothing could be moved, hidden, or removed before the main team got there.

A bus carrying forty-five uniformed ATF agents arrived right behind the SUV's. It stopped at each building that had a black SUV parked out in front and unloaded six to eight additional uniformed agents at each location. They were easy to distinguish; their jackets had "BATFE" written in bold yellow letters on the back. Those additional agents were directed by the suits to help secure the building and then to carry out a search of the premises. Appropriate keys were obtained through maintenance and a thorough inspection began that dug into all storage rooms, lockers, closets, and hallways including every drawer and shelf. Nothing was left unchecked. Hicks believed there was a cache of illegal weapons hidden somewhere on campus and he was determined to find it.

Digging further into the receipt that Gentry had given Hicks depicting the sale of the weapons and researching his story was time consuming. They followed a paper trail from one dealer to the other who claimed they had purchased and then sold the weapons to another private dealer. When the last registered owner was located and confronted, he pointed to a police report filed the day before that claimed the weapons were stolen from a container in a Boston shipping yard. He said he was about to ship the weapons out of the country. Hicks didn't buy it.

After securing the Administration building, Hicks drove over to personally participate in securing the range building. That's where he suspected he'd find what he was looking for. Part of his team headed right to the basement, Hicks and the rest of the team went up to Major Monett's office on the second floor and took it over. It was used as his own temporary command center. His men moved the Major and his staff into the conference room amongst assurances that they were not under arrest, but they were restrained to the point where that's exactly how they felt.

The Major, his assistant Harry Coin, his secretary, two staff members, two teachers and two students, who were unlucky enough to have gotten caught in the office at the same time of the raid, were cautioned to remain in place. "You're just being detained" they said. "You're not allowed to leave or to communicate with anyone on the outside". One cell phone and two BeepX communicators were confiscated from the group, they were not allowed to make a call and if they had to go to the bathroom, they would have to do it in the presence of one of the agents. They were determined to keep any news of their operation from leaking out.

Classes for the rest of the day were cancelled and they weren't allowed to make phone calls or post the news on the internet. The Feds made them make cardboard signs that were taped to the exterior doors of the building. The plan was to minimize any type of contact that could produce a warning, a warning that would tip off the conspirators and give them a chance to hide the illegal weapons they were after. It would be a big feather in Hicks' cap if he could just find the weapons cache.

Guards were placed at the buildings' front doors with orders to let students out but not in. Then three of the uniformed ATF agents went down to the basement and walked up to the equipment room where Carl Roughett happened to be on duty as acting clerk for today's session. People had just started arriving in the men's and women's locker room and were milling around getting their gear together, all were in various stages of dress before class. Already Carl had signed out rifles to the early birds for today's target practice when his routine was rudely interrupted.

Three men bullied their way up to the front of the line by physically pushing aside the students waiting at his window. One of them grabbed the rifle the clerk had just handed out and yanked it out of the Cadets hands. He took another off the counter and handed it back to one of the other men. At the same time, he flashed his identification badge and shoved it at Carl. It was a laminated badge with his picture on it. There was his name- Rolf Wiggum, a fancy government symbol and ATF written in bold letters across it. When Carl saw that it matched the same emblem on their jackets, he believed it was legit. He'd seen that jacket before.

"What do you want this time?" Carl said.

"Direct orders from the ATF are for you to stand down and shut down immediately! Cease all operations of this facility and prepare to cooperate with a search. This place is now closed!" he yelled to everyone standing around.

"Please take your hand off the counter sir" Carl said to him.

"What?" The agent said looking surprised but unconsciously he picked his hands up off the counter between them.

Carl hit the two panic buttons simultaneously underneath his side of the counter and a large sheet of bulletproof glass slid down from the top and slammed onto the countertop with a bang. In less than a second it had sealed off the room by putting two inches of glass between the agents and Carl. Carl just stood there and stared back at their shocked faces. Luckily, the agent had moved his hand or else at this moment he'd be minus fingers.

All any equipment manager on duty had to do was to push both buttons at the same time to spring the glass. One was located at each end of the counter within arm's reach, this ensured that the clerk would have to separate both hands and place one on each button to go into lockdown mode. That procedure guaranteed that both clerk's hands would be on the safe side of the counter when the glass fell. The manufacturer of the device didn't give any consideration for where the hands of the person threatening you would be.

"Holy shit!" the agent screamed, shocked from the "bang" of glass on counter and the audacity of this kid. He had just come way too close to having his fingers cut off. All three agents reacted by jumping back and pulling out their guns. All three drew a bead on Carl's body and for a second thought seriously about trying to shoot through the glass. You could see two sets of three red laser dots nervously dancing around in small circles. One set of dots was on Carl's chest. The other set was a reflection of the same on the glass in between them.

Carl stood defiantly on the other side feeling safe even though there were now three Sig 45's pointing right at him. The barrel of Rolf's gun was shaking badly even though he held it with two hands. Carl shrugged his shoulders at the agent and tried to yell loud enough so that they could hear him through the safety glass "Sorry, got to verify this, its procedure!" He picked up a phone next to him and dialed a number with a smirk of a grin on his face completely ignoring the fact that there were three guns trained on him.

Agent Hicks answered the phone that rang on the Major's desk. He told the clerk on the other end who and what he was, but Carl insisted on speaking to the Major.

Hicks took a call from Rolf on his mobile phone at the same time. Rolf explained the resistance he was running into, and the nature of the problem became apparent. If the clerk couldn't be swayed, it would be a major obstacle to completing a timely search of the most important room on campus. He tried to explain the situation slowly and carefully to Carl, but it was useless, Carl wasn't going to cooperate. He'd have none of it and insisted on speaking to Major Monett. Hicks relented hoping that it would speed things up. Since the phone in the conference room had been removed, he brought the Major back into the office and handed him the phone.

"Carl, its Major Monett. Yes, it's legit, they have a warrant and it's legal. Stand down and open the armory for them. Let them search it... No, I can't come down there they won't let me; they're holding me here".

Hicks took the phone away from the Major and spoke briefly into it. "Now open the God damn door son before I arrest you for impeding a Federal investigation". Smiling, he hung up, certain that he would get his way. Then he yelled angrily into his mobile phone at the agent on the other end "...and bring that kid up here to me!".

Carl contemplated what the Major said. He moved away from the window and walked over to the armory door. Yes, he was going to obey his commander "but before I do..." he paused and quickly sent out a single text message from his BeepX. He hit the send button, removed the bar across the door, turned the handle and opened it.

Two agents burst through the door and pushed past Carl. Rolf walked in next and paused in front of the desk clerk. He looked at him and with a tilt of his head he snarled "I'm very disappointed in you". Then he punched Carl square in the face. Carl reeled back with his hand skimming across the top of the counter as he tried to catch his balance. He only succeeded in knocking everything on it onto the floor. His body continued and smacked back up against the wall behind him. As he hit, the BeepX dropped from his hand and tumbled on the ground along with all the stuff from the counter. He crumpled to the floor in agony as his vision went blank.

Two agents splintered off from the group at the range building and walked around to assist with its evacuation. Whenever they encountered students, they announced that the building was closed and that they were to vacate the premises immediately. All were then escorted outside. The three agents in the armory went to work cataloging the type of weapons stored there and the rest of the ATF team members split up and started searching their assigned section of the building. The hunt focused on the basement because the armory and locker rooms were the most likely place they would find what they were looking for. It was a maze of hallways and doors down there along with storage areas and closets in every room. But every room including the gymnasium had to be scrutinized and methodically gone over. The gym was an easy search, but it became particularly slow going when they got to the student locker room. All three hundred and fifty lockers had to be opened with the master key and its contents gone over. Hicks urged his men to be thorough and carefully inspect every one of them.

A BeepX went off. It sat there on the counter next to Kenny's bed buzzing and moving around in a circle from the vibration. A BeepX isn't a phone it's a combination beeper/text message device, every student has one. The device was more popular than a phone because the school supported it with their own in-house server. To use one was a quarter of the price of a phone, both in initial expense and in monthly fees, hence its popularity. All it did was text messaging but that was all it needed to do. No one carried phones much anymore, especially around campus. Service was almost non-existent up here in the mountains even before they shut the Delhi tower down. That tower didn't carry enough traffic to be profitable and only the most profitable towers were maintained these days. At least that was the excuse they gave. Many conspiracy theorists thought it was part of the government's drive to blind rural sections of America to help restrict communication.

The BeepX device was a perfect solution. It uses a microwave connection to a transponder located on the roof of the maintenance building. That transmitter sends the signal to a transponder on top of Mt. Tenny which broadcasts it around campus with about a 10-mile range radius. It runs independently off a solar power array located next to the transponder. Even the BeepX beeper itself has a small solar panel that charges the battery by sunlight or artificial light. Some people (who aren't maniac texters) can go months without needing to charge it. Nowadays, kids don't ever bother with full length phone conversations, a simple text message is all that's needed. Everyone uses the "Standard shorthand method" for communication. The official dictionary can be accessed in the menu, or you can get it in written form from the booklet included in the 'standard kit' issued to every student upon enrolment. It defines and or deciphers the many abbreviations used for frequently used words. Many took it to an even higher level and have made up their own language on the thing, which can be saved in an individual's personal dictionary. Your dictionary can be downloaded by another to enable them to decipher private messages between you. One only needs to know what dictionary you are using and click on the abbreviation to get its meaning. This feature turns the device into a secret code transmitter.

Kenny sat up in bed, grabbed the BeepX off the counter and glanced at the digital display. It was 8:45 and he was just getting up. Sitting on the bed for a moment he rubbed the sleep from his eyes to see better. He knew he was late. Kaiden had come back from Tai Chi practice and was already dressed in uniform ready to go. He'd shaken Kenny a few times before to wake him, but it just wasn't happening.

Kenny looked at the message again. It read "T ATF r hre. Tking ovr Rng Bldg serch n lockrs!"

Kenny didn't quite get it at first. He slowly got up, looked at the BeepX again, looked away, thought about it, yawned, and then started doing the "not awake slow shuffle" over to the bathroom. In the middle of the room, he stopped and looked at the beeper again. Then it dawned on him that ATF meant Bureau of Tobacco, Alcohol, Firearms & Explosives.

"Holy shit! Kaiden!" he yelled. His eyes bugged out as he moved fast towards the bathroom.

Kaiden and one of their neighbors were in the bathroom at the sink. Kaiden was brushing his teeth while looking in the mirror. "Kaiden..." Kenny yelled anxiously. "I just got a text from Carl over at the Armory. He says the Feds are here and they're searching the building!".

Kaiden looked up and through a mouthful of toothpaste exclaimed... "They're what!".

"They're searching the Range Building man! It must have to do with weapons, there's nothing else the Feds would be interested in there. I'm getting on the waves to put out the word. I'll see if I can find out more about what's goin on".

Kaiden said "I'm heading over now. I'll beep you if I see anything". He immediately changed gears and walked out of the bathroom grabbing his hat on the way to the door.

Kenny spun around and looked at his computer and all the technology on his desk. Noting that the message from Carl came in at 8:26; he looked and saw 8:37 on his digital clock. Instantly he tapped out a quick reply to Carl's message and waited for a response. Nothing came back and a look of concern came across Kenny's face. He ran into his neighbor's room through the connecting bathroom and yelled at "Money" and "Peck" who were both standing there looking out the window, their eyes following a drone that hovered above one of the buildings. Money's real name was Carleton Forbes, his last name being the catalyst for the nickname. Peck got his nickname because he was an aspiring body builder with a fantastic upper body physique.

In a frantic voice Kenny yelled "I need your help now!".

Agent Rolf went back over to Carl who was just coming too on the floor. He rolled him over and searched him but found nothing of importance. Carl moaned as he became aware of the expanding pain in his nose and cheekbone. Rolf pulled him up and sat him against the wall. He took hold of his shoulders and shook him while staring into his face. "Where are the automatic weapons kid?".

Carl just looked at him dazed and confused. "We don't… have any… automatic…" is all he could muster.

Rolf threw him back against the wall totally disgusted with his answer. Just then one of his men searching the armory called out from the back "Rolf! Get over here and look at this. I got something!".

Rolf perked up and walked away with the expectation that his man had found something juicy. Just after turning away from the floor next to Carl's feet, a BeepX went off. Carl glanced at where he thought it might be amongst all the junk on the floor. He could hear the familiar humming sound of its vibration indicating an incoming message but didn't know where it was. He glanced back up at Rolf who had stopped in his tracks and cocked his head trying to listen to something he thought he heard. Carl didn't dare look back towards the sound which might give away its location; he just placed his foot over the spot where he thought it was. He closed his eyes and let out a moan and while trying to cover the sound of the BeepX. Agent Rolf turned and looked down at Carl. Another moan from Carl's lips was convincing enough to dispel any suspicion he might have had as to the origin of the sound.

"Rolf! Get over here man. Where are you?" his fellow agent called from the parts room.

"I'm coming" he said and walked away.

When Carl opened his eyes, he thanked God that the agent had continued his trek towards the back. He moved his foot off the spot and saw the last few flashes of light on the beepers digital display.

What the agents found wasn't exactly the automatic weapons they were looking for but even still there was excitement in his voice. "I'm going to call this in and bring the kid up to Hicks. I'll be right back".

In the back of the armory underneath the bench, where the gunsmith worked, was a multitude of bins with all kinds of spare rifle and handgun parts in them. Next to the bench was another door going into a separate 10 x 15-foot parts room that had the same type of bins ranging in all sizes from tiny to large. They filled the shelves that extended from floor to ceiling with even more bins on shelves in the center of the room. The whole set up was very neat and each bin was nicely labeled, which made it easy for the agents.

Many of the bins had stickers labeling the parts as belonging to the "Remington 700". Some described the contents as various pieces of the "Kel Tek SU16" and still others as "Ruger model 77". They must have had multiples of every spare part you'd possibly need to keep these guns in working order. The ones marked AR-15 and SU-16 were bins the agents were attracted to. There they found spare rifle barrels, upper and lower receivers, trigger mechanisms, stocks and many smaller pieces like springs, screws, and bolts. There were enough spare parts that if assembled, it could probably complete three or four of the illegal rifles.

Agent Rolf Walked briskly back into the main storage room of the Armory speaking loudly over his shoulder. "I'll bring the kid up and deliver the good news to Hicks". He grabbed Carl up off the floor and pushed him toward the door. Rolf scanned the floor where Carl had been laying. The BeepX wasn't there.

Pushing him continuously in front of him, Rolf escorted Carl up the stairs into the Majors office and sat him down in the chair in front of Hicks. "Damn did you have to rough him up?" Hicks said when he saw the swollen eye and red-blue-green rainbow of colors developing on Carl's cheekbone.

Rolf said "He resisted sir, but... (he tried to change the subject) the good news is... we found enough spare parts in the parts room to assemble about four working AR-15's sir". He said it with a smile as if he thought he'd get a reward for his effort.

Hicks got up and yelled "That's it? Just four unassembled rifles? I can't believe this shit!". Then Hicks rained on the guy's parade. "Get back down there and find me those guns god damn it; or do I have to do it myself? Don't come back here until you find em! Tell Charlie to bring Monett back in here on your way out".

The Major walked back into his own office a minute later. Immediately he glanced at Carl and quickly walked over to him. He looked at Carl's face closely and bent down to speak to him face to face.

"You Ok son? The Major said in a sympathetic voice.

"Yeah, I'm Ok Major. Thanks, don't worry about me. I'm sorry Major". Carl said it with a tear starting to form in the corner of his good eye.

"You're sorry? Don't be, you did exactly what you were supposed to do". The Major touched Carl on the shoulder. Then he stood up, walked over to his own desk, and looked down at Hicks who was sitting in his chair. "You'll hear about this you piece of shit. You contain your men you understand, or I'll make it my mission to see that you regret it. Bring that agent back here and let him try that shit on me!".

Hicks stood up and snapped his fingers. Two of his agents entered who were standing just outside the office door. They looked like they'd attack if they heard just one more click of his fingers. With that backup, Hicks got right back in the Majors face.

"Don't talk to me like that you fucking synthetic soldier. All you're doing here is playing army like little kids in a sand box with Tonka toys. You think you're better than me? You think you can beat the ATF? You and that asshole Gentry. Well, I've got your immediate future in the palm of my hands, and I can crush this little romp-a-room class you got going here. Just give me an excuse!". They stared each other down with plenty of disdain before Hicks continued.

"We found enough parts down there in the storage room to make four AR-15's. That's felony possession Monett!".

"Hicks those are just overlooked broken parts that we haven't gotten rid of yet. They're nonfunctional, unintentionally saved. You can't charge us for that".

"Oh yes, I can, and if you're not a good little boy scout, I'll do just that. Now are you going to tell me where they are, or do I have to get it out of the kid?" There was no response. Hicks snapped at his men. "Take him back!".

* * *

Beepers were going off like crazy all over campus. The buzz quickly got around with the news of the Feds raid on the Academy. Small groups gathered in hallways, on sidewalks and in dorm rooms as the word spread. These small groups turned into larger ones as the students searched for answers to what was going on. People who were turned away at the range Building, or by the agents guarding the doors of other buildings, started to gather on the walkways outside directly in front of the building. Rumors were rampant. One was that Major Monett and his staff had been arrested, another was that the school was being closed. Chancellor Gentry was under arrest too. You could see anguish and fear in their faces as they learned about the situation. Some girls were crying. Others turned away angry when they realized that this could be the end of their school.

Moments before, during the search of the range locker room, agents found a semi-automatic Kel-Tec SU16-C rifle with two hundred rounds of ammunition and a twenty-round magazine in one of the student's lockers. It was the same model that was reported to have been issued to students at the shooting range and was one of the Cadets favorite weapons. Only now it was illegal to own under the ban and was exactly the type of weapon that Hicks was looking for. Hicks had his men hauled the Major back into his office for another conversation.

The Major was adamant and swore "How the hell would I know. I don't know how any student could have gotten one of those or why he hadn't turned it in".

This wasn't exactly what Hicks wanted, but he'd take it. At least he found something. Up until now they'd come up without the evidence they were looking for. Namely a large stash of AR-15's. He really thought he'd catch them with a cache of weapons in the Armory and disappointment showed in his voice when he yelled at his own agents.

"This is all you got? We need the mother fucking load not onesie twosies! Get back down there and find it God damn it!" Hicks turned to the other black suits standing around the Majors office with nothing to do and yelled "Bring the kid who owns that locker to me!"

Agent Hicks turned to the Major. "It would be a whole lot easier if you'd cooperate and show us where they are. If we find it on our own, it's not going to be good for you". Then he got in the Majors face "This is your last chance Monett, where are they?".

"I've already told you. We sold them. We're in complete compliance with the law".

"The 'law' Monett?" Agent Hicks backed down but made another subliminal point by walking over behind the Majors desk. Grinning like a Cheshire cat, he sat down, put his elbows on the desk and folded his hands together in front of his face. He paused for a long moment to let it sink in.

"Well, it's certainly not in line with our rights as granted by the Constitution's second..." the Major started to say.

"Oh, that bullshit again? The Constitution? We have come to the conclusion... ha, 'I' have concluded, that document was written over two hundred years ago by a bunch of white angry old men that had no idea of the intricacies of today's society. It's as outdated as the wigs they wore when they wrote it. We've outgrown it and it needs to be brought into the twenty-first century. THE LAW does that Monett".

Monett jumped on his statement. "You think we're stupid, that we want to go to jail? It's against the law to own those rifles so we got rid of them as the law states. This is an outrageous breach of our rights. What is it with you… we're guilty until proven innocent?"

"We shall see, won't we? I have a feeling that before the end of the day the ends will justify our means". Hicks said it with total confidence and total lack of concern for the possibility of failure.

Kaiden ran out of his dorm and ran smack into a group of his fellow dorm mates who had gathered outside. They had formed a circle in front of the courtyard and were discussing the news. Kaiden started to inform them of Carl's BeepX message and the fact that the Feds were searching the range building when one of the sinister looking SUVs pulled up in front of their dorm. True to form, six agents in black suits got out. Kaiden and the other students stood there and watched as the occupants walked briskly toward them. Their black suits, sunglasses and white curly wire in their ears made it obvious who they were; they were the "enemy" and now they knew the rumors were true. Federal Agents were raiding the campus. The group stood there and turned their attention toward the intruders as a sniffer drone descended upon their building.

For just a moment, the agents stopped and spoke quietly to each other. They hadn't expected a welcoming committee and looked around nervously as the group in front of them started to grow. It turned into a crowd from a steady stream of students exiting the front door of the building. The crowd quickly absorbed the fact that the agents were there to search the building. The enemy was not only on campus, but they were also at their doorstep.

A conclusion was reached, and the suits formed up. They moved forward forcefully parting the throng with authority. The two in front moved students out of their way with a wave of their arms saying

"Alright move back, ATF comin' through, move back... nothing to see here". They strode up to the dorm's front door and entered as if they owned the place. Some students responded with contempt. The black suits were chastised as curse words and insults followed them in. One suit remained and stood outside the front entrance barring people from going back into the building. After checking IDs to see who they were, the agent would let them out, but not back in. The rest of the agents went up to the second floor. Unknown to any of the other students, they had been called to initiate a search for the owner of the illegal Kel-Tec rifle. Kaiden witnessed one of his friends being rebuffed at the door. The agent held out his hand as he approached and told him he wasn't allowed back in. The student was incensed that these guys could just come in here and block the entrance to his own residence. He stood there for a while fuming along with his roommates while they ranted about the injustice.

"What the hell are they doing here?" someone said. "What are we gunna do?" said another.

They all watched as the sniffer drone flew just feet away from the second-floor windows pausing for a moment at each to peer inside. "They're looking for something or someone" one of the Cadets answered.

Kaiden suddenly said "I'm going to find out!" and took off running down a worn-out path in the grass that led around the corner of the building to the back entrance. Two of his friends followed and ran behind him. The back door wasn't blocked. Kaiden chuckled to himself thinking about how useless their tactics were. They went in through the back garage door where bicycles and Rat Packs were parked.

Meanwhile, the agent stationed at the front door became increasingly worried. That large crowd of students outside the door he was guarding was getting louder and more animated. The ranting and raving started to escalate. A half-filled soda can sailed through the air and hit the door. It landed and hissed and sputtered spewing soda like it was a live grenade. The agent started to panic and spoke into his radio

"Guy's whatever you do 'hurry the hell up' find him and get the hell out a there, the situations getting hot down here".

Without bothering to take the elevator, Kaiden leaped in bounds up the three flights of stairs to his second floor. Out of breath, Kaiden busted through the stairwell door on the second floor and skidded out across the hallway's smooth tile. His momentum took him into bouncing off the opposite wall. When he looked up, he froze and came to an abrupt stop. There in the middle of the hallway were five agents escorting Kenny to the elevator in handcuffs. His hands were behind his back and Kenny's head hung low from the humiliation; he didn't even look up. Some students were standing in their open door with heads peeking out just enough to see. They were watching the procession but when the agents saw them, they yelled "Get back inside, the shows over". Each of the agents held a large box in their hands and another agent held a duffel bag that Kaiden recognized. "They must have confiscated a bunch of shit from my room!" he thought.

The hallway cleared when the agents walked through making their way to the elevator door. On que the doors opened and the group of them shuffled in.

Kaiden ran up and shouted "Where you takin him?" just as the elevator doors were closing. He could see the face of his friend in the diminishing space between the doors. Kenny looked up and their eyes met for a moment. His solemn expression said it all. The doors shut cutting off the connection to his roommate.

Kaiden ran back to his room. His door was now taped off with plastic yellow "DO NOT CROSS" tape like it was some sort of crime scene. He only paused a second as he contemplated ripping it down but thought that it might somehow get Kenny in more trouble. He shook his head at the stupidity of it all. Kaiden ran to his neighbor's door, turned the handle, and walked in. There was Money and Peck standing at the window. Peck was shouting down to a group of students below on the lawn.

"They're taking Kenny! They took him! Money turned toward Kaiden when he heard the door open "Oh shit Kaiden!" He felt relieved that it was only him. "Man, they took Kenny, they took Kenny!" Money had a baseball bat in his hands and was looking scared enough to use it on someone. Kaiden bypassed him and ran to the connecting bathroom door. He had to unlock it to get into his room.

His room had been thoroughly ransacked. Things were all over the place. His bed was turned upside down and the blankets thrown about. Instantly he noticed that his knives were gone. Kenny's UTG tactical vest and ammo belt were missing as well, along with his Mod Gear Rifle Case. "That must have been what the agent was carrying" he thought. Luckily Kaiden was wearing his uniform, they couldn't' steal that from him! He always wore his uniform to range class and both he and Kenny were supposed to be there at nine. All the rest of his stuff was strewn about the floor and ... "Shit!" he yelled out loud. Kenny's computer was gone.

"What right do they have to take our shit?"! Kaiden yelled to no one in particular, he turned and saw his two neighbors standing at the bathroom door looking in. "They took his computer?" It was a question because Kaiden couldn't envision how they could have gotten it out of here. It didn't look like they were carrying all that with them. Kaiden was stunned and tried to think.

Money came over to him and put his hand on Kaiden's shoulder. "Wait, come here man" he said in a quiet voice like he didn't want anyone else to hear and guided Kaiden back into their room. "Look" Money said and pulled a blanket off a bunch of stuff stashed in the corner of the room. It was Kenny's computer, all of it, three large screen monitors and the hard drive. Money looked at Kaiden and Kaiden smiled ear to ear and hollered "Yeeeaaahhh! Holy shit you got it!".

"Yeah, we locked the door, and they didn't come in here". Money and Peck high five'd each other enthusiastically and then giggled and laughed like schoolboys.

Kaiden's demeanor changed, with intense seriousness he looked Money in the eyes and grabbed him by the shoulders. "You gotta pack Kenny's computer up and get it ata here; quick, they might come back to get it. Pack it up and hide it somewhere else. Take it to Candy in

Rio Linda, give it to her only, she's in Village E. Someone there will show you where she lives and what to do with it. Try not to be seen, if you are, take off in the opposite direction from where you're actually headed. Then circle back around".

"Damn right!" Money said without hesitation, he turned to Peck. They smiled at each other like they were ecstatic about being able to do something. They high five'd each other again and got busy. Kaiden grabbed anything of value from his room that he could carry, or at least all the stuff that the agents hadn't taken and added it to the pile of stuff that the boy's would take to Candy's place. In his mind he was forced to take it somewhere away from here to protect it. Suddenly, he didn't feel very safe. Kaiden quickly left through the bathroom and ran out of his neighbor's front door leaving the boys to their task.

On the way out Kaiden met the same group of students milling around the front door of the dorm. A bunch of long faces were watching the Feds drive away with Kenny handcuffed in the back seat. Kaiden ran up to them, everyone wanted to know what was going on.

"Kaiden, what's up? Why are they taking Kenny?".

Kaiden stared at the SUV with intense concentration as it disappeared down the road "I don't know, but I heard they're searching the range building right now. Let's get over there and see what's goin on". The whole group took off with a new sense of camaraderie and ran together in the direction of the range building.

A drone circled above and four black suits circled Kenny who walked in the middle of the group with his hands cuffed behind his back. The five of them marched past an alarming number of students that had gathered out in front of the Range building. Onlookers quickly got the gist of what was going on, one of them screamed "Now the bastards are arresting us! Look!".

Someone else yelled "Hey what did he do to you? Assholes! Go back to your pig pen!".

That started it. More than a few students scrambled around looking for something to throw. There weren't many rocks available, but someone found some. That and every soda can in the vending machine soon became projectiles that flew through the air and struck the agents and the pavement around their feet. One of them found their mark and hit one of the agents in the back. The procession of black suits sped up and approached the front door of the building in a hurry. A rock went sailing over their heads and hit the front door. The drone was seen dodging something with a quick maneuver that took it up to a higher level but not high enough before a well-aimed can of soda struck it. When propeller met can, the drone blew up in a watery midair explosion. Drone parts and the spray of orange soda rained down on the agents below. Much to the dismay of the drone operator, his monitor went blank.

The procession quickened their pace and ducked into the building just as the need for shelter became urgent. The agent guarding the door closed it as fast as he could behind them ducking as a rock followed them in. It just missed the guy and bounced off the floor, but the agent was shaken. He was lucky to have gotten the door closed before more rocks hit the outside of it. Standing on the inside, he looked out helplessly through the glass at the students shouting pejorative insults. They formed up and banged on the door while shouting angrily. The agent turned and yelled to his cohorts, pleading with them as they walked fast down the hallway "Hey can I get some help here?".

None of the agents volunteered to stay behind and help. It wasn't their job. And at that moment there was no way to lock the students out. There were two sets of doors with a long bar handle of the type that needed a special Allen head wrench to lock it. Only the maintenance man had it. The guard resorted to using his handcuffs to bind one door to the other, effectively locking it as he called his commander to report the developing situation.

Desperation radiated from the guard's tone as he spoke to Hicks on the radio. Hicks got the message and dialed in the drone's video feed to see it for himself on his phone only to be informed that it had been compromised. He was taken back by the news and surprised by the students' reaction. "The nerve of them to attack my men!" he thought but then he wondered "How far out of hand could this get?". Then he smiled realizing that this confrontation wasn't a setback, it could be a career boosting opportunity. This could make the news. In his mind, he pictured himself being interviewed by a reporter on TV about the student's antigovernment riot. He hadn't seen this coming but now it brightened his face as he savored the idea. There's nothing he'd like more than to get a chance to go down and knock some heads. Even though his boss wanted this to remain "low profile" he could still make some arrests. That'd be even better, then he'd be able to publicly denounce this rabble and start to expose this place for what it is, a terrorist's nest of right-wing radical fundamentalists.

"No, TERRORISTS!", Hicks corrected himself. "First, I'll mobilize campus security and get the State Police involved. That will add some beef into the mix and give me backup if push comes to shove" he thought. Hicks picked up the Major's phone and made a quick call. It made him feel like he was in command of the place. The call went to the maintenance man on campus. When Mr. Sanchez got on the phone Hicks ordered him to drop what he was doing and come up to the front door of the range building with the tools to lock it. "In fact, lock all the doors on campus starting here and now. Lock this place down!" he demanded. Then he called Campus security and spoke to Adrian Phillips to solicit his help to control his unruly students.

"Phillips…" he said after explaining his concern (Hicks never gave anyone on campus the dignity of calling them by their title. Only someone above him in his own organization got that kind of recognition). "…I want them arrested for assaulting a Federal officer or whatever charge you want but keep them away from us so we can do our job".

Phillips responded "You called me this morning and told me in no uncertain terms to 'Stay out of your way' and how did you say it 'Don't even come out of your cave' yeah that was it. You even referred to us as a 'Little security force'. Now you want me to assign my men to help protect you and your operation? Hell, you ordered me to stay out of it and that's what I'm going to do. I'll monitor the situation and do my best to keep the students from damaging any of the buildings but other than that, you're on your own. In fact, if there IS (!) any damage or injuries, I'm going to hold you personally responsible!!!" Captain Phillips was now yelling into the phone. "And oh yes, I suggest that you go back to YOUR cave ASAP to stop the escalation of anything that might happen here on this campus. You have been warned. If you refuse to listen- ITS YOUR ASS!!!" Click. The phone went dead.

Unfortunately, none of Major Monett's staff who overheard the call could hear Captain Phillip's response. If they did, they would have snickered into their hands trying their best not to laugh.

Hicks didn't hang up right away; he hung onto the phone after it went dead making it look like he was still in total command of the conversation. "Thank you, Captain, have your men stationed around the campus and await my orders" then he hung up. Next, he calmly called "Welch" the head of his onsite State Police support. Lieutenant Sergeant Welch had remained at the administration building with Chancellor Gentry and had his men patrolling loosely around campus.

"Welch, get your men over to the range building we have a situation brewing. I need backup, there's a mob outside that thinks it's OK to throw rocks at us. I want you to take care of it".

"First of all, my name is 'Lieutenant Sergeant Welch'. I might even allow you 'Trooper Welch' but that's the basis we're gunna work from now on, got it?".

Hicks was taken back by yet another avenue of resistance and was now visibly upset.

"What is this?" he said throwing his hands up in the air "Can't I get any cooperation around here?".

Lieutenant Welch went on as if Hicks hadn't said anything. "What's your rank Agent Hicks, I mean- what are you in the hierarchy of the ATF?".

Hicks had the look of surprise on face- a degree of frustration given away by the widening of his eyes. Internally there was a corresponding rise in his blood pressure. "Hell, I know where this is going" he said angrily into the phone. He stood up and replied in as serious a voice as he could muster while trying to sound as commanding as possible "I am 'Special Agent in Charge' Mallory Hicks and don't you forget the 'in charge' part. That's the basis you're going to work from Welch. Your orders are to back me up. Don't give me any of this rank shit. What I need right now is back up, so BACK ME THE FUCK UP!".

There was a slight pause. "Alright Hicks..." If Hicks was going to call him "Welch" then he damn well was going to return the snub. "I'll get my men over there but keep a low profile will ya, no sense in stirring up a hornet's nest".

"That's more like it" he said. Hicks hung up the phone and stared off into space. "Hornet's nest huh..." he said with a wild look in his eyes. "Well then I'm the fucking beekeeper!".

Riding in a marked Dodge Charger officer Bastone was driving down the main road on campus when he suddenly stopped. The scene in front of him made him pick up his radio and report in to the Lieutenant.

"Lieutenant this is Bastone, I just drove up to the range building parking lot and I can see from here that there's a whole lot of people out here standing around outside the building, over".

"Bastone how many and what's the demeanor, over".

"There must be a hundred or so now with more on the way. There's civvies and blue uniforms mixed, about 50/50 I'd guess students and Cadets. There're a few older men and women but I assume it's mostly students. I'm trying to determine... but I don't think this is a happy occasion sir".

"Are they armed?".

"No sir, not that I can see but like fifteen of them are pulling that cart of theirs. I don't know what's in them. Otherwise, they're just standing around. Some are in groups. I'm pulling up to the front entrance behind the mobile units now. Oh, I can see the ones up near the door. It doesn't look good Lieutenant; some of them are banging on it, looks like they're trying to break in".

Lieutenant Welch called his second officer "Officer Moran, come in, what's your twenty?".

"Lieutenant I'm on Main Street on the North side of campus. We got a hundred people walking around outside of the buildings and on sidewalks, must be from the Feds closing 'em down and shutin 'em out. It looks like they had a fire drill or something and they're all milling around outside waiting to go back in, over". Officer Moran drove slowly past the crowd outside the Administration building. Groups of them stopped what they were doing and stared back at the police cruiser with blank faces.

"OK. Moran; meet Bastone over at the range building. See if you can keep a lid on that situation over".

Moran's cruiser turned around and drove the half mile to the entrance of the range building parking lot. He pulled up right behind Bastone. Both got out to discuss the situation. "The Lieutenant said to keep a lid on this but what the hell are we going to be able to do? I'm not wading into that mess without backup. If things turn south here, we're screwed" Moran said.

"Hell yeah, I agree. I've been in plenty of crowds before and at some really crowded affairs where I've waded through thicker ones than this, but this is different. Those blue uniforms are militia..." Bastone motioned his eyes toward the group. "... They give me the creeps. You never know what kind of weapons they have. I mean that's why the Feds are here ain't it? And shit we can't count on the Feds for backup".

Moran got back on the radio "Lieutenant, I think we're gunna need some help down here".

A half hour had passed when AIC Hicks came into the conference room where all the "detainees" were held. All his teams had reported in and now he was feeling the need to wrap this up. Two agents trailed behind him as he entered the room and stood by as back up. Without saying a word to the others in the room, Hicks calmly walked over to a large painting on the wall at the head of the conference table and stood in front of it trying his best to give the impression that he was studying it and contemplating its story. A smile broke out on his face as he digested the meaning of information he had just received from his field teams. He really enjoyed having the upper hand and he was sure he had it with this new discovery. The search had turned up another Kel Tec SU16 rifle in another student's locker. Already a team had been dispatched to bring in its owner. That made a total of two operational assault rifles among the four unassembled ones with about two hundred forty rounds of confiscated ammunition. That was a far cry from the number he had hoped to produce but it was enough to prosecute. The raid had produced some positive results that were certain to please his boss. It was a whole lot better than coming up empty handed.

But that's not why Hicks was smiling. With his hands behind his back, he stood facing the rather large painting that depicted an artist's rendition of the famous Civil War battle of Gettysburg. For a few long moments, Hicks pretended to study the painting without acknowledging anyone else in the room. It gave him a prelude to his triumphant summit he was about to hold with the leader of this illegitimate Militia.

Out loud he said to Monett "If we could only go back in time and just whisper in his ear 'Don't send Picket's division up the center! They'll get massacred and you lose the entire war". Agent Hicks spoke to the painting and then he turned to face the Major as if he had just made a major esoteric point.

His comment about the painting referred to General Lee who commanded the Confederate Army of Virginia in 1863. At the battle of Gettysburg, Lee sent his forces against the newly appointed Union General Meade. To attempt a quick defeat, Lee sent General Pickett in as the spearhead of a full-frontal assault against the middle section of the Union lines. In hindsight, it was a suicide mission, but at the time General Lee had confidence that it would succeed. General Picket ended up losing 3,000 of his men which was over half of the entire Division under his command.

Hicks continued "Man think of how that one statement could have changed the entire outcome of the battle, or even the war itself! The entire political landscape too. They say we might still have slaves today if Lee won at Gettysburg. If he destroyed the Union Army there..." he pointed to the painting "...there would have been nothing between him and Washington D.C... Could have marched right up and camped out on the White House lawn. Whew! Thank God they stopped him. Thank God for the Union soldier, for the man who stood up for the Federal Government when our enemies would have torn it down" Hicks said it with emphasis and a high degree of admiration in his voice.

"You see Monett, just because you're a rebel doesn't mean you're on the right side". He turned and faced him. "We found the mortar launcher".

The Major didn't respond. Everyone else looked at each other wondering what he meant.

Hicks said "You've got a fucking 60mm mortar in the storage room out at that rifle range". He said it seriously and then laughed. "My agents are packing it up now and bringing it in along with the bombs".

"What! Hey there are no explosive rounds out there, those cases are just target rounds. Some with smoke but we don't have any bombs! Besides it's not on the list of banned weapons in EO-129-52A".

"Come on Monett, if not, that thing's definitely on the ATF's list! We're confiscating it. That thing certainly shouldn't be in the hands of rogue civilians".

"Cadets Hicks, we're 'Cadets', not civilians".

"Whatever. I'm afraid I'm going to have to bring you in for questioning. You've got some explaining to do about where you got that thing".

"Oh what, I'm under arrest?".

"Yes, but you don't have the right to remain silent".

Major Monett stared at him in disbelief but was done saying anything more; he knew this would play out independent of whatever he would say. Hicks stood in front of the Major with a pair of handcuffs in his hands and told him "Turn around and place your hands behind your back". The Major turned around and the click of the cuffs was the final say.

"What am I being charged with Hicks?".

They patted him down and took his keys and wallet.

"Ok" Hicks said and then spoke to his men so the Major could hear "Charge all three of them with subversion and the fourth one if we get him in here with possession of illegal firearms. Throw in 'with terrorist intent' for good measure. You..." he looked over at Carl. "You'll also be charged with impeding a Federal investigation". He turned to his agents "Take them and put them in a separate room, get 'em ready for transfer. Let's wait to see if we can get the owner of that second rifle before moving out. Get the weapons boxed up. Then we'll move them all to the bus".

Carl was punching buttons on his BeepX as the agents started to handcuff the Major. Previously he was able to get out a couple of messages but there really wasn't much to report until now. He didn't think he'd be arrested and thought he'd have more time. Previously he had been hiding the BeepX underneath the table and out of sight, now he was trying frantically to punch buttons and complete a message without them noticing. The agents finished with Kenny and turned to Carl motioning for him to "come here" just as he hit the send button. He stood up and came out from behind the conference table and placed his hands behind his back. They searched him but didn't find anything. The beeper was sitting out of sight on the seat of his chair.

Just as all three of them were about to be escorted out, the Major stopped and turned to Hicks "I see you know a little about Civil War history Hicks, but conveniently you have forgotten the most important fact about that Union soldier. I'm talking about the ones who chose to fight in the battle of Gettysburg".

"Oh yeah Monett and I suppose you're going to enlighten me".

"The irony of it is that the Union soldier you spoke so highly of..." the Major paused and let his eyes wonder over to the painting and stared at it for a moment before he spoke with respect. "...that soldier knew all too well about the possibility of dying for his country. Maybe not so much in the first battle of the war but certainly by the time that battle rolled around, he knew". The Major looked back at Hicks and paused until Hicks returned his gaze. They both locked eyes as adversaries would.

"He chose to fight anyway, out of an innate sense of obligation; first to their fellow soldiers, second for their families and third for their country so that all of them could live the way they wanted to... as free men. They fought desperately for it! God bless them all".

"Yeah, yeah, I know all of that Monett; you don't have to lecture me on it. I identify myself with that exact cause; it allows me to feel at one with what I'm doing right now". Hicks turned away to end the conversation, but the Major turned him back around with one last statement.

"The thing you don't realize, is that the Union soldier you feel so 'at one' with, the very same one that repelled Pickets charge and held the perimeter saving the day at Cemetery Ridge, and the blocking wedge the Union Army formed that stood in the way of the rebels marching right into Washington DC? They stood there in the face of all that carnage, incomprehensible to you and me. And during it all, immersed in that hell with the possibility of death just moments away, he still refused to run!

Those men were from State Militias all across the north. The 20th New York State Militia from right down the road here in Kingston, the 71st New York State Militia, the 14th Brooklyn Militia, the 22nd New York, the Irish Brigade, the 14th New York Independent Battery, New York Sharpshooters, and that's just the ones from New York. All of them fought in the battle of Gettysburg. There's also the 26th Pennsylvania Emergency Militia out of Harrisburg, the Independent Battalion Militia, Beal's Independent Company Militia, Huffs Militia, Zell's Battalion Militia, the 13th Pennsylvania Reserve, the 29th Massachusetts, Logan's Guards. Shall I go on?

"No Monett" Hicks said. "I'm talking about the regular army, not the untrained fucking boy scout Militia".

"That's my point" Monett fired back at Hicks and his ignorance. "At that time in 1861, there was an insignificant number of trained regular army. Every single one of the infantry units that fought at Gettysburg was assembled in 1862 at the beginning of the war. 'Assembled' I might add from the 'untrained' civilian population. Gettysburg was fought just one short year later in July of 1863. In fact, the only men that had any kind of experience at all were the older Militia units themselves like the 71st New York State Militia formed in 1850 or the 20th out of Kingston, formed in 1851. Because of the lack of experience, the war went very badly for our Union heroes and our cause. So many died in that one battle alone. Gettysburg took out 23,000 Union soldiers, killed, wounded, or missing. Wouldn't it have been great Hicks... to have been able to have whispered in their ears long before the war started; 'train your Militia!' Prepare yourselves! You're going to need them".

Agent Hicks broke in "Ah I see where you're going with this Monett and it ain't goin to work. To hell with you people and your Militia, the more trained they are the more of a danger they are to society. Don't you see that? Why would we want a trained Militia? So, they can rise up against us?".

"Rise up against who Hicks? Who are you?".

"WE ARE THE FEDERAL GOVERNMENT GOD DAMN IT!" Hicks yelled and moved toward the Major aggressively getting inches away from his face. "And you better start showing some respect!".

"Yeah, well 'WE ARE THE PEOPLE!'" the Major yelled back in his face. "The whole Cadet organization is made up of 'people' just like that Union Soldier! What you're doing is pitting the Government against the People. Just like England did before the revolutionary war!" Major Monett stood back and shook his head "Big mistake".

Hicks stared back at him for a moment and Monett took the opportunity for one last statement "Hicks, what you're doing is the exact opposite of what the 'Government' is designed to do. It's not your job to fight us; The Government was formed to protect us. Not to take away our rights. It's not the American way!".

"Don't tell me what the Government was designed to do Monett. Take him out" he said to the man holding him. "I'm going to disassemble this illegal rabble" he said to anyone listening. Hicks effectively ended the conversation by leaving.

"Lord help you Agent Hicks" the Major said to a closing door. But only the two agents standing there next to him in the room heard him. The agents both glanced at each other with a hint that for a brief second at least they questioned their own loyalty and wondered which side of this argument they should be on.

Two State Police officers were standing next to their patrol cars watching the students. A large group of them had formed in front of the range building and everyone was talking about the absurdity of the ATF's actions. The rhetoric started to ramp up which made the cops nervous.

"Why would they treat us like criminals and infringe upon our rights? We're not the enemy!" one of the students yelled.

Kaiden and his dorm mates made it over to the range building and joined the larger group of students forming in front of the cops. Most of them were wearing the same matching Cadet uniform.

"I can't believe the ATF are here searching our buildings" a student said. "What'd we do to deserve this? Aren't we on the same side?".

"I feel betrayed by my own people" another added.

"Kaiden!" a classmate said when Kaiden walked up and joined the group. "What's happening, what's going on with Kenny?".

"Damn Feds came and got him. I don't know why, they just did. They searched his room and took most of his electronics and some other stuff, some of mine too. The bastards got my knives".

"We saw Kenny, they brought him in. He was in handcuffs man! They took him inside".

"Here! Kenny's in here?" Kaiden asked.

"Yeah, about five agents brought him in just now".

Another Cadet Kaiden didn't know came over and asked him "Hey you're Kaiden Sawyer, Kenny's roommate?".

"Yeah, well at least I was Kenny's roommate. I wonder what they're going to do to with him?".

"Well, they got him hold up in the range conference room with a bunch of others right now, the Majors in there with him".

"How do you know that?".

"You know Carl Roughett, the guy who clerks the armory desk?"

"Yeah of course I know him".

"He's a good friend of mine, used to be my roommate. He just beeped me telling me that they got Kenny for possession of a Kel Tec semi auto rifle".

"What? Really!" Other Cadets perked up and crowded around to listen.

"Carl said that they found Kenny's rifle in his locker. He got caught holding on to it man".

"Holy shit!" another Cadet in the crowd said loudly. Everyone turned and looked at him. "I've got a rifle in my locker too". The beginning of panic formed on his face. I never thought they'd come and find it here!"

Kaiden turned to the guy who knew Carl and asked him "What's your name?".

"Orie".

"Orie" Here let me punch my number into your shotgun list on your beeper. Forward me anything else Carl sends you will ya?".

"You got it".

"Can you get a message back to Carl?".

"No, well I don't know he's not responding. I tried. Maybe they're watching him, and he can't beep out or something".

"Someone make sure that Captain Oberman gets this and knows what's goin on. Anyone got his number?

"I do" someone in the group yelled.

"See if you can get him" Kaiden said to the Cadet. Try and get an indication as to what he wants to do".

"I'm on it".

"And you... what's your name?" Kaiden spoke to the kid who said he had a rifle in his locker.

"Mark".

"Mark don't go back to your room. They'll be looking for you there. Stay here, they won't find you in this crowd. If you can get a hold of your roommate or your neighbors, get them to grab any of your gear that they can before the Feds get there and search your room. Tell 'em to hide anything that pertains to the Cadet organization or else it'll be gone when you get back". Then Kaiden spoke to the crowd "Does anyone know how many agents are here in the building? Do we have any intel?".

Another Cadet spoke up "I saw at least twelve bad guys go in".

"Twelve? What else did you see?" Kaiden asked him.

"Well, I was waiting for class out here when they pulled up, six guys got out of each car. Their SUVs are right there. There's a large capacity bus of theirs somewhere on campus too. It pulled up just after the first group went in and dropped off another six or so then left. One of 'em is guarding the front door. They won't let anyone back in now".

"That means there's what about seventeen or eighteen of'em in there now. Shit! Anyone know what other buildings they've taken over?".

It was natural for Kaiden, he took over and gathered as much information as he could and rattled off orders.

"I need someone to go around back and watch the doors. There's three of them, can I get two volunteers with beepers?".

"I'll go". "I'll go". "Me too" someone said.

"Good. Everyone, take my number and report in. Let me know what goes in and out of there". He called out his beeper number and each of the three volunteers saved it in their address book.

"Go!" Kaiden told them.

The three Cadets took off. Then Kaiden sent a text message to Ciera and warned her that a sizeable force of Feds had invaded the campus and were snooping around looking for weapons.

* * *

All five of the Feds search teams reported in by radio. The shakedown of about ninety-five percent of the buildings on the list had been more or less completed. Hicks was satisfied that the work was done but just livid that his search teams hadn't found anything more than they did. Luckily one of his teams found a mortar in the storage room out at the range. That would be his saving grace. He could now report a successful mission to his boss and praise would surely be forthcoming. Already Hicks was planning to secure the evidence and order the departure of his team. Only the plan just got a little more complicated with the appearance of a mob.

Hicks spoke into his radio "This is agent Hicks… What happened to my drone feed? I want all ATF personnel in the range building to converge on the front main lobby in five minutes. All other teams wrap up what you're doing and pack up what you've got. Then meet me at the front of the range building, I repeat, meet at the front of the range building. Team five, don't come back into the building, finish loading the mortar on the bus and drive over to meet me at the front of the building, we'll meet you there in five. We'll converge and convoy out in fifteen. Let's get to it people! All units prepare to leave, over".

"Team four to Agent Hicks, over"

"Come in team four".

The agent was looking out the dorm window at the angry crowd. "We're at Mark Olin's dorm room sir… no sign of the suspect and have found no additional weapons, just a bunch of military paraphernalia. We're searching through that now. It seems like someone's been here and taken a bunch of stuff out of here. How do we proceed over".

"Does he have a computer?"

"Well, it looks like he had a computer, the hard drive's gone".

"Confiscate any other pertinent evidence and bring it with you. Then join the convoy, over" Hicks ordered.

Kaiden got a BeepX message from Orie which was forwarded mail from Carl Roughett. It said "Mjr. M, Kenny, me- un Arst! Thy fnd 60m Mortar! Tak'n it! Chrg Mjr M fr posetion!".

Kaiden turned to the group of Cadets in front of him. "The Major's under arrest. They found a 60mm Mortar? I didn't even know we had one".

"I did. We got one all right. I've fired it" Brute said as he walked up to the group Kaiden was talking too.

"Brute! I'm glad you're here. They got the Major under arrest for possession of an illegal weapon! Shit, they're taking him!" Kaiden said.

Everyone turned and looked toward the front door of the building.

"What're we going do?" a Cadet yelled.

"Who's the one trying to get a hold of Captain Oberman?

"I am".

"No luck?".

"Not yet".

"Send him that same message. Try again".

"Ok, sending it..." he pressed a few buttons on his beeper.

Hicks, his crew, and the detainees all walked out of the elevator onto the lobby floor and moved briskly down the hall towards the front door. Four of his men were standing there waiting for him. One of the agents hurriedly walked up as he entered the foyer and reported that they were still waiting for two others and that they would be there shortly. Then he turned and motioned toward the glass door "But we got a problem".

On the other side of the locked doors in the exterior courtyard were a hundred students yelling, pumping their fists, and banging on the glass door between them. The news that Major Monett was under arrest had spread quickly through the crowd. Beyond the agitated crowd they could see their SUV's parked in the street waiting for them. It only took Hicks a second to come to a conclusion- "We're going out the back. We'll board the bus there". The entire group reversed direction and started walking toward the stairs while one agent spoke rapidly on the radio trying to coordinate and change the way point. "Mobile one, lead team is changing pickup location; we'll be exiting the building at the back and will board the bus there at the rear of the range building. Meet us there for further orders, be prepared to move out quickly".

Kaiden's beeper vibrated again. It was a message from one of the volunteers watching the back door. He read it, looked up and then said "Got confirmation that they're taking something from the rifle range storage room. Our man back there can see them bringing it out. There loading it on a bus".

"Shit we're losing our Mortar!" someone yelled.

"Got a message from Oberman!" another Cadet yelled with excitement. "Says to try and stall them. He's on his way. Says try not to let 'em take it till our lawyer gets here".

Kaiden turned and addressed the crowd trying to get as many Cadets as possible to hear his voice. "CADETS! CADETS! CADETS!" he shouted at the top of his lungs, about twenty-five of them turned their heads in his direction. "The Feds have found an automatic rifle, arrested Major Monett and confiscated the 60mm Mortar from the rifle range". Murmurs rippled through the crowd.

"We've got orders from Captain Oberman to try and stall them for as long as possible until he gets here. We can try to block them from leaving! I need your help!".

"YEAH!!! Hoo yah!" many in the crowd yelled back.

"Then FOLLOW ME NOW!!! COME ON Let's GO!" Kaiden took off running with the mob moving in a wave right behind him. It seemed like the entire crowd of Cadets moved as one and took off at the same time. Students and Cadets who had heard about the Majors arrest were coming in from all over campus and converging on the range building. When they saw Kenny's group start to run, they joined in and followed the crowd around back. Over two hundred Cadets (and counting) all ran around back to the rear of the range building.

One of the cops standing there watching witnessed a wave of blue uniforms swarming over the sidewalks and the yard picking up speed and getting louder as they went. The scene alarmed him. He ran over to his squad car to report it.

At the back door of the range building an ATF agent cautiously peered out of the open door and looked around. When he saw that it was clear he ventured out further. Quickly he assessed the situation and saw the ATF bus parked out on the other side of the parking lot about two hundred yards away next to the rifle range storage room. There, agents could be seen loading the confiscated 60mm mortar into the bus's luggage compartment. With just a quick duck back into the building and a short consultation with Hicks they decided not to waste any time and make a run for it. Doing something beat standing there waiting for the bus to finish and pull back around to pick them up. With that decision, the entire contingent of sixteen agents plus prisoners burst out through the double doors in the back and moved briskly down the sidewalk. They walked two abreast except at the center of the column where Hicks led his three prisoners with agents surrounding them on all sides.

The column of ATF agents only made it halfway to the bus before hearing the noise and seeing movement on their left. When they looked up, a surge of Cadets came rolling around the far corner of the range building and streamed across the lawn like a blue wave flowing over the gentle slopes of the landscape. Green grass turned blue as the multitude of Cadets poured across it and raced into the parking lot. The human upsurge flowed between the cars and moved right up to the fleeing column of agents. Minus the swords and spears it looked like a scene right out of the movie 'Braveheart'.

Hicks and his team froze in place as they glanced at each other wondering what to do. He only had seconds to respond and quickly calculated that his team would never make it to the bus or back to the safety of the building before being overrun by the mob of Cadets. He looked at the building and then at the bus. Neither one was obtainable; the Cadets were upon them before a decision could be made. Before they could respond they were surrounded.

At first all the Cadets could determine was that they had stumbled onto a group of agents. They only realized the significance of their encounter when they saw their beloved Major standing amid them with his hands bound behind his back. Kaiden saw Kenny among them and instantly started thinking about how to pry him away from their captors. It was an absurd thought to interfere with a Federal investigation, but that same thought permeated the crowd and infused itself into their overriding mindset.

Cadets surrounded the agents on all sides and started screaming and yelling and waving their hands to disrupt their forward progress as if somehow, they had the power to stop this. It ended up that they did.

All the agents drew together and huddled against the perceived threat. They became nervous and placed their hands instinctively on the grips of their guns. The horror of what might happen next showed in Major Monett's expression. They were backed into a corner. The situation had become a ticking time bomb.

From out of the center of the group, Hicks pushed aside his own agents and barked with the attitude of a wild boar. He stood there looking at the students who were blocking his way with a twisted lip and a look of righteous indignation. He said to his men "Follow me" and kept shouting "GET OUT OF MY WAY! GET OUT OF MY WAY!" as he attempted to force his way through the crowd and move in the direction of the bus. But a wall of Cadets blocked him and held him in check. Hicks realized they weren't going anywhere, and he got mad as hell. He spat out orders trying to get them to obey but he only succeeded in fueling a return volley of shouts and obscenities. The Cadets pointed their fingers at him in both horizontal and vertical gestures while shaking their heads saying "No way! You have no right! Let 'em go!".

"MOVE!" Hicks yelled waving his arms like he was Moses trying to part the sea, but he only got more frustrated by their inaction and their audacity to interfere with him. Agents moved up and stood next to him looking like they were ready to protect their leader and jump into the fray that was about to develop. Major Monett moved up behind Hicks so he could see what was going on even though he knew there wasn't much he could do if a fight broke out, his hands were literally tied. Two agents tried pushing Cadets out of the way, but the Cadets pushed back, and they got nowhere. Then an agent punched a Cadet in his face, and they got into a brawl. Another Cadet stepped in and punched the agent. The scene became chaotic, no one was backing down. It was about to go to the next level on a grand scale at any moment. Seeing no other alternative, the agents resorted to the only other card they had to play. To obtain the upper hand, they pulled their weapons and threatened the crowd with the end of a barrel.

Kaiden muscled his way up to the front of the line of Cadets who were confronting Hicks. He was just in time to see the guns come out. Without thinking he stepped out of the ranks into the danger zone and stood between the Cadets and the agents. Without knowing if it would have any effect at all he held up his hands to both sides and yelled "STOP! STOP! STOP!"

Surprisingly both sides backed off a little, but Kaiden had to go up and down the line shouting to the Cadets "Everyone be Quiet! Be quiet! Calm down!" He put up both hands toward his Cadets and repeated "Be quiet, calm down!".

To a considerable extent most of them did. But there was still an underlying murmur and shouts of insults that went back and forth from both sides. When he achieved a slightly better level of control he turned around and faced the person who looked like he was in charge-Hicks. He walked up to the man and got in his face. Looking into the eyes of his adversary made him smile to himself. He'd been up against some mean ass gang members before who looked a whole lot tougher than this guy. He thought how ironic it was that someone had given so much power to this one asshole.

The Major looked on intensely wondering what the hell he could do to stop the progression of violence that was about to be unleashed on his Cadets. He was glad to see Kaiden step in and somehow get a grip on the cork that was about to pop out of this bottle.

Kaiden yelled "If you want to get out of here in one piece, I suggest you back off and put away the guns".

"What!" Hicks said incredulously. "You have one minute to get your shit eating faces out of my way and cease with impeding a Federal investigation or else things will get very bloody amazingly fast around here. I'll shoot my way out if I have too! You want that?".

Captain Oberman had also succeeded in making it through the throng and had overheard that last statement. He too muscled his way in and stepped out from the front line of Cadets entering the gap between the two factions. Ciera was right behind him but was taken back when she saw the agents brandishing their pistols.

When he saw her, Kaiden thought that this was no place for her even though there were quite a few women in the crowd. He knew that somehow; he had to neutralize the gun issue and went with the first idea that popped into his head. It was a desperate attempt to disarm the situation, but Kaiden played it up anyway.

He stepped up to Captain Oberman and gave him a salute in precise military fashion as if reporting to his commander. Kaiden got his attention just before he was about to speak to Special Agent Hicks "Captain Oberman sir" he said loudly so that all could hear. "I'm glad you're here, our snipers are in place and ready for your orders" he said it with emphasis on the word "snipers".

His Captain frowned not quite understanding the full ramifications of that statement as well as showing a little disbelief as he stared back at Kaiden. Hicks and his men heard it too and frowned. They turned and looked all around them and then at each other with doubt but acknowledged the possible consequences if there really was a sniper with a rifle trained on them.

"Yes" Kaiden said. He purposely made an obvious gesture so all could see when he turned and pointed to the balcony of the range building.

Everyone's eyes turned and looked in the direction Kaiden was pointing. Off in the distance on the second floor of the gymnasium there were doors that opened onto a second story open terrace. The Terrace overlooked the rear of the building and the parking lot itself. It was used as an "outside" option for parties or a place that one could go for fresh air during dances or special ceremonies held in the gym. Two Cadets were leaning on the wall looking down over the parking lot watching the incident materialize about 100 yards away. Both rested their arms on the wall and looked back down at the crowd totally surprised that the group in the center was now looking up at them. Someone in the middle of that circle was even pointing in their direction.

Kaiden made a show of it and waved his arm at them like it was a signal of some sort. The two Cadets on the roof looked at each other mystified. One of them said to the other "Hey that guy's waving at us" and reluctantly, he waved back inadvertently returning Kaiden's signal.

From that distance and angle no one could see whether they had a rifle or not.

Oberman got it. "Thank you, Cadet," he said knowing that Kaiden had just handed him an ace in the hole. Now he spoke with authority "You see gentlemen..." he glanced around and then focused on Hicks "...I think we can put away the guns. That's just going to end up with you and any number of your men getting shot dead, oh and by the way..." he said quickly before Hicks could say anything "...they're trained to shoot the leader first and my men are excellent marksmen, they don't miss".

For just a second, Hicks' first reaction was to get in this kids face and berate him up and down in front of everyone for the insolence and for the audacity to threaten an agent of the ATF. But the thought of a trained sniper with its crosshairs focused on him right now kept creeping into the forefront of his consideration. Once he got the feeling that a bullet was about to rip into his body at any moment, his demeanor changed. "To contribute to the escalation of hostilities might not be such a good idea" was his second thought.

"Stand down and put away your guns" Hicks told his men while staring into the eyes of this kid standing in front of him. His men were slow to obey. He turned toward them and yelled at them "Stand down and put away your guns I said". Slowly they did as they were told and holstered their weapons. Hicks turned back to Oberman defiantly and said "Now stand aside and let us through".

Captain Oberman responded with confidence in his voice "You are violating the Constitution of the United States of America by confiscating equipment and arresting these individuals under false pretense".

"Don't you know kid; it's against the law to possess these weapons. It's a felony!" Hicks said.

"It's a felony for a 'citizen' to own one of these weapons" Oberman replied, "not for a member of the Cadet organization. We are allowed to bear arms sir; semi-auto military weapons are included under the definition in our Charter. Even still we got rid of many of our weapons just so something like this would not happen, but since it has, we still stand on our constitutional rights to bear arms. Release these men, NOW! They are innocent of criminal intent!".

The two of them looked like they'd come to fists at any second and this would end in a huge brawl with the whole ruckus starting back up again when Major Monett pushed his way out from between two agents. They weren't watching him closely enough and he had edged his way up to the source of the confrontation.

"Atten-tion!" he commanded. He said it so sharp and loud that even agent Hicks straightened up a little. Captain Oberman as well as all the Cadets who saw him came to a crisp stance and saluted the Major. The crowd became quiet. Major Monett couldn't return the salute so instead he gave them an "At ease" order.

"I truly doubt that we can successfully argue this point right here and now in this parking lot" he said to his Captain and all the Cadets who could hear him. "All we can do is to trust the justice system to rule on our behalf. I am confident that when everything comes to light, I will be exonerated. Captain Oberman!".

"Yes sir" he said coming back to attention.

"Form up! Parade line right, parade line left. Sweep out the center all the way to that bus, that's an order".

"Yes sir" the Captain said in conjunction with a salute. Then he did an about face and yelled an order at the top of his lungs at all the blank faces of Cadets that stared back at him "PARADE LINE RIGHT! PARADE LINE LEFT!" and motioned with his arms to define the parade line parameters.

It started slowly; one cadet at a time coming to attention and lining up on each side of the path that started to form as the crowd parted. Another Cadet stood shoulder to shoulder with the previous one forming a ten-foot-wide gap between the two. Cadets lined the perimeter on both sides forming an open pathway down the center. With the Major in the middle and Captain Oberman and Kaiden on each side, they marched forward together one step at a time allowing the path to develop as they went. A Cadet standing in front of them would come to attention, salute the Major and then step to the side. That Cadet joined the previous soldier standing at attention or slipped into the crowd behind the line.

Hicks looked at his men and smiled knowing that he had won and then fell in line behind the Major. All the members of the ATF followed eagerly behind him. It was as if the Major and consequently all the ATF agents, walked under a military honor guard.

One of the agents who had previously come to blows with a Cadet was so pleased with the turn of events that he walked with a strut, laughed, mocked, and chided them all as he walked by them. When he saw the same Cadet he had previously fought with standing in line at attention, he walked up to him and got in his face with a shit eatin grin and said "Alright little soldier boy now that's more like it". He did that quick little motion pretending to punch him in the face but stopped at the last second just to see if he could provoke him, then he laughed hysterically and moved on. He was beside himself with the knowledge that they wouldn't move or respond while at attention. When he turned back to one of the other agents, he gave a celebratory high five with a laugh between the two of them. At that same moment, a full can of soda flew from the crowd in a precise arch and smacked him dead center on the base of his neck with a thud. You could tell it hurt by the agent's reaction. He stopped and turned around with scorn on his face and a hand rubbing his neck while trying to see who threw it. You could see it in his eyes; he had full intention of going after the perpetrator and would have if a rather large black agent behind him didn't give him a shove that almost knocked him on his ass.

"Come on Jenkins, get the hell moving. If you get this crowd throwing shit at me, I'm gunna kick your mutha fuckin ass!". Jenkins looked back at him and thought about it but then decided to go along and get along. It wasn't the right time to argue with one of his own. He got back in line without further incident.

The procession made it to the bus upon which they loaded everything and everyone on board as quickly as possible. Under the watchful eyes of a sea of blue uniforms standing around them, the bus slowly made its way through the throng and out onto the main campus road.

By that time, every Cadet on campus had heard that their leader Major Monett was under arrest and had scrambled to make their way over to the range building. The crowd and every Cadet the bus passed paused, came to attention, and brought the ridge of their hand up to their forehead in salute and a show of respect for the man inside.

There were four State Police patrol cars and five campus police security vehicles parked at the curb. Three more backup State Police vehicles had just arrived on scene and were driving slowly around observing the crowd. The troopers and even Academy campus security were standing out in front of their cars calmly talking to their partners oblivious to the degree of fear that the throng of ATF agents had just experienced. It was obvious that they weren't about to wade into this mess with the limited resources they had. At least not until more backup arrived.

Hicks got on the radio and coordinated their withdrawal "All teams meet at the exit point and form up; we're rolling out of here now! Over".

27

New Reality

No one knew what this meant. Cadets were stunned that this could ever happen. Their commander had been taken. How long would they hold him? Everyone knew him as an honest benevolent man and loved him like a father. What has this world come too? He was held in such high esteem that their sorrow quickly turned to anger. People thought of him as so far removed from the definition of "criminal" that this just didn't make sense. Now they were forced to re-evaluate the concept of right and wrong and they developed a strong sense that the government was generating a new kind of wrong, a wrong that became real for each one of them. One could argue that this wasn't a new phenomenon. This kind of intrusion on individual liberty had been developing for quite some time. Now it touched everyone at the Academy in a personal way. It hit home. What type of people are those who would consider the Major and what he stood for as somehow being "a terrorist"? And these people are the ones in power? How did this happen? The realization was sobering. Each one realized that if the government could do it to him, they could do it to any one of them.

At first there wasn't a noticeable change at the Academy, at least not on the outside. On the inside you could just feel it. A week went by without news concerning the Major. No information could be found on the government's website or any ATF public bulletins. The last word was that the Major, Kenny and Carl were being held without bail on terrorist charges. This could only be done if they were labeled as domestic terrorists and charged under the provisions of the National Defense Authorization Act.

Classes resumed as usual with substitutes filling in on classes that the Major taught. There was a new clerk at the rifle range, yet Kaiden was still minus all his stuff that had been taken out of his room and of course, his roommate too. The threat of them coming back to get Kenny's computer was always on his mind.

Finally, the Major's name showed up on an internal ATF report. They didn't even bother to have the decency to inform the school's administration before releasing it. The notice confirmed that the action they were taking was part of the "anti-terrorist" campaign enforced by the Patriot Act(s) and authorized by the "Enforcement Act" which was a rider added on to the amendment passed two years ago by executive order. This initiated the crusade against home grown terrorism and gave the president the power to "operate freely and openly within US borders in a more aggressive manor against all enemies both foreign and domestic". The report went on to justify their action by linking the listed groups and individuals as part of an underground terrorist organization and labeled the capture of these men and women as proof of success in the war against what they called "Home grown terrorism". All of it in defense of a possible "Revolution" by right wing underground forces. Any group that touted a strong belief in the limitation of power as it applies to government and prescribed in the American Constitution, was a target.

The report read "We have made progress against a growing insurgence perpetrated by various Militia groups across America". It then described the groups and their areas of operation and cited the activity as funded by outside foreign terrorist organizations and Mexican drug cartels. Major Monett or the man listed as Jazz R. Monett, had been charged with "subversive intent" and mentioned his position as the head of the "Cadet Militia operating in central New York". They described the area of central New York as "a hot bed for political unrest".

* * *

Another dark day for the Academy occurred two days later. The suits came back and rolled into campus unannounced the same way they had done before. This time it was low key with only two SUV's. They cruised up to the administration building and a group of five men from one of the cars walked into the Chancellors office just like they did before. One member of the group pushed a dolly in front of him.

Men in the second vehicle drove over to Parker dorm and attempted to recover Kenny's computer. They too brought a dolly with them.

At the administration building, one agent confronted the Chancellor's secretary while the others burst into the Chancellor's office. They got right to the point and surprised Chancellor Gentry when they informed him that he was under arrest. He was immediately handcuffed and escorted out of the building and into the SUV before any trouble could develop. Under protest from Mary Sterling the remaining agents took files and the hard drive to both his and her computer. Within minutes they had what they wanted and before anyone knew what was happening, the equipment was on a dolly, and they were gone like thieves in the night. It would have been a much more significant event if people had known it was happening or if more people around the country realized that this same scenario was playing out in an alarming number of incidents just like it all across America.

Agents in the second group failed to find Kenny's computer. They busted down the door to Kaiden's room (It was locked) but found nothing of interest. Their search flowed through the bathroom and into Kaiden's neighbors' room where they confiscated any Cadet paraphernalia that Money and Peck had.

* * *

A secret meeting with all the Cadet Leadership and Officers was held the next day in the Bunkers conference room. Only this time

Security was beefed up to the max. Chester Fairmond, second in command of the Cadets, spoke up after a general discussion of the current atmosphere.

"Gentleman and ladies" (he nodded to Lieutenant Irene Stalouti). "We've heard the situation report. Now the question is 'what are we going to do about it?'. If the decision is to resist, we must be prudent and understand that our enemies are going to bring pressure to bear against the organization to shut us down. Are we going to roll over? Or do we stand our ground? I give the floor to Captain Phillips".

Captain Phillips stood and looked around at all the people seated. "I do not think we should disband. By doing so we would be agreeing with our adversaries that we are the problem. The problem lies with the people who seek to steer this country towards a socialist/communist form of government. The burden it has placed on the American people is crushing us. We need to fight back as hard as they are pushing us. The livelihoods of hundreds of people depend on the system we have developed here at the Academy. We must make sure that our way of life is passed on to the next generation and impress upon our sons and daughters that freedom is worth fighting for. The Cadets are well suited for this endeavor. We just need to decide as to whether we are going to activate and use our skills to secure the future of this country. Are we going to protect the hand that feeds this community? Or succumb to the hand that takes from it? It starts here, it starts with us. I say if we go down, they go down. Either way we choose, our community is going to need everything this school and this organization has to offer to survive. This is it people. You must decide".

They took a vote. It was unanimous. From this point on the Cadets would band together, tighten up and prepare for whatever comes.

28

Reset

Agent Roy Atkinson was promoted to Commander of the IRS-ART. His bosses gave his team a second chance after the misfortune of losing three agents. They chalked it up to just plain bad luck. The new improved and "approved" tactics were no-nonsense techniques designed to achieve results without the risk they were previously exposed to.

The scene looked eerily familiar. The same as it did just minutes before Agent Minolta got blown away two months ago. Only now Minolta was dead and his boss, Agent Roy Atkinson, was forced to step down into the position and personally take command of the team. It was imperative to fill the gap and quickly get things back on track. Once it was rolling smoothly again, he could slip out of direct involvement and oversee operations from the comfort of his office. At least that was his goal.

Atkinson sat in his unmarked car with his partner; both wore dark sunglasses and were watching a house in a suburban neighborhood in Wilmington on the outskirts of Philadelphia. The entire procedure was revamped and brought up to date. No longer were they going to take any chances. Their technique was refined to facilitate a higher degree of success; success being defined as "No loss of life, with maximum control". Conveniently, agent Atkinson no longer required his own participation in the raid itself. He would stake out, watch, and give the signal for his team to go in. That was, not surprisingly, the first change in procedure. Also, they no longer went through the hassle of obtaining a warrant or having a warrant officer assigned to the recovery raid. Nor were they going to bother with local police backup. All that was taking too much time to coordinate, and they were running into a lot of resistance, even more so after the death of two police officers. The reputation of the IRS-ART was tainted by that tragedy and now the police were reluctant to participate. But it also helped in a way, now they didn't need to worry about paperwork or even public perception. All they had to do was point to the tragedy to justify their new strong-arm tactics. To hell with public perception. After their team was ambushed by a well-armed army, they had their excuse which allowed them to circumvent any further restraint that might hamper their team's effort and place them in danger. Sympathetic government officials and politicians gave them permission to do whatever it took to avert a repeat of the appalling incident. In response the IRS brought the whole operation "in house" and codified their own dedicated team. Blood had been spilled and from now on there'd be no more Mr. nice guy.

Atkinson and his partner had just witnessed a car leaving the target location five minutes before. They determined that it was the owner, but they allowed him to leave. One of his mobile units was responsible for tailing the vehicle and to eventually apprehend it, especially if the vehicle turned around and headed back to its point of origin. Although they knew that this didn't mean the house was empty, the fact that the owner's car left lowered the number of occupants in the home and that was something that helped lower the risk assessment.

"Go!" Atkinson yelled into his phone.

Seconds later an armored personnel swat van rolled up fast and screeched to a halt in the driveway of the house Atkinson was watching. It came out of nowhere and he was pleased with the speed in which his men could ascend upon the target. The rear doors blasted open and just like the Marines out of an armored personnel carrier, a six-man team poured out the back and hit the beach. Dressed in their cumbersome tactical response gear complete with heavy bullet proof vest and helmet, they moved with surprising agility. Some took cover but others kept going so as not to lose momentum and the element of surprise. When they reached the front door one of them produced a shotgun door buster. It had a handle on it that gave the handler stability while placing the muzzle up to the door lock. The thing fired a slug that busted through the lock and the door jamb itself all at the same time. One shot brought to bear on almost any door and the team was through. Knocking was no longer on their list of things to do before influencing entry. They didn't even try the handle first to see if it was open for fear that it would alert the occupants.

"Bam!" The door flew open and team members moved in with rifles poised shouting "IRS! Police! IRS! Police!".

You could hear continuous shouting echoing through the door from inside the home. Atkinson heard it from the speaker in the dashboard of his unmarked car. He was picking up audio from a microphone on one of the agent's helmets and heard everything that was going on inside. Some voices were sharp, others were muffled. Then "Clear!" was heard twice over the radio before the sound of a gunshot broke through all the commotion. Immediately after, Atkins heard an excited voice come over the radio "Perp down! Perp down!".

A female's high-pitched scream came from somewhere inside the home. It permeated the air and then suddenly came to an abrupt stop along with the muffled sound of people wrestling.

"Clear!", "Clear!" came over the radio again and then "We got a live one here". Moments later the "All clear" was officially declared for the entire residence.

"Three minutes fifteen seconds" Atkinson said to his partner while looking at his watch and then "Great job guys!" he said into the mike. "Do we need an ambulance?".

"Yeah, but he'll be DOA sir".

Atkinson turned to his partner and said "Better him than us".

His partner repeated the IRS motto "No loss of life with maximum control, at least not on our side" he added.

"That's how we do it" Atkinson said with a smile.

Atkinson switched back to his mobile phone and spoke into it "Mobil unit one what's your status?".

"We got him at the corner of Realm and Whitney sir. Isolate, surround and take 'em down! Worked like a charm. No resistance he's in custody now".

"Ok, bring the car back here, included it in the inventory along with everything else on the property. Take the perp to the station and hand him over to Detective Mack, he'll hold him for the cool off period and deal with all the legal shit. I'll inform him of the situation here.

"Roger that, we're on our way".

Atkinson looked at his partner. "Ok Jim, they're ready for you. Tighten down security and be prepared for hostilities from outside sources, neighbors, relatives; whatever. Secure the perimeter and do the inventory".

With clipboard in hand Jim got out of the car and closed the door. The passenger side electric window rolled down "...ahh Jim!" Atkinson pulled his glasses down so Jim could see his eyes. "Everything in the house gets written down on that sheet. All of it. Nothing disappears or I'll have your ass up for redemption".

"Don't worry chief, got it".

"Yeah, that's what I'm afraid of". Atkinson mumbled to himself as he rolled the window up. He rolled the car forward and looked around at his men who were starting the next phase of the reclamation process, securing property, and taking inventory. He smiled and said "Now that's how it's done!".

* * *

Over the next few months Atkinson reveled in the degree of success his operation had achieved as measured by the increased flow of cash and assets without the loss of life. The level of income from this project was questionable and was thought of as possibly insignificant but their accomplishments turned it into a major ever-increasing river of flowing assets. His superiors started to take notice. They were achieving four to five times the predicted earnings they had estimated. It seems that Americans were hoarding valuables at home and neglecting their payment of taxes. Who would have thought?

Any civilian confronting the IRS initiative with condemnation was thwarted with a stern lecture on how the IRS was only collecting money duly owed to the United States Government. It was their inherent right to recover it and the methods they used only reflected the times and the need for a more efficient way of getting the job done. The number of ART members under Commander Atkinson's control expanded in tandem with the greed of its creators, and why not? There was no major opposition coming from the media. And if it worked in one state, ditto the arrangement in all the others and multiply the results. Consistently, millions of dollars flowed into the hands of its benefactors every week. Atkinson's boss and all the beneficiaries involved were smiling like Smurfs playing in a blue pool. Everyone was pleased with the results. The degree of cooperation the United States government displayed bode well with all parties involved. Knowing that obligations might at least be addressed rather than simply written off was assuring. The venture turned into an exceedingly popular method of addressing foreign debt obligation.

President Richmond even took it to a new level. Through Executive Law, he decreed that the IRS was exempt from having to satisfy any state taxes levied on property seized for the purpose of reclamation including any claim of "Estate tax". This assured that the Federal Treasury would realize the full property value and effectively barred the State from any monetary gain.

A beneficiary of the Asset Reclamation Program could opt to take possession of a certain property as payment, which surprisingly became an immensely popular choice. Many foreigners wanted a piece of America, and this was a great inexpensive way to inherit property. They too enjoyed a tax-exempt status for acquiring property in this manner. Nowadays Real estate was worth a whole lot more than holding on to the same value in deteriorating American dollars. The program was so popular that the Chinese government requested (and got) their own men placed on the IRS-ART team under the guise of being "advisors" or "trainees" claiming that they needed their own people to uphold the interests of the Chinese government. Recovery teams became extremely popular indeed. Federal land in America was now "on sale". The current administration was selling off federally owned land and assets to the highest bidder to rid themselves of the burden and to generate some desperately needed cash. Foreign countries purchased large tracts of farmland and buildings across the country. America was for sale.

29

Kaiden's Run

Two days had passed since the invasion. Students referred to it as "The day of Major loss".

Ciera urgently beeped Kaiden and asked him to meet her at her Hogan in Rio Linda at 2:30. It was an odd request at an odd hour, but Kaiden was able to oblige so he beeped her back "Ok".

Kaiden was late, but not because he couldn't find it, it just took a little longer to get there than he anticipated. Ciera was in Village F, known to all affectionately as "F Troop". Only those who had seen the ancient re-runs on TV knew about the implied reference to the ancient sitcom that ran in the 60's. Kaiden had never been to F troop's village before, but it wasn't hard to find. "Just follow the signs" is what everyone always said. It was the village right next to village E where Shiloh lived. He knew his way there quite well.

"You're late!" she said when she saw him walking up the path to her Hogan.

"Yeah, there was a red light at the biffy, so I had to stop".

"Well, I'm glad you got that out of the way, I just hate it when a good man pisses me off". Kaiden laughed at that.

"Ciera, no true 'man' would ever run out on you".

She smiled and looked at him with appreciation. He had said it with such sincerity. She moved toward him and hugged him.

"Kaiden" she said "If I ever need a compliment all I have to do is call you".

"Wow, I'll take that as... a compliment" Kaiden said.

"Yes, but I'll be honest with you" Ciera said pulling back. "I am trying to butter you up because I have a favor to ask of you".

"Now I know it must be important because you know that I'll go to the ends of the earth and do anything you ask even without any butter". Ciera smiled back at him. She was trying to be serious but then she broke out with a laugh.

"Oh boy, I needed that" but then she got serious again. "I really like you Kaiden... and that's why it's hard for me to ask".

Now Kaiden got serious. "Alright what do you need".

"I need you to ride escort for a shipment. It's dangerous work, that's why I'm hesitant to ask. But I need someone I can trust. Last night we had a truck that was hijacked. We think more like 'confiscated' but we can't confirm it now".

Kaiden caught on to the seriousness of the situation "What happened?".

"They're watching us" she walked over to the stove and put the kettle on the hot plate. "That's why I'm meeting you out here. A week ago, they sent us a government liaison from the FDA. His name is Rickert, Shawn Rickert, and from the get-go he's acting like he owns the place. He and his assistant just showed up one morning. No one even called to let us know he was coming. He's come in, more like moved in, under the guise of an advisor. That was about a week before the Chancellor's arrest. Since then, he's all but taken over and gotten aggressively involved in everything. He's even moved into the Chancellors office. That assistant of his, the government administrator, who we suspect is really his bodyguard. They claim they are here to help in the Chancellors absence, but we know that they are both just government spies. Already he's setting up board meetings and putting his two cents in where it doesn't belong. Rickert contacted me right off and was asking all sorts of questions about the Humanitarian Relief Organization. We know it's a blatant attempt to infiltrate the Academy; they're looking for dirt and for information. They need it to shut us down, but I think they want to find out our financial infrastructure first".

Kaiden broke in with disbelief "Wow I can't believe it. The government sent an agent to physically inject their two cents into a private business?".

"Yes, we don't quite know what to do about it yet, our lawyers are still trying to decide the best course of action".

"I know what to do, we bar his ass from entering the Academy. Stop him right at the gate and send him packing. Thanks, but no thanks, get your slinky ass at a heea".

"That'd be great but can't do that without repercussions. We've already complained to the State Governor, she claims he's part of the regulatory agency assigned to monitor certain food production businesses. Supposedly all large agricultural companies have one now. And oh yeah, he's going to help make it safer by 'helping' us conform to Federal Food Drug and EPA regulations.

Rickert has already asked to see all our purchase orders and requisitions for the last year. He won't accept the last inventory we did but wants to personally take an inventory of everything we have. That brings me back to why I brought you here.

Our security team escorting the rig we sent to pick up our last order reported that they were being followed, not by the police but by the ATF.

"How did they know it was the ATF?".

"I don't know. Maybe they saw an emblem or something. The last thing we heard was that the transport was being pulled over, more like forced over. The escort team turned around to assist but... we haven't heard from them either".

"They're missing? No police report or nothin?".

"Nothing yet, we've been searching local and state police reports all morning. Kaiden, they knew where we were going and what we were doing".

"What were you doing Ciera?".

"Oh, no nothing like that!" she cut him off from thinking there was some kind of nefarious activity on her part but then said "At least not that time anyway" Ciera looked up at Kaiden and paused to let that sink in fully aware of the implication.

"This run was just for a load of construction material, copper wire, pipe and food items, nothing illegal. At least nothing that should be considered illegal. The Unions have become aware of our operation and have complained about us using non-Union labor. It seems they don't like being left out of the loop. They claim that only Union labor can transport cargo across state borders as stated in the Federal Transportation Act. We think that this is why many of the trucks are disappearing. They don't like the competition".

The tea kettle started to whistle. Ciera took it off the stove and poured two cups of tea. She stirred them with a spoon and handed one to Kaiden. He took it but Kaiden smiled knowing that she must be deep inside her own thoughts about this; he never asked her for a cup of tea.

"I still can't get my delivery of diesel fuel for the farm because my supplier had a truck hijacked over on 88 near Oneonta just five days ago. They found the driver, dead. It spooked all the others so now I can't get anyone to deliver. Luckily that was after the delivery of an unleaded gas drop that we had just received at the school or else we wouldn't even have that.

"Thanks for the tea" he said. "So why do you need me?".

"I have a pickup to make. It's... an extremely important one. It's imperative that it makes it back here in one piece without being hijacked. It's very valuable and we need this shipment to get through. I need someone I can trust to go down and get this one".

"What is it I'd be picking up?".

"I can't tell you now. I don't want it to leak out about the nature of the cargo. If you get caught you can truly claim ignorance. It'll help your case".

"My 'case'? Wow you really are expecting trouble, aren't you?"

"I don't know, but things are really getting tight out there. We have to act fast and get as many of these shipments in as we can before things get even worse".

"I'll do it. When do I go?".

"Tomorrow night. You're traveling with another Cadet from security. You'll be driving down in just the cab, and you'll pick up your rig fully loaded at your destination. All ya gotta do is hook up and get the hell out a there and get back up here in one piece".

"I'll be driving the truck?".

"Yeah, we can't trust the Union drivers anymore, we're gunna have to do it ourselves, that's why I need you. We think the drivers might be the source of the leak. This way the Union won't get wind of it and we'll have a better chance of success".

Kaiden had been using the cup of tea to keep his hands warm. He sat it down next to the stove and walked to the front door of the Hogan. For a quiet moment he stared out at the cold leafless forest.

Finally, he turned to Ciera "OK but I need to take care of a few things first. So, I'd better get going, I don't have much time". He left but turned and talked over his shoulder "Thanks for the tea, I'll beep you".

Ciera moved to the door and looked after him, concerned because she hadn't quite finished talking to him the way she wanted to but was satisfied that he picked up on the severity of the problem. Kaiden was no dummy, she was counting on that. Then she sat on the bed with a big sigh of relief like the weight a major problem had just been lifted off her shoulders. Still, she was saddened because she had to use him like that.

* * *

The ride down for Kaiden and his new partner "Remy Horton" was no big deal. They started out at 3:00 o'clock in the morning and drove down in the cab without the big rig behind them. It was Ciera's idea to pick up the semi-trailer at the pickup point. That would make the trip down and the pickup a whole lot easier. Besides, Kaiden was able to practice driving without all that weight tacked on. He got the hang of it only after figuring out that with no load you can start off in second gear instead of first. Starting in first gear made the cab shutter and kick back and forth violently until disengaging the clutch and switching into second.

The rig made it down into southern New Jersey in eight hours due to a few detours needed to avoid reported roadblocks and inspection points. It wasn't so much that they had to avoid the inspection points; after all they weren't hauling anything. But they did it to become familiar with the roads and to find ways around certain trouble spots for the way back.

After six hours of driving, they were both in need of a pit stop, it was just after 9 o'clock and breakfast sounded like a great idea. Stations that were open for business were getting scarce; they had to go miles out of their way to find this one. That "old school" gadget the CB radio was great for finding places and getting information on the best food, gas, and of course updated reports on road conditions. It proved even better than the internet since roadblocks could appear in odd places at odd times. Truckers always had the most up to date information; it was like a direct connection into road drama. The only problem they found was that there was a lot of disinformation on the radio as well. It seems that some people had an interest in doing their best to muddy the water.

The only major concern on the trip so far was that Remy got nervous when he thought he saw that they were being followed. "Kaiden I could swear that I've seen the same car appear behind us on three separate occasions". From then on Remy kept looking in the rearview mirror and got more and more jittery about the prospect.

"Don't worry about it" Kaiden said confidently. "We'll lose them before we get there".

"Alright but where are we going?".

Kaiden knew Remy Van Horton from seeing him at various Cadet functions as well as working with him on multiple hunting parties. But he didn't know him well enough to confide with him and give him details of the mission, even if he was a Cadet. Ciera had conveyed that "all precautions should be taken" and he took her warning very seriously.

Kaiden told him "I'll let you know when we get there".

The same car appeared behind them again and then disappeared behind traffic. Kaiden noticed it now, but you couldn't tell by his demeanor. He just looked at his watch and said "We're going to make a try for gas up ahead at this next truck stop. We'll get some breakfast too, all right?".

"Yeah alright, I'm starving" Remy told him.

Twenty minutes later they let the CB radio guide them to a well-known truck stop near the border of New Jersey and Pennsylvania. Quite a few places along the way had been closed; this one was open, but it was jam packed. Cars and trucks filled every parking spot with people double parked and waiting for someone to leave. There was also a lengthy line to get fuel on both the truck and car side. Even with all that mess Kaiden insisted on going in anyway. "We can speed this up some if we get on line for gas and you go in to eat while I try and get us up to one of the pumps. You go first. We might not need to park if we time it right. If I get re-fueled before you finish eating, I'll park the cab over there" Kaiden pointed to the parking lot filled with semi's sitting in rows idle with their drivers either asleep in their cab or in the restaurant eating.

"Ok, I'll be back in fifteen, can I get you anything?".

"Nah. Hey take your time, sit down and eat" Kaiden said.

"Yeah, I could use a break from this seat" Remy said as he slid out of the cab and hit the pavement, his cramped legs desperately needing a stretch.

Neither of them noticed due to the number of vehicles that were moving in and out of the parking lot, but that same car they had suspected of following them turned into the car section of the rest stop and parked in a position from which it could observe their truck. Its occupants saw Remy exit and then walk into the restaurant. One of them got out and followed him in. Innocently enough, all he observed was Remy buying a farmer's special breakfast and sitting down at a table to eat. When he was done, he got up and hoofed it back out to the truck. Remy found Kaiden still waiting on line for fuel. At least he had moved up to near next in line at the pump. Now there was only one semi in front of them.

"My turn" Kaiden said.

Remy jumped in the cab and took over the wheel. "Great, I gotta hit the bathroom and I'll get some breakfast too" Kaiden said. "You'll probably be refueled before I get back; I'll meet you over there". Again, he pointed to the trucker's parking lot.

First things first. Kaiden walked toward the public bathroom in the center complex. Seemingly unknown to Kaiden a man followed behind him just far enough so as not to lose him in the steady stream of people walking beside Kaiden on the sidewalk. Kaiden looked like he was deep in his own thoughts. When he got to the bathroom and passed the double door entrance, he suddenly sped up and started running toward the exit on the opposite side of the men's bathroom. The bathroom was one of those large ones with two convenient entrances with one on each north and south bound side. At the same time, Kaiden took off his jacket, turned it inside out and put it back on. The color of his jacket changed from black to tan while beelining it out the other side. To top it off he pulled out a baseball cap from his back pocket and put it on. By the time he came out the other side the man following him was just going in. As the man walked in the bathroom, he happened to see two stall doors close in front of him. He was forced to guess that one of them was Kaiden; he had no reason to think otherwise.

Kaiden walked fast around the outside of the building and quickly got back over to the trucker's side of the parking lot. He could see Remy dealing with the pump but instead of walking up to their cab, he took a right and walked down the sidewalk that took him into the lot where all the other semis were parked. The man with the tan jacket and baseball cap walked between the rows until he disappeared among the multitude of semi-trucks.

It took about five minutes before the person following Kaiden started to panic. A different guy came out of one of the bathroom stalls-it wasn't Kaiden. Realizing he had lost contact with his assignment he immediately walked up to the second possible stall, grabbed the door on the top with his hands and pulled himself up to peak over the top. It was the only other place he thought Kaiden could be.

"Hey what the fuck?" echoed off the bathroom walls as its occupant voiced his opinion of the intrusion, but that man wasn't Kaiden either. The agent turned around with a frantic look on his face and dialed a number on his phone as he ran out.

A thick line of trucks and cars drove out of the rest stop and onto the highway, luckily the out was moving a lot faster than the in. An old Mack truck cab with a faded red paint job, minus its rig, merged slowly into the line of traffic building up speed at the same pace as the truck in front of him. Its driver, happy to be moving again, turned up the radio and started singing an old rock and roll song by "Jet Black" in a thick heavy New York accent. The driver was about twenty years old yet already had tattoos that covered his arms making him look like a long-time trucker. A cigarette dangled from his mouth as he sang.

"Do you wanna be my girlfriend?" He yelled out and then banged on the steering wheel in sync with the beat of the song. Between phrases the transmission grinded into gear and he glanced in the rear-view mirror. Then he'd go back to banging on the wheel and singing his song in an elated tone.

It was only after the semi pulled out onto the highway and reached cruising speed did Kaiden pop up from his hiding place on the floor of the cab. His new driver yelled with all the excitement of seeing a long-lost friend and they gave each other an overjoyed high five and a gang-style handshake.

"Damn it's great to see you again gringo" he said. "We've missed you, you son of a bitch. Where've ya been? Some hermits cave in the mountains somewhere?".

"Romondo, thanks man, you still got my back and I'll never forget this". His full name was Romondo Latoya Velez, a friend of Kaiden's from the old neighborhood. Kaiden hadn't seen him since he'd left the city.

"You better not forget you son of a bitch cause I'm gunna remind you every chance I get". Then he looked at Kaiden with a wry smile and sang out with the song right on cue "Are you gunna be my girl?".

Kaiden cracked up and then joined in the singing as they cruised down the highway.

1, 2, 3 tell me you're gunna meet with me
Because you look so cool I don't' want to be nobody's fool.
Big black shoes- with eyes that stare-
she's so fine I'm guna spend all my dime.
I can't complain... you're driving me to despair...
you keep sayin you already got one down there. Yeah.
I know you... don't want to talk
Believe me when I say I want you to stay... yeah.
I just need to know "You gunna be my girlfriend"?

Remy finished checking the oil and refueling the truck and looked around for Kaiden before hopping back into the cab. Kaiden was nowhere in sight. He started the truck and drove it out of the station and into the trucker's parking lot and luckily found a place to park. Twenty minutes went by before the phone rang and woke him up from his nap. The ringing was coming from Kaiden's backpack sitting on the passenger's side floor. He grabbed it and fumbled through it trying to find the phone. "Got you" he said and quickly tapped it open.

"Hello?".

"Remy, this is Kaiden".

"Kaiden? Where are you?".

"Listen to me carefully and follow my instructions, this is important. I won't be going with you for the rest of the trip. We're being followed. I need you to look in my pack, you'll find a yellow envelope".

Remy rummaged through the pack and sure enough he found a large yellow envelope. "Yeah, I see it". He pulled it out and looked at it.

"Open it, read it, and follow the instructions. Do exactly what it tells you too and do it in the same order that it tells you. I'll meet you there. Do you understand?".

"Ah yeah I guess so... but what's goin on?".

It was too late, there was no reply. Kaiden had already hung up. Remy stared at the phone and then at the manila envelope for just a second before opening it. He read it and then looked up and looked around.

The truck's engine came to life with a loud diesel "ping" that made it sound like the engine was broken. Probably bad gas had something to do with it. Remy edged the cab forward and got online to exit the rest area. The instructions told him to consult the handheld maps they carried instead of using the GPS. He was to travel to three different waypoints before meeting Kaiden at the last one twenty-four hours from now. Remy gave out a sigh and then raised his eyebrows and shook his head saying "I hope you know what you're doin".

The agents observed the rig starting to move. "What the hell! They're on the move. I didn't see the second guy get in did you?" They both looked at each other wondering what was going on.

"You idiot, you had to lose him didn't you. Shit! Now we don't know if he's in the truck or not".

"It doesn't matter" the second agent said. "We're supposed to follow the cab to its destination and record all its stops. That's our job. We just need to know where they're going and we sure as hell can still do that".

"Yeah, but you better report it. I got a feeling they're not goin to like this". The agent glanced at him with a dubious look and then reached for his phone.

Four hours later Romondo's cab pulled into the parking lot of some warehouse in the southern part of Camden, New Jersey. Kaiden jumped out and took care of the formalities with the warehouse foreman. The man directed Romondo as he backed up into bay #14. Romondo's familiarity with the big rig was obvious. He had been working for Gator transport for two years now and like a pro he backed the cab up to the cab-less rig parked in #14. After that the rest of it was easy. They made the connections from cab to rig which had been sitting there loaded and ready to go. This was a whole lot easier and faster than bringing in their own and having to load up when they got there. After making a payment they were rolling out of the parking lot just twenty minutes later with a heavy load. Romondo had to use first gear to get the weight of the truck moving, after that it drove just like before. As far as they could tell no one had observed them making the pickup.

The plan was never to meet back up with Remy. He was the decoy to throw off whoever was following them. Unfortunately, Remy had to be left to fend for himself. Kaiden didn't know if anyone would be tailing them but devised the plan to ensure the success of his mission. It wasn't just that he wanted to prove himself to Ciera, although that did weigh heavily on his mind, it was more from a desire to keep himself from getting captured or even killed. He was aware of the frequent truck hijackings in the news. Ciera never told him what he was transporting. She just repeated that it was unbelievably valuable and that it had to get through. That was all that needed to be said for Kaiden to take the precautions that he did.

Romondo and Kaiden headed West on 76 through southeastern Pennsylvania instead of going North to be unpredictable. It was risky, the route was new, and they didn't have all the information like Kaiden had on interstate 87. But they figured that they, whoever "they" were, would be expecting them to take the same route back and would be looking for them. They also avoided interstate 81 North due to reports of an inspection point at the Pa/NY border. Trucks were being pulled over and inspected causing a major traffic jam both ways. Instead, they meandered their way through Pennsylvania over to Harrisburg and found their way up Route 15 north which ended up being a secondary road with a nice scenic drive as it follows the Susquehanna River. It was such a beautiful road; it almost made them forget about the hard changes going on in America while driving through such a beautiful area. Yeah, it was a lot farther and positively out of their way, but they felt safer and figured that they'd have a lot better chance going this way.

Ciera was worried. It was 3:00 in the afternoon. She hadn't heard from Kaiden or Remy all day and he wasn't answering the phone she had given him for communication. As far as she knew he didn't have his own, so it was a pleasant surprise to get a call from him, but not under these circumstances. Only the call wasn't from Kaiden, it was Remy. He told her in a desperate voice "I'm making this call just as the ATF are swarming around my cab. They just pulled me over and I figure I got just enough time to let you know!" He told her where he was and explained that Kaiden had disappeared about an hour before when they stopped at a truck stop for lunch. He didn't have time to say anything more. The next thing she heard was Remy saying "Hey guy's what's all the ruckus about?" Then she heard "Hey what the fuck!" There was the sound of scuffling and then the phone went dead. Ciera flipped her cell phone closed while staring at the wall with tears in her eyes.

Diesel fuel was available just off the Highway near Milton Pa... But Kaiden and Romondo were only allowed twenty gallons' maximum and were charged $12.45 a gallon. They took what they could get. Next, they decided to take the lesser traveled road '220' north instead of following 15 all the way up across the border into New York. Even though 15 was a much better improved road with sections that looked like a highway, and 220 a rough secondary two-lane road, they decided to take 220 because it connected into their target (I86) a lot farther east of their intended destination. If all went well, they might even shave off some driving time. As it ended up, it was a big mistake.

Sayre Pa. was the last town they'd pass through before crossing into NY and they would have made it without incident if it wasn't for Pennsylvania's Local Transportation Union #242. Nowadays they manned and operated a roadblock on Route 220 just outside of Sayre's Town limits. It was designed to catch truckers doing exactly what Kaiden and Romondo were doing, circumventing the major roadway.

Route 220 turned into a four-lane highway complete with a divider about five miles before intersecting with interstate 86. A roadblock was strategically placed at that transition point. It was set up on both sides of the road to catch traffic going in either direction.

Kaiden had taken the wheel and relieved Romondo just after they passed through Milton Pa. They expected smooth sailing and had no information to cause them concern even when Kaiden ran into traffic just outside of Milton. Delays such as this were common except for the fact that it slowed them down to a crawl. Romondo had fallen asleep with his head against the window. Still Kaiden got on the radio and gave a shout out for a "Look over the shoulder" to any southbound rig they could catch.

An initial contact was made but then the radio's static changed, and something drowned out the voice. It hissed and squelched and then a clear voice came over and said "All's OK North bounder, you'll just run into a little heavy traffic that's all. Keep your heading and you'll get through with only about a half hour delay, over".

"Ah, roger that south bounder" Kaiden replied with a frown on his face. "Where did you say your 20 was?

There was no further response, just static with a much more subdued level of white noise. Kaiden was suspicious, something wasn't right. He reached over and tapped Romondo hard enough to wake him from a sound sleep.

"Romondo, I think they're jamming the radio signal".

"What, what's going on?" For a second it was hard for Romondo to comprehend. He tried to shake the sleep from his brain by shaking his head.

"The radio, a strong voice came over it and said 'it's all clear up a head' but he stepped all over my southbound contact. I think he was drowning out our chatter on purpose. Something's not right".

Romondo took a few seconds to respond. "Let me check dis map for another way at a heea" he said in his thick New York accent. After consulting the map, he looked up "We pass the toin off for Milton yet?".

"Yeah, that was a few miles back" Kaiden informed him.

"Shit. All we can do now is look for an exit, maybe at 'Athens'. We sure as hell can't toine around eea, not on dis road and if there's a road-block before or at Athens we're screwed".

"Hell, maybe I can turn around in one of these driveways here...".

"No. Your skills at backin iss thin up are nonexistent. If we get stuck eea we're just as screwed if not woise, we'd be dead in the water. Let's keep rollin and hope for a legit toineoff. Look, I see a possibility up a head".

The map showed one last turn off at Greens Landing. Even though that road took them west through a rural area and in the opposite direction of their intended route, it was their only alternative. It was a two-lane State road that traveled up into the rural areas of North-western Pa., which wouldn't have been a trucker's third choice under normal circumstances, but they decided to take it. As luck would have it, there were three pickup trucks and men standing around the inter-section when they approached it. The trucks were parked on both sides of the road.

"Ut oh. Shit what's this" Romondo said.

"Doesn't look like a roadblock. More like they're just watching traffic" Kaiden noted.

Up at the turnoff on the left they saw eight men standing off to the side of the road. When a vehicle ahead of them turned at the inter-section three men strolled out from the side of the road and waved it down. They approached the driver's side and signaled the driver to roll down the window. Clearly the men scrutinized the car, its occupants, and its contents. They must not have seen anything of interest because they waved the car through. But would they allow a semi-truck?

Kaiden had no choice but to follow and turn off at the same inter-section. The men repeated the procedure and flagged him down. On their shirts in big letters read "UAW Local 248". The man in the street motioned for him to roll the window down. Kaiden did and leaned out asking "Hey what's up, you boy's looking for terrorists?".

The Union man shrugged off the question without answering. "Where you headed?".

"Oh, ahh..." Kaiden said with a pause as he tried to listen to Romondo saying something in the background.

"Bentley Creek" Romondo said as he read off the next town up the road they were attempting to take.

"Bentley Creek" Kaiden repeated to the man. "We're headed for Bentley Creek".

"Bentley Creek?" the man said. "What you got a delivery for them or something?".

"Ah, yeah, yeah..." Kaiden said thinking that this might get them through. "...we got a delivery for them".

"A delivery up at Bentley Creek?" The Union man scratched his beard. Why there's no one out there to deliver too. It's just a big parking lot next to the bridge overlooking Bentley Creek. That's just a fishin spot. What would you be delivering there?".

Romondo spoke up so that the man could hear him "No the delivery's not there we're just passing through there to get to Wellsburg".

"No, we're just goin through to Wellsburg" Kaiden corrected.

"Wellsburg? That's near interstate 17. No trucker in their right mind would travel this road when you can go right up here to 17, take a left on 87 and head over to Wellsburg. It's right off the highway".

Another man climbed up onto the running boards of the cab on Romondo's side and peered into the window. Romondo turned and stared into the hardened face of an unhappy red neck Union man. If it wasn't for the glass between them, he'd be smelling the man's breath. Romondo depressed the door lock and gave him a big smile.

"What Union are you with? You are Union, right?" the first man asked Kaiden.

"Ah, yeah of course. We're with Local 59 out of New Joisey".

The man looked at him suspiciously. "Get out and come down here".

Kaiden didn't know what else to do so he opened the door and hopped out of the truck while desperately trying to think of a way out of this. He left the door open to maintain a quick escape route and to allow Romondo to get out and come to his aid if necessary.

"I need to see your papers then".

"My papers? What is this, World War II Germany? Paypas please" Kaiden joked in his best German accent, then he laughed trying to lighten the air with his newfound friends. Two more men walked up to Kaiden. One stood on each side of him effectively boxing him in against the cab of the truck. They scrutinized his every move with a menacing glare.

"Yeah, your card, your Union card" the one on the right said.

Romondo shuffled over and sat in the driver's seat of the cab to get a better view. He'd been in many a street fight and could sense that this was shaping up to be trouble. He stared out the open door with his body moving ever so slowly like a cat maneuvering to pounce. Plan B was to put it in gear and drive out of there quickly if needed. This scene had all the makings of a fight.

"Oh that, my Union card" Kaiden said while looking up at Romondo with a big, forced smile. "It's a funny thing about that Union" Kaiden laughed "they don't ever send me my new card on time...".

"Hell, son you don't look like no Union to me, I think you're just one of those scalper drivers tryin to cut us out of work ain't ya!". The man pointed his finger and took a step closer to him.

With that Kaiden realized that he wasn't going to get through this with a standard line of BS. "We don't take kindly to that". The man in front of him cocked his arm back and took a swing at Kaiden's face. It would have landed too if Kaiden didn't quickly jot his head backwards. One moment his head was there within range, the next it was not. As his head traveled backward Kaiden's right foot shot forward delivering a strike to the man's groin. Kaiden kept it loose and whipped his foot like a towel just before it hit. To someone watching it looked like just a tap but being dead on target magnified the results. The man's face changed from anger into a painful cringe where his eyes faded off to the side as every sensory nerve in his groin radiated with pain. It was so overwhelming that it was all his mind could comprehend and deal with at one time. He gripped his crotch with both hands, dropped to his knees and fell over.

At the same instant the two men on both sides of Kaiden reached out and grabbed his arms to hold him. Kaiden set his kicking foot back down on the ground for a solid connection and then twisted his body sharply clockwise. The action pulled his arm loose from the guy on the left. The guy on the right held on but was pulled forward and off balance by doing so. Kaiden followed through raising his left fist to the level of the guy's face. Fist and face met in the middle with a crack of knuckles against nose. Again, it wasn't so much the power of the punch but the fact that it was delivered to such a tender spot. Even still the guy felt like he had just run into a wall. Martial artists jokingly call it "blocking a punch with your face". Tears filled his eyes and instantly clouded his vision. He let go and stepped backward.

The guy on Kaiden's left recovered quickly and switched from grabbing to throwing a left punch. Kaiden turned counterclockwise to face him and was fast enough to catch the punch with his left arm and parry it to his left side. In practice that block is always followed immediately by a right palm strike to the opponent's body or face, but in this case Kaiden wanted to cause damage that would end the fight quickly. The fingers of his right hand darted out and poked the guy's eyes. For him the lights went out like a dark shade being pulled down with painful shards of pulsing white light complete with spikes around the edges. He reeled back in pain. Kaiden felt the retreat and pushed while trapping the man's rear leg. He made it look easy; the man was off balanced and fell backwards hitting the ground with the thud of his own weight against pavement. The force of the fall knocked the wind out of him.

Kaiden quickly turned around and was about to jump back up into the cab, but as if that wasn't enough, the guy with the broken nose came at him again holding his nose with one hand and swinging with the other. Kaiden sidestepped the punch and dropped down into a solid stance placing one hand on the guy's elbow and one on the guy's body. Slowly (at first) he started to push. Having an arm trapped like that causes one to naturally pull back to try and get out of the hold. Kaiden used that "help" from his opponent and pushed him hard at the same time, in the same direction. The result was amazing. The guy lifted off his feet and sailed backwards in the air for about two feet before touching the ground. Without being able to change his plight in midair the man landed way off balance. He tumbled backwards and fell down landing on his lower back. All three of them were slow to get up.

The Union man standing at Romondo's window sensed something was wrong and climbed down to go help. By the time he got around to the others it was too late. Kaiden was back up in the truck and the semi was already kickin it out. All he could do was to try and help one of his friends get up. The one he was helping got mad and started pointing saying "Follow them damn it, follow them!".

Romondo slid back over into the passenger's seat to let Kaiden climb back in. Kaiden saddled up, depressed the clutch, shifted, and hit the gas. The semi shuddered as it took off. He was ecstatic "I was gunna help ya dude, but it didn't look like you needed it. Damn you're still in your game man that was awesome. I love watchin you beat up on red necks, yeah!" They both slapped hands with excited smiles between them.

Kaiden shifted gears quickly continuously nudging the truck up to a higher speed and looked in the rear-view mirror to see if anyone jumped on it. "We're not out of it yet, one of those trucks is pullin out fast. Yup, he's following us".

"Shit!" Romondo said. Elation deflated into concern while looking into the rear-view mirror. "What do we do man?".

"Well, all we can do is git the hell ata heea" Kaiden said.

The cab kept shuddering from the stress of Kaiden's desire to move faster. A truck loaded like it was didn't move "fast" in any sense of the word, but it didn't matter. Soon they were haulin ass up a narrow secondary road with curves and turns that would naturally dictate the top speed they could go. It was a dangerous road for semi-trucks and even more dangerous for cars traveling in the opposite direction. If any car coming the other way met up with Kaiden as he cut a curve short, they would plow right into the side of the rig. And on a road like this there's no option, a semi would be forced to cut a corner due to the size of the rig. They did have one advantage though. The Ford F150 following them couldn't pass them either. Kaiden could block him on the straights, and they would have knocked the guy off the road if he tried to pass on a bend.

Romondo started reading the map again. "We'll be comin up on a intersection. We can go right which will put us back on 220 but much foither up. It'll bypass Athens. If the roadblock is there, den we'll miss it. Left takes us even foither west but we'll have a few more options goin that way".

"Get on the radio and see if you can get the 20 of that roadblock".

Romondo put out a request for a south bounder but only static came back.

"Shit" Kaiden screamed. "We need to lose that truck. Either way we're turning West at the next crossroad you mentioned. If we go back to 220 this guy could have his friends waiting for us. This'll take us out of our way but it's definitely a safer bet".

"Oh yeah, what if he's got friends up there in them thar hills?"

Kaiden thought "We could use a few friends ourselves right about now" It gave him an idea. "Romondo, get my beeper and use the phone to dial the number in my address book listed under 'Peace Core' then hand it to me.

Romondo got the phone but protested. "I don't think dem guys is gunna wanna help us Kaiden". Kaiden smiled at the miss conception but didn't bother to explain.

Romondo hit the call button. "Aay! Can't get through we ain't got no soivise out heea".

Kaiden frowned and pounded the steering wheel. But then he thought of another way. "Try using the beeper; send a message that Kaiden Sawyer needs help".

Romondo punched the keys and sent the message. "How's this gunna get through if the soivice is down?".

"Well, we're getting into some altitude here. If we somehow get line of sight to a transponder, it'll go through. Anythin?"

"No, nuttin yet".

"Try sending it again when we get to the top of this mountain".

As they crested the peak of a ridge off to the left was a beautiful view of the sun setting on the rolling hills of Northwestern Pennsylvania's countryside. The scenic view would have been a lot more appreciated under any other circumstance. Romondo punched the correct keys and sent the message again.

There was no response. They almost stopped thinking about it when the beeper suddenly beeped. With a surprised look on his face Romondo looked at Kaiden.

"Answer it!" Kaiden shouted.

"It woiked!" Romondo shouted. "It's a guy named McKinney. Says 'can you call me?".

"Tell him CB radio" Kaiden said.

Romondo sounded out the words as he punched it into the beeper "No service, CB radio" and sent it. Seconds later it beeped again.

The message said "Channel 10".

Romondo switched the CB radio to channel 10. To Kaiden's surprise he heard Allen McKinney's voice come across the speaker. "Break 10 calling Kaiden, Kaiden this is Ogami".

"Is that Allen? This is Kaiden Sawyer come in".

"From this point on no names, call me Ogami, but yes it's me".

Kaiden breathed a sigh of relief. "I can't believe I got you. I don't have a lot of time, I'm in trouble and I need help…".

It was a shot in the dark, but Kaiden ended up making the right call. Allen McKinney's voice somehow came in clearly on channel 10 but then faded out as they drove into a valley. It was back and forth like that as they drove through hilly terrain. After a few attempts Ogami was able to get the gist of their predicament and immediately recognized the seriousness of the situation.

"I'm glad you were able to reach me, I knew of your assignment and for a while there we thought we lost you. How the hell did you end up in my neighborhood?".

"Dun know Mr. Ogami man. We're just passing through".

"From now on your call sign is 'Gatlin' got it? Now Gatlin this is important, under no circumstances are you to give up that cargo, do you understand? It is imperative that you get to us. I just so happen to have people in your area that can help. Wait, give me five minutes. I'll be right back". Then there was only static.

A message came in on the beeper ten minutes later, it just said "channel 6".

When they switched to channel six, they heard "Gatlin, come in Gatlin. This is Ogami". McKinney quickly laid out a plan and asked Kaiden to meet his "Patriots" at a location that both could arrive at congruently. They were going to attempt to pry the truck away from their pursuer by a simple blocking maneuver with their own vehicles. If they could put some space between them and the truck, they could buy some time and then Kaiden could slip away on a predetermined route that McKinney laid out.

"Ogami I'm looking in my mirror, our pursuer just turned into pursuers. There's more than one truck behind us now. I'm afraid they might have the police on their side, they could get a roadblock set up somewhere in front of us and then we're screwed!".

"Yes, they'll probably try to block you or force you off the road, but I don't think they're going to involve the police. They'd have to cut the police in on the take so it's not as profitable that way. It'll probably be just us against them. Hang in there kid, help is on the way. I want you to take as many turns on side roads as you can so you will stay unpredictable. That way the enemy won't have time to get a roadblock set up. Check your watch, exactly forty-five minutes from now make sure you're driving on..."

The beeper beeped and Romondo looked at it. It read "South on Route 14 between Roaring Branch and Ralston".

Ogami continued "Find it on your map. Watch for it, our vehicles will pick you up and fall in line in front of you. Leave space for them, let them in. I'll describe the good guys for you, if you make a mistake and let the bad guys in it won't go well for you. Don't let them in front of you if you can help it. My guys will let you pass them and then they'll fall in line right behind you and block your pursuers. If it works, they'll put some space between you, you'll be able to make the next turn and lose them".

"What happens to your guys after that?".

"Don't worry about them, they know what to do. My guys can take care of themselves".

Luckily, the traffic was light on the back roads. A few slow pokes they encountered gave them the scariest moments of the ride. Without hesitating Kaiden blew his horn, turned into the oncoming lane and passed them. In one case they were incredibly lucky that the driver of the car they were passing cooperated and slowed down to allow them to pass. But in another they weren't so lucky. As Kaiden was passing he saw the headlights of a car coming right at him! A crash looked like it was unavoidable. If at the last moment Kaiden didn't crank the wheel and turn back into his own lane they would have crashed. Horns were blaring as he cringed. There was a bang and the truck shuddered. Looking in the rear-view mirror Kaiden saw the car careening off the road and into the ditch. He cleared the oncoming car by inches and made it without a head on but had just clipped the car behind him.

Kaiden drove fast taking as many turns as possible without losing the load or losing sight of the main goal; Route 14 south. Now there were four pickup trucks that stayed on their ass no matter what turn they took. They were just waiting for a chance to pull up alongside them and somehow force the semi to pull over. They got their chance at the next intersection.

Romondo and Kaiden thought it was odd to see traffic in front of them after arriving at the intersection of 514 and 414. Two cars and one pickup were stopped at the intersection. They had their blinkers on and were waiting to turn but no one was moving. Kaiden pulled up slowly but didn't dare stop; their pursuers could block them in from behind, then get out and swarm the truck. To avoid that scenario, he kept going and attempted to pass the waiting cars on the left figuring he'd move to the head of the line and take the turn without stopping. At the same moment, an old Ford Bronco with big fat tires turned into the oncoming lane and slowed down right in front of them. Kaiden slowed down too but kept creeping forward hoping to force the Bronco to back up. The driver stopped the truck, put it in park and emerged from the vehicle. In his hands was a roll of something that Kaiden couldn't quite make out. He looked up at them with a cigarette in his mouth and smiled slyly as he threw his bundle on the road. It unwound and quickly rolled out across the road in front of their truck.

Romondo shouted "Watch out it's a spike strip!".

Kaiden had to stop. The truck was no good to them with blown tires. He looked in his rear-view mirror just as trucks behind him filled in any space he might have had to back up. Forward: blown out tires, backwards and he'd have to plow through a couple of pickup trucks. Kaiden didn't know what kind of damage he'd do to the load with that maneuver, so he just sat there and hit the steering wheel in defeat.

"Quick, Romondo, get a message out on the beeper!" Kaiden yelled as he picked up the CB microphone. "Gatlin to Ogami, Ogami, May Day, May Day they've stopped us at the intersection of 514 and 414 we're boxed in. I'm sorry, they got us. I guess we lost the load. I repeat. We're at the intersection of 514 and 414...".

Romondo was busy punching keys on the beeper sending the same thing. Kaiden didn't know if anyone received the message or not before that same red neck climbed up on the truck and re-appeared at Romondo's window. This time he had that "got ya" snarl that clearly showed he wanted their ass bad. When Kaiden looked out his own side window there were two men standing there beckoning him to come down.

Kaiden and Romondo sat in the cab with the doors locked not wanting to step out into a dire situation.

"Damn, looks like they got us bro" Kaiden said.

"Yeah, I don't think we're gettin at a dis one skappy".

"Sorry I got you into this mess Romondo".

"Hey dun wurry bout it, I was lookin ta see new places, meet new people..." Romondo said as he turned, waved, and smiled at the guy outside his window. He turned back to Kaiden and put out his fist. They butt fists and then elbows with one of their gang salutes. Kaiden looked out the window again; now there were more of them standing there.

"Holy shit one of em's got a rifle!" Kaiden shouted.

The next thing he heard was "Come out now or we'll put a bullet through the door".

Kaiden didn't have to think very long. The thought of a bullet coming through the door, or the glass generated pictures in his mind that made him open it without any further delay. He raised his hands in the air as he exited the truck to keep from getting shot. Trying to climb down without using his hands and the fact that a gun was pointed at him made it a clumsy undertaking. He slipped and slid down the last step but luckily his feet landed underneath him on the pavement.

Two men appeared at his side. Kaiden recognized one of them as the one he kicked in the groin during their first encounter. The man was frowning with revenge pasted all over the corners of his face. He stood there looking like he was dying to get even. Both grabbed Kaiden and threw him back up against the cab as they had done before, only this time it was different. It's amazing what invisible bonds a gun places on the situation. He couldn't react like he did before but was forced to just stand there and take whatever was coming. More men came around until a small crowd stood around him. This time there was no small talk. They started to wail on him right away with punches and kicks that came from every angle. He was able to absorb the first few blows by filling his body with chi. He blocked the first flurry of kicks to his groin by turning his hips. That effectively closed the gap between his legs and kept them from delivering direct hits. A baseball bat appeared in the melee and struck him with pain racking accuracy into his stomach and ribs. A body seemed to fall out of the sky and land on the attackers. Kaiden didn't remember a strike to his head which turned out the lights.

30

Where Do We Go From Here

(Now That All Of The Children Have Grown Up)

At Tenny Hill Academy, people were simmering in a dark emotional cloud. It affected each member of the student body and the Cadet organization in an unusual way. Some were somber, some were elated with a feeling that something big was happening or was about to. Before recent events they all thought of themselves as belonging to something important, this was something that gave them profound meaning in their lives. Each one of them would drop everything and use their skills for the benefit of the Nation if called upon to do so. The entire student body felt in their hearts that they acquired the ability, knowledge, and skills for the express purpose of supporting their country in time of need and would endeavor to use them to help friends and neighbors alike. Now their Captain had been arrested and the Chancellor too. They were being labeled as part of the problem, as terrorists, by the very government that was supposed to be protecting them. Today it became obvious that Uncle Sam currently perceives them as the root of the resistance. They are part of the underlying wave forming against the new government. How absurd it was to all who knew the truth.

From this point on no one could argue that fact, all they had to do was read it in the ATF's report. The process had begun; the student body, teachers, staff, administration, all of them- had to choose sides.

In their minds when they thought about fighting against "enemies both foreign and domestic" they always pictured themselves shoulder to shoulder with the police and government agencies. Now they stood dumbfounded that the concept had flip-flopped and left them staring back at their government with contempt. It was the main topic of discussion in every corner of campus just as it would be tonight at the Emergency Board Meeting. It wasn't a regular session board meeting, this time everyone was invited to come and voice their opinion. Even Mr. Rickert, the FDA rep, and his partner were invited. The meeting was hastily put together and held in the Bunker's auditorium three days after Chancellor Gentry was arrested.

Professor Jing had taken over and seemed to be in charge. When it appeared like everyone who was supposed to be at the meeting was in attendance, he officially began. In a serious tone he got right to the point.

"This Academy is at a crossroad where our very existence is at stake... both as a member of this school, the Cadet organization, and even as citizens of the United States of America. If it wasn't clear to all of you before, it should be crystal clear to you now; the government has taken a step, albeit over a prolonged period, but a step that has positioned themselves so that they are now standing at a distance looking back at us from the other side of the red line. They are now squarely facing the very people they are sworn to protect. The result is sobering. They have defined us as the opposition, and they are starting an initiative to dismantle the Cadet organization.

I must inform you that there are some of our students and staff members who couldn't handle our side of the line, this 'reality' or the burden that comes with it. They decided to quit, opting to cut their ties and become as 'disconnected' with the situation as possible. About ten percent of the campus population, including some staff members, have packed up and left. I invite you to do the same if you feel so inclined, for if you have not already decided to dedicate yourself to our cause, we won't be in need of your presence".

There was a buzz around the audience as everyone digested that statement. Agent Rickert was there too along with his assistant. They both squirmed in their seats due to the way this meeting had pole-vaulted out of the box.

"One thing is certain, there will be more butting of heads with the government. We believe this is just the beginning. We have a government administrator in our midst right now that has been sent to 'help' us during Chancellor Gentry's leave of absence. We know his real capacity is to gather intelligence on this facility. In other words, he's a spy. He's in the audience now I believe. Agent Rickert? Where are you?".

Rickert raised his eyebrows, opened his mouth, and looked around like he was appalled.

"This man has already taken steps to shut us down and dismantle this school and its curriculum as it stands. He has stated, and I quote 'Mt. Tenny farm is in direct competition with commercial traffic and will not be allowed to compete with established businesses. People it has begun. They are going to shut us down in lieu of their good old boy corporations and businesses. The question is 'are we going to let them'? We are here tonight to decide a course of action and to determine what you, the student body, are willing to do about it".

FDA agent Rickert immediately stood up and walked briskly over to the podium in the center of the room and grabbed the microphone. He broke in and not only addressed the board in front of him but turned around to the audience as well. "My name is Rickert..." he said.

A "boo" welled up from the audience.

Professor Jing stood up and told everyone "People this is the government... ahh... representative".

The 'Boos' became louder and gurgled up from the crowd, Mr. Rickert changed tact quickly and made his point before the "boos" could build up into a significant problem.

"You people don't get it. We have a crisis here; businesses are going under. To protect them and direct more business their way we are eliminating small time competition. Don't' you see, this will be good for business and good for the community".

The audience responded with deep murmuring that built up into an even stronger reaction. "Boooo!" could be heard coming more strongly from people scattered around the audience.

Rickert got mad. "You fools..." he said directing his resentment to the ones who dared to show such disrespect. "...this will help keep them in business! You will always have a supplier to buy from! We will make sure they stay open".

Someone in the audience behind him stood up and yelled "At what price? Your price? Any price you feel like charging?" Another yelled "Yeah you and your good old boys, your company, your preferred cronies?".

The negative response accelerated as people started to stand up and shout. Something sailed through the air and just missed hitting Rickert's head. The administrator ducked and recognized that this had become hostile way too fast. He looked even more nervous yet allowed his frustration to bring him to the point where he almost continued his assault on their stupidity. But he thought better of it and was smart enough to see that it was time to make an exit before this really got out of hand. He held his tongue, threw the microphone down and walked briskly out with his assistant falling in close behind him.

Professor Jing apologized "Sorry about that but I had to get the first thing on our agenda out of our way". The audience laughed and then cheered and clapped like they had just won the first battle.

For the rest of the night many people spoke at the podium, yet it was far from boring. Everyone spoke passionately and everyone listening wanted desperately to hear the opinions of their peers and come to a consensus about what to do. Everything came to a head; years of frustration were laid out. The overwhelming majority thought that the direction this government was going couldn't go unchallenged. Some even talked about a revolution. A portion of the discussion evolved around the serious business of going down that road. Others wanted to petition the government. But one underlying view was clear; the government needed a course correction, and just how to steer this was the topic of heated debate. Yes, it had been the topic of debate for quite some time, but tonight the students made an internal decision that they had to finally do something about it.

It was typical; the student body was split into three factions with three different viewpoints with one clearly outweighing the other. One side proposed to get involved with the government in a more active political role to help enact policy that was more in line with established Constitutional boundaries. The other side spoke of failed policy and politicians who were "breaking the law" as it was. Strong opposition against cooperation was the dominant opinion, the majority was against allowing the government to shut the Academy down. The other third of them just didn't care one way or the other.

The next student speaker who stood up said it best. "Our politicians are violating and ignoring existing policy and basic human rights as it is. They're not just arresting people for what they've 'done', they're arresting people for what they 'might do' and their only crime is voicing their opinions! Opinions that happen to be in opposition to what the government is doing. So why would they follow new laws and new regulations if they're not following the laws we have on the books right now? Freedom of speech! What happened to that? We don't have freedom of speech in this country anymore. And the new flag with President Richardson's party emblem in the corner? This is exactly how it started in Germany with Hitler's Nazi party. The only way is to rise up and forcefully remove these people from office".

Another stood up and said "More policy won't matter! We must show that we are willing to fight for strict interpretation of our Constitution. The government's actions are inconsistent with its original intent. Our political opponents have become so entrenched in the system that it is now impossible to peacefully remove them. We have the right to change our leaders. Politicians are like diapers; they should be changed regularly and for the same reason!". It took a while before the laughter died down from that one. The man continued. "We must use force to oust those who seek to violate our rights and who strive to disregard our God given freedoms. The Constitution is the basis from which our freedoms thrive, and from which this country has thrived. When that is breached, when that is gone, we have been fundamentally altered and you can no longer describe American's as living in the 'land of the free' and the 'home of the brave'. Today is the day where fifty percent of that famous statement is no longer true! This is too much to bear; this is too much to lose! We have observed that our politicians have set us on a path toward socialism. Well, my friends; we are no longer just 'on the path'. We have arrived! And we are now being forced to live in a socialist state! For a long time, they have endeavored to ignore our rights and have secretly and openly promoted a Marxist style of rule. It has slowly filtered in; blanketing and smothering the founding fathers' spirit and original intent. They've taken our gun rights away and they've taken all the profit out of our business. The Union thugs won't even let us transport goods across state borders anymore! We're forced to bail out every country that has failed and pay for their workers' compensation. Bankers have run the banking system into the ground and bureaucrats continuously bail them out with trillions of dollars to the point where the dollar is now worthless in today's market. It's time we fight! We must fight with every means at our disposal before we are choked to the point where even fighting is impossible. If we don't do something now, together, then where will each one of you be when they come to get YOU when you're all alone with no one to help! For they will come, that is now obvious after all this. They came and got Major Monett and Chancellor Gentry. They're trying to eliminate what they believe to be the source of their opposition. Next is to force you to submit to their ideology. Are you ready for that? Or are you ready to fight? This has become as serious as it can get. It's time to respond".

"YEAH ALRIGHT! Woo, woo, woo!" the audience stood up and clapped and shouted with a loud long stream of enthusiasm.

"Then let's get it on! Restore our freedom! Restore it NOW!" The speaker shouted his last statement with a clenched fist in the air. The crowd cheered for a full two minutes straight. Professor Jing didn't even try to bring them to order.

After everyone settled down, what scared every one of them the most was the realization that it was now up to them, their generation. It was obvious that each American Citizen who shared the same love for America's original intent and its founding principles had to be called to action. It was the key to saving the essence of the country, which everyone agreed was held in reverence above all else. The continuation of the American free market system depended on it. They had to stand up and take action of one type or the other if they wanted to save the greatest country the world has ever known. That much was clear. It fell to them, and people like them. It fell upon this generation; it fell on their shoulders. Tonight, they voted overwhelmingly 825 to 142, to make a stand and keep the school running at all costs.

A secondary private meeting was held after the assembly broke up. A request had gone out over the loudspeaker that all attending board members and Cadet Officials meet in the conference room after the main vote. All through the night and well into the early morning hours the discussion continued. At around two thirty, decisions were finalized, and a preliminary course of action decided upon.

* * *

A light came on in the back of Kaiden's mind when he came too in the back seat of a strange car. There was a ringing in his ears, and he could barely see out of the slits in his eyes. His body ached all over. He could tell they were driving fast by the way the car was swaying and the lights and trees were zooming by. Not knowing where he was or who was driving was puzzling. He couldn't figure it out.

"What happened?" Kaiden thought he said it out loud but didn't know if it actually came out of his mouth. It didn't, what Romondo heard from the front seat was just a mumble. He leaned over the car's front seat and looked in the back; his face appeared within the realm of Kaiden's vision and hovered over him.

"Don't worry bro, help is on the way. Hang in there" Romondo told him. Just after he spoke the words Kaiden passed out again.

* * *

The next morning agent Rickert and the so-called Government Administrator came into the Academy's administration building on time at nine o'clock. Immediately he started running around the building with his bodyguard in tow barking out orders to the secretary and staff. Rickert had conferred with his superiors about last night's hostile meeting, and they decided to issue new directives to speed up the takeover of the Academy. With the way things were sounding it was imperative to move things along at a faster pace. They had studied the situation enough; Rickert was directed to start the process of dismantling the structure of the school by beginning the process of disbanding the Cadet organization.

"No more fooling around" Rickert thought. After that episode last night, he was determined to flex some muscle. The new directives from his boss spurred him on to do just that. A smile formed on his face backed by the knowledge that he didn't have to deal with any of that crowd who were so vehemently against him; he pictured their faces and reveled in the thought that he could take this place down from within without anyone being able to do anything about it.

"I'll smite you all" Rickert said out loud to no one in particular. Then he stormed out of his office. A minute later he stood at a desk in the accounting records room and directed the clerk sitting there to pull all the old files they had on the Cadet organization. He wanted to make sure he had everything in hand that he could have on the organization and was going to bring the old files up to his office to enter them in as evidence. He wanted to use them to dig deeper into the history of the people who ran this group. He needed to know more about how far the organization reached, and exactly what to do to break this institution down. When he looked up, staff members were standing around staring at him without responding to his demands. They just stood there looking at him with a blank stare. He repeated his demand but there was no reaction.

"You idiots, I'll get it myself then" he said as he walked over to the file room door. He tried to open it, but it was locked. "Open this door!" he demanded.

The clerk just shrugged his shoulders and gave him that same blank stare.

Rickert realized that this was evolving into a banner statement against his authority. He looked at one of the other staff members who was intimidated enough to inform him "I'm sorry sir; you don't have the clearance to access those files".

Frustrated beyond belief, he turned and stormed out of the room with his sidekick in tow and bee-lined it down the hallway to his office where he could place a private call.

"All right for you, you sons of a bitches" he said. Then he turned to his aid "I was hoping it wouldn't come to this, but I guess I'm going to need a little more muscle. I'll get them in the end, oh I will. No matter what!" he said with a flare of anger. He passed the secretary standing at her desk. Mary just stood there looking at him incredulously as if she pitied him.

Agent Rickert stared at her indignantly as he passed her desk and went back into the Chancellor's office. He was so enveloped in his own anger that when he walked in, he didn't see anyone sitting at his desk. He closed the door, turned around and was quite startled when he looked up. As his vision expanded, he saw two people standing on each side of his desk. Rickert had come to consider the desk to be "his". They all stared at him in a way which gave him pause.

"What is the meaning of this? Don't you make appointments…?".

"Like you did the day you arrived?" It was Captain Phillips, head of campus security. He spoke while sitting in the Chancellors chair with his hands folded in front of him and his elbows resting on the desk.

"I don't need an appointment; I'm acting head of this Academy appointed by the Federal government to oversee its…".

"...Destruction?". Phillips finished the sentence for him. On one side of the desk stood Captain Oberman, on the other stood Professor Jing. All three of them stared at Rickert decisively with a cool sense of confidence.

At that moment there were strong voices coming from outside the door in the secretary's office. Rickert quickly opened the door with the intent of calling his sidekick in for support. He was going to ask his guests to leave, and if there was any trouble, he'd... but what he saw shocked him. His bodyguard was standing in the middle of the reception area surrounded by four Cadets in uniform. He was protesting loudly as two Cadets manhandled him. Two of them held his arms; a third was cuffing his hands behind his back while another stood in front frisking him. They found a concealed weapon in an ankle holster and immediately confiscated it. They escorted him out of the office with the man looking over his shoulder yelling at Rickert for help.

One of the Cadets stayed behind. He turned around, folded his arms across his chest and stood in the middle of the doorway. Rickert didn't have to ask, he knew what was happening. He slammed the office door shut, cutting off the dominant stare of the Cadet in the only act of defiance he had at his disposal. Then he turned back to face his adversaries. He took an aggressive step toward them as if that would somehow strengthen his position. "What do you think you're doing, you fools! Do you think that somehow you have the power to stop us? You and your little band of insignificant rebels will be wiped out with just one phone call. I'll see to that!".

Captain Phillips stood up and matched the administrator's aggressive action with his own. He strolled around the desk and walked right up to Rickert and got in his face.

"You let 'your people' know that from this point on your assistance is no longer needed here. Security!" he called. The security officer opened the office door and entered the room. "Please escort Mr. Rickert along with his assistant off the property. Mr. Rickert, your job here has been terminated. Do not come back or I'll have you arrested for trespassing and throw you in the stockade if you do".

Rickert was so mad that a vein bulged out on his forehead from the pressure building up inside. He was unable to speak or even act. Before he realized it, a security officer was standing next to him pulling on his elbow and motioning him towards the door. He stood there breathing heavily, staring at Captain Phillips without knowing what to say or who he could call that might be able to turn this situation around and end this contest of power. Captain Phillips signaled by nodding his head toward the officer and the officer ended the stalemate by grabbing Rickert's arm. Rickert pulled his arm away sharply and paused looking around angrily at all four of them. It looked like he was about to say something but instead concluded that there wasn't anything he could do about it. Rickert turned and walked briskly out the door.

The four Cadet Security officers escorted the two government officials to their car and were about to follow them to the front gate in their own campus security vehicle when Rickert rolled down the car window.

"The gun?" he demanded with his hand out.

"That gun is an illegal firearm sir. It's got a magazine with more than a five-round capacity. I'm going to have to confiscate it".

"That is government property..."

"Bill us" the Cadet said.

31

No Way, New Way

In the Chancellor's office, Captain Phillips spoke to Captain Oberman and issued the directives that were sanctioned by the board during last nights' emergency meeting. The direction they were taking had been defined and their course of action empowered by the overwhelming vote from the student body. There would be a few changes made around campus starting immediately.

A temporary guardhouse was ordered to be constructed at the intersection of Mt. Tenny Rd and Academy Drive. The Academy's Board members were already looking to contract for a permanent structure but ordered the small shed to be installed immediately "Until a permanent one could be arranged" they said. Within days a small wooden shed appeared in the middle of the road at the entrance to Academy Drive. Lines had been painted on the pavement to direct cars to either side of it. The shed was just big enough to house two guards. In it was a short desk and a small closet with a composting toilet, the latter chosen because it didn't' require any plumbing. Two exterior doors were installed to allow access to both lanes of traffic on each side. A long plastic PVC pipe was used as the arm for the barrier. It had a thick diameter section at its base and a smaller diameter from the mid-way point on out. The sections were glued together and painted with black stripes. One was installed on both sides of the road and for now it would be manually operated until a permanent electric gate could be set up. Both were a pain in the ass to use so the exit barrier was hardly ever closed for that reason.

"Due to recent events, I want two Ops' (observation posts) set up..." Captain Phillips was saying as he walked over to a large map of Tenny Hill that hung on the wall. He showed Captain Oberman two approximate locations. This one's about a mile from the front gate... "I want it around here. Place it on this ridge by the front access road and here on the back side of Tenny Mountain to cover our back door. Both need to overlook the road at a distance where we can obtain about a twelve-minute warning of any traffic from either end. Oh, make sure they cover them with thermal protection to hide their signature from above. From these points I calculate a possible sixteen-minute warning if they come through the back door and a twelve to fifteen-minute warning from the front. See if you agree and feel free to adjust the locations to make it so.

Cadets will man the OPs round the clock. Use your best men and keep it a tight knit circle of trusted people only. Keep the locations and the fact that we are observing, a secret. It won't do us much good if the enemy knows we're there. Use a minimum of two observers and back em' up with an electronic warning, one down on the front gate as well. Camouflage them smartly so nothing can be seen. Cut a trail between the OP and the front gate and between the OP and Security's central office here. Do not make the trail entrance points obvious; see what you can do to hide them. Create a main gate check point at the entrance to Academy Drive and man it twenty-four. We don't need to be able to defend it so much as we need to be able to stall anyone looking to roar in here quickly. I want a soft barricade built with a more solid movable barricade available that can be rolled into place quickly when needed. You'll have to be able to set up an effective blockade within the twelve-minute window and any barricade design should be able to effectively inhibit or detain the flow of traffic through that point. Run a com line between the three of us, the front gate, the OP, and security headquarters too as a backup in case the phones and or BeepX goes down. I want to know who's comin and who's goin and be able to screen out the people who don't belong here. From now on, no more surprises".

In the approximate location that Captain Phillips indicated the two observation posts were set up the very next day. Permanent trails to the locations would be cut through the woods and marked once the locations had proven themselves to be effective. For now, they would simply set up camouflaged hunting blinds and mark a temporary trail. Oberman's patrol was able to find sites that were selectively chosen due to their ability to overlook about a quarter mile stretch of unobstructed roadway at both the front and rear approaches to the property. Over time they planned to dig in and upgrade the OP by building a bunker style hide complete with a berm and natural vegetation as camouflage.

No one could predict what the government's reaction would be, but the majority agreed that it wasn't necessary to arm the guards at the Academy's front gate. An early warning system was the main goal. The transformation of the front gate wouldn't be quick; this might take a week of work to complete. The Lock Construction Company was contracted to install one-way road spikes and an electronic gate where a vehicle could drive out but couldn't drive back in without losing all its tires. The only problem was that the company estimated that it might take three months to get the equipment installed. No solid date of completion could be given, everything revolved around the availability of product and only then could an actual delivery date be set. Until then the Academy would have to make do with a temporary wooden gatehouse and a pull up barricade that would be used until a permanent structure was built. It would be manned by two Cadets around the clock from this moment on, all incoming traffic would be scrutinized, and IDs checked. The campus was put on 'alert 4' status which just meant that security was now in 'serious' mode.

* * *

Lyle Koneham, head of the ATF, brought in Special Agent Mallory Hicks to Washington DC for a briefing on Tenny Hill Academy. After the run-in with IRS representative Rickert, the Academy popped up on the agency's radar. It came down from high up that something needed to be done to stem the flow of resistance to the government's policies. Immediate action was prescribed for this case.

It was a meaningful trip for Mallory who walked across the huge Homeland Security symbol embedded in the marble floor right at the entrance to the building. "You can't walk across that without being inspired" he thought as his shoes touched it.

Agent Hicks found himself in a plush office sitting across from the boss of his boss. He had a file on his desk and the man was leafing through it as he spoke. "Agent Mallory Hicks, thank you for accepting the assignment. I'm getting pressure from some especially important people to take care of this so I'm glad that I have someone I can count on to get the job done. I am assigning you as the AIC on this one. Are you Ok with that?

"Yes sir, I am ready to go".

After a moment of awkward silence Lyle Koneham looked up from the file and said "They call themselves the 'Cadet's', somehow, they got the state to license the organization, but we know they've turned it into a full-fledged 'Militia'. Just yesterday they were added to the domestic terrorist list, and we believe that they are the ones behind the attacks on legal roadblocks in the central New York area as well as supporting other covert activities. We suspect that they are the ones behind the hijackings too. I see here that the IRS is extremely interested in this case. They've cited multiple violations of the tax code.

These people have an accredited school in the Catskills; somehow, they've been influenced and taken over by this militia organization. They masquerade as an 'Academy' while promoting dissention against the Federal Government, they openly practice above ground militia training exercises and I'm looking into evidence of an underground network as well. They revere liberty, are against taxes and hold the constitution up as their bible, especially the Second Amendment.

Full-fledged constitution thumpers for sure. The Militia has multiple violations of gun laws and there have been two arrests so far of individuals involved with the possession of illegal firearms. The school is actively engaged in the trade of canned agriculture products, and they are suspected of using gold and silver as monetary exchange. That's what's got the IRS on their ass; of course, they're interested in this case from a tax evasion standpoint.

All the above are highly illegal. On top of that they have resisted the insertion of an IRS administrator who went undercover as a representative of the FDA. They used the acronym 'FDA' to draw less attention. The DT's (domestic terrorists) sent the guy packing just a few days ago".

"Well, they fit the definition of domestic terrorists to a tee" Agent Hicks commented. "I didn't know that the IRS sent administrators in to work with companies".

"They've been doing that for quite a while now. But normally they send in real administrators, in this case the FDA administrator was an IRS agent named Rickert. Looks like we've had to resort to undercover operations to try and get more tangible evidence on these people" Koneham said.

"Without success?" Hicks asked while raising his eyebrows.

"They're a tightly woven well organized group that looks completely legit on the surface. It has required additional resources above and beyond standard procedures to dig deeper and find the crime. They surprised us, but we know that the rabbit hole goes deeper.

Hicks, we can't let this get out of hand. The ATF wants to step up efforts to disband this Militia and the IRS wants to confiscate the property".

"What are they delinquent on their taxes?".

"Not in this case, but the higher ups want this taken care of. Even the President's gotten involved; it's priority one coming down directly from him. He wants to nip this problem along with others before it becomes a major force to be reckoned with. I'm sending you in because you're familiar with these procedures, I'm entrusting you with the job.

We figured that to do this with force would require men, money, and assets that we would like to retain for other more important endeavors like what's going on down in Florida. Right now, the State of Florida is threatening to secede from the Union with others threatening to follow their lead. We might have another civil war on our hands if they do".

Hicks was flipping through his copy of the file they had on the Academy unmoved by the bombshell dropped by Koneham about the threat of a Civil War.

"Why don't you just bring in the National Guard and get it done with?" Hicks asked directly.

"Thought about it, but we're short on personnel and assets. Most of the Guard has been sent to the Middle East and North Africa. Besides, we don't think this will require all that. We don't want the place destroyed and we don't want any publicity. The IRS has stuck their two cents in too, they want to inherit the property in good condition, you know, for resale value. Remember the uproar about bringing in the Guard after the Chicago Mall massacre? They blew up the entire building getting those people out, killed a lot of civilians doing it too. That mall may never be rebuilt".

"It wouldn't have gotten so out of hand if they hadn't declared martial law and stayed on. I just read a report on it. Since the incident, the police have shot and killed an average of forty-three people… a week. They're still patrolling the streets of Chicago as we speak. It's a war zone out there" Hicks said.

"Exactly, and we don't want another war zone here. We think there's an easier way to do this" Lyle replied.

"Yes, sir I understand. How have we been getting our intel on this organization?".

"We have an undercover agent enrolled at the school. His name's Remy Horton. But so far, he's been unable to get us any incriminating details on the underground. We'd like to have that before we take them down. And we figured you could do it with a little more finesse than the National Guard. Your job is to get all the names of these domestic terrorists and the evidence we need to prosecute. Hicks you've been ordered to disrupt and disband this organization ASAP".

"Yes sir, I can handle it".

"Good, I wanted to get your commitment before I told you about my little side note, I need you to investigate IRS statements about the hoarding of gold and silver. The IRS says that they've been paying some of their employees with gold and silver coins and trading it for years now. See if you can find their horde, I want it confiscated and its contents brought to me immediately. Don't let the IRS get it understand?".

"I see, yeah using gold for monetary transfer is illegal sir" Hicks stated.

"Not if it's spent at face value it isn't, but the IRS is complaining about the inherent loophole. State law in Utah, South Carolina, Colorado, Georgia, and others have allowed gold and silver coins as monetary exchange for years now. It's perfectly legal if the coins are passed off at face value..."

"Then what's the beef?" Hicks asked.

"First, New York's not one of those States and for good reason. Let's say the Academy paid an employee with a one ounce $50 gold piece. That's legal yes but you me and the IRS know that an ounce of gold is worth $2,943 in today's market. The person receiving it can legally claim they received $50 as income and then turn around and sell the coin for thousands without paying taxes on it. We suspect that that's exactly what they're doing. Or at least it's what the IRS believes these people at the Academy have been doing; they're breaking the law and evading taxes on these transactions. Yes, it's an IRS problem but we can use IRS resources to put some pressure on the Academy which will help take down the Militia. We believe if we take out the bank that's funding them, the Militia will fall without much effort at all. Besides it's those people we really want anyway. Any confiscation of gold will pay us back for the effort. First and foremost- find and identify the people involved, have plans ready to take them down, use force as a last resort. If you encounter armed resistance, then you are authorized to use whatever force you need to address that. But please, we do not want this operation to become another Waco Texas or Chicago mall massacre is that clear. We don't need to go in with drones and guns blaring, this is a simple matter. We should easily be able to take these clowns down just by removing their leaders and their source of income. I don't want this to end up in the public eye as an attack by the government against law abiding citizens. And Hicks... try not to turn this into a major raid that ends up with a lot of dead agents or dead 'students', which would be even worse. If casualties occur, make sure you feed the media so that they are described as dead terrorists. Let's prove these people to be criminals and present our case especially in the court of public opinion, then we can move on them more aggressively with anonymity. I'm just trying to cover all my bases here".

"Yes sir. What resources can I count on?".

"You will have a limited budget. Things aren't flowing down from above like they used to. The whole damn country is going down the tubes. Those damn Republicans: they've pushed through spending cuts that are cutting our resources to the bone. Revenues are down, that's why the government is going after people like this. I've been asked to make some significant cuts in our department and your boss is feeling the pinch. If you perform well here Hicks, I can personally assure you 'job security'. You'll always have a place in the ATF.

Luckily, we acquired all that SWAT equipment, armored cars, bullet proof vests, full auto weapons and over a billion rounds of ammunition with stimulus money years ago. You'll have access to a helicopter, a technical surveillance vehicle, a BearCat armored troop carrier and as much ammunition as you need but that's about it. I don't have any more assets I can put into this at the moment. We're busy on all fronts. Besides you won't need them. As I said, this is a simple matter of closing a school so please don't screw this up! Don't count on the calvary showing up to help you either, do it smart. Deal with this with the available agents in your area and get any assistance you can from local police. Agent Hicks..." Koneham said with emphasis "Remember the Alamo".

"I understand sir".

"Oh yes, you'll have an IRS Agent along as an observer..." he looked down at the files "... ah, it's IRS Agent Rickert. He requested the assignment. He'll be contacting you to assist in this endeavor. Give him your full cooperation. That is all, keep me informed of your progress".

"Yes sir".

* * *

Captain Phillips got an immediate urgent phone call from the FDA within hours of the expulsion of their agent. They requested a meeting and offered to discuss the situation to find out why their representative wasn't working out. The meeting occurred two days later:

"Captain Phillips, Professor Jing, thank you for meeting with us to straighten out what must be a huge misunderstanding. I am Agent Mallory Hicks with the ATF, you already know Mr. Rickert from the FDA, I also have with me Mr. Murray Adel from the FDA, and this is Mr. Creaton from Proclamation Insurance Company's compliance division. Hicks purposely paused to let that sink in as he and the other three associates sat down in chairs across the desk from them.

Hicks had contacted the insurance agency and the FDA and brought them in on this to apply as much pressure against the Academy as he could. Manpower from multiple agencies would go a long way to help make his point. The IRS was already on the case and not too happy that the ATF was now involved but they were willing to join forces to bring this situation to a profitable conclusion.

The meeting was held in the Chancellors office in the Administration building. The memory of getting kicked out the last time was still burning in the synapses of Rickert's mind.

Hicks didn't know it, but his car was one of the first that the newly established OP had picked up and identified as an incoming concern. From the new OP located on the ridge above Mt. Tenny Road and through a fine set of X-12 Benelli binoculars, his men observed an incoming Ford Taurus missing the green THA campus parking sticker in the upper left-hand corner of its windshield. After spotting the government license plate a shout of "Incoming" triggered an immediate phone call to security. When he got word, Captain Phillips timed their arrival to see how well his OP and early warning system worked. He smiled when they arrived right at the anticipated twelve-minute MRT (minimum reaction time). For the first time they had confirmed the gap on an actual unannounced visitor.

"Thank you for meeting with us and actually making an appointment this time" Professor Jing said. He couldn't help but stick that one in and glanced at Rickert as he said it.

Agent Hicks disregarded the professor's comment and proceeded to launch into pleasantries designed to defuse the tension in the air and then got to the point. "As I said Captain Phillips, Mr. Creaton here is from Proclamation Insurance. I'm sure you're aware that he's representing the insurance company that carries your liability insurance for the Academy". Hicks motioned to Mr. Creaton to proceed.

"Mr. Phillips..." Mr. Creaton began.

"That's Captain Phillips" the Captain corrected him.

"Ah yes, Captain Phillips. Well, Proclamation Insurance is a government owned subsidiary which must obey current laws for issuance policy coverage as all government agencies are relinquished to do. I'm sure you understand. I need to ask you; do you still operate a gun range on premises?".

"Yes, we do".

"I'm afraid I must inform you that the new law states that we cannot issue insurance for this property if guns are contained within the liable sector coverage area. We have overlooked this in the past but from this point forward..." he glanced over at Hicks "...the possession of firearms on the property will be cause for automatic termination of your mortgage liability insurance".

Hicks backed him up "Captain Phillips, you are hereby notified that Tenny Hill Academy must vacate all firearms and close the range on premises within seven days or face cancellation of coverage".

Captain Phillips listened and sat there with an unaffected look on his face for a long moment. Then he responded. "Mr. Creaton, cancel our insurance and send us a refund check for the balance of the year. We are no longer in need of your companies' services".

Mr. Creaton looked around shocked. He wasn't expecting that at all. He was used to his clients squirming under pressure and scurrying to find ways to satisfy his demands. "But Mr. Phillips, the lender requires you to have liability insurance. You just can't cancel your insurance; the lender will drop you...".

"Mr. Creaton, leave that to us, at this very moment we are planning to make a major final payment on our loan which would satisfy our obligation. From this point on we will be self-insured and will no longer need to comply with your rules and regulations. Please cancel our policy. I'll give you the request in writing before you leave". Captain Phillips looked around defiantly and said "What else can I do for you gentlemen?".

Creaton gave Hicks a "bolt from the blue" look. Hicks glared at the Captain indignantly. The first salvo of his attack had been defused, but then he smiled and sat back in his chair knowing the screws had only begun to turn.

"Alright, let's change the subject" Hicks said. "Mr. Adel will you discuss the FDA's point of view please".

"Yes certainly. Um, Captain, we know you had problems with our previous envoy Mr. Rickert here. I assure you he was just trying to work with the Academy to implement the new federal laws concerning food production. I have spoken with Mr. Gentry in the past about this same issue but being that Gentry is no longer here I must take this opportunity to speak to you and impress upon you the new rules and regulations that apply to your situation".

Captain Phillips didn't change the expression on his face or move to acknowledge the FDA rep at all. There was a long moment of silence with no reaction.

Adel cleared his throat and continued... "Ah we know that Mt. Tenny Farms is producing various items that you are selling on the black market...".

Professor Jing jumped in "Excuse me, the black market?" he said with raised eyebrows.

"Yes, you call it the 'flea market'. Same thing. Anything sold in a non-licensed environment like that is illegal. Produce can only be sold by approved licensed facilities that have satisfied the insurance requirements and have installed proper safety and sterilization equipment. This is to protect the public from botulism outbreaks and salmonella poisoning of course. Anything grown on unlicensed farms will be considered contraband and will be dealt with accordingly.

"But we've never had any poisonings" the professor said. "I know of no instances in the entire county".

"Yes, there has been but no matter, it's the law. We also know you are participating in illegal commerce on the black-market Professor, and I am here to tell you to cease and desist. What you're doing is illegal, so consider yourself warned. But I'm not here to slap fines on you for past transgressions, we are reasonable people and we're here to help you. I can get you the license you need and guide you in setting up the proper equipment to conform to the new regulations. That's why you need our help. I'm sure you won't be happy about the $9,200 license fee but if we can get past that the rest of it's a piece of cake".

The professor and the Captain glanced at each other with incredulous looks on their faces wondering why they were still entertaining this charade.

Professor Jing spoke up first "Mr. Adel, I know the cost of some of the ultraviolet sterilization equipment that the FDA requires for sterilizing milk and beef, I also know about some of the upgrades we would have to make to our kitchens such as the installation of an all 'professional commercial grade ventilation system'. Then we have the upgrades, which in our case would be the installation of larger pipes and new fire suppression sprinkler heads to replace the old on our existing fire suppression system. Not to mention the additional sprinkler heads that must be installed as per the new spacing regulations. These upgrades alone would cost the school somewhere in the neighborhood of $175,000. And I'm sure there are other regulations that you will inform us of that will only add to that figure. We are still reeling from the effects of 'guv cov' health care which has made our health insurance cost twice as much as it had before. Then on top of that there are the new regulations on employment. We are forced to pay laborers $22 per hour, kitchen staff $27 and managers no less than $39. They are then forced to join the Union and pay dues each month. We're not allowed to cross hire, meaning a farm laborer cannot work as a cook and a cook cannot work as a cleaner. And the new rule where there must be one paid worker for every volunteer? What the hell is up with that! How do you expect a small farm to afford to do this without going out of business?".

Hicks interjected "Guv Cov' as you call it has been documented to be less expensive. Besides, those of us who can afford it should pay more so that those who can't, can have insurance too. Isn't that the American way... to help others in need?".

Captain Phillips couldn't help but comment. "Let me be the one to inform you that it would be 'the American way' if the money was given freely, by one's own free will. This is nothing more than a forced contribution which equates to the re-distribution of wealth through taxes. It's a socialist concept that is far from the 'American way'. The cost of the policy is only cheaper for about forty percent of the population; the other sixty percent pay a whole lot more than they were paying under the old system. But that's beside the point; the main problem now is that every employee must be covered by the Academy...".

Hicks broke in "Ah and isn't that a good thing Professor. Now everyone is covered".

"Well before the government got involved everyone had access to healthcare too, only they had the freedom to purchase it on their own. If it wasn't supplied by their employer, they could simply buy it themselves".

"But Professor it was way too expensive! Hicks broke in again. "The government had to step in and help change that".

"Help? That is precisely my point, too expensive for whom? That is the real question. Previously an employer had the ability to add that cost in as consideration upon determining the dollar paid per hour for any employee. If the cost of the benefit was let's say two dollars per hour, then the employer could pay the employee two dollars an hour less to cover the cost. Benefits were always intended to be included as part of an employee's pay, not in addition to it. Now with the minimum wage at the levels they're at, an employer can't pay someone less to cover any additional expense. It places the full burden of the benefit's cost right on the company's shoulders".

"Yes, and that's exactly where it should be!" Hicks countered.

"Well now the Academy is forced to pay for everyone's insurance out of the profits we make. Since everyone is now covered, our total health care expenditures have gone up by a staggering seventy-five percent".

"...and that's a good thing Professor" Rickert chimed in. "That's a good thing for all the workers out there who are struggling to pay their bills. You and all those corporations out there make too much profit from your services anyway. You can afford it. Besides shouldn't you be contributing more for the good of the community anyway?".

"You are wrong on every point except the fact that we should be contributing more to the community. This government policy doesn't just affect the corporations you speak of, and now we get to the crux of my argument. It hits the small mom and pop businesses and the farmers even harder. Their expenses go up and their profit goes down. As if they weren't struggling before, they sure are struggling for their survival now. So, they try to make up for it with higher prices but as you know, people can't afford higher prices therefore sales diminish, and no one wins".

"Yeah, thank God the government has stepped in and set prices for some of those items. Thank God for some semblance of control that keeps things in the realm of affordable" Hicks said.

"But the effect that has is now there's no way that farmers can raise prices to recoup the loss. The result is that they go out of business or just stop growing that item commercially. And here we are with the shortages of food that this type of policy causes. All of us are paying exorbitant prices for everything".

"Professor Jing" Hicks said leaning forward in his chair. "If the Academy cannot afford to produce food according to the law, then you shouldn't be in the business of producing it. It's not fair for everyone else".

Jing threw his hands up and sat back in his chair "Oh my god, your only reaction is 'it's not fair' and 'get out of the business'? Since it's not 'fair', then you must make it so that none of us can do it? Don't you see this is exactly why we have such shortages of food and supplies? You're choking us off to the point where we can't produce for the good of the community. You just said your regulations were designed to protect the community but here you are functioning as the main cause of the problem".

Rickert said "I can't speak to that Professor Jing, but I know the supply problems will iron themselves out in time. For example: as you know 'Sanmonto' is the official supplier of seed, pesticides, and fertilizer for the US now, all purchases must go through them…".

The Professor broke in "Sanmonto only sells genetically modified seeds…".

Rickert explained "Yes of course, how can a seed company stay in business if everyone can produce their own seeds for free? This just ensures that business flows back to the parent company. They supply you; we supply them. We need them. I'm sure everyone knows how important food is. We just can't let a company of this size and of this importance go out of business. Besides by selling specific types of seed to select farmers each year we can more effectively balance the type and amounts of crops that are grown. You can apply for the types of crops you want to grow but the final say will be in the type and quantity of seed you are allowed to purchase. This way we don't have an over production of certain items but can maintain a uniform growth of products all along the market spectrum…".

"What you mean to say is that the government now has complete control over the previously 'free' agricultural market sector". Professor

Jing said without being able to hide his contempt for the man and his regulations.

"Oh no, no, no listen, I'm not here to butt heads with you on philosophy. That has been decided long ago by people a lot smarter than me…".

Captain Phillips broke in without letting him finish "Yes but I am here today Mr. Rickert, caught between a rock and a hard place, because we are butting heads not only on philosophy, but directly due to your violation of free market principles, principles that have proven historically to have produced the richest economy ever achieved in the world to date. What you and your cronies are engineering is a complete dismantling of that system and our ability to generate a profit. Don't you realize that profit is what allows individuals and corporations to contribute to the greater good of the community? I thought you just said that's what we should be doing?".

"I don't mind you making a profit as long as it's not 'excessive'" Hicks sneered.

Jing got visibly upset. He slammed his hand down on the table "That's the problem with you people, you think you have the right to tell us how much we're allowed to make…".

"Jing hold on, hold on" Captain Phillips tried to reign him in, but the professor continued.

"…The 'free market system' was chosen and promoted by people way smarter than the political hacks you just eluded too".

Hicks was done addressing the professor's comments, he turned to Phillips "Captain no need for disparage. I think the only thing this great country of ours has produced is the very profit you speak of which has led to run away greed which led to the downfall of the very system you are now propping up on a pedestal like it has done no wrong".

The professor stuck his two cents in "Speaking of 'doing no wrong', the first thing out of your mouth concerning the benefits of your strategy was that it didn't create any over production. Do you realize that over production in a free market creates prices that drop dramatically?

All you have done is guaranteed that consumers will pay inflated prices consistently at all times of the year".

Agent Hicks tapped his pen on the note pad he held in his lap after getting an indication about how this meeting was going to go, then he said calmly "I can't do anything about the laws Captain Phillips, but as with you, I am entrusted with enforcing them. It is my job to make sure that your facility is not in violation. I need to check your inventory and determine if you are in possession of illegal seeds as well as to make sure you are not growing the items on this list". He slid a piece of paper onto the desk in front of the Captain for him to read. Then after a moment, Hicks slid another piece of paper in front of the Captain on top of that one.

Captain Phillips turned to the professor "I just got a feeling of de ja vu Professor, didn't you?".

"Yeah, all this seems a little familiar" Jing said. "Just like the conversation our Chancellor had with you Rickert on the day you came in here and started harassing us".

Phillips immediately recognized the photograph in front of him as an aerial shot of the fields at Mt. Tenny Farms. It must have been taken last summer by a drone. Apparently, the government was still using satellite mapping technology that had been banned from public use. All satellite viewing systems had been taken down because they had become classified as a potential "terrorist tool". Through the Patriot Act, they had been removed from view for the good and safety of the public.

Hicks went on... "We need to bring this facility up to current standards and I need your help to implement the laws we have on the books now. For example, we calculate that you are growing seventy-five acres of corn in the area marked on the photograph. By law you are only allowed to grow twenty-five acres of corn".

"What! This is crazy!" Professor Jing cried out in protest.

"I think it's rather generous Professor" Hicks said with a pompous flare. "Small businesses and homes aren't even allowed to grow corn at all but with a facility of your size and the fact that you are a large corporation, you qualify for a twenty-five-acre maximum. You should be grateful".

"And what happens if an entity such as ours makes the mistake of growing twenty-six acres of corn Mr. Rickert?"

"Well, you will be held in violation of the Federal Food and Drug Standardization act. The people involved could be arrested and I will confiscate your stock and burn the illegal field" he raised his eyebrows. "But come on now, it's not going to come down to that now, is it? I'm sure we can reach an agreement for the good of the community".

Jing said to Phillips "There's that 'good of the community' again. I love how these guys talk". He turned and said to Agent Hicks "You don't really mean that we actually come to an agreement, at least not one that is mutually equitable, what you really mean is that we must come to agree with 'you' don't you".

Mr. Adel acted like he hadn't heard that and continued reading from the papers in front of him "Now on another note, as required by law and again due to the size of your facility it is required to have a FDA field office and a field officer on premises on a full-time basis. The new rule is that the officer is required to become your employee and he is to be placed on your payroll. We apologize that Mr. Rickert wasn't working out. I have brought him back here today so we can discuss how to integrate him more adequately into the Academy in a more acceptable manner.

"No" Captain Phillips said without diverting his eyes from Agent Hicks.

"What do you mean 'No' Captain? This is not negotiable it's required by…".

"I mean No. No one from the FDA or anywhere else is allowed to come onto these premises and set up residence. Not without our permission. If anyone from your office is found to be setting up here, I will arrest him, confiscate his gun and burn your 'field'… office".

"Cute Captain, but I don't think my superiors will think very highly of threats. Let's avoid the repercussions of a stance like that and …".

"Agent Hicks..." Captain Phillips said. He spoke with a deep breath and a sigh "Please inform your superior that I have your list of demands and I will pass it on to my superiors for consideration". He stood up. "This meeting is over. My people will escort you out".

Hicks stood up too. "I'm not done yet Captain" he said in a stern voice. "There's more that we need to go over". It was a tense standoff that Hicks was going to make sure he won. "I'm going to inform you now that Mr. Rickert here is not actually here from the FDA's office, he's actually with the IRS...".

"Yes, we know. It's still 'no' Mr. Hicks, especially if he's with the IRS" the Captain spoke and then turned to Mr. Rickert "Now even more so... we're done".

Hicks shot him a cold glance that hung in the air for a long moment. You could see the debate going on in his mind and his tact change as he concluded that the Captain was serious. The pressure built up until he spat it out through clenched teeth "You ungrateful leaching mother fuckers!" he glanced at the professor too. "All of you! You think you can refuse the office of the ATF and the IRS? This will have major repercussions for all you phony freedom loving patriots!".

The scene repeated itself. The door to the office opened behind them and Sergeant Pointer entered with two guards. Rickert turned and looked at them. He canceled the speech he was about to launch into, stood up and said "OK, have it your way Phillips. This was my last attempt to do it equitably. Now it will go down my way". He quickly grabbed his things, threw his coat over his arm and once again stormed out.

Hicks followed but couldn't resist, before he left, he turned around and said one last thing. "The only problem with it ending like this Captain is that when I come back it will not be a cordial visit".

Captain Phillips responded "As far as I am concerned agent Rickert, this wasn't a cordial visit". He allowed them to leave without uttering the comment that burned on the tip of his tongue.

* * *

Everything was on the up and up for Roy Atkinson and the IRS-ART. His boss, Anthony Knowles, was back on his good side. Changes he had made to the operation started showing up as increased revenue on the bottom line of the weekly reports he submitted. "Results! Results! Results!" That's all his boss ever talked about. Now his teams were bringing in millions of dollars' worth of recovered assets each month without so much as a negative headline on the front page of the news. Roy had fine-tuned the team's recovery policies and honed their techniques until they were running as smooth as a grocery store cash register. His teams no longer relied on local law enforcement; now they were made up of recruits pulled from either ex-military, ex cops, mercenaries, or direct appointments from his boss. "Appointment" was a polite way of saying "forced to hire". Those in that category made up most of his recent recruits. The sharks smelled money and started swimming ever closer to his operation. Chinese beneficiaries all seemed to have a friend or a friend of a friend that needed a job. There was no shortage of Asians who wanted to participate in taking wealth away from Americans. Asian recruits now made up about half of his team's roster.

Roy, as well as many of the American members, couldn't stand it. Besides the fact that many of them didn't speak English, Roy suspected that they were somehow stealing a portion of the jewels, cash and coins. It was getting to the point where Roy believed that this was the main reason why they were hired. It was evident that the Chinese were inserting members of their military into the operation to infiltrate and gain a foothold into this highly profitable business. It also gave the people involved the ability to "skim" profits off the top. But there wasn't anything he could do about it nor did he feel compelled too. If his bosses didn't care, then why should he?

One of his team leaders was of Chinese descent, his name was Shenki Kadisu. Originally Kadisu was assigned to the team as a G5 entry level agent at the request of an influential Chinese beneficiary. But no one acquired the position of leader unless they earned it. From the start Kadisu exhibited traces of an "A" type personality that set him off like a greyhound after a rabbit on each assignment. The ability to effectively implement tactics and bring the tools of the trade to bear on numerous successful conclusions got him the job. Most likely he was military; positively he was an asshole.

Most Chinese when they come over to America, adopt an 'American' first name, not Kadisu. If you weren't part of his team, he insisted you called him by his full name Shenki Kadisu. If you were a member of his team, you didn't call him at all, he called you. He wasn't interested in adopting anything that smelled American except if it had the aroma of money. The guy was hard core. He was strict and gung-ho on busting ass whenever he could during recovery operations. At first his dedication and skills were appreciated, but once Roy promoted him to TL (team leader) his demeanor became downright belligerent. He had little finesse when it came to dealing with his men, and even less with clientele. It was either his way or the highway and that was the last place any of them wanted to be. The Americans did their best to put up with him. Besides, his strict no-nonsense approach meant he got the job done and so far, no one's gotten killed under his command.

After five months of operation the IRS had sixty-five teams operating in forty-six cities with more to come. Some teams doubled up on the larger cities and some would be flown to various locations for special recovery missions. The missions ranged from small single-family homes to large commercial properties to wealthy estates. No one was exempt from the wrath of the IRS hit teams. After a property was secured a secondary holding crew would come in, take over the assets and relieve the initial recovery team. They secured, held, and maintained the property until the estate could be sold off.

* * *

It was in the news yesterday. President Richmond pushed the "button" and shut down all four of the major ISP's with more to follow. He pledged to purge the airwaves of misinformation, lies and deceit while claiming to be protecting the American people from "mendacity". Their plan was coming together nicely for the Progressive Socialists.

The government had tentacles growing into Oil, Healthcare, Agriculture, Gun, and the communication industries. But "don't worry" the president said, "It's all for the good of the people".

Shutting down the internet was inevitable. Internet content had already been restricted through a campaign by big brother to stem the tide of stolen information posted by whistle blowers. Back in 2010 Edward Snowden started it all. He fled to Russia after exposing evidence of the NSA's spying techniques on the American people and was just the first of many high-profile cases. There has been a growing number of them ever since. All involved are called "traitors" by the government and "heroes" by the people whose eyes have been opened by what they had discovered the government was doing. Since then, there has been a steady stream of defectors from government ranks. Homeland Security went to work to restrict the ability of these "traitors" to distribute and expose the information they stole. In response Congress pushed through HB154 to "Protect Cyberspace as a National Asset". It was a blatant attempt to clamp down on right wing rhetoric like zero-degree weather on a Macy's Day parade. The bill was sold as a defense against propaganda, and it easily passed. In it "kill switch authority" was given to the President to use to effectively shut down portions of the internet when deemed necessary which just meant that it brought all the major ISPs (Internet Service Providers) and a handful of smaller independents under the government's direct control.

What was even more alarming was that it empowered the government with the ability to police content and shut down any perceived opposition at their whim. But policing the internet is a monumental task and it is impossible to plug all the possible routes upon which information flows. Word got around.

Through the underground, Americans heard conspiracy theories about IRS teams that were going around confiscating civilian property. Editorials and articles about it appeared and then disappeared. You had to look hard to find information about the murder of Mr. and Mrs. Claymore by an IRS swat team. At first only die-hard conspiracy theorists believed it, many others didn't bother or just didn't care. After all it was just tax evaders that were being targeted right? And they deserved it. Didn't they?

* * *

The ban on guns was responsible for a growing wave of violence and the emergence of strong anti-Government sentiment. Right off some of the States like Texas, Arizona and Montana rebelled and refused to enforce the law, but only in the few States where angry citizens had some influence over policy. Once again there was a growing divide among American citizens with an intensity that hadn't been seen since the Civil War. Only now there was no well-defined North and South border.

America no longer has repercussions from a slave problem but there were plenty of people seeking new ways to stoke the flames of racism. Guns became a tool used to divide the masses and muddy the water so that opinions could not focus and coalesce against the real prominent issues. As it was before in the first American Civil War, animosity didn't boil over just from the slave issue. Today gun control replaced it as the catalyst. States' rights vs. Federal control were about to come to a head once again. President Richfield warned the "rogue State Governments" and threatened to treat "noncompliance" with the loss of the offender's job and or arrest. The president implied that (someone) would come in and remove them from office if they didn't toe the line.

"We have plenty of people looking for jobs now that will gladly obey the law and do the right thing for the citizens of your state" the President said on the issue. That quote did more to fill the ranks of the opposition than anything else. It put all politicians on edge because it was now clear that the central government was willing to act to replace any troublemaker with a more obedient Fed supplied civil servant.

Voluntary surrender of weapons wasn't happening to the degree the Feds desired so they put pressure on the State governments to crack down and attempt to remove guns from the hands of law-abiding citizens. State governments were forced to uphold the law and carry out

Federal policy all under the threat of withholding State subsidies. More and more citizens began to protest and resist not only the efforts of the Feds but also efforts presented at the State and local level too. The hornet's nest was starting to buzz.

Gun shops/dealers went out of business or vanished and went underground. That little thorn in the side of the government took care of itself. Local Police started going down a list of licensed gun collectors as well as owners and singled them out for a visit. Police went in and successfully took a huge number of weapons out of public hands through vigorous "search & seizure" missions.

After the news got around, tens of thousands of cases of "stolen gun" reports filtered in from citizens all across America. Law abiding people were suspected of lying and the Feds still believed they were harboring illegal weapon(s). Automatically without due process, they were labeled "criminals" and treated as such. Police came in and searched their homes without a warrant because they were guilty until proven innocent. Metal detectors were used to scan attics and yards to find illegal guns. Most of the searches conducted by the Police turned out successful, some turned out disastrous. Police soon found themselves in an ever-increasing number of violent incidences with the very people they were sworn to protect. Serious confrontations resulted in the deaths of citizens and police officers alike. It forced them to abandon passive measures and moved to "SWAT' style search & discovery raids. One day they were law abiding citizens and the next day they were felons. People were shocked by the aggressive tactics, never thinking that their own police would turn on them like that. More and more of the public, started to turn on the Police.

END BOOK 1

Exposed to a possible paradox in your beliefs, you must realize that there is another path besides the one you have sanctioned. To maintain your course in lieu of new contradictory evidence disregards the intellectual mind and removes yourself from guidance by truth.

Stephen S. Hoag

To know and not to do, is not to know.

Author unknown

Look For:

UPHOLD AND DEFEND Book II

Everything was tightening, markets were constricting, leaving Tenny Hill Academy searching for ways to continue under strict government oversight. The American government, teetering under the weight of a tremendous ever increasing financial burden, was also searching, searching for new ways to fill their coffers.

Can Tenny Hill Academy, as well as the free market system, survive with a government that is slowly transforming into a socialist, communist style regime? This is what happens when those two forces collide.

Book Two describes that fight, that battle for survival as Kaiden and Ciera spiral deeper into the effects of total government control.

About the Author

Many aspects of the novel Stephen S. Hoag has written are drawn from a lifetime of great experiences. The best experiences taught by his two children, a wonderful wife, and a best canine friend by the name of Dixie, "All of whom I am very proud of" he wants them to know. Stephen never joined the armed services or held an occupation in emergency response but has immense respect for those who did. Having a keen interest in the tools of war and the art of survival from a civilian's perspective was surly the catalyst for the dream he had that inspired him to write this book. He believes wholeheartedly in the value of the Bill of Rights, significantly the first and second amendments, and endorses the American Constitution 'as written".

Being a practicing Martial Artist for the last forty years has given Stephen a unique insight enabling him to see firsthand the value in acquiring the ability to defend oneself. That path encouraged good physical health and has been the vehicle for spiritual awakening. Stephen has studied the art of Wing Chung, Choy Lee Fut, Hsing Yi, Bagua and Tai Chi and is now a teacher of the Arts for some twenty years. For many of those years he owned and operated a company involved with solar energy and is a follower of the light.

www.ingramcontent.com/pod-product-compliance
Lightning Source LLC
Chambersburg PA
CBHW070645310726
48982CB00001B/417

* 9 7 9 8 9 8 8 4 6 6 3 1 4 *